MW00397750

THE VIRTUES
of SCANDAL

THE VIRTUES
of SCANDAL

A NOVEL *of* LORD BYRON

Richard Henry Abramson

AESCHYLUS PRESS
San Francisco, California

Printed in the United States of America

Library of Congress Cataloging-In-Publication Data
Abramson, Richard Henry
The Virtues of Scandal / Richard Henry Abramson

First Printing, 2020

Trade Paper: 978-1-7349918-0-2
Hardcover: 978-1-7349918-1-9
eBook: 978-1-7349918-2-6

Cover Design and Interior Design: Glen M. Edelstein,
Hudson Valley Book Design

PRINTED IN THE UNITED STATES OF AMERICA

This novel is dedicated to my father Robert Abramson, who loved a good story, and to my mother Hilda Abramson, who loved a good book.

AUTHOR'S PREFACE

BEFORE WE start, Reader, there is something we need to discuss.

The novel you are about to begin is, I suppose, a work of historical fiction. But what does that mean? Is the story *true*? Did these characters exist? Did they take part in the events I describe, or speak the words I have bade them speak? In the end, how much of this can you believe?

As a genre, historical fiction is often described as involving a story that takes place in a historically recognizable past. By that bare definition, *The Virtues of Scandal* is indeed a work of historical fiction. But still, *what here is true?* The film *Cowboys and Aliens* – which, if nothing else, proves that even Daniel Craig has boat payments – takes place in an identifiable historical period, the American Wild West. But it would distort the definition beyond recognition to characterize as historical fiction a story about cowboys and Indians heroically fighting off an extraterrestrial invasion. Why? Perhaps it is because the departure, nor merely from what *actually happened*, but from what might *conceivably have happened*, is simply too great. This does not imply, of course, that a story featuring men on horseback engaged in a running gunfight with space aliens might not be entertaining. But, at least to my mind, it would best be classified as fantasy.

In the present novel, I have endeavored to be faithful to the known character of the real historical figures I describe, and to the customs and speech of the Regency era within which much of the novel takes place. This is not, however, a work of historical scholarship. Rather, it is, first and foremost, a work of the imagination. In writing it, I was less interested in strict adherence to the historical record than in telling a compelling story.

As a consequence, there are events depicted in the novel that did not occur in the way they are described, or that did not occur at all. Further, while many of my characters are based on real individuals, others were entirely imagined. For better or worse, the elements of setting, character, plot, dialogue and conflict are animated in *The Virtues of Scandal* both by the actual and by the fanciful; and, within the body of the novel itself, I have chosen not to distinguish the one from the other.

Like any story-teller, my hope is that you will give yourself over to the tale, and will enjoy the historical context and period detail without believing it in every instance to be an accurate depiction of historical events. And, in return for your indulgence, I promise to clarify in the novel's *Afterword* what major aspects of the novel are and are not faithful to the historical record. This, I believe, is a bargain that will in the end leaven the imaginative with the factual without detracting from the intoxicating experience of being immersed for a while in a previously unfamiliar time and place.

Richard Henry Abramson
Palo Alto, California

PROLOGUE
Missolonghi,
Ottoman Greece – 1824

THE RIOT of battle. Adrenal cries of rage, fear and pain. Guttural curses, pants of effort and exhaustion, rising screams, cut off in an instant. The whinny and snort of frightened horses, and the heavy stamp of flailing hooves in the dirt. The ring of clashing blades, and the pulpy thud of pikes on flesh. The broken groans of the dying, who rattle and cough like wounded geese. The air is palpable, thick and moted with dust. The sharp stink of shit is overpowering.

At the edge of the tumult, two men circle, probing for advantage. Their narrowed world consists of raised blades, the opportunistic flex and slide of legs and feet, and the quick flicker of eyes that may betray intention or disguise it. One – a Turkish janissary by his uniform – feints to the left and whips his curved *kilij* forward, seeking the exposed flank of his adversary. The other, whose pale complexion marks him as an Englishman, parries the blow with his saber, then slashes at the Turk's right arm. The razor steel slices through fabric and flesh as the Turk, grunting with pain, shifts the *kilij* to his good left hand.

The opening is brief, but fatal. With a sharp thrust, the Englishman drives the point of his weapon deep into the Turk's belly. The janissary slashes desperately as the Englishman struggles to withdraw the blade, then silently doubles over and, as if in prayer, drops to his knees in the dark, clotted mud.

Time seems to pause. The janissary lists to the side, falls over, and lies still in a spreading pool of blood. The Englishman's heart pounds as he stumbles backwards, recoiling from the dead man at his feet. His chest heaves as he gasps for breath. His eyes are wide, and he struggles to suppress a rising nausea. Only then does he feel the wetness in his side, and a burning pain. He looks down, astonished, and with a peculiar sense of detachment wonders at the brightness of his blood. He feels cold. Turning away, he sees two men running towards him, one solidly built with thinning red hair, the other slight, pale and oddly dressed in silk jacket and pleated trousers. He tries to speak, but can make no sound. A wave of weakness washes over him, the world spins, and he struggles to keep his feet. As the two men half-carry, half-drag him away from the fighting, the ruddy one mutters a soft oath. "God damn you, Byron, how the hell did you talk me into this?"

CHAPTER 1
Almack's Assembly Rooms

Our ridicules are kept in the background,
Ridiculous enough, but also dull.
Professions too are no more to be found
Professional; and there is naught to cull
Of folly's fruit, for though your fools abound,
They're barren and not worth the pains to pull.
Society is now one polished horde,
Formed of two mighty tribes, the Bores and Bored.

DON JUAN, CANTO XIII

ALTHOUGH ITS quarters were unpretentious – a dun, two-story structure constructed in the *Palladian* style and located on the south side of King Street in the heart of London – Almack's Assembly Rooms regularly hosted the cream of London's nobility. On Wednesday nights between April and October, the peerage and its hangers-on gathered in the Almack ballroom under an imposing crystal chandelier to dance, mingle and be seen. Wealthy young bachelors sought pretty young brides, while those without means focused on annual income. Married couples flirted with premeditated spontaneity, though never with each other. Musicians, composers and poets vied for the largesse of patrons and patronesses. Alcohol was prohibited, as the eruptions of the surprisingly vomitous Countess Cutribaud a few years past had not been forgotten. But it was hardly needed – ambition supplied the necessary lubrication as social climbers reached for lofty peaks of title and prestige. And if, in ascending, they stepped on the grip of a fellow climber, there was solace in knowing that everyone ultimately arrives at their appropriate station, or is deservedly cast into the social abyss.

On a crisp autumn night, fashionable couples whirled across the polished dance floor. The ladies' formal dresses made a faint rustling sound, while the men dressed in the modern fashion, with fine black wool trousers and fitted single-breasted tailcoats, their silk cravats wrapped above ruffled pearl-white linen shirts and tied elaborately at the chin. At tables near the dance floor, men and women nibbled on delicate *fairy* cakes, the icing flaking off in a gentle dandruff of crumbs. Some of these salaciously burrowed into plunging valleys of cleavage, where they slowly dissolved. As one octogenarian noted wistfully, it was an end to be envied.

Towards the side of the room, three men and a woman were engaged in animated conversation. Two of the men stood side-by-side, their backs to the dance floor.

William Wordsworth, the taller of the two, was in his early forties, though his gleaming pate and silver sideburns made him look older and more than a bit like a balding crane in a bad suit. With the publication of *Lyrical Ballads* in the last years of the 18th century, Wordsworth had established himself as the progenitor of a new, imaginatively introspective style of poetry, one in which the poet's subjectivity, particularly as expressed in his feeling response to Nature, was itself the subject of the poem. But his talent had withered on tangled vines of personal sorrow and political reaction; now, his finances secure and his politics and religion relentlessly orthodox, his imaginative triumphs were ten years behind him.

Robert Southey, Wordsworth's contemporary and colleague, was also a poet and essayist, although of a lesser order. In his youth, Southey had supported the anti-monarchist ideals underpinning the French

Revolution, and both his poetry and his essays championed republican reform and individual liberty. But like Wordsworth, his politics and outlook had shifted – with the political winds and the financial allure of patronage, claimed his critics -- and he now decried as seditious those who questioned the primacy of the Anglican Church or the conservative policies of the Tory government.

Standing beside the taller Wordsworth, Southey may have seemed unremarkable to some, but that impression was quickly dispelled by his sharp intelligence and aggressive posture. Southey had curly brown hair, an aquiline nose, close-set eyes and eyebrows that seemed constantly to arch in disapproval. In conversation, he had a way of accentuating his points by puffing out his chest and jutting his chin. Marring an otherwise well-reasoned critique of Southey's interminable paean to John Wesley and Methodism, one critic uncharitably observed that Southey resembled nothing so much as an irascible pigeon.

There was no need to rely on the arch in Southey's brow to recognize the loathing he felt for the man with whom he and Wordsworth were conversing. To Southey's way of thinking, George Gordon, the 6th Lord Byron, personally embodied most of the vices against which Southey and his fellow Tories felt themselves arrayed.

Dressed in a tailored black waistcoat, ruffled shirt and blood-red cravat, Byron stood facing the dance floor, his grey eyes flickering away from the conversation as attractive couples spiraled by. He was of medium height and, though he sometimes struggled with his weight, his posture was straight and his stance athletic. His dark hair was thick, curls slipping carelessly past his collar. Pale of complexion, Byron's nose was straight and his cheekbones high and well-defined.

As the men conversed, an elegant young woman, only a few weeks wed to a self-important peer from Kent, caught Byron's eye and smiled at him from across the room, drawn by his reputation, his countenance, and by a palpable self-confidence that to some seemed arrogant. Byron, who missed little, returned a hawk's smile.

In Almack's ballroom that evening, discussion had given way to argument.

"Execute the Luddites for the crime of damaging machines that deprive them of their livelihood?" Byron's tone was cold. "Is this really your proposed solution? Oh, and should we hang them, or simply leave the beggars to starve?"

"Sentiment in matters such as this is dangerous," Wordsworth replied, peering at Byron down his thin, sharp nose. "It would give me little satisfaction to make an example of the frame-breakers, Byron. But a breakdown in public order serves no one's interest. I'm astonished you don't feel the same way."

"I suppose I should," Byron sighed. "Though I sometimes wonder, is cruelty that dresses itself up as policy any less callous?"

"If the government is shown to be impotent, progress of any kind becomes impossible."

"Oh, please William, spare us the platitudes. Hang them if you must, but don't pretend that they dangle to vindicate principle."

Byron glanced at Lady Caroline Lamb, the slight, vivacious young wife of the politically ambitious Lord William Melbourne. Lady Caroline followed the conversation with interest, her blond curls cascading in disobedient ringlets down her delicate neck. He'd seen her for the first time several months previously and, his interest piqued, had asked a mutual acquaintance to introduce them. To his surprise, she had declined, referring to him as "mad, bad and dangerous to know." He thought her characterization was entirely unfair, and it pleased him very much.

"America," he continued, "to whose existence I expect you are by now resigned, emerged from riot and rebellion. If history tells us anything, it is that progress comes not in spite of a breakdown in public order but because of it."

Southey snorted. "Our Lord Byron's disrespect for the law, like his contempt for protocols of every kind, is most evident when its subject concerns the sanctity of the Church or the security of the State."

"There is some truth to that," Byron acknowledged. "Try as I might, I can think of no regimes more concerned with their own self-perpetuation than the Church and the State."

"You take such views to an extreme," Southey huffed. "How else to explain your continuing admiration for Napoleon, who most now acknowledge to be nothing less than a tyrannical atheist."

"Nonsense, Southey. It should be obvious even to you that the Corsican isn't an atheist. He believes *himself* to be God!"

As Caroline laughed, Byron changed the subject. "Before I forget, Robert, please accept my belated congratulations. *Poet Laureate* of England! It is a great honor, and one for which you are quite well-suited. Hard to believe Walter Scott turned it down." He raised a contemplative finger to his lips. "Perhaps he didn't recognize its significance?"

"Lord Byron," Caroline interjected, "had you no designs on the position yourself?"

Byron grinned, nodding his head towards the glowering Southey. "Robert has given us so much; it is only meet that his labors be recognized."

Caroline suppressed a smile. She recalled one of Byron's verses – *"O Southey! Southey! Cease thy varied song! A bard may chant too often and too long!"*

Southey's face was flushed, and his fists were clenched. Byron wondered whether it might not be politic to defuse the growing tension. But, glancing at Caroline, he decided against it and turned back to Southey.

"Robert," he asked, "in your travels on the Continent, did you ever play *bouts-rimés*? It was quite popular in Paris prior to the Revolution."

"Yes, I am familiar with it. I last played at a party almost eight years ago in Avignon." He turned to Lady Caroline. "It's an old game, actually. Each player must construct a short poem using the same four rhymed endings – hence the name *bouts-rimés*, or 'rhymed ends.'"

Wordsworth gave Southey a warning glance but said nothing as Byron, looking pleased, suggested they play. When Southey hesitated, Caroline leaned coquettishly into the *laureate*.

"My brave, brave knight. I, Lady Caroline of La Melbourne, shall be your Sancho Panza!" Drawing herself up, she cast a theatrical finger towards Byron. "Slay the Black Knight," she exhorted, "and glory shall be yours!"

Southey bared his teeth in what Caroline took to be a smile. "As you wish, my lady." He dabbed at his forehead, his kerchief fluttering like a limp banner on the field of battle. "And will you do us the honor of selecting the rhyming ends? That is, if Lord Byron has no objection?"

"I've no objection," Byron replied with a grand sweep of his arm. "I would ask only that your lovely squire select words in English, rather than in her native Castilian." Caroline laughed, her eyes bright. The more he saw of her, the more interesting she seemed.

After thinking on it while the men talked, Caroline cleared her throat, seemingly pleased with her choices.

"As your firearms are lyrical, let these serve as semantic ammunition: Hut/smut, ragged/jagged, crown/clown, poet/know it. I realize that the last is not one word but two," she added, "but as it *is* the last and will complete the rhyme, I deem it a rhymed ending nonetheless."

After a pause to allow for objections, Caroline signaled agreement with a sharp clap of her hands. "Gentlemen, take ten minutes to compose your rhymes." Gracing Wordsworth with a smile, she asked whether he would escort her to the bar for a refreshment, a request with which he appeared delighted to comply.

As they strolled away, her bare arm linked in his, she glanced back at Byron. "Lord Byron," she admonished, "we are confident that you will be artful in your verse. Do not disappoint us."

CHAPTER 2
Bouts-Rimés

I think that were I certain of success,
I hardly could compose another line.
So long I've battled either more or less
That no defeat can drive me from the Nine.
This feeling 'tis not easy to express
And yet 'tis not affected, I opine.
In play there are two pleasures for your choosing:
The one is winning and the other losing.

DON JUAN, CANTO XIV

WHEN CAROLINE and Wordsworth returned, they were accompanied by a clustered murmur of nobles, eager for a show. While a good hanging might have generated a bawdier crowd, in this setting a battle of wits between Byron and Southey was a promising diversion. Their mutual antipathy was a matter of public record, and attention now rested on the two poets, who stood facing one another like pugilists.

Caroline asked who would like to proceed first, and Byron inclined his head. "I defer to Mr. Southey's august office, and to his greater years." Everyone recognized his sly reference to Prince Regent George Augustus Frederick, to whom Southey owed his appointment. Byron nodded to Lady Caroline with a smile that Southey thought impudent and that Caroline found charming.

"Thank you, Lord Byron," replied Southey. His eyes, calculating, scanned the notables. "I accept your deference in the spirit with which it is given. I would expect no less from one who descends from the storied Byron line."

Caroline hesitated, taken aback. As Southey well knew – as everyone knew – Byron's family was tainted by scandal. Although the charge was never proven, his great-uncle was reputed to have murdered a neighbor, and his father was a dissolute rogue whose marriage to Byron's mother staved off financial ruin only for a time. Fleeing to the Continent to escape his creditors, he died at thirty-six, tubercular and penniless, leaving his wife and young son nothing but the obligation to pay his funeral expenses and his debts.

If Byron was offended by Southey's slap at the family name, he didn't show it. He made no reply, and seemed less insulted than amused. Seemingly disappointed to have been unable to escalate the confrontation, Southey extracted from his coat pocket a sheet of paper, which he squinted to read:

> *His clothes are dirty, torn and **ragged**,*
> *Much worse, they say, his crumbling **hut**;*
> *His yellowed teeth are broken, **jagged**,*
> *The mouth they guard croaks wicked **smut**.*

> *The poor and broken, sings the **poet**,*
> *Still serve the glory of the **crown**,*
> *Whose mercy graces lord or **clown**,*
> *And sanctifies all those who **know it**.*

Southey looked up to see a few ancient heads nod sonorously, and was gratified to hear several calls of "bravo" and "well done." In her capacity as mistress of ceremonies, Lady Caroline bestowed what Southey took to be an approving smile. "England is fortunate indeed," she said with a solemnity that almost made Byron laugh, "to have a man of such talent as its newest *poet laureate*." Watching from the rear of the assembly, Wordsworth rolled his eyes.

The string quartet, which had been slogging its way through what passed in London for a Virginia reel, completed its exertions and fell silent. Seizing the moment, Byron took a pace forward and turned to face Southey.

"You never disappoint, Robert. No matter the master or fashion to which you swear fealty, your subservience is always unconditional."

Southey flushed as Byron turned to the crowd and began to recite. "*Southey!*" he declaimed,

> *The Prince, impatient heir to the maddened* **crown**
> *To which clings George, his raving father and incumbent* **clown**,
> *Demands only that your verses, no matter how forced or* **jagged**,
> *Glorify his name and policies, no matter how absurd or* **ragged**.
> *Laureate! Garbed in fine Latin you sit, our purchased* **poet**,
> *Albion's paid for font of fawning* **smut**.
> *Still, captive to the gilt of your position, you strive not to* **know it**,
> *Yes, even the dimmest hound knows better than to foul his meagre* **hut**.

As Byron recited his *bouts-rimés*, Southey's dark eyes narrowed, his breath contracted to stuttering gasps, and his fists clenched. His posture was rigid – Caroline thought the man might be having a stroke. At last, Southey could contain himself no longer. Enraged, he exploded like a champagne cork and leaped forward, his hands raised towards Byron's throat.

Byron, who was well-practiced in the art of provocation, had been watching and saw him coming. With Southey almost upon him, he sidestepped and, with a subtle shift of his hip, deflected the flailing *poet laureate* towards the dance floor, where he collided with a whiskered banker who was smoking a cigar and furtively sipping from a silver flask.

The banker bellowed – Southey sprawled – the brandy spilled – the cigar dropped – the alcohol ignited – and a lovely blue-tinged blaze, rich with the scent of fine cognac, flared gently on the polished floor.

As the languid flames licked at his feet, Southey looked up in horror as the crowd regarded him with what Caroline later described with delight as an 'exquisite' mix of amusement and disapproval. His mortification, however, was not yet complete. As Byron took Caroline's elbow and steered her towards the door, they stepped carefully past the prostrate Southey. Byron paused, clearing his throat. His voice could be heard across the spacious room, and over the tittering assembly.

"Once again, Robert, congratulations on your new position."

CHAPTER 3
The House of Murray

There is a commonplace book argument,
Which glibly glides from every vulgar tongue
When any dare a new light to present:
'If you are right, then everybody's wrong.'
Suppose the converse of this precedent
So often urged, so loudly and so long:
'If you are wrong, then everybody's right.'
Was ever everybody yet so quite?

Don Juan, Canto XVII

RETREATING UNDER fierce attack, Byron parried his opponent's slashing blade and recovered to the *en garde* position. Sensing an advantage, his adversary recklessly pressed forward. With a deft parry, Byron deflected the renewed attack and made his own *riposte*, feinting to his left and then, in a blur, thrusting over the responsive parry. The tip of his ebony cane came to a sudden stop, hovering just inches from his opponent's chest. "*Touché*," he crowed, looking down at his opponent in triumph.

Crestfallen, his foe threw down his wooden sword and, to Byron's consternation, began to cry. John Murray, who had been sitting behind his cluttered desk, partially obscured by scattered stacks of pamphlets, periodicals and assorted *literaria*, looked up in annoyance. "Byron," he muttered, his unlit pipe clenched between his teeth, "must you butcher the children?"

"Only history determines whether the conqueror is an instrument of carnage or a champion of principle," Byron demurred as he squatted to comfort Murray's vanquished five-year old. Rubbing at his tears, the little boy took back his sword, stood up ramrod straight, and returned Byron's salute. "In fact, Murray, I am teaching your boy skills – including how to accept defeat with dignity – that he will one day find invaluable. You may thank me later." Byron tousled the boy's hair and, smiling broadly, plopped down in the cracked leather armchair that faced his publisher's desk.

A decade older than Byron, Murray was a man of even features and temperament. He had been Byron's publisher and friend for almost ten years, and had prospered from the publication of *Childe Harold's Pilgrimmage*, whose unprecedented success had made Byron famous. The first two cantos of his newest work tucked under his arm, Byron had arrived unannounced on a damp November morning just as Murray was sitting down to breakfast.

"It will be called *Don Juan*," he had announced airily, tossing the manuscript onto Murray's desk. Loose papers took to the air like startled butterflies, then softly resettled. "Not that gaudy Spanish libertine – you know, the Tirso de Molina version? Mine is pronounced 'Ju-Wan,' rhyming with 'new one.'"

For the next hour, Murray said hardly a word as he devoured the manuscript, squinting from time to time to decipher Byron's handwriting. Cold as a stone, his eggs and mash lay untouched on his plate, which teetered precariously on a stack of Joshua Reynolds lithographs. Finally, Murray sighed and lowered the manuscript. He shrugged at Byron, who as usual was resplendent in blue quilted waist-coat and white nankeen trousers.

"Only a shrug, Murray? I don't know what I expected, but it wasn't indifference."

Shaking his head, Murray tapped the sheaf of papers that sat before him like some kind of poetical incendiary.

"Byron, you know how reluctant I am to further inflate the ever-ascending bubble of your self-estimation. But this – this ...." He paused, searching for the right words. "*This* is original, and outrageous, and provocative, and – best of all for one in my position – wildly entertaining." He gestured towards a bookshelf to the left of his desk on which, slumming alongside military histories, the narrative journal of an archeological expedition to the Azores, and *A New System of Domestic Cookery* by Mrs. Eliza Rundell, stood bound leather volumes of poems by Pope, Dryden, Swift and Milton. "In its own way, I daresay it is as good or better than anything I've read, and much better than anything I've published – including *Childe Harold*."

While Byron thought about whether to take that as a compliment or an insult, Murray did some quick mental arithmetic, multiplying canto by advance and comparing that to a corresponding product of canto and retail price. He was pleased with the outcome.

"What is your plan going forward?" he asked. He adjusted his glasses, which had become essential to his reading and not unkind to his image. "You do have a plan?"

Byron grinned, amused by Murray's unusual blend of keen business instinct and literary broad-mindedness. "These first two cantos are just the beginning. I don't exactly have a plan – Murray, you need to eat something, you don't look well – but what I do have is *material*, a lifetime of it."

"What's unique here–" Murray started to say, then paused. "Well, actually, there's much here that's unique." He paused to chew on his spectacles, gathering his thoughts. "One thing that strikes me is the narrative character of the work – I tell you, Byron, already this is a hell of a story! That you can tell it in verse is impressive."

"Pleased that you think so. But you raise an interesting point, and one I've been thinking on. Perhaps *Don Juan* might translate well to fiction?"

Murray frowned. "Fiction? For-the-masses fiction? You?"

"Why not? *Waverley* and *Ivanhoe* have done quite well, haven't they? If Walter Scott can churn out a chapter or two every month, why can't I? And to your point, it would play to a larger audience; and did I already mention the money?"

Murray shook his head. "I don't know, Byron. While I admire how well you manage to tell a story here, already this is much more. It succeeds as verse in part because you have a genius for it, but also because the form allows you almost unlimited freedom."

Byron shrugged. "You're probably right, Murray – my God, did I just say that aloud? Excepting Walter's and a couple of others, most of these serial fictions aren't worth the time it takes to read them."

"Precisely. Your reputation is as a poet; no matter how well you craft it, a novel would alloy brass to your gold coin." Murray grimaced. "Besides, I'd need to find a new printer – Thomas Davison does good work, but he isn't set up for the volume that a serialized novel would entail."

"Well, Murray, that's a problem you may need to solve in any event. I have enough material for at least another forty or fifty cantos, so we'll need a printer who can keep up."

Murray nodded, trying to appear blasé. In fact, he was flabbergasted both by the scope of the project and, at least as executed in these first cantos, by its audacity. He had always been impressed by Byron's imaginative brilliance, which from the start had blazed through his client's verse like lightning. But with the exception of the third and fourth cantos of *Childe Harold* and a few savage stanzas of *English Bards and Scotch Reviewers*, Byron's voice had been undisciplined, and his genius uneven. At least, judging from these first cantos, until now.

"Is this your *Divine Comedy*?" he asked, hoping to draw Byron out. If this was as important a project as he now suspected it could be, he needed to better understand its scope.

"No!" Byron exclaimed, shaking his head. Rising from his chair he began to pace, deftly navigating through deep canyons of stacked volumes whose collapse, though quite inevitable, he usually resisted the urge to hasten.

"I've no interest in writing a *divine* poem – there are plenty enough of those, though except for *Paradise Lost*, none of the scope or quality of Dante." Byron plucked a book from the top of a teetering stack. "*Pride and Prejudice* – I like the title!" He examined the title page. "A handsome print run, and a third printing! Worth a read, Murray?"

Without waiting for a response, he returned the book to its place. "An epic poem? No. I want to write a *human* one. I'll leave it to Wordsworth and Coleridge to parse the workings of the Divine, whether expressed in Nature or ... I don't know, herring. And Southey – damn his apostate soul – Southey has the market cornered when it comes to fawning paeans to England, the Anglican Church, and anyone else who might butter his bread." A little half-smile. "He may have written them, John, but when I read them, the *paean* is mine!" Byron guffawed, pleased with himself.

Murray leaned back and crossed his arms. "Southey's not without talent, Byron. Wordsworth and Coleridge as well. You're too well-read to believe otherwise."

"If only his mien was as modest as his talent," Byron muttered, looking up in annoyance as a horse-drawn cart bearing paving stones and bricks clattered loudly down Albemarle Street.

"It's not his politics I detest so much," he continued over the din, "though they are appalling. It's the hypocrisy! He spends the first half of his life in self-righteous defense of liberal causes, and the second half championing a point of view – and often the very same measures – he previously denounced. And in the most pompous and judgmental style imaginable." He threw up his arms and, gazing out the window, appealed to a passing clutch of school-girls. "Who does that," he shouted, "and then demands to be taken seriously?" The girls continued on their way, paying him no mind.

Pivoting, he advanced on his publisher. "I tell you, Murray, we're gripped by a barely-suppressed malevolence. The poor are tolerated only to starve, while the nation's wealth is squandered on foreign adventures. The nobility – ironic what we call ourselves! – respond as you might expect, bemoaning all disturbances to decorum and looking away as the government sodomizes the rotting corpse of our hard-won freedoms. Yesterday the Catholics felt the legislative lash; today it is the Irish and the tradesmen. Parliament does nothing, or worse, legislates away the rights of those it's meant to serve. Did you read my maiden – and quite possibly, my last – speech to the House of Lords?"

"Opposing the bill to hang the frame-breakers? I did. In a very short time you managed to abuse a great many."

"And well they deserved it! Thousands of jobs lost to 'improvements' in mechanism that enrich only the owners. And when, in their hungry desperation, the workers turn on the machines, the government's solution is to hang the poor sods?"

"The bill was appalling indeed. How many voted against it in Lords?"

"A dozen or so, all Whigs. Passage was never in doubt. Castlereagh's taken Malthus to heart, don't you see? For the wretched few who survived the wars, he offers nothing more than unemployment, starvation and – for those bold enough to protest – the hangman's noose."

"Was he there? When you gave your speech?"

"Oh yes. In fact, after I finished, he rose in reply."

"He answered you directly? I'd have wagered a thousand pounds that he'd ignore you."

"No, although your instincts are right. He spoke only a few words – I remember them exactly. 'My Lord Byron,' he said, 'I wish to thank you for your remarks, which remind us that mawkish sentiment – especially when dressed in fine clothing by a tongue as skillful as yours – has no place in the debate of issues critical to the long-term welfare of the realm.'"

Seizing the arms of his chair, Byron leaped to his feet to resume his circumnavigation of Murray's office, his gait only slightly troubled by his congenitally turned out right foot.

"I have some fine stanzas reserved for Castlereagh," he confided. "Who would have thought the ruthless suppression of the Irish Catholics qualifies a man to be Foreign Secretary?"

"He's the devil to the Whigs these days, isn't he? Although I expect they blame him less for the substance of the government's policies than for the efficiency with which they are carried out."

Byron grunted. "No less blameworthy. By the way, I'm going to dedicate the poem to Southey, though I suspect he may be less than appreciative."

Murray sighed. "You may be able to insult Southey without consequence, Byron, though I would caution you to be careful even there. But I'm not sure you realize that neither the government in general nor Castlereagh in particular are likely to respond to criticism as gracefully as you."

"You should avoid sarcasm, Murray; it doesn't become you."

Murray said nothing, but shifted his pipe from mouth to hand, then tapped it on his knee. Pursing his lips to speak, he instead looked away.

"What, Murray? Spit it out, man."

"Your poetry is brilliant, Byron; that much even your critics concede. But your talent will shield neither you nor this publishing house from reprisals."

Byron stiffened. Knowing Murray as he did, he had expected his publisher to have some misgivings. Still, anticipating Murray's timidity made it no less irritating.

"What do you find troubling?" Byron asked coldly. "Is it the politics? The carnality? Is it a resemblance, real or imagined, between my characters and my character? Or do you object that I have cast as villain or fool men with whom you hope to break bread?"

"I object to nothing. But as your publisher, it falls to me to ensure that neither you nor the Murray house are embarrassed by unnecessarily provocative candor, political or otherwise."

"Unnecessary? Since when is candor excessive? Do we suffer, in these regressive times, from an overabundance of Truth?" He glared at Murray. "Or is it Hypocrisy that must be held safe?"

"The torch of truth tends to flicker out in the Tower, Byron. Must I remind you of the writers who have been prosecuted for libel against the Crown?"

"Is it the poet for whom you're concerned? Or the publisher?"

"I'm suggesting only that you tone down some of the more inflammatory passages. Titillation is one thing – it sells. But scandal is too easy a target for prudes and critics who would like nothing more than to take you down a peg." He pulled out an old editor's trick. "*Don Juan* is too good – too *important* – to risk the censor's pen."

Setting his jaw, Byron stood. "You underestimate the virtues of scandal, Murray, and not merely because scandal *titillates*. Has it never occurred to you that men – and women too, for in this, gender plays no part – who reason from first principles, and do not blindly confuse what *is* for what *might be*, are inevitably vilified as *scandalous*?"

"It's a matter of degree, Byron."

"Degree? Open your eyes, Murray! Those who profit from depraved convention conspire to call it virtue; cling to it like a king to his crown; and condemn as *scandal* all deviations. Luthor, Swift, Pope – need I go on? Show me a man of truly original thought whose ideas or conduct have *not* been vilified as scandalous!"

"Precisely my point, Byron. Unless its martyrdom you're after?"

"Hardly. But I will not water down my verse, nor make a eunuch of *Don Juan*! The poem will please if it is lively – if it is dull it will fail – but I will have none of your damned cutting and slashing."

As Byron turned to go, he gestured towards the bookshelf. "Another thing, Murray," he said acidly. "If you would prefer a less controversial engagement, I suggest that you publish another cookbook by the estimable Mrs. Rundell. Her recipes, at least, have the virtue of offending only the stomach!"

CHAPTER 4
The Waltz

Seductive Waltz!—though on thy native shore
Even Werter's self-proclaimed thee half a whore;
Werter—to decent vice though much inclined,
Yet warm, not wanton; dazzled, but not blind—
The fashion hails—from Countesses to Queens,
And maids and valets waltz behind the scenes;
Wide and more wide thy witching circle spreads,
And turns—if nothing else—at least our heads.

BYRON, THE WALTZ, PUBLISHED ANONYMOUSLY, 1813

AS HE approached Melbourne House, crossing St. James Park heading towards Whitehall, Byron considered his friend John Cam Hobhouse's warning about Caroline Lamb. "You'd best be careful with that one, Byron. She's one of the few women in London who could damage even your reputation." Hobhouse was preternaturally cautious, which was one reason why Byron appreciated his company. The benefits of Hobby's caution were clear: either Byron would corrupt his friend, obtaining some small vindication of vice over virtue; or he himself would be restrained, which often spared him trouble. Still, he had to admit to some misgivings about Caroline.

For one thing, she was thin and flat-chested. With her curly blond hair cut short, she had the look of a tomboy. Physically, she wasn't his type.

More troubling, she was married to William Lamb, whose rising political connections within the Regency government led some to speculate that he might one day be the King's First Minister. Byron was rarely deterred by the risks of seducing the wives of important men; through neglect or cruelty, the cuckolded husband usually had it coming. He made it a point, however, never to seduce their mistresses, which he had found to be a far more dangerous enterprise. But Lamb – Lord Melbourne, by title – was not merely well-connected; as far as Byron could tell, he was both thoughtful and, at least for a Tory, progressive. And he could detect none of the self-righteous posturing that always set his teeth on edge and made him ache for the righteous intervention of a vengeful God or a mocking critic.

Caroline could also be difficult. "Your latest lover must be the leading lady," the Irish playwright Thomas Moore had observed one evening as he and Byron shared a bottle of brandy, "and is the type who complains constantly about the script." Still, once charmed, Byron tended to give himself over to the performance and was inclined to overlook small flaws in the production. His letters, sometimes two or three a day, sparkled with wit, and he lavished her with the attention she craved. She, in turn, was uncommonly clever, and practically vibrated with sexual energy. But he had discovered how volatile and demanding his newest lover could be; she was insecure regarding his affections and required frequent assurances and expressions of tenderness. At times it could be exhausting.

And yet ... there was something about Caro that was enticing. Byron paused to avoid a collision with a large sheepdog, which hurtled past him with a panting young boy, stick in hand, in hot pursuit. For one thing, she didn't seem to care much what people thought of her. Depending on his mood, Byron found this alternately exciting and alarming. While concerns over appearances and conformity to convention were not unique to the English, they were so tightly woven into the social fabric that – should a loose thread be tugged just so – the entire garment seemed sure to unravel. Byron liked to think himself indifferent to sacred cows, and Caroline was not the first to confide that his willingness to mock those he found pretentious was part of what made him so interesting. Still, he cared about appearances more than he liked to admit. Recklessly – perhaps even heroically – Caroline seemed not to care at all.

She's rarely dull, he reassured himself as he approached Melbourne House, which stood like a fortress separating Downing Street and Whitehall from the grey Thames beyond. But when Caro became enraged at seeing him at parties with other women, threatening to make a scene at the door or in the street below, he was sometimes of a mind to reconsider.

A disapproving butler – Byron thought it grand that his name was Calvin – opened the heavy wooden door and stepped aside. With a perfunctory nod, Byron brushed past the white-haired steward and stepped into the foyer, his boots clicking on the polished marble. Lord Melbourne was off to Scotland for a hunt and would not return for a fortnight. Still, Byron never felt altogether comfortable coming to Melbourne House. Caroline had assured him there was no reason for concern – her husband knew of their affair, as she knew of his dalliances. As for Caroline's moth-er-in-law, whose spacious apartments took up most of the ground floor of the imposing mansion, the formidable Lady Melbourne and Byron had been friends and *confidantes* for several years. Not only did she know of his affair with Caroline, she encouraged it, hoping that it might eventually result in the dissolution of a marriage she had always considered unwise.

When Byron had described this tangled web of sexual and familial relationships to Moore and Hobhouse, Moore shook his head. "You couple with the wife, cuckold her husband, and confide in his mother. Shakespearean, wouldn't you say?" Hobhouse, who had known Byron too long to be astonished, merely looked glum.

Closing the door behind Byron, Calvin inclined his head toward the stairs. Byron knew the way. As he ascended the carpeted staircase, his bad foot turned slightly outward, Byron heard piano music above him. At the landing he turned down a narrow Greystone hallway until he reached a set of doors fronted by twin curved mirrors. His reflection expanded grotesquely as he approached; was this poor craftmanship, or someone's twisted sense of metaphor?

The room was a large studio, trapezoidal shafts of sunlight streaming in through high windows on its southern side. Aside from a few chairs which lined one wall, the space was bare, and the pale beechwood floor was scratched and worn. A piano and bench occupied a small platform on the west side of the room, the pianist's hands flying over the keyboard as his feet worked the pedals and his head swayed in time to the music.

Squinting against the glaring reflection of the sun off the floor, Byron turned his attention to a dancing couple, their bodies tight, who swirled in unison to the rhythmic strains of the waltz. Caroline smiled as she danced, her body lithe and graceful as she whirled and spun. Although Byron was a superb swordsman and a champion swimmer, as a dancer he was indifferent, and he felt a small tug of jealousy as he tracked Caroline and her partner across the floor. *The woman can at times be unendurable, but by God, she is alluring!* At times he could barely refrain from taking her right there on the dance floor. The music rose and fell as the pianist's fingers caressed the well-worn keys.

As the waltz drew to a close and the music faded, Caroline's partner bent forward and, his lips close to her ear, whispered something that made her laugh. Retreating a pace, he bowed to kiss her proffered hand. Brushing the sweat-damp curls off her forehead, Caroline dismissed him with a smile and strode over to greet Byron. "It's about time you got here," she scolded, hoping to sound cross. "How many bottles of Margaux did you and your insufferable friend consume?"

"Margaux? Never at midday, and Hobhouse would drink ale if given the choice. We had a passable Calon Segur, and only the one bottle." He leaned close, pressing his lips to her ear. "To drink more would risk too much."

Caroline laughed, her voice throaty for one so small. Rising on her toes, she pushed him away. "You presume too much."

Byron gestured towards Caroline's dance partner, who sat across the ballroom on a stool, changing his shoes. "What did he say to you just now?"

"He asked whether next time he might lead."

Taking Byron's hand, she turned toward the door and led him back down the hall and up a second flight of stairs to her rooms, whose solid oaken doors she closed behind them. They remained closed for several hours.

CHAPTER 5
Devising a Plan

A DOZEN goats watched impassively as Hobhouse and John Polidori set Byron against a low wall of sun-bleached stone. "It's barely more than a scratch, Byron," huffed Hobhouse, his round face flushed with exertion, his thinning hair damp with sweat. He and Byron had been friends since their student days at Cambridge. They had traveled together in the Balkans during their post-graduate 'Grand Tour,' and had extricated themselves from a few scrapes, though nothing quite like this.

"Polidori will fix you up good as new," Hobhouse said encouragingly, "Won't you doctor?"

Polidori nodded. He was several years younger than Byron and Hobhouse and, in white trousers, blouse and jacket, seemed oddly overdressed for a battlefield. His dark hair was caked with dirt, his lips were cracked and swollen, and his pale skin, better suited for the fogs of London than for the searing Grecian sun, was a sunburnt crimson.

"He looked worse the morning after Lady Oxford's Waterloo party." Pulling a cravat from a leather pouch at his waist, Polidori pressed it against the wound. He noted Byron's complexion, a sickly white, and leaned in to check his pupils.

"We need to get him someplace where I can clean and properly bind this wound. I think I saw some clothes on a line at that farmhouse across the field. Maybe you can find something we can use as a bandage."

Byron coughed, wincing at the pain. He managed a weak smile. "If you manage to pilfer something, Hobby, make sure it doesn't clash with red."

"Your sartorial requirements," muttered Hobhouse, rolling his eyes, "will be my primary consideration."

As Byron leaned back and closed his eyes, Hobhouse pulled the doctor aside. "Tell me this is something you can deal with, Polidori."

"I'll do what I can. But unless the Turks clean their weapons meticulously – and I've seen little evidence that anyone in this rotted cesspool of a country has ever had so much as a bath – the risk of fever is high." Raising his arm, he wiped the sweat off his brow. "He's at risk of shock as well. Once I get a field dressing in place we can travel, but where are we going?"

Hobhouse glanced at the goats, who gazed right back. Reaching for a stick, he squatted down to scratch a rough map in the bare dirt; the Greek mainland to the north, the Ionian Sea to the west, the Aegean Sea to the east, and the Peloponnesian peninsula to the south. In the far southwest of the mainland he scribed a small circle.

"We're here, in Missolonghi." To the southeast, on the north central coast of the peninsula, a second circle. "Patras. Except for a Turkish garrison holed up in the citadel, the city's in rebel hands, at least for now. If we can get to Patras, we should be safe. The French are running weapons in from Italy –maybe we can find a place on one of the returning ships."

Polidori considered the rough map. One of the goats, braver than the rest, sidled over and appeared ready to cross the Aegean in an attempted incursion against the Greek mainland. With a dismissive wave, Polidori repulsed the invasion. The goat bleated crossly as it retreated.

"Two questions," said Polidori, pointing at the gulf Hobhouse had drawn in the dirt. "First, how do we get across to Patras?"

Hobhouse shrugged. "We'll figure it out when we get to the crossing point at Antirrio. It's not that far from there to Patras. I'm pretty sure we can find a way across." Polidori looked skeptical but only nodded. With a grunt, Hobhouse got to his feet. "What's the second question?"

"Who holds the territory we'll need to cross?"

Hobhouse squinted as a gust of wind flung particles of Hellenic soil in his eyes. "A goddamned division of godless goddamned Turks," he replied. Turning away from the wind, Hobhouse checked to ensure that no troops were in sight. Seeing none, he set off, cautiously making his way across the dry, wind-blown field.

CHAPTER 6
A Young Man of Seville

IT WAS mid-summer in Seville, a city famed for the bitterness of its oranges and the beauty of its women. The heat of the Andalusian day dissipated slowly – in this season, it often felt like the fat Spanish moon generated as much heat as light. Side-stepping hopeful vendors and hopeless urchins, starry-eyed poets and star-crossed lovers, preoccupied students and unoccupied vagabonds, a young man weaved his way through the Casco Antiguo with purpose that was evident even to a casual onlooker. No more than seventeen, the boy was slender, his narrow waist encircled by finely-tailored black trousers that disappeared into rich calfskin boots. His shirt was white, the Egyptian cotton luminescent in the pale light of the rising moon, and he was handsome – there are some, jealous perhaps, who might have called him pretty – with energetic dark eyes, high cheekbones and delicate features. His black hair was full and, to one who hadn't watched his meticulous preparation for this evening, seemed to fall carelessly over his collar.

As he walked along the Calle Arfe, Juan Pedro Calderón de Castilla passed ornate fountains and crumbling walls that dated from the occupation of the city by the Moors, who conquered Seville in 712 and ruled the city for five hundred years until, as was then the fashion, it was retaken in the name of Christ. To Juan's right soared the imposing Alcazar Cathedral, built on the foundation of a magnificent mosque, and the young man admired for the thousandth time its intricate array of Moorish arches and iris-blue tiles that seemed cut from the flawless summer sky. As always, he found it odd that so singular a monument to Christ should be grounded on so prominent a pillar of Islamic faith.

Juan hurried north as the Guadalquivir River hurried south, intent on its journey from the Carzola Mountains in the northeast to the Gulf of Cadiz and the salt-grey Atlantic in the west. One of Juan's tutors said that there once stood near the mouth of the Guadalquivir an ancient city, Tartessus, whose people worshipped Astarte, the goddess of sexuality, fertility and war. He told Juan that, despite prodigious effort, archaeologists had been unable to locate its ruins, nor any trace of the sacrificial temples that were said to have flourished there a millennium before the birth of Christ. As he was both young and unmarried, Juan could not fathom how Astarte could be the goddess both of sex and war.

Following the river, he passed La Giralda, the ancient minaret that, in an architectural auto-de-fe, had been forcibly converted in the fifteenth century to the present Cathedral bell tower. Its bells, his tutor told him, had tolled to mark the burning of heretics in the square below. His tutor's eyes had been filled with such great sadness that Juan felt as if their pyres had burned only yesterday.

Juan turned east and entered the fashionable La Macarena district, passing the Conventa de Santa Ines, where a young nun was said to have disfigured herself with boiling oil in order to discourage the amorous advances of King Pedro the Cruel. Past the Convent and set back from the street stood a villa, fronted by a stone wall and black wrought-iron gate. Behind the gate, but visible through its filigreed bars, spread an enclosed garden, painted in vivid pinks and blues by the Spanish sun and fragrant in the spring and summer with the perfumed scents of jasmine and lavender. Juan paused to cast a cautious glance up and down the street, but nothing stirred save for a stray black cat, whose eyes glowed psychotically in the moonlight. With a shiver, Juan made the sign of the cross.

Opening the gate, Juan passed through the garden and crossed a courtyard whose bleached stone matched that of the paladin wall. Before him stood the villa. The ground floor, framed by pink and white oleander, gave way to an upper story featuring six windows, each one flanked by Moorish arches and black wrought-iron balustrades. If one were young, athletic and sufficiently motivated, it would be possible to climb from one of these windows and drop to the courtyard below.

The door opened as Juan approached. "Come in, Senor Juan," whispered a young servant girl only a few years older than he, her frown giving way to a shy smile. "Good evening, Esmerelda," Juan murmured, inclining his head with respect. Checking again to make certain that no one had followed, Esmerelda latched the door and led Juan up the leftward half of a graceful double staircase.

As they mounted the stairs, Juan looked up at the imposing portrait of Don Alfonso, the master of the house and husband of Dona Julia. Those on whose livelihood it depends understand that a good portrait reflects and, if necessary, fashions the perpetual youth, virility and power of its subject. This portrait did not disappoint. Dressed in military uniform, Don Alfonso's head was large, his chin prominent, his hair black and cropped short like a soldier's. His dark eyes and furrowed brow gazed past the viewer, intent on a distant prize. His tight lips were framed by a thin mustache and dark pointed beard that hinted of casual cruelty. His right hand rested on his hip, his left on the jeweled hilt of a sword sheathed in a silver scabbard. Juan admired the portrait and the skill of the painter, whose art had miraculously rejuvenated one whom Juan knew to be a pocked and bloated relic of fifty years. Still, the splendid villa that Don Alfonso surveyed from his wood and canvas station at the top of the stairs also reminded Juan of the Don's power, and of the blood with which his wealth had been purchased. Esmerelda averted her eyes as they passed, silently leading Juan across the wide hall to the door of her mistress' bedroom.

Esmerelda knocked once and then quickly three times. She jumped back, startled, as the door flew open and a slender young woman with bright eyes and long, shining black hair reached out, grabbed Juan by the front of his coat, and pulled him into the room. Esmerelda frowned disapprovingly, but Dona Julia just laughed. "Do not be cross with me, Esmerelda – love is not a river to be made placid behind a dam. No! It is a waterfall whose beauty depends on its plummet from soaring heights to foaming depths." She cast a conspiratorial smile at the girl. "Alfonso is away on a hunt, but keep close watch." Biting her tongue, Esmerelda nodded and backed away. As the heavy door closed with a thump, she reflected that rivers are something to drown in as well.

CHAPTER 7
The Evolution of Desire

SHE REMEMBERED *every moment. How when Juan was fourteen and Julia eighteen, her brush of his cheek was as chaste as a young maiden's heart, and as pure as the snow that falls early in the morning, when the wind is still. To her older friend, Juan's mother Dona Inez, Julia would confide that Juan was a lovely boy who would grow ever more handsome. Inez would nod a little sadly, reminded that the rise of life's arc is so much shorter than its fall.*

Julia held a special place in Inez's heart, for had Juan's older sister lived she would have been only two years younger than Julia. Luna – named for the unusual crescent moon birthmark just below her left shoulder – was just a few months shy of her second birthday when she died. But she had already displayed a quick and lively intelligence, and her mother thrilled at the proud spirit she saw in her young daughter's clear blue eyes. Inez's husband, who traced his ancestry to the Kings of Aragon who ruled the island of Malta in the fourteenth century, was every bit as proud; he had insisted on bringing Luna with him to visit his parents, who still lived on the island. Both had perished when their ship was lost in the Mediterranean, just off the Barbary coast near Tunis. Inez was pregnant with Juan and, despite her devastation, resolved to raise her second child to be as strong and fearless as her first.

The boy to whom Inez first introduced her was awkward and shy, as boys of that age often are, but Julia saw in him an emerging strength of character that she admired. "When he laughs," Inez would sigh, "he reminds me so much of Luna." Looking to the sky, she crossed herself. "May she smile on us from her perch at God's side."

Julia recalled Juan at sixteen; tall, willowy and darkly handsome. How, when she and Juan saw each other, their glances had grown tentative and indirect, their eyes cast downward. In his youth, Juan was confused by this strange rush of feeling. Julia, two years wed to the hidalgo Don Alfonso, understood better, but resolved for the sake of honor, virtue and faith to resist temptation – she would see the boy no more. Solely to test that resolve, she called upon Inez the following day, angling her chair to face the parlor door. So often did she glance up that Inez thought her friend had business elsewhere.

She remembered how she had been impatient at her weakness, and had determined to confront the passions with which she struggled. She would face Juan, and would overcome the impure whispers of her heart. He would be like a brother, their connection forged by the familial fondness that puts closeness between siblings beyond reproach. And were he to ask or, not asking, stoop to kiss her face or neck or lips, she had but to reject his advances, as she had the advances of other men when she too was less than twenty.

Further, any touch they might share would be innocent, and as platonic as the love that the goddesses have for Man, excepting of course that of Venus for the handsome Adonis, which was quite a different thing and of no present account. If first a hand be kissed and then a lip, she would still her passions as firmly as she reined in the Andalusian mare that Don Alfonso had given her on their wedding day. Still, despite her efforts to distract herself with other things, these thoughts left her flushed and unsettled.

Juan too had felt the stirrings of love. He spent days wandering in the woods and along the grassy banks of the streams he knew far better than the uncharted island of his heart. Of Julia he thought much; of her large, expressive dark eyes, her full lips and kind smile, her high cheeks flushed a soft sunset crimson – and of her breasts, concealed and yet ripely conspicuous, their gentle rise and fall visible against the unblemished cotton of her blouse.

Upon greeting or bidding him farewell, Julia's touch now lingered for seconds that seemed like minutes, and he felt a shiver and a stirring that must surely be obvious to all. Yet no one spoke of it or seemed to notice, though he felt its effects for days. He felt all at once helpless, lost and joyful.

Julia smiled as she recalled their courtship's culmination. How finally – and with her husband in Madrid on business, purposefully – she had invited Juan to join her late one sunny June afternoon for a glass of fine manzanilla pasada. Juan drank little, but, not wanting to offend, downed several glasses of the salty, tangy sherry as Julia sipped her own. When they kissed, at first tentatively and then in a colliding rush of hands and lips, all hesitations, resolutions and promises were forgotten. Breaking away with her thick black hair in tangles, Julia led Juan out of the parlor, up the curving staircase, past the handsome portrait of Don Alfonso, and down the upstairs hall to her bedroom.

Where, on a night almost six months later, they lay panting from the exertion of their lovemaking. Juan rolled over onto his side so that he could face Julia, who dabbed at her glistening neck with the sheet. "Don't do that," he growled, pretending to be fierce. "It is known that he who licks the sweat of love from the neck of a beautiful woman will never tire, and can make love until the dawn."

Julia laughed. "This is known?"

Juan assured her that it was, demonstrating with his tongue how the precious dew should be harvested. Julia tossed her head back onto the pillow and, with a satisfied sigh, informed Juan that greater reservoirs could be found further south. But before an expedition could be launched there came a sudden knock on the door – once, and then two times in quick succession. In unison, Juan and Julia bolted upright, their wide eyes fixed on the door.

"Esmerelda, what is it?" Julia's voice was tight.

"It is Senor Alfonso," whispered the girl. "There are men with him. Hurry!"

CHAPTER 8
One Way Out

THERE WAS *no time to flee, little time to hide. Only moments after Esmerelda's warning, they heard the sounds of men climbing the stairs. Despite the girl's protests, the door burst open and Don Alfonso strode into the room. Behind him were two men, one of whom Julia recognized as Carlos, a decommissioned Valencian foot soldier whose loyalty to Alfonso apparently compensated for his paucity of wit. With him was Don Alfonso's lawyer Miguel, a slender man who fairly twitched with a calculating nervous energy – Julia referred to him as El Ardilla, the Squirrel. Alfonso was breathing hard and his face was flushed, either from exertion or from wine, perhaps both. His eyes darted about the room and settled on Julia, who sat upright in the center of the wide bed, blankets and bed covers clumped around her, the fine linen sheet clutched tight against her breasts.*

"So, is this how you greet your wife after a time away, Alfonso?" Julia's voice dripped with scorn. "Perhaps you thought it might be amusing to humiliate me before your friends, eh?"

Alfonso ignored her. In two strides he crossed the room to the closet, whose twin doors he pulled open with a flourish, the frames banging against the plastered wall. He peered in – dresses, coats, skirts, several large hats and a startling assortment of undergarments peered back. Holding his short sword before him like a taper, he shifted the dresses first to one side and then the other, revealing nothing but bare wall. He turned back to his wife, who continued to berate him.

"What exactly do you plan on doing with that sword, Alfonso?" Julia laughed bitterly. "Will you run me through? No doubt it's the hardest thing you've brought to this room in many weeks."

Alfonso blushed an even deeper red as his lawyer diplomatically examined the room's fine Venetian carpet. Carlos, his lupine jaw agape, simply stared at the half-naked Julia, apparently hoping that she might relax her grip on the concealing sheets. Alfonso gave Carlos a withering look, then bent low to peer under the bed.

"Yes, Alfonso," Julia mocked, "that is where I keep my lovers – it is so convenient to have them close. Sometimes they come up and, if they ask nicely, sometimes I go down." She addressed the lawyer. "Miguel, don't you agree that it is the logistics that make infidelity so complicated?"

Miguel shrugged but said nothing. He recognized a deteriorating case when he saw one, and considered the mitigation of loss a crucial aspect of his services.

With a touch of desperation, Don Alfonso again surveyed the room and then – his eye falling on a slight gap in the curtains framing the window to the left of the bed – raised an eyebrow to Miguel and motioned. Miguel looked doubtful but, heeding the instructions of his client, murmured an apology and eased his way around the bed toward the window.

"Ah, Alfonso," said Julia, her sarcasm biting, "you have solved the riddle of the disappearing lover! In the few seconds it took you and your imbecilic companions to enter our house and rush up the stairs, my lover gathered up his clothes, leaped barefoot and naked from my second-floor window onto the cold stone below, and ran away while I closed the window behind him and returned to my bed." She regarded Miguel sadly, as if his involvement in this matter were a vast disappointment. "Miguel, open the window."

Miguel glanced at Alfonso, who nodded. Sweeping the curtains aside, the lawyer grasped the thin iron handle and lifted. The window did not budge. Using both hands, Miguel tried again, with the same result. He turned toward Alfonso and shrugged. "It appears to be stuck."

"Yes, it is stuck, they are all stuck, the handiwork of the idiot painters your brilliant client hired to save a few escudos." She turned back to Alfonso. "But if you manage to get one open, Alfonso, perhaps you will be so kind as to toss me out of it, as I would rather fall to my death than be humiliated further by my own husband." Julia's lip trembled and, with a soft, throaty sob, she began to cry.

Deflated, Alfonso started to stammer an apology. Julia, her breath coming in gasps, would have none of it. "Go! Get out, all of you, before I seize my husband's useless sword and wash these tears away with my own blood!"

Alfonso motioned to his men, who backed out of the room, apologizing as they withdrew. Promising to return and explain himself, he turned and followed, pulling the door shut behind him.

At the sound of the latch, the bed linens, blankets and sheets billowed like a sail, rose as though enchanted, and then fell like a punctured soufflé. From within, half-suffocated, emerged young Juan, who had been curled up in hiding, his head enveloped by Julia's thighs. His face was red and his dark hair tangled – Julia thought he looked adorable. But she was not insensible to the continuing danger, and quickly pushed him towards the open closet. "Remain still!" she whispered. "In a few hours it will be morning, and when Alfonso leaves you can slip away!"

Juan grinned and stole a quick kiss, then slid into the closet and closed the door behind him. And just in time. Within seconds Julia heard a light tapping on the bedroom door. She waited, and the tapping was renewed. Pausing for a few moments more, she finally called out her assent, and Don Alfonso – this time with neither men nor sword – edged into the bedroom. "My darling Julia," he offered soothingly, "I know you must think me mad." Looking heavenward, he made the sign of the cross. "May God strike me down where I stand if I lie ..."

Julia crossed her arms over her chest and turned away. "I hope he does so quickly, my husband, so that I do not have to bear the insult of your excuses on top of the humiliation you have caused me already."

Alfonso was contrite. "Julia, my love, my gentle angel." He was beseeching. "I own twice as many years as you, and the price I have paid for each of them is written in the lines of my face. There are times when I cannot believe that a woman as young and beautiful as you could ever be faithful to one such as me, and when these dark thoughts arise, they consume me. Every sign – a drawn curtain, the tread of an unfamiliar horse, a lightness to your step when I have been away – leads me to suspect the worst." He bowed his head. "Such thoughts are unworthy, my love .... "

He did not complete the thought, for as he approached the bed he stumbled over a pair of shoes half-hidden by the overflowing bed linens. This would not have been remarkable, nor would its consequences have been ruinous, but for the fact that the shoes in question were not women's shoes and they were not Alfonso's. He looked at the shoes, and at Julia, and once again at the shoes. Then, uttering the foulest of oaths, he bolted from the room to retrieve his sword.

Leaping from the bed, Julia ran to the closet and threw open the doors. "Juan, run before he gets back! Run!"

Needing no encouragement, Juan raced for the door, hoping to make his escape before the enraged Alfonso could return. Alfonso had moved quickly, however and, sword in hand, met Juan near the top of the stairs, Alfonso heading up, Juan heading down.

While Juan may not have occupied the moral high ground at this critical juncture, his tactical position was superior. With a forceful shove he pushed Alfonso down the stairs, the Don's sword scattering away as he fell. Without pausing, Juan flew down the stairs three at a time, leaped over the sprawling Alfonso, and ran out the front door and through the open gate to the street.

From her window above, Julia watched her handsome young lover's flight, and followed his racing form until it disappeared around the corner. Retreating from the window to her bed, she fell back onto the pillows, the tears hot in her dark brown eyes.

CHAPTER 9
Castlereagh

'Let there be light,' said God, and there was light!
'Let there be blood,' says man, and there's a sea!

DON JUAN, CANTO VII

THE MORNING light in London, brooded Lord Castlereagh, Foreign Secretary of His Majesty's George IV's government, invariably promised more than it delivered. Castlereagh had arrived at his office at dawn on a brisk November morning and had drawn aside the heavy drapes on either side of his desk, hoping the morning sun might dissipate the night's lingering chill. But the winter sunlight offered no more warmth than a harlot's smile, and hours later the Foreign Secretary's spacious office was as cold as when he'd arrived.

He seemed always to be cold these days. A handsome man in his early-fifties, Castlereagh's pale complexion and perpetually tousled auburn hair hinted at his Dublin roots. As a child, Castlereagh had been sickly but extraordinarily able. He excelled at Cambridge – unusual for gentlemen peers, who by tradition preferred to coast – and returned to Ireland intent on a career in politics. His outlook was for the most part progressive, and the first years of his political career were spent as a Whig, supporting political reform and opposing the repressive Irish policies of the Tory government.

But, like so many of his contemporaries, Castlereagh had been shocked by the chaos of the French Revolution, the bloody Terror that followed, and the rise of the autocratic Napoleon. By the time he entered government service in the last decade of the 18th century, his fear of a French invasion in Ireland, and the forceful separation of the Emerald Isle from England, outweighed his disapproval of England's mistreatment of Ireland's Catholic majority. Called upon to take a leading role in the suppression of the Irish Rebellion of 1798, he displayed a ruthless efficiency that impressed his superiors and chilled his critics. Yet Castlereagh's instincts were not authoritarian – he generally preferred the carrot, not the stick, and was capable of great subtlety when he thought it useful.

Leaning forward in his chair, Castlereagh contemplated the dispatches that had arrived in a steady stream from Constantinople and were now deposited in a diplomatic alluvium on his desk. As he re-read them all, he was once again reminded of the endless complexity and brutality of international affairs. Sifting through the dispatches, he found what he was looking for and, sighing, read it again:

26 April
To His Lordship, Viscount Castlereagh

His Lordship will recall my reports of atrocities committed both by rebellious Greek subjects of the Ottoman Turks and by the Sultan's janissary corps. Within the past month, the janissaries burned two Orthodox Christian churches with its congregations inside, and publicly executed another twenty-three local prelates, whose heads were then displayed in Adrianople's Grvelsi Square. Similar barbarisms have occurred in many of the towns and cities through which the uprising has advanced.

In accordance with your directions and the policies of His Majesty's Government, I have managed to prevail upon the Porte to refrain from more systematic and widespread persecution of the

Orthodox Christian community. To that Government's credit, it has for the most part done so, to the extent consistent with its legitimate interests in quelling a rebellion of subjects within its borders.

Three days ago, the restraint thus far exercised by the Sultan gave way. In the Sultan's name and, I am informed, on his orders, the Ecumenical Patriarch Grigorios V was seized from his quarters in Constantinople. Begging for his life, he was hanged in the public square, and his defiled corpse dragged through the streets. He was eighty-two years old and, despite the Porte's claims that he was complicit in the present insurgency, had publicly condemned it. These barbaric measures, visited upon the principal prelate of the Orthodox Church, would without more be likely to inflame sectarian passions both here and elsewhere; that they were carried out on Easter Sunday, a coincidence that could hardly be accidental, was an additional insult ....

Castlereagh shuddered. He had seen violence like this before, in Dublin; had watched the fevered mob advance; heard the shrieks of its victims; smelled the blood that ran in sluggish streams through the narrow streets, staining the ancient stones.

Metternich had seen it all coming. He always did, was always a step or two ahead, even when his own hand was weak.

Castlereagh recalled his first meeting with the Foreign Minister of the Austrian Empire in February, 1813, less than a year before representatives of the major powers met at the Conference of Vienna. The winter had been mild in Vienna until shortly before Castlereagh's arrival, and not even the local tributaries of the Danube had frozen over. But the snows had blown in from the north the previous week and when Castlereagh arrived, shards of ice clinging to the flanks of the horses that pulled his carriage, two feet of fresh snow blanketed Vienna's cobbled streets. It was several days before the snow stopped falling, and travel within the city had come to a soft and muffled halt.

He recalled their initial discussions. The drifting snow having made it impossible to reach the imposing Schönbrunn Palace, their meeting had been shifted to a modest but well-appointed private residence owned by an older brother of Metternich's wife Eleonore. Stamping the snow off their boots and brushing it from their coats, they had settled in without deputies in a cozy downstairs study lined with books and warmed by a blazing fire in a deep stone hearth. "Ah, Viscount Castlereagh," Metternich had asked in greeting, "how do you like our winter?"

"Well, Foreign Minister, my attitudes on such matters have evolved. I've always detested the cold. But ever since the Corsican's armies foundered on the Russian steppes, I have become more appreciative of Winter's virtues!"

They'd sat for hours in comfortable armchairs around a heavy wooden table, drinking first tea, then wine, then a fine, aged Irish whiskey that Castlereagh had brought with him as a gift. It had taken only a few minutes for the British Foreign Minister to recognize that Metternich's reputation as a strategist was well-deserved.

"You must think us foolish," the Austrian had observed with a disarming smile, "to have entered into an ostensible alliance with the Corsican."

"No, not so foolish. Your armies' valor didn't prevent the French from occupying Vienna. Had I been in your position, facing renewed French threats less than three years later, I can't say I'd have done any different."

"Our choices were unattractive."

Castlereagh saw an opening. "Prussia is in the ascendency, and in Russia Tsar Alexander practically bursts with restless ambition. Perhaps Austria is more open than before to the possibility of a closer alliance with England?"

"It's a fool who clings to a strategy that has outlived its use. Circumstances have changed, and I concede that such an alliance may have advantages. But there are risks as well."

"You mean the French?"

"I mean the Russians." Metternich leaned forward, his hands clasped and resting on the table. "What are *your* views on such matters, Foreign Secretary?"

"Fortunes wax and wane, both of men and states. As France contracts, competing empires will be emboldened, and it won't be long before we find that one threat has been replaced by another."

"Precisely. Your solution?"

Castlereagh chuckled. "You're Metternich. Isn't that a question I should put to you?"

"I have no answers, only questions. But at least our objectives are clear."

"*Our* objectives? So, you agree that we are aligned on these matters?"

Metternich waved impatiently. "Oh, there will be particulars on which we disagree, questions of emphasis and degree. On the major issues, however, I see only common interests. We both fear Alexander's expansionist ambitions – a re-invigorated Russia is a threat to Austria in the Balkans and to British interests in the Mediterranean."

"And these other common interests?"

Metternich grunted. "Come now, Lord Castlereagh – you ask a question to which you know the answer." He paused, waiting for the Englishman to commit himself, but Castlereagh merely smiled.

Metternich arched his brow and nodded to Castlereagh's glass. "Are you just going to sniff that good whiskey, or do you intend to drink it?"

"I suppose that depends on your answer."

Metternich sighed, gazing out the window at the drifted snow. "So be it; I will tell you what you already know." He gestured at the drifts. "There will never be enough snow to soak up the blood of revolution. None of us, myself included, understood what was happening in Paris until the heads were gathered in baskets by the hundreds, and fires blazed that could be extinguished only by a decade of war."

Metternich rose to throw another log on the dwindling fire, which offered its thanks in a shower of sparks. Brushing bits of bark from his hands, he stood before the hearth, staring into the flames. "The threat is hardly limited to the Continent. Your government underestimated nationalistic forces in the American colonies, and has paid a price that it will take centuries to calculate."

The Austrian crumpled a sheet of paper and tossed it on the fire, where it quivered for a few moments before bursting into flame. "Embers are smoldering all over Europe: in the incipient German states, in Italy, in Spain, in the Balkans – even in your own Ireland. You ask about common interests? We – the great empires – are threatened by the fires of nationalist revolution, and the inciting winds of ethnic and religious rivalry. If we're not very careful, they may immolate us all."

Now, six years later, Castlereagh shook his head, forcing himself to return to the present. The crisis Metternich had predicted had arrived. Addressing the Eastern Question – what to do about the damned Greeks' incipient rebellion against the Turks, and the escalating massacres that threatened to degenerate into a broader, destabilizing conflict – could no longer be postponed.

Absently, the Foreign Minister sipped his tea. It wasn't that he cared a whit for the Turks; the sclerotic Ottoman Empire had been disintegrating for decades, and its dissolution was inevitable. But a slow and controlled dissolution could be managed. A precipitous collapse was quite a different matter, posing a serious threat to the equilibrium upon which peace in Europe depended. If the present crisis could not be contained, Castlereagh feared that a broad, major power conflagration might be unavoidable. This was an outcome that had to be avoided, no matter what the cost.

The Foreign Secretary rose and called for his assistant. In a few moments, Thomas Reilly, a rail-thin, earnest young Dubliner fresh out of Cambridge, appeared in the door. "Yes sir?"

"Lord Strangford's in London, visiting with his family. Send him a message that I want to see him right away."

"Here, sir?"

"Yes, Reilly, here. In London. In my office."

"Yes, m'lord. Shall I tell him what it's about?"

Castlereagh sighed. "I'm the bloody Foreign Secretary, and Strangford's the Crown's envoy to the *Porte*."

Reilly looked blank.

"The Ottoman central government – do they teach you nothing in university these days? I expect he'll manage to puzzle it out."

Reilly blanched. "Right away, m'lord."

"And when you've attended to it, Reilly, see what you can do about reviving this fire. It's bloody cold in here."

As his assistant withdrew, Castlereagh pressed his fingers against his temples, hoping to relieve another of his headaches. There seemed to be no good solutions to the Eastern Question; only solutions that were bad and solutions that were even worse. Despite the reputation for ruthlessness with which he had emerged from the chaos of the Irish Rebellion, Castlereagh considered himself a man of principle. Yet in order to protect Austrian interests, even Metternich had been willing to enter into a marriage of convenience with the hated Napoleon. If their situations had been reversed, would Castlereagh have been willing to do the same? Just how far was he prepared to go to protect God, country, and the lives of a generation of Englishmen?

CHAPTER 10
Scandal Sells

They accuse me – me – the present writer of
The present poem of – I know not what –
A tendency to underrate and scoff
At human power and virtue and all that;
And this they say in language rather rough.
Good God! I wonder what they would be at!
I say no more than has been said in Dante's
Verse, and by Solomon and by Cervantes.

DON JUAN, CANTO VII

A CROWD – orderly, expectant and for the most part well-mannered – was gathered outside Hatchard's, on Piccadilly. Founded in 1787, Hatchard's had long been London's preeminent book seller. The shop catered to the affluent and the powerful, and generally looked down on the middle class. The poor and dispossessed it ignored entirely. It was not Hatchard's practice to ride cresting waves of popular culture, and its proprietor saw no reason to indulge the latest passing fancies.

It was therefore surprising, shortly after 10:00 a.m. on an overcast morning in late November, to see scores of customers queuing up within the book shop and spilling out into the street. Regulars could not remember a time when the shop's titles had generated even modest popular interest, much less this morning's frenzy. Even more surprising was the publication that had attracted so many customers to its doors.

"'S'it true what they say about 'im?" asked a stout woman in a garish, ill-fitting yellow dress, the strings of her matching bonnet lost in the fleshy folds of her chins.

Her companion, as skinny as her friend was stout, laughed. "It can't all be true, Janie. If it was, you and I would be carrying his pups, and he'd not get a minute's sleep!"

At the front of the line, an angry patron was arguing with a lanky young clerk whose frameless spectacles rested crookedly on his thin nose. "I came here to buy four," insisted the red-faced customer, mopping sweat from his brow with a damp hankie, "and that is what I intend to do. Are you in the business of selling these volumes or not?"

"I understand, sir," the clerk explained patiently, "but as you can see, we have more customers than volumes, and the sign very plainly says one to a customer." He pointed to a neat, hand-lettered placard that sat on the counter. *Don Juan, by George Gordon, Lord Byron: One to a Customer.*

"I've waited in the queue for fifteen minutes, and saw your sign only when I got up here to the front. If you had put the sign where it belongs, I'd have seen it right off."

The clerk looked past the man's shoulder. "The queue is to the street, sir; perhaps we should have posted it on a passing carriage?" He lowered his voice. "I will sell you one now and place one on hold for you in the back. You can pick it up tomorrow."

Reckoning that half a loaf was better than none, the customer grumbled his assent and, to the clerk's relief – he'd half expected the blustering fool to drop dead on the spot – the transaction was completed. In less than two hours' time, Hatchard's allotment of three hundred bound volumes – Cantos I and II of Byron's latest – had been reduced to less than thirty, with more customers waiting to buy.

The clerk considered cutting off the line, but Mr. Hatchard was very strict about encouraging patrons to peruse the shop's titles broadly.

Perhaps those who missed out on the Byron might be interested in Cuninghame's latest revelations regarding the Anti-Christ, whose origins the meticulous cleric had traced to the year 533, when Justinian I granted universal rule to the Papacy. Co-marketing the two titles, the clerk reflected, would be inspired; a number of this morning's customers had made it a point to declare, their voices raised so that all might hear, that Byron's *Don Juan* was only the most recent sign of England's continuing moral decay. A few others, fearing perhaps that they themselves might be questioned, signaled their agreement with dour nods of disapproval.

Well, the clerk conceded with a wry smile, it is vital indeed that the arc of the realm's spiritual descent be monitored closely. Resolving to soldier on to the last volume, no matter the cost to public decency, he turned to assist his next indignant customer.

CHAPTER II
Melbourne

A real husband always is suspicious,
But still no less suspects in the wrong place,
Jealous of someone who had no such wishes,
Or pandering blindly to his own disgrace
By harboring some dear friend extremely vicious,
The last indeed's infallibly the case,
And when the spouse and friend are gone off wholly,
He wonders at their vice, and not his folly.

DON JUAN, CANTO I

WILLIAM AND Caroline Lamb's suite of rooms at Melbourne House were directly above those of the formidable Lady Melbourne, who had situated her son and daughter-in-law in close proximity, the better to monitor their turbulent marriage. Caroline liked to blame her husband for having corrupted an innocent maiden, but it was her disastrous affair with Sir Godfrey Webster, the son of Lady Melbourne's contemporary Lady Holland, that justified Byron's admittedly cruel observation that he could never be accused of having corrupted Caroline – her reputation was in tatters before he ever met her.

William Lamb had been an idle but promising dilettante when he met the nineteen-year old Caroline Ponsonby, whose aunt was said to have run up gambling debts of more than £1,000,000 before her death at forty-seven, and whose mother was so sexually promiscuous, and so indifferent to her daughter's welfare, that Caroline's grandmother felt compelled to remove the child from her care. More than ten years her senior, Lamb was tall, handsome in a wavy-haired, straight-nosed, strong-chinned aristocratic sort of way, and rich. She had been charmed by his modest forays into verse, which Byron – with uncharacteristic restraint in the first days of their affair – carefully praised as "earnest." Like Byron, he was a Cambridge man, and though he had yet to achieve prominence, he was intelligent and sophisticated and already inclined towards politics. But, only two years from their wedding vows, the volatility which had once made Caroline so interesting had become a problem.

Although Caroline's affair with Webster was messy – and to her husband's dismay, publicly so – Lamb had tolerated it and had defended her to his mother, who was not nearly as forgiving. Indeed, Lady Melbourne was the topic of a simmering quarrel that had now boiled over.

"Your mother," charged Caroline, her voice shrill, "has detested me from the day we met; a disregard which I assure you is entirely mutual." Glaring at her husband, she took a deep breath. "I can live with her contempt; I can tolerate her sarcastic asides; I can even put up with her prattling lectures, though I may have to kill the woman if those continue." She lowered her voice, aware that Lady Melbourne might be listening downstairs. "But I can no longer abide her continuing efforts to tarnish my name with everyone in her preposterous social circle which, unfortunately, happens to be our preposterous social circle as well!"

William laughed, which only made Caroline angrier. He straightened his face. "Yes, my mother is a woman of strong convictions."

"Strong convictions? One has convictions on matters of philosophy, or on the political issues of the day, or perhaps on the relative merits of mutton and pork. Your mother's feelings toward me have nothing to do with conviction; she hates me because I embarrass her, and am not nearly good enough for her brilliant son!" Furious, she slammed her palm on a side table, knocking over a glass figurine – a swan, William believed, or maybe a duck – which shattered on the dark oak floor.

"She has her devious fingers in countless pies! Byron knows her, even calls her his friend – he's said as much!" She paused. Although William – together with most of London society – was aware of her affair with Byron, she generally tried not to rub his nose in it. At the moment, though, she didn't really care what he thought.

But if he was upset or angry, he didn't show it. Instead, he crossed the room to a side table, on which sat a silver tray holding glasses and a dozen bottles. Selecting a smoky Highland single malt, he poured himself a drink. He glanced inquiringly at his wife, who shook her head.

"I understand how you feel, Caroline," he said softly, hoping to drain some of the emotion from the room. "I'll speak to Lady Melbourne." He doubted it would make the slightest impact on his mother, who was as strong-willed as his wife.

He lifted his glass and took a healthy swallow, which must have pleased him because he took another. "This matter with Byron, Caroline, has become an embarrassment." His voice hardened. "Do you not realize that his reputation adds no luster to yours?"

Of course, thought Caroline. *His concern is with appearances. I could fuck a horse, and so long as the stable door was shut he wouldn't say a word.*

"Is it my reputation that concerns you, William?" Her voice dripped with sarcasm. "Where was your concern for my reputation when poor Aunt Georgiana couldn't repay your father's loan, and was interrupted in her London apartments by the gruesomely public service of a writ?"

"My father acts to protect his interests according to his own judgment; he does not consult with me beforehand." William drained his scotch and gazed longingly through one of the tall windows that looked out on the Melbourne House gardens and beyond them to the Thames. "Your reputation and mine are not entirely independent, wouldn't you say? And I would have no wish to see yours sullied even if they were." Setting the heavy crystal glass down on the table, he nudged fragments of shattered figurine aside with his foot.

"For God's sake, Caroline, you and I both know that this thing with Byron will run its course – it will burn out like one of those magnesium *fusees* that Davy displayed at the RS last year."

Caroline hesitated. William's belief that her affair with Byron was nothing more than a diversion misapprehended the intensity of their feelings. But it was convenient to have him think so; were he to believe otherwise, his infuriating aristocratic tolerance just might give way to jealousy. While the spectacle of William in a jealous rage would be satisfying, it might also be dangerous, not only to Byron, but to herself. She underestimated neither Lady Melbourne's influence nor her spite.

Besides, she had to admit that William was not the only one who thought her rash, and her passions fleeting. Shortly after their first meeting, Byron had sent her a rose with an accompanying note: *"Your Ladyship, I am told, likes everything that is new and rare, if only for a moment."*

William reached out and smoothed Caroline's hair, tucking a wayward curl behind her ear. As rebellious as its owner, it promptly escaped. "We mustn't fight, Caroline. I'm no good at it, and am certainly no match for you." He glanced downward, indicating his mother's rooms below. "Lady Melbourne," he confided in a low voice, "calls me a pushover. She says that you have your way with me too often, and that she fears for my safety!" He brushed her cheek with the back of his hand, trailing it softly along her neckline.

Shuddering, she felt her anger dissipate like the sudden breaking of a fever. Determined to tap the last of its energy, she heaved an exasperated sigh. "There are times, William, I have been tempted to blow my brains out, but for the recollection that it would bring pleasure to my mother-in-law. *Even then*, if I could be certain to haunt her ...."

He laughed – she had always liked his laugh. "You do know that I love you, William; you *know* that I do. That will never change." Stepping close to her husband, she stood on her toes to kiss his lips, her delicate hands clinging to his coat for balance. As always with Caroline, William felt his annoyance metamorphose into something else, and Caroline felt it as well. Releasing her right hand from his coat, she caressed him through his trousers, tracing his stiffening manhood with her fingers. "If your mother is listening," she whispered huskily, "let's at least make it worth her while."

CHAPTER 12
Strangford

All that the mind would shrink from of excesses,
All that the body perpetrates of bad,
All that we read, hear, dream of man's distresses,
All that the devil would do if run stark mad,
All that defies the worst which pen expresses,
All by which hell is peopled, or as sad
As hell, mere mortals who their power abuse,
Was here (as heretofore and since) let loose.

DON JUAN, CANTO VIII

ONLY TWO weeks after Lord Strangford's appointment as His Majesty's Ambassador to the Sublime *Porte*, all hell broke loose in bloody Constantinople.

At first, Tsar Alexander's reluctance to intervene on behalf of the Orthodox Greeks seemed likely to doom the incipient rebellion to failure. But as word of the uprising reached cities, towns and villages that had long chafed under Ottoman rule, crowds became mobs and, before long, hundreds of Muslims were driven from their homes or burned inside them. Reprisals were swift and the violence escalated, provoking further atrocities on both sides. Within a few frenzied months, thousands were murdered in alternating violence that pitted Greek subjects against Turkish overlords, Greek peasants against Turkish landowners, and Greek Christians against Turkish Moslems.

Strangford had anticipated an unsettled situation, though not this level of violence. A boyish-looking young man in his mid-thirties, Percy Clinton Sydney Smythe – after his father's death, 6th Viscount, Lord Strangford – had done well in his initial posting in Portugal and had welcomed his new posting. Yet it was neither Constantinople's might nor any illusions of imperial permanence that appealed to the newly-appointed ambassador. To the contrary, it was precisely the precariousness of the Ottoman Empire, and the opportunity to play a role in managing its dissolution to England's advantage, that he found intriguing.

Strangford stood awkwardly at the door, waiting for Castlereagh to acknowledge his presence. He had been in London visiting family, and the summons to meet with the Foreign Secretary had been a surprise.

After a few moments, the Foreign Secretary's assistant finished stoking the fire and took his leave. Castlereagh, a sheaf of dispatches in his hand, crossed the room to shake the envoy's hand – "Good of you to come, Strangford" – and gestured towards the twin Queen Anne chairs facing the crackling fire. "Sit," he commanded, as though to a loyal dog.

As always, the Foreign Secretary was polite and solicitous, but Strangford didn't miss the faint circles beneath Castlereagh's piercing green eyes. It had been only a few months since he'd seen him last, but Strangford was shocked to see that much of Castlereagh's Irish auburn hair had turned grey as the London sky. The older man was elegantly attired in a cream-colored waistcoat of fine Lambeth wool and a royal blue jacket, but Strangford noted that some of the weight of his obligations had migrated to his waist.

"It's nice to be back home for a time," Strangford ventured. "It's a relief from the incessant heat in Constantinople." He knew better than to plunge into matters of substance, or to profess opinions without leave.

"I've been cold all morning," Castlereagh grumbled, "but it keeps one awake, no matter how dreary the reading material at hand." He waved the sheaf of papers at Strangford, whose heart sank as he recognized them as his dispatches from Constantinople.

"Actually, Strangford," Castlereagh reassured him, "I appreciate your reports. Unlike so much of the teeter-totter nonsense I usually receive – on the one hand this, on the other hand that – yours possess relevant factual details, display close observation, and, from time to time, actually venture an opinion." As his boss openly appraised the young envoy, Strangford fought off the urge to shift in his seat. "In any event, you seem to have a talent for cultivating useful sources of intelligence."

Pleased at the unexpected compliment, Strangford inclined his head. "If my reports have enabled his Lordship to appreciate the import of recent events in the Levant, I am glad of it. In all candor, sir, it's the complexity of the *Porte*'s internal politics that makes the situation so difficult to assess."

"What do you mean?"

"The *Porte* is rife with intrigue, various factions fighting for influence with the Sultan, who carefully plays one off against the other. Meanwhile, the Greek Orthodox Patriarch was encouraged to believe himself secure enough not to need the Tsar's protection, but not so secure that he felt at liberty to defy the Sultan. The *reis effendi* referred to him only two months ago as the Sultan's Cardinal Wolsey."

"The *reis effendi* is a student of English history?"

"Apparently, although which version I cannot say."

"Wolsey was cast aside when he couldn't procure the divorce Henry demanded. The *reis effendi* was saying that Gregory's position – and, as it turned out, his life – depended upon his ability to deliver? And to deliver what?"

Strangford shrugged; he wasn't sure what the *reis effendi* intended.

"Well," Castlereagh sighed, "whatever the Sultan expected, it would appear that Gregory failed to produce it."

Nodding, Strangford pressed on. "The janissaries who make up the core of the empire's military are arrogant and debauched – they don't so much fight as plunder. While the Sultan has taken steps to curtail their worst excesses, for the most part he tolerates them, perhaps in the hope that their cruelty may intimidate the rebels into submission. If so, it's a miscalculation; all it's done is to remind the insurgents how much they hate the Turks. The entire situation is getting out of hand."

"And the Greeks? How do you assess their capabilities? And their will to fight?"

"These Greeks? They're beset by faction and divided by ethnic and family loyalties and hatreds. Regional chieftains vie for power, as suspicious of their countrymen as they are of the Turks." Strangford shook his head. "Perhaps this is what comes from four hundred years of subjugation."

"Hmm. Shared hatreds do have a way of papering over differences – in Scotland, the only thing that kept the Highland clans from slaughtering one another was their greater loathing of the English." He waved the dispatches at Strangford. "You've tried to prevail upon the Turks, through their *reis effendi*, to soften their approach and keep the janissaries in check. Has that done any good?"

"Perhaps a little. But unless the Sultan puts a strong hand to the janissaries, there isn't much the *reis effendi* can do."

With a weary sigh, Castlereagh reviewed the bidding. "To sum it up then, this is a popular insurrection, inspired by nationalist fevers, fueled by pent-up religious and ethnic hatreds, encouraged by the weakness of a corrupt regime, but hamstrung by ethnic and tribal rivalries, as well as by a paucity both of resources and of leadership. Do I have it right?"

"Yes, your Lordship. Not to put too fine a point on it – it's a mess."

"How do you see this playing out?"

"The problem is the Russians, my Lord. The insurgents are Orthodox Christians, so every measure taken by the *Porte* – and every massacre committed by the janissaries – is viewed through the lens of religious persecution. The Turks contend they're putting down a rebellion; the Russians, that they're persecuting a religious minority."

"What does the Russian envoy say of Alexander?"

"That he is horrified at the wholesale slaughter of Christian communities and the destruction of churches and religious icons."

"What do you say?"

"Alexander surely sees this as an opportunity. By leaping to the defense of beleaguered Christians in Greece, he can seize both the moral high ground and – if war with the Turks results – large chunks of their empire."

Castlereagh nodded, his expression grim. "How much time do we have?"

"I'm not certain, my Lord. There are already heavy snows in the Caucasus. I doubt the Tsar will have much appetite for a winter campaign."

"That would give us until at least May, maybe June," mused Castlereagh, staring into the fire. "We are caught on the twin horns of a dilemma, are we not?" Uncertain as to which horns the Foreign Secretary was referring to, Strangford remained silent.

Breaking his gaze, Castlereagh returned to his chair. "If the *Porte* continues on its present course," he explained evenly, "it is unlikely to be able to bring the insurgency to a speedy conclusion. We can therefore expect that countless Greek Orthodox Christians will be slaughtered. The Tsar will rely upon this as a pretext for intervention, and will either declare or provoke war. Either way, Alexander will have his conflict and, sooner rather than later, an advantageous position in the Levant, in the Balkans and, worst of all, in the Eastern Mediterranean."

Tossing Strangford's dispatches onto his desk, Castlereagh rose and wandered again to the hearth, where he stood, extending his hands towards the flames. "On the other hand, if by some miracle the Greeks manage to outlast the Turks, not only will the Ottoman Empire likely collapse, it will fuel nationalist and anti-monarchist passions in the Balkans and quite possibly elsewhere in Europe."

He rubbed at his eyes. "Neither of these outcomes is satisfactory. We have to find a more orderly solution, one that preserves the Ottoman empire in something resembling its present form, and brings a swift resolution to this unpleasantness with the Greeks."

Gesturing towards a bottle of port on the credenza behind his desk, Castlereagh murmured an apology. "I should have offered you a drink, Strangford – would you like one? When Strangford shook his head, Castlereagh looked a little disappointed. "But we also have a political problem; don't we?"

"My Lord?"

"The Tories, who cling so fiercely to conservative orthodoxy that they would sooner be orthodox than right, perceive their cause to be served by the preservation of Ottoman suzerainty over Greece." He shook his head in exasperation. "Stunningly, they're oblivious to the fact that Russian intervention is likely to destroy the Ottoman bulwark they wish to preserve."

"Meanwhile, the Whigs reflexively support nationalist movements as consistent with their vague notions of 'liberty.' They adhere to these views even when the striving nationalists are self-evidently mendacious, or likely by their liberty to deprive others of it." Castlereagh snorted. "While men like Fox, Byron and Sheridan prattle on about the Rights of Man, it's up to us to keep the whole bloody thing from burning to the ground."

With a shrug, the Foreign Secretary turned to escort his envoy to the door. "Reilly," he called, "summon Lord Strangford's carriage."

As the two men shook hands, Castlereagh gripped the ambassador's shoulder. "Continue your reports as before. Do what you can to moderate the Turks' response to the rebellion, particularly with respect to actions involving Christian churches and clergy. Determine how the Russians respond to suggestions of compromise. And – this is of the utmost importance, Strangford – I want you to find a janissary officer with whom we can do business. Someone independent enough to seize an opportunity. It is possible that we may have need of such a man in the months ahead."

Releasing his shoulder, Castlereagh met and held the young envoy's eyes. "You have a bright future, Strangford – you have my trust, which is more than can be said for some of your colleagues. Be sure that you do nothing to make me regret it."

As Strangford departed with young Reilly, Castlereagh thought of the words that opened Byron's *Don Juan*, which he considered scandalous and found that he enjoyed immensely. "I want a hero," Byron declared in the opening stanza of Canto I. *As do I,* the Foreign Secretary of His Majesty's Government murmured to himself thoughtfully, chewing on the beginnings of an audacious idea. *As do I.*

CHAPTER 13
The Partisan

THE ROAD from Missolonghi to Rio was crowded. There were women on foot, their narrow skirts and loose white blouses embroidered at the hem and sleeves in brilliant blue; donkey carts carrying everything from stacked firewood and sunbaked bricks to sharp black olives and golden rounds of cheese; herds of long-haired goats tended by shepherds younger than many of their flock; and, in the region east of Missolonghi, roving patrols of janissaries, their waist-coats blanketed with dust. As sometimes happens, when the Greeks and Turks weren't trying to kill one another they exercised a grudging tolerance that accommodated the mundane requirements of commerce and daily life. Greek blacksmiths shoed Turkish horses; Ottoman administrators levied Greek taxes; Christian and Turkish shepherds tended to their flocks in adjoining pastures. In hilly villages and spreading towns, the hated janissaries could be seen haggling with villagers over the price of olives, tobacco and dates.

In early May the weather in western Greece was temperate, the grass on the hills still green from the winter rains. As evening faded into night, Byron woke with a start. Hobhouse reached over and put his arm on Byron's shoulder.

"It's almost dark," he said. "Time to move." Hobhouse peered at Byron. "What is it, the pain?"

Byron shook his head. "No, it was a dream, a good one. But things began to get ticklish at the end, and I awoke to find you beside me." Byron pressed gingerly at the edges of his wound, which was covered by a white bandage – formerly a woman's blouse – wrapped tightly around his waist. He offered Hobhouse a weak grin. "You're a bit of a disappointment in comparison, but don't blame yourself."

"You're lucky we're still here," sniffed Hobhouse." He gestured toward the doctor, who knelt nearby, peering out through the trees towards the road below. "Polidori wanted to sell you to the Turks, but I told him we'd hardly get enough to make the effort worthwhile."

Byron started to laugh, then winced. "Careful, Hobby. I probably represent half your electoral base."

"You mock my reversals? Were it not for you, the only knives I'd need fear would be political, and wielded not by Turks but by Tories. I lost count of how many times my opponent invoked your notoriety. 'He runs about with a radical poet of doubtful virtue – if his morality is not in question, is not at least his judgment?'"

"Don't despair, Hobby. God won't always be a Tory."

Hobhouse scowled at his old friend. "Did you know, Byron, that not everyone likes you?"

Byron looked astonished. "Perhaps the voters were misinformed? I've been told I'm charming."

"You're skeptical of so much, Byron – why not this?"

Before Byron could respond, Hobhouse turned to Polidori, who had risen to his feet and was gathering what little food and water remained. "Is it clear?"

"Well, no one's in sight right now, and the last Turk patrol passed hours ago." Reaching for their dwindling sack of figs, he took one and passed the others to Byron and Hobhouse. "I suppose we should get started." Hobhouse and Polidori helped Byron to his feet, and together they stepped through a gap in the dense oleander bushes behind which they had sheltered and clambered down the rocky slope to the road below.

In deference to Byron's wounds they walked slowly, heading east toward Rio. They were constantly alert to the smell of fires or the sound of laughter from janissary encampments. When on occasion they smelled wood smoke or grilling meat, they abandoned the road and traipsed in darkness through thin woods or rocky fields. As a consequence, their path was circuitous and, guided only by the waning moon, they stumbled into thorny shrubs, tripped over half-buried stones, and ducked to avoid head-high branches of the occasional terebinth tree.

Stopping for a moment's rest, Hobhouse lifted his nose to the wind. "Do you smell something burning?"

Squinting through the darkness, Byron saw a faint pin-prick glow which just as quickly vanished. Polidori made a circling motion, silently urging a detour. Ignoring him, Byron made his way forward, navigating around scattered rocks and twisted roots. Whoever it was, it didn't look to Byron like a Turkish patrol, and if he didn't need to hide, he didn't want to. After a moment's hesitation, Polidori and Hobhouse followed.

Within a few paces they were able to make out the dim outline of a man sitting on a fallen tree. Not a man, really, so much as a boy of perhaps seventeen, who wore an amused grin as he watched the three Englishmen approach. Boy or not, Byron could see that he was armed with a dagger in a sash around his waist and an over-and-under two-barrel pistol in a leather strap across his chest. Byron thought he might be Greek, though he couldn't be sure; he sometimes found it difficult even to distinguish an Irishman from a Scot, unless you could get him to a bar and see what he was drinking.

As he approached, Byron extended his arms, his palms turned up to the night sky. "*Kalispera*," he said – "Good evening." The boy said nothing, but extended his own hand, which held between thumb and middle finger what looked like a wrapped cylinder of tobacco. Within the past few years, the French had coined a term for such miniature cigars – *cigar-ettes*.

Byron accepted the offering and cautiously took a shallow puff, releasing it quickly. Rolling his eyes, the boy shook his head. "No – I can

THE VIRTUES OF SCANDAL / 63

show." He reclaimed the burning cigar and drew the smoke deep into his lungs, holding it for a few seconds before exhaling. The smoke was sweet in the warm night air. Byron, Polidori and Hobhouse watched with interest; they had never seen a cigar inhaled this way, but then again, this did not smell like most cigars. The boy proffered it once more to Byron, who drew in the smoke, holding it until his lungs burned. He exhaled and coughed, the pain sharp in his wounded flank. Tears welled in his eyes.

The boy laughed. "I hope you sleeped well in the glade behind the oleander," he said in passable English. "It is wise you travel in night. The Turks are often during the day, but at night they drink and eat like pigs."

The Englishmen looked at one another with astonishment. "How did you know where we slept?" asked Hobhouse. Byron was still recovering from his coughing fit and couldn't speak.

"We know who you are," the boy responded, gesturing at Byron. "You are By-roon, the English who gives money and guns to the Greeks; this is the true?" The boy offered the smoldering little cigar to Hobhouse, who eyed it with suspicion and shook his head. The boy shrugged and passed the smoke to Byron, who carefully took another puff.

"Byron," he said, exhaling a thin cloud of smoke, "not By-roon." He pointed at the boy's pistol. "Nice weapon – where did you get it?"

"My uncle took it from a Turk, a janissary who didn't any more need it. It wasn't new, but it shoots enough good." He pointed to the two barrels. "Good when there is not the time for to reload."

Byron felt a little dizzy, and his mouth was unaccountably dry. Reaching into the canvas ammunition bag he carried by a strap across his chest, he pulled out a goatskin *boda*, tipped his head back to drink, then wiped at the splash on his chin with his sleeve. "Water," he said to the boy, offering the *boda*. The boy took the bag and, tilting his head, expertly shot a stream of water into his mouth. He handed it back to Byron. "I have watching you now two days. Your hurt is bad?"

"I'm a doctor," responded Polidori. The boy looked skeptical, but chose not to challenge the claim. "Lord Byron has a nasty gash in his side,

and we need someplace to rest where I can clean and dress the wound."
Polidori noticed that Byron was having trouble with the clip that fastened
the flap of the ammunition bag. "Is your village nearby? Can you take us
there?"

The boy considered. "I can take you close, but I must for to ask before
enter into the village."

"Ask who? Uh, whom?" Byron felt a little funny, like he'd had a drink
but not quite like that, either. He shook his head, hoping to disperse the
fog. "The leader of your partisan band?"

The boy laughed – he seemed to laugh easily. "It is the leader, yes, but
not a man. It is my *mitéra*, and you can hope she trusts, or you will not
so long live."

"Your mother?" Byron almost laughed, though he wasn't quite sure
why. Not wanting to offend the boy, he tried to focus. "We'll take our
chances, my side hurts like hell. What's your name? You know me," he
said, and gesturing towards Polidori and Hobhouse, introduced them
with a wide grin as "my physician and my aide-de-camp." He thought this
was hysterical and giggled – Hobhouse stared at him like he'd gone mad.

With a flick of his fingers, the boy discarded the smoke. "I am Panos.
My village from here maybe is a day, maybe two. We stay away the road –
I show you the where."

As Panos turned, heading away from the road towards a thin copse
of trees, Byron motioned towards the discarded smoke. "Panos, what the
hell is that?" he asked.

The partisan didn't turn around. "Medicine. Now walk and keep no
noise."

Byron, Polidori and Hobhouse exchanged glances. "I do feel a little
better," Byron offered with a shrug. They followed as the boy moved off
through the darkness.

CHAPTER 14
Maniac Wind

DURING HIS *studies of art, history and the classics, Juan's concentration would sometimes slip, and at such moments he often found himself dreaming of the Grand Tour he would undertake when he came of age. He imagined himself standing at dawn on the polished aftercastle of a gleaming galleon, gazing at the receding Spanish shoreline as his friends and family strained to keep him in sight. As a crisp wind gathered in the swelling sails, the crew, their white pantaloons spotless and their shirts as blue as the infinite sky, efficiently worked the lines while the captain and his officers maintained a watchful eye. He imagined – for in daydreams, there is nothing to be gained by skimping – that the captain's lovely daughter, on her way to Genoa to spend the summer with her cousin, would have need of a companion and tutor for the long voyage. As twilight caressed the drowsy sea, she and Juan would stand together against the rail, sharing slices of sweet Galician orange.*

In the event, it had turned out differently. Alfonso was well-connected in Seville, and had the power to make great trouble for Juan. The scandal was an embarrassment for Alfonso, but neither had Juan covered himself in glory, nor added to the lustre of Inez's proud family. It had therefore been decided that Juan should leave Seville and Spain for a time, and quickly.

It had been impossible to secure a berth on a proper passenger ship on such short notice, but Inez called in a favor and managed to book passage for her son on an aging brig – the Angelica, after the poem by Lope de Vega – that had long carried oranges, olive oil and other agricultural goods between Iberia and ports throughout Europe. The Angelica was set to sail from Cadiz in a matter of days, and it was determined that Juan would be upon it.

He packed a few things in a trunk, bade farewell to Dona Inez, who hugged him close and admonished him to write, and left his home under cover of darkness, accompanied only by a yawning coachman who drove the carriage and tended to the drowsy mare that led it down the old merchant's road to Cadiz.

As for the heartbroken Julia, she dressed in dark cloth and a concealing veil, stoically accepting her banishment to La Conventa de Santa Paula, where with God's grace she might expiate the stain of scandal. Juan would never see her again. But, shortly before his departure, he received a letter that with Esmerelda's help Julia had managed to conceal inside a figurine of the Holy Virgin. "My Juan," she wrote,

> *"they tell me you depart. No matter how far you range, no matter how my passions may be quieted, my heart will always echo the beating of your own. Live, my love, with the grace and pride that are your gifts, and that – at least for a time – you shared with me. Though we may be apart, now and forever more, in spirit we shall remain together always, no matter how great the distance or lonely the seclusion.*

Six days out of Cadiz and bound for Genoa, Juan found himself at the corroded rail of the Angelica, his Julia convented and the imagined captain's daughter nowhere in sight. Instead, as he leaned over the rail, his face a convulsive green, he stood shoulder-to-shoulder with a perspiring ceramics merchant from Madrid named Sanchez, who groaned as he bid farewell to the remnants of his supper. The ship lurched once again as water poured in sheets off the rippling sails. Juan wrapped his arms tightly around the rail to keep from being tossed. Sanchez did not move quickly enough and was lifted in the air and flung to the foredeck, where he flopped about like a fish until his flailing arms found purchase in a coiled line, to which he clung for his life.

The ship had encountered stormy weather two days out from Cadiz and, as the north wind strengthened, the sea grew violent. The captain tacked southeast in an attempt to evade the worst of it, but an ill-tempered Poseidon had other ideas. By the sixth day of the voyage the captain and crew were exhausted and the passengers terrified. Still the winds howled, and the mountainous waves, whose snowy crests Juan could almost touch, buffeted the ship.

Though Juan was a strong swimmer, he had little experience as a sailor. He was pressed into service nevertheless, and spent hours below on the pumps, attempting to expel water faster than it could accumulate in the hold. At this he and the other men were unsuccessful, and as the ship continued to take on water it became less maneuverable and more vulnerable to the constant assault of the waves.

A rising sense of panic seized both passengers and crew, the stale sweat of fear as palpable as the stinging spray that lashed their faces. Still, Juan managed to remain composed. During a brief lull in the storm, the first mate remarked on Juan's steadiness to the captain. "He's young," replied the captain, "and believes himself immortal." He rolled up his navigational chart, which offered no solutions. His grey eyes were tired, and his shoulders ached from the weight of the many lives resting upon them.

"As a young sailor on my first voyage," he confided in a wistful tone, "I was swept off the deck by a wave, and managed to save myself only by catching onto netting rigged to the side of the ship. I remember that I was angry – at the storm, at my mates who failed to catch me, at my own clumsiness. But I do not remember being afraid – in my youth, I knew no better." He grinned, salt water glistening in the grey stubble of his beard. "A quality I find increasingly annoying now that I own it no longer."

Somewhat to Juan's surprise, Sanchez the merchant endured both his intestinal woes and the ship's increasing peril with stoic acceptance. Between bouts of nausea which left him gasping as he clung to the rail,

Sanchez clung with equal fervor to a leather-bound bible, though Juan never saw him open it.

"Be of good faith," he shouted to Juan, his voice barely audible over the screaming wind. "One way or th'other, salvation awaits us." He released his hand from the rail and tapped the Good Book, almost losing his balance in the process. "They that go down to the sea in ships, that do business in great waters; These see the works of the Lord, and his wonders in the deep." He offered Juan a beatific smile, the collar of his coat turned up against the storm. Flecks of vomit stained the dark, soaked fabric. "Psalms 107." Juan smiled back politely. He did not wish to be disrespectful, and saw no point in emphasizing his preference for earthly over heavenly salvation.

Sometime in the night on the seventh day, a violent swell struck the Angelica broadside. With a pistol crack the mainmast split and, within seconds, splintered. The mainsail, which had been trimmed as far as possible while still keeping the ship under sail, surrendered itself to the storm, the loose canvas snapping and the untethered rigging writhing like an angry snake. Two unfortunate swabs on the foredeck, neither of them as much as twenty, were struck by the twisting lines and flung into the churning sea, while another was crushed by the falling mast. Men cried out in terror, but could not be heard over the howling of the maniac wind.

Juan, who had been trying to catch a moment's sleep in his tiny quarters, jolted upright and raced up a narrow companionway to the deck. All was in chaos. A jagged splinter of the shattered mast, driven like an arrow by the wind, was buried in the chest of the captain, who lay in a heap on the fore-castle deck, his lifeless eyes wide. Suppressing his own panic, the first mate ordered the remaining mainmast to be cut away, and two men with axes leaped to the task. In almost the same breath, he ordered the lifeboats to be readied, and several men ran to untie the lines and to unwind the capstans that held the two skiffs in place.

The captain had ordered a reach to the west, seeking to point the bow of the Angelica into the wind. But with the mainmast gone the ship's progress slowed and it became almost impossible to steer. Hoping to generate more *speed, the first mate screamed to raise the foresail. But before his order could be carried out the ship climbed to the summit of an enormous swell from which, after an instant of weightless stasis, it fell like a stone.*

As it bottomed out in a watery canyon, the broken ship was briefly sheltered from the tempest. For a moment, all was calm. Though he knew better, Juan allowed himself to hope that the ship might miraculously be spared, and with it their lives.

It was not to be. With a thunderous roar, a massive wall of water surged over the heaving deck of the crippled Angelica, sweeping a dozen men to their deaths. As the ship heeled violently to port, Juan flung himself to the deck, which rose steeply as his flailing hands found purchase on a metal cleat. The ship continued to list, until the foremast and broken mainmast touched the waves. Men were tossed from the deck and holds and, like bread, were cast upon the roiling waters. Some screamed, while others wept.

Juan's panic hit him with an adrenal jolt. Drawing on strength he did not know he possessed, he somehow managed to maintain his hold on the cleat, his legs kicking spasmodically as his body dangled in space.

The Angelica's keel was now wholly visible, the ship's deck perpendicular to the water. It hung suspended and, for a few seconds, seemed like it might right itself. Then, with a low, irrevocable groan that Juan could hear over the wind and rain and panicked shrieks of drowning men, it toppled over as if nudged by God's unsparing hand. In moments, the Angelica slipped forever beneath the devouring sea.

CHAPTER 15
'It Has Made You Rich'

My days of love are over, me no more
The charms of maid, wife and still less of widow
Can make the fool of which they made before;
In short, I must not lead the life I did do.
The credulous hope of mutual minds is o'er,
The copious use of claret is forbid too.
So, for a good old-gentlemanly vice,
I think I must take up with avarice.

DON JUAN, CANTO I

DOUGLAS KINNAIRD, Byron's friend and banker, looked up from a leather-bound ledger that lay open on the desk before him. "Good God, Byron. Your expenses are extraordinary." Kinnaird, whose sage financial advice Byron habitually ignored, had been introduced to Byron by Hobhouse at Cambridge. Unlike most of Byron's friends, who generally managed to convert substantial inheritances into meager ones, Kinnaird had prospered in the banking trade, and had recently been named managing director of Ransom & Morland's Bank. Kinnaird's curly hair was red, his cheeks were soft and round, his eyes lively and alert, and he was unaccountably fond of the sideburns that swept halfway down his cheek. Byron thought his friend resembled an oversized Irish chinchilla.

"If you mean that as a compliment, Kinnaird, thank you. I do try." Byron sat on a couch in his banker's spacious office, where he'd settled in to work on some revisions while Kinnaird reviewed his finances. "But if you intend to chastise, I would remind you of what you told me only eighteen months ago. 'Byron,' you said – rather expansively as I recall– 'not only has *Childe Harold* made you famous, it has made you rich.'"

"And so it did. But while your income is more than adequate, it isn't limitless." He gestured at the ledger. "Is all of this really necessary?"

"Absolutely. What in particular do you consider excessive?"

"Oh, let's see," Kinnaird responded, sliding his spectacles into place. "Maybe I can find something." He bent over the ledger, his eyes tracking back and forth as he scanned the entries. "Hmm," he said after a moment, "allow me to list just a few of the more extravagant items:"

- *Napoleonic traveling coach (£500)*
- *Albanian dress uniforms (3), with gold thread (£70)*
- *White quilted waistcoats (15) (£65)*
- *Olive, silk-lined coat w/ 24 polished steel buttons (£40)*
- *Architect's drawings, Yacht (scaled down three-masted schooner) (£35)*
- *Artist's commission (portrait) (£45)*
- *Complete Works of Alexander Pope (leather bound and signed by the poet) (£40)*
- *12 cases Château Haut-Brion (1812), 12 cases Château Margaux (1809), 12 cases Château Petrus (1810) (£290)*
- *Abraham-Louis Breguet jeweled movement pocket watch (£100)*
- *Newstead Abbey renovations (£1730)*

Byron leaned forward, setting his papers aside. "This *is* concerning," he said, his voice grave. "I ordered the 1808 Haut-Brion, not the 1812.

The '12 – have you tried it? – is dense as India ink. I doubt it'll be drinkable while I still draw breath."

Kinnaird shrugged. "Joke all you want, Byron. But your creditors aren't laughing, and will not be patient much longer. You need either to reduce your expenses or increase your income – if possible, both."

Byron raised his hands in surrender. "You're right, of course. But the problem needs to be addressed on the supply side of the equation; I find it easier to reduce my weight than my expenditures."

Kinnaird gestured at Byron's revision sheets. "The first two cantos of *Don Juan* are selling well. Didn't Murray pay you an advance?"

"I've worn, drank, sat for, commissioned and ridden in the advance. The rest I receive as sales accrue."

"Murray's confident that sales will be robust?"

"He is. But I can spend much faster than I can write."

"Write faster." Kinnaird tapped the ledger. "Most of your worth is locked up in Newstead Abbey. Have you thought further on what we discussed last year?"

"That I sell my ancestral home? And betray I don't know how many generations?"

"You don't even like the place – last time we were there, you threatened to burn it to the ground."

"Whether I like it or not is of no consequence. It's the bloody family seat." Byron cocked his head to the side like a spaniel. "Remind me, what do you think we could get for it?"

"Hard to say. As you know better than anyone, it's been neglected for years, and will be expensive to renovate." He stroked his sideburns. "Perhaps £75,000, if to a buyer of means. If not ...."

"I'd have expected more for a property that dates from the twelfth century," Byron grumbled. "Then again, every peer with a pot to piss in owns a crumbling estate away from London – the countryside positively teems with the neglected and the ruined." He paused, timing the punchline. "And then there's the properties themselves!"

The men brooded in silence until, brightening, Byron raised his head. "You needn't worry, Kinnaird. I'm thinking of prostituting myself –"

"Hard to make much in a labor-based transactional business like that, Byron – just not enough hours in the night. And aren't you a little past your prime?"

Grinning, Byron made an obscene gesture. "... prostituting myself," he repeated, "by taking a page from Walter Scott's book. He's done quite well with serialized fiction, and with *Waverley* and *Ivanhoe* in particular. He gets 'em hooked and then trades for years on the appetites he's created, feeding his readers a bite or two a month. Walter tells me that *Blackwood's* pays well for such trifles."

Kinnaird looked dubious. "Byron, I should be the last to dissuade you from increasing your income. But as you've said yourself, your talent is more for poetry than for prose. Would novelizing be wise?"

Byron shrugged. "No, not really. Murray thinks it an atrocious idea, and likely to sully my reputation."

"Heaven forbid that reality intrude," Kinnaird ventured, with a hint of a grin, "but isn't your reputation a wee bit sullied already? Through no fault of your own, of course."

"In the present, yes. But my eyes are trained on the future, in which I expect to be vindicated gloriously."

Kinnaird laughed. "Unless Murray's right, and future generations come to know you as 'that odd fellow who wrote such amusing little stories.'"

"Come now, Kinnaird, who says I can't have it both ways? This serialized fiction is nothing more than *Don Juan* – or portions of it anyway – converted from poetry to prose fiction. With some changes, of course; otherwise, I'd go mad with boredom. Those who like the poem may like the book, or hate it, but they'll pay to find out which. And for those who haven't the patience or taste for verse, this may be more to their liking. Their coin is as good as any other."

"I don't know, Byron. I agree with Murray. With a dusty thump, Kinnaird closed the ledger. "I'd sooner lend you the funds you need than see your name tarnished by a work too trivial for your talents."

Byron frowned. "I am already in your debt, Kinnaird – and, as you know, this is meant literally, and not merely as a figure of speech. I will not impose upon you further. But I appreciate your sentiments, and shall weigh them fully before committing myself to any measures that might lead to protracted solvency."

"Come now, Byron. Surely you can increase your income through more traditional means? You're not without charm, and there are women who seem to find you irresistible. Find a rich woman – a spinster if necessary – and marry her." Kinnaird snapped his fingers. "*Poof!* Problem solved."

"Don't think it hasn't crossed my mind. I could do as you suggest, or simply blow my brains out – it doesn't much matter which, as the remedies are nearly alike." He sighed, enervated by a species of financial fatigue peculiar to the offices of bankers and accountants. "More than once, my late mother urged me to 'marry a woman of fortune.' It must have slipped her mind that her husband – my father – did precisely that, and then proceeded to abscond with the largest part of her inheritance." Byron permitted himself a wan smile. "Or perhaps she remembered it well, and simply reckoned that if it was good enough for old Jack it should be good enough for me."

He gathered his revision sheets and rose, nodding to Kinnaird as he turned to leave. "Make payments of ten percent to the most insistent of my creditors – twenty if absolutely necessary. Tell the rest that I expect to make them whole within the next few months. Who knows?" he shrugged. "Perhaps *Don Juan* will exceed expectations; and I will write more quickly; and you will once again assure me that I am not merely famous but rich."

CHAPTER 16
Dedication

He had sung against all battles, and again
In their high praise and glory; he had call'd
Reviewing 'the ungentle craft', and then
Become as base a critic as e'er crawl'd –
Fed, paid, and pamper'd by the very men
By whom his muse and morals has been maul'd;
He had written much blank verse, and blanker prose,
And more of both than any body knows.

BYRON, THE VISION OF JUDGMENT

ORIGINALLY FOUNDED as a chocolate shop in 1693 by an Italian *chocolatier* named Bianco, White's was the oldest and had long been the most exclusive gentlemen's club in London. Like many of the clubs, White's catered to aristocratic men who gathered to gamble, socialize, discuss politics and affairs of state, and escape the demands of wife or mistress.

Since the late 18th century, White's had also served as the informal headquarters of the Tory party, which meant that most of its members were committed monarchists who despised political and social agitation; feared the destabilizing influence of the French Revolution and were suspicious of reform of any kind; opposed Catholic Emancipation – the extension of social and political rights to the untrustworthy Papists; and were intent on suppressing the desperate and increasingly violent labor unrest in England's north, where the so-called Luddites, whose jobs had been sacrificed on the alters of industrial productivity and technological progress, were taking crowbars to the mechanical looms they blamed for falling wages and vanishing jobs.

Most of the activity at the club took place in a spacious drawing room framed by opposing black-mantled hearths and furnished with oriental carpets, short-backed armchairs of cracked brown leather and more than a dozen pentagonal tables, each topped in red felt.

On a December afternoon so damp and dreary that one could almost sympathize with the realm's insatiable hunger for foreign soil, Southey – whose membership came as one of the perquisites of his timely conversion from reformer to Tory – sat with Wordsworth near one of the fireplaces, a bottle of Portuguese tawny on the table before them. Both were absorbed in identically bound manuscripts.

Finally, Southey slammed his volume on the table, nearly knocking over the port, which wobbled for a few moments as though itself besotted. "This is tripe!" he hissed, ignoring startled septuagenarian glances from a nearby table. "The bastard calls it poetry, but I think it nothing more than libel dressed in satire's clothes! And you and I, William, are among its targets."

He picked up the bound sheets and waved them at Wordsworth. "Did you read the 'Dedication?'" Wordsworth shook his head. Adjusting his spectacles, Southey turned to the opening pages:

> Bob Southey! You're a poet, poet laureate,
> And representative of all the race,
> Although 'tis true that you turned out a Tory at
> Last, yours has lately been a common case.
> And now my epic renegade, what are ye at
> With all the lakers, in and out of place?

A nest of tuneful persons, to my eye,
Like 'four and twenty blackbirds in a pye ...'

You Bob, are rather insolent, you know,
At being disappointed in your wish
To supersede all warblers here below,
And be the only blackbird in the dish.
And then you overstrain yourself, or so,
And tumble downward like the flying fish
Gasping on deck, because you soar too high, Bob,
And fall for lack of moisture quite a dry Bob.

Wordsworth burst out laughing. "Well – Bob – you must admit he has a certain wit."

Southey glared at him, unamused. "So, you admire his wit, do you William?" Clearing his throat, he turned back to Byron's verse:

And Wordsworth in a rather long Excursion
(I think the quarto holds five hundred pages)
Has given a sample from the vasty version
Of his new system to perplex the sages.
'Tis poetry, at least by his assertion,
And may appear so when the Dog Star rages,
And he who understands it would be able
To add a story to the tower of Babel.

"There are critics who've said as much, Robert; by comparison, this is mild stuff."

"Just wait, there's more."

I would not imitate the petty thought,
Nor coin my self-love to so base a vice,

For all the glory your conversion brought,
Since gold alone should not have been its price.
You have your salary; was't for that you wrought?
And Wordsworth has his place in the Excise.
You're shabby fellows – true – but poets still
And duly seated on the immortal hill.

For me, who, wandering with pedestrian Muses,
Contend not with you on the wingèd steed,
I wish your fate may yield ye, when she chooses,
The fame you envy and the skill you need.

Wordsworth yawned, affecting indifference. Nevertheless, he did not long delay in turning to the Dedication, which he read while Southey glowered at the smoldering fire, his arms crossed tightly across his chest.

"Well," Wordsworth finally sighed, his grin vanished, "he's made no secret of his admiration for Pope. This might have been written by the dwarf himself." Leaning back in his chair, he shifted with discomfort. White's chairs had been designed for the short and fat, and the lanky Wordsworth owned too much leg and not enough bottom. "Quite a chip he seems to have on his shoulder. It's sad, really."

"Sad? This isn't sad, it's bloody malicious."

"Come now, Robert; don't you see? He's envious – of you for having been appointed *laureate*, of me because *Lyrical Ballads* represents an evolution in verse that he does not understand. He's lashing out like an angry child who wants attention." Looking up, Wordsworth nodded politely to Lord Brookdale, who wandered past bearing a stain on his jacket that looked like porridge. Mumbling in what Wordsworth took to be Latin, the old man shuffled on.

"The worst thing we could do would be to indulge him. We should ignore it – he'll be shattered."

Southey was not convinced. He had seen the crowds lined up at Jarndyce and at Hatchard's. He had never seen people queue up to buy a poem, and sales of his own works had always been modest. In fact, had it not been for his income as a contributor to the *Quarterly* and, of course, as *laureate*, he would have a hard time making ends meet. From what he could see, Byron had no such difficulties. He leaned forward, jabbing at the pages with his finger.

"This is about more than us. Byron's not content to prick his rivals; he's got his sights set on bigger game. Somewhere in here," he hissed, flipping pages, "yes, here it is – he calls the Regent a tyrant, and Castlereagh an 'intellectual eunuch!' That may be the nicest thing he says about the Foreign Secretary -- listen to this, you can practically taste the venom!"

> *Cold-blooded, smooth-faced, placid miscreant!*
> *Dabbling its sleek young hands in Erin's gore,*
> *And thus for wider carnage taught to pant,*
> *Transferred to gorge upon a sister shore,*
> *The vulgarest tool that tyranny could want,*
> *With just enough of talent and no more,*
> *To lengthen fetters by another fixed*
> *And offer poison long already mixed."*

Southey tossed Byron's poem onto the table. "He calls George Augustus a tyrant and Castlereagh a killer, complicit in the violence both in Ireland and now in northern Italy! This is an affront, not merely to art, but to the realm."

Wordsworth winced; he considered Southey a friend, but sometimes found him almost unbearably pedantic. Still, he agreed that Byron had crossed a line. "Yes, well, I suppose it is. But what would you have us do about it? And why is it our responsibility anyway?"

"It is our responsibility because we are poets whose art has been defamed. Because we are members of a party, and adherents to a philosophy, that is under attack. And because I just can't stand that arrogant, entitled, debauched son-of-a-bitch." Draining his glass, Southey set it on the table. "As for what to do about it, I haven't figured that out just yet. But somehow, we need to drive our good friend Lord Byron from England's shores."

"Oh? And how do you intend to do that? Byron is a peer, and quite the celebrity. He has friends, some of whom have influence." Wordsworth gave Southey a thin smile. "Are there powers invested in the *poet laureate* of which I am unaware? Had I known I might have tossed my own hat into the ring."

"This is an Anglican country," Southey snorted, "and the so-called 'reforms' that have been championed by the Whigs change nothing. The government has been resolute in punishing acts of sedition – just ask William Hone how he enjoyed the Tower! If *Don Juan* isn't an act of sedition, I don't know what is."

"Pope, Dryden, Blake, Swift, Milton – especially Milton – were no less subversive, and none of them were run out of town." Wordsworth rubbed the bridge of his nose. "In fact, I'm not sure I'd be comfortable advocating banishment as retribution for a poem. I seem to recall you expressing strong opinions in your younger days."

Southey hesitated. Long ago, he had written a passionate tribute to Wat Tyler, whose Peasant's Rebellion in 1381 had given quite a fright to King Richard and the English nobility before it was ruthlessly suppressed and Tyler beheaded. Southey lowered his voice to a whisper. "I was a young man when I wrote *Wat Tyler*. Few would indict any man, much less the *poet laureate* of England, based on the forgotten verses of an impressionable youth." Wordsworth nodded, though he doubted that Southey's critics would be quite so understanding.

"Besides, whatever I may have written long ago, there is nothing in my personal behavior that leaves me vulnerable to attack. Can the same be said for Byron?" Southey poured himself another glass of port and offered the bottle to Wordsworth, who shook his head.

"To call him dissolute," Southey said with an intensity that took his friend aback, "understates the quality of his perversion. He cavorts with prostitutes, drinks to excess, champions radical causes, and has had affairs with more women than I can count, including most recently our good friend Catherine Lamb, whose own reputation is more than a little tattered."

"Except for the radical causes part," Wordsworth smirked, "many of the men in this room have done the same, although not nearly as successfully. As for the placid and sexually conventional character of our lives, well, I suppose you're wise to make of it a virtue."

Wordsworth reached into a pocket and extracted his timepiece; he had work to do. With a low grunt and a crackling of joints, he pocketed the watch, unwound himself from his chair and stretched his neck like a giraffe. He took up his volume of *Don Juan*. "Thank you for the port, Robert. I'll look for you at the *Quarterly's* dinner next week. In the meantime, I'll read Byron's latest more carefully, and will think upon it."

Rising to his feet, Southey reached up to place his hand on Wordsworth's shoulder. "You do that, William, keeping in mind that a libel unrebutted is what succeeding generations call history. And, as you imbibe this heretic's poison, ask yourself this – do you want your history written by a jealous, posturing radical with a talent for perversion?"

"For God's sake, Robert, we're poets! We'll be judged by our work, as will Byron. It is all that matters." He clapped Southey on the shoulder. "Don't you see? We have the good fortune to be able to write our own history."

"Maybe. But I've got a new poem coming out, a tribute to George III—"

"*The Vision*,' or something like that?"

"*A Vision of Judgment*. It's almost done, and I'm going to include a preface that condemns in the harshest terms the blasphemous poison that Byron and his friends peddle as verse."

"It's a dangerous business, Robert, publicly trading insults with Byron. He's good at it." Remembering a particular evening at Almack's, he almost smiled.

"I won't be intimidated, William, not by Byron." Southey's eyes narrowed. "I think he's dangerous, and I'd be willing to wager he's got much to hide. Were his perversions to be exposed, I expect it would bring ruin upon him. And will, if I have anything to say about it."

Wordsworth had no great fondness for Byron; not for his politics, not for his verse, and certainly not for the scathingly personal broadsides that Byron seemed to relish. But at his core, Wordsworth wasn't a malicious or vindictive man, and the festering hatred that he observed in Southey made him shiver. *God help you, Byron. And, Robert,* he reflected, assessing his colleague as if for the first time, *God help you as well.*

CHAPTER 17
The Predictability of Vice

And after all what is a lie? 'Tis but
The truth in masquerade, and I defy
Historians, heroes, lawyers, priests to put
A fact without some leaven of a lie.
The very shadow of true truth would shut
Up annals, revelations, poesy,
And prophecy, except it should be dated
Some years before the incidents related.

DON JUAN, CANTO XI

HOBHOUSE MAINTAINED a comfortable set of rooms on Upland Mews, not far from Hyde Park. Less comfortable was the £200 annual rent, but he liked the sunlight that streamed in through the tall front windows on those few glorious mornings when London wasn't dreary or blanketed in fog.

His house guest lay prostrate on Hobby's scuffed leather couch, his left hand shielding his bloodshot eyes from the sun. Moonlight, he told himself as he squeezed his eyes shut, would still be too bright.

"By the mercy of the Almighty, I beg you Hobby, close those drapes before my head splits open and what little brain remains spills out over your hideous rug." Hoping to clear his head, Byron rubbed at his eyes with the back of his hand, igniting a cerebral explosion of blinding splinters. Quickly abandoning the effort he groaned, which he found didn't hurt so much.

"Good God, Byron, what were you on about last night?" Hobby pretended concern, which Byron immediately recognized as amusement. "If you die will I need to have you embalmed, or did you drink enough to make that unnecessary?" Hobhouse put a glass of soda water and a hot cup of tea on the table next to Byron. "Drink one or the other, though I must warn you, there's no liquor in either."

With a prodigious effort, Byron managed to sit up and swing his legs onto the floor. He slumped forward, burying his face in his cupped hands. Like a convict, he peered at Hobhouse through the confining bars of his fingers. "I dined with Sheridan, Colman, Kinnaird and I can't remember who else. Like many of these affairs, it was first silent, then talky, then argumentative, then disputatious, then unintelligible, then altogethery, then inarticulate, and then finally and irretrievably drunk."

With tremulous hands, Byron managed to raise the soda water to his lips, downing half the glass in a swallow. He looked for a moment as though he might retch, but in the end merely belched.

Hobhouse watched disinterestedly; he'd seen this show before, nor was this the first time Byron had stumbled through his door well past midnight. "How did Sherry fare?" Their hard-drinking friend Richard Sheridan was as entertaining a drunk as Hobby knew, and was usually good for a story or two in the wake of one of his benders.

Encouraged by his modest success with the soda water, Byron had turned to the tea. But his hands were not yet steady, and the Delft Blue saucer gradually harbored a tepid pond of Earl Grey. "Oh, he was in fine form as usual. Maybe you heard about his response to the watchman who found him wandering one night recently, drunk and for the most part senseless? He – the watchman – asks 'Who are you sir?' – no answer. 'What's your name?' – a hiccup. 'I say, sir, what's your name?' – Answer, in a slow and deliberate tone – 'William Wilberforce!'"

Laughing – the Reverend Wilberforce was well-known as a champion of the temperance movement – Hobhouse opened the cupboard and peered inside. "There's nothing here that might safely be eaten. Feel up to going out for something to eat?"

"Good idea. But we need to stop at Abigail Falkland's on our way. Her husband John died a few months ago in a duel, and I need to pay my respects." Hobhouse assented and, in excruciating sunshine, he and Byron walked down the cobbled street in the direction of Hyde Park.

Captain John Falkland's residence – still owned by the Widow Falkland, although Byron feared a bank or two might be lurking – – stood back from the street, protected by a black wrought-iron fence. As Byron and Hobhouse passed through the gate and made their way to the house, an ancient mastiff lying by the fence lifted a drooping eye in greeting.

Byron nudged Hobhouse. "Reminds you of Smut, doesn't he?" In their college days, Byron had had a large bulldog named Smut. With a quiet arrogance that Byron found infuriating, the Trinity College administration had banned Smut from Byron's rooms, pointedly invoking the applicable paragraph of the voluminous *Rules for Gentlemen at Cambridge* that was distributed to all incoming students. After making arrangements for Smut, Byron – who had since made it a point to read the *Rules* from front to back – acquired a small bear, with respect to which the rules were silent. Unamused, the administration threatened expulsion. "If you expel him," Byron had warned Master Mansel, "so much your loss, as he shall simply matriculate at Oxford."

"He does look a bit like Smut. I loved that dog – I remember him lying by my side at Amicable Society meetings."

"Ah, yes – the Amicable Society. Which dissolved, as I recall, due to the incessant quarreling of its members!"

Standing at the door, which like many in this neighborhood had been painted bright red in the current Georgian style, Byron drew a deep breath, smoothed his rumpled coat, and knocked.

Captain Falkland's widow answered the door herself. In her thirties, she was a colorless woman, her tired hair imprisoned in a bun and her black dress fastened tightly below her chin. "My condolences, Abigail," Byron murmured, inclining his head. "We all miss John." She gave him a weary smile. Byron could hear children in the rear of the house, and wondered how she would manage.

Ushering her guests into a front room, the widow Falkland asked Byron if she might get them something to eat or drink.

"I'm afraid we haven't the time, Abigail, as we're headed to an appointment. But I wanted to come by to extend my sympathies and to see if there's anything you need." He pressed her arm. "As you know, I had nothing but respect for John; we enjoyed many pleasurable evenings together." Tactfully, he omitted the details, which on a number of occasions had involved good wine and less good women.

Thanking him for his kindness, Abigail embraced him with a touch more zeal than Byron anticipated. As she turned to bid farewell to Hobhouse, Byron slipped £200 into a bowl on a table by the front door. For months thereafter, the widow Falkland sent him letters that were discreetly but unmistakably amorous. "This is why I so rarely act with virtue," he complained to Hobhouse as he deposited her latest missive in the bin. "I greatly prefer the predictability of vice."

CHAPTER 18
A Note from the Front Desk

What a strange thing is man, and what a stranger
Is woman! What a whirlwind is her head,
And what a whirlpool full of depth and danger
Is all the rest about her! Whether wed
Or widow, maid or mother, she can change her
Mind like the wind. Whatever she has said
Or done is light to what she'll say or do –
The oldest thing on record and yet new.

DON JUAN, CANTO IX

In 1820, Reddish's Hotel, St. James, was one of the finest lodgings in London's West End. Favored by members of what might be described as the middle nobility, the hotel was small but tastefully appointed, and the fashionable location just off St. James Square was convenient to White's and to White's Whig counterpart, Brook's. What's more, when treated with the generosity expected of a gentleman, Reddish's staff were alert to scandal and scrupulously discreet.

Byron was reminded of the value of the hotel's discretion on an unseasonably warm evening in December when, as he dressed in anticipation of an intimate supper in the hotel's gilded dining room, he was interrupted by a soft tap at the door. He rearranged his cravat one last time, exchanged a final glance of mutual admiration with the dashing fellow in the mirror, and opened the door to find a young bellboy in spotless white uniform and round black cap waiting patiently. The boy smiled shyly, bowed –– Byron noticed that he angled his neck back to avoid losing the cap – and extended a small silver tray bearing a sealed envelope. A nod of thanks and several shillings later, Byron closed the door, the opened note in his hand.

"What is it, Byron?" called Caroline, who sat at a small writing desk near the window, looking out on the cobbled, tree-lined street that fronted the hotel. She half-stood; rearranged with an efficient wiggle the bunched blue folds of her silk gown; stole a quick glance at her hair in the mirror above the desk; and plopped back into her chair.

Before her sat a stack of handwritten sheets, a draft of Byron's most recent poem, a gothic romance he was calling *Lara*. Without waiting for a response, she grabbed the sheaf of papers and waved them at Byron. "Is this not a bit, oh, I don't know – *obvious*? I mean, the writing is clear and the images well-formed, I grant you that, you never disappoint in such things."

Leaping to her feet and clutching Byron's draft, Caroline began to pace the room. "Is this truly your self-portrait?" she asked. "It's so dramatic!" Sweeping the back of her hand across her brow, she began to read aloud. *"There was in him a vital scorn of all,"* she declaimed, raising her free hand skyward,

> *... as if the worst had fallen which could befall,*
> *He stood a stranger in this breathing world,*
> *An erring spirit from another hurled.*
> *A thing of dark imaginings, that shaped*
> *By choice the perils he by chance escaped;*
> *But 'scaped in vain, for in their memory yet*
> *His mind would half exult and half regret.*
> *With more capacity for love than earth*

bestows on most of mortal mould and birth,
His early dreams of good outstripped the truth;
And troubled manhood followed baffled youth;
With thought of years in phantom chase misspent,
And wasted powers for better purpose lent.

She paused in her reading but continued to pace, circling Byron like a wolf. Retreating, he took refuge in an upholstered leather chair.

"Caroline, it may indeed be 'obvious,' but is it not true? Does it not reek of wasted promise and misspent talent? Is it not – Miltonic?"

Caroline laughed and, squinting as though blind, bent forward. "Better to rule in hell," she thundered, thumping the floor with her imagined staff, "than serve in heaven!"

Abandoning the role as quickly as she had assumed it, she bounded over to Byron and unceremoniously toppled into his lap, from which he hurriedly extricated the newly-crumpled note. "Well," Caroline conceded, leaning in close, "in all your narcissistic magnificence, you are the closest thing to Milton's Satan that I've encountered this side of *Paradise Lost*." Judgment delivered, she bit Byron's ear and jumped from his lap, sending the *Lara* pages flying.

Byron rubbed his ear and scowled; he liked to seek Caro's reaction to his poems, but so often found her comments, like the woman herself, excessive. *Still*, he reminded himself, *I'm a fine one to decry excess!*

Reclaiming her seat at the desk, Caroline pointed at the envelope. "Does yonder missive bring news, my lord?"

"I suppose you could say that, Caroline. Were you aware that your husband would be dining in town this evening?"

Caroline swept aside one of her blond curls, which, like a cat, had settled on her forehead seeking attention. She dropped her hand to her lap, then raised it to pull at her ear. "I had no idea," she responded, avoiding his eyes. "As you know better than most, his social calendar and mine do not often overlap."

"True enough," Byron conceded. "Still, I'm surprised you would be unaware of his plans this evening, as they are extraordinary." Raising the note, he read aloud:

> "This establishment has the very great honor to host this evening a party that includes the Prime Minister, Earl of Liverpool as well as the Foreign Secretary, Lord Castlereagh. The party includes as well Lord Melbourne, with whom you are of course acquainted. As, under the circumstances, it is in the interest of all concerned to avoid any embarrassment, I await your instructions as regards any alternative arrangements you may wish to make."

Byron lowered the note. "How many times, Caroline, has your husband dined with Jenkinson and Castlereagh? Quite a feather in his politically ambitious cap, I'd say, and not something hastily arranged." He looked hard at Caroline, who looked away. "I would boast at least to my friends were I to be invited to sup with Walter Scott or William Grenville. Yet William breathed not a word of this to his wife?"

The room was silent, save for the soft clopping of horses on the cobblestones below. Caroline stared at the floor; she looked deflated, like a bird trapped in a cage. Byron remained silent, waiting for her to gather herself. At last, she looked up at him, her eyes red and wet.

"I wanted–" she said hesitantly, her voice a whisper, "– I wanted them to see me with you." She clutched at the diaphanous silk of her gown. "Please," she pleaded, "don't be angry with me."

Byron stood and strode toward the door, then back toward the bed – it was his turn to pace. "What did you think would happen, Caroline? How did you think your husband would respond were you and I to waltz into supper, hand in arm, while he dined with the bloody Prime Minister and the bloodier Foreign Minister? Who, incidentally, I just excoriated in print as a 'cold-blooded, smooth-faced, placid miscreant,' and as an 'intellectual eunuch!' Perhaps you imagined he'd invite us to join them for the fish course?"

"I didn't – I don't care what they think. I may love him, I cannot deny my heart, but it is a summer wind. With you, it is a tempest." Rising, she stepped close, her hands reaching for his chest. He grasped her wrists and pushed her arms away.

"Caroline, I need to live in the world. I have no difficulty troubling powerful men on my own, I don't need you to toss hot peppers into the soup. Yes, we have loved; yes, there is passion, that too is undeniable. But you seem determined, not merely to warm yourself by love's fire, but to be devoured by it ... like a *Jean d'Arc d'amour*." He regarded her coldly. "How often have I begged you to observe basic rules of decorum, to be discreet, to avoid – for your sake as well as mine – public scandal?"

Caroline's eyes, wet with tears, flashed with anger. "You dare lecture *me*, Byron, on decorum? On scandal? You, who have made a career of it, have elevated it – literally! – to an art form? My behavior may not meet your expectations, nor those of my family and husband. But it is at least honest, and unadorned by hypocrisy. In this we have always been kindred souls – or would you prefer that pretty artifice with which more proper women are clothed?"

Byron took a deep breath, controlling his anger. "It is one thing to poke the lion, Caro, but quite another to offer oneself up as its supper. If – when – I choose to offend, I alone pay the price, and that is a bill I am willing to make good. The theatre you create may feature you as the leading lady, but it requires me to stand on a stage not of my choosing."

She flailed her arms, her loose sleeves whipping like flags. "Oh, don't play the victim with me, Byron! Who seduced whom? Did you not notice that I was married? Or to whom? You cannot go about making women love you, and then demand that they display their passion only in private, and within the four posts of your bloody bed!"

"I do not make women love me, any more than I make them read my verse. If, in reading, they are carried away, that is hardly my fault." He shook his head. "This is beside the point, another of your skillful deflections. This is not about me, Caroline, but you, who must at all times be in *extremes*, at one moment of passion, at the next of jealous rage. In private, it is merely exhausting. In public, and in light of my unwarranted but undeniable notoriety, it is dangerous."

"Unwarranted? I don't think so. I tell you Byron, if the public knew how feckless, how reckless, you really are– "

"What? They'd stop lining up to buy my verse? Realize I'm no Bob Southey?"

"If they knew you – knew you as I do – they'd probably throw you out of bloody England, and set me up at a nicer Bedlam in the Cotswolds!" She wiped at the tears on her flushed cheeks. "You accuse me of staging our – whatever this is. You're the writer, Byron; how does this play end?"

"All tragedies end with a death, Caroline, all comedies with a marriage. It isn't clear to me what you planned for tonight's performance. But if this is a tragedy, the death won't be mine. And if it's a comedy, the marriage won't be mine either."

Byron gathered his coat and cane. He approached Caroline, who stood in the center of the room, at once defiant and forlorn. He looked down at her ridiculous curls and at her slight shoulders, bare above her gown. She raised her eyes, wet with tears, and sneezed fiercely. For a moment or two he wrestled with himself; then, sighing, he pulled her close and kissed her on the forehead. As he stepped toward the door his voice was low, almost a whisper. "I am no martyr; or at least, this is not my cause. I won't follow you into the flames, Caro. There's too much still to do."

CHAPTER 19
A Prisoner of the Sea

HAD DAYS passed? A week? Juan wasn't sure, not that it mattered. To the lone survivor of the wreck of the Angelica, the passage of days was measured not in hours but by the depletion of his dwindling store of dried figs, cured pork and soda crackers. In the panic that attended the urgent loading of the lifeboats, fresh water was overlooked, but some misguided tar had heaved in an oaken cask of rum, and thus Juan managed simultaneously to slake his thirst and buoy his spirits.

Nights flashed past like reflections in a distorted mirror, the moonlight refracted in the rolling prism of the waves. The rocking of the sea, steady and relentless, sickened Juan for most of the first day, but he gradually got used to it, and the endless waves seemed as sand dunes on a vast, featureless desert of water. Juan felt himself a camel, endlessly trudging up dune after dune, each indistinguishable from the last. He recalled that, during the Battle of Thymbra, the Persians used camels to scare off the Lydians' horses at close range – it seems that the smell of camels frightens horses. Sharks circled Juan's small boat several times, and he hoped that they too might be put off by his sea camel scent.

The sun rose on the eastern horizon, the canvas sky brushed in pinks and reds. Juan's thrill at the glory of the sunrise was short-lived, as the maiden dawn was quickly despoiled by the day's ravaging heat. Juan's lips chapped, then parched, then cracked and bled, his blood as salty as the sea. He took what cover he could under the boat's canvas tarp, but the suffocating heat drive him into the open. Had he an oar and some line he might have fashioned a sail, but neither were to be found. Juan assumed they were tossed into the sea when the lifeboat hit the water, and reminded himself to be thankful for the rations and the tarp.

It was miraculous that he survived at all. As the Angelica teetered in the storm, its broken masts parallel to the water, Juan had clung to a cleat, his legs dangling high above the waves. He knew that the ship could not be saved but, like a man in a raging river who stubbornly clings to a log as it topples over the falls, he refused to let go. Finally, as the ship groaned in its death shudder, he lost his grip. As he fell, the deck rushing by, he glimpsed the first mate, who had lashed himself to the ship's wheel. The man appeared to be laughing, his face contorted in a convulsive scream, but the sound was lost in the storm. Below, Juan could see at least a dozen sailors who'd been swept off their feet by the waves and the impossible angle of the ship. Most were bunched against the rail, drowned or drowning. Juan had no time to consider their plight further, hitting the water with a concussive slap. He was stunned, but somehow managed to fill his lungs with air before a powerful backwash of wave pulled him beneath the surface.

Miraculously, the backwash also carried him clear of the doomed ship. After what seemed like minutes but must have been only a few seconds, he was able to kick his way to the surface where, surrounded by debris, he watched the ship slide into the depths. Treading frantically and fighting both his panic and the suction exerted by the sinking Angelica, he turned the other way and was almost struck by one of the lifeboats, which two crewmen had managed to untie in the moments before the ship pitched over on its side.

The craft must have slid off its platform and over or through the rail, and by luck landed upright. No one had managed to climb aboard, but the boat had a rope ladder attached to its side. With a desperate lunge, Juan seized the bottom run and held on as the lifeboat rose and fell in the violent sea. With the last of his strength he pulled himself up the ladder, rung by rung, and tumbled into its well, where he lay exhausted, gasping for air. He could hear the faint cries of drowning men, but they soon subsided and then vanished, lost in the frenzy of the storm and the dark fathoms of the sea.

When he awoke it was daylight, and the storm had passed. A soft wind blew, and it seemed to Juan that the boat was moving. But without sight of land there was no frame of reference and, as far as Juan could tell, the boat might be drifting in circles or farther out to sea.

He spent much of the first day scanning the horizon in the hope of spotting land, but eventually he gave up, trying instead to sleep and to conserve his energy and supplies. It rained one night and Juan managed to collect a few cups of fresh water in the tarp, which he drank sparingly, touching his moistened fingers to his lips. But the rainwater was almost gone and his food had run low. Baked by the sun, weak from hunger and increasingly affected by even small amounts of the rum, he drifted in and out of consciousness, his sleep restless and uneasy.

Night fell, the darkness pocked by stars. He dreamed he was again a child, an energetic boy of ten whose dark curls and long lashes attracted the attention of bullies and women alike, each with a different though no less predatory intent. He was swimming in the river, the Guadalquivir swollen with spring melt, the current cold and swift. A girl of perhaps thirteen watched from shore, warning him more than once not to venture too far into the river. From her blue eyes, sharp tongue and the distinctive crescent-moon birthmark below her left shoulder, he knew her to be his lost sister Luna, though they had never met.

Heedless and trying to impress her he dove deep, straining to make out fish and submerged boulders in the dim, refracted light. When he surfaced, he found himself captured by the current. He struggled to swim toward shore but the current was too powerful, and he could taste the acid panic rising in his throat. As he struggled, he caught a glimpse of Luna running along the riverbank, her hair flying and her eyes wide with fear. She was calling to him; he could see her lips moving but couldn't hear a word. He began to weaken and, kicking as hard as he could, felt the cold of the river pierce him like a thousand tiny daggers. He faltered, swallowed a mouthful of water and coughed, the panic overpowering. His head slipped beneath the water. With an adrenal surge, he kicked his way back to the surface, crying and coughing and not yet ready to die.

Voices. He heard voices, at first distant, then closer. He twisted his head, struggling in the rushing current to find their source. His chest was pounding, his vision little more than a red haze. Again, he heard the voices – they seemed to be speaking in a language he did not understand – and frantically he tried to rise up high enough to see. The sound of the river had changed, no longer roaring but instead slapping at regular intervals, more like waves than rapids.

Juan opened his cracked and bloodshot eyes, then quickly closed them, the sun blinding. He tried again, squinting into the glare, and fifty yards away saw an approaching skiff and beyond it a three-masted mistiko, its forward gun protruding from the ship's sleek bow. The skiff was manned by three sailors, two hauling on long wooden oars, the third standing in the bow, silhouetted against the rising, burnt orange sun like some kind of Apollonian deity. Juan wondered what they were doing in the Guadalquivir, then realized that he had dreamed of the river but was still a prisoner of the sea. The man in the bow of the skiff called out, but Juan could not understand his words. He tried to stand, but his legs were rubber and he got no further than his knees. And so it was that, from his knees, in the posture of a supplicant, Juan spread his arms and greeted the Cypriot pirates into whose custody he was about to pass.

CHAPTER 20
The Choreography of Indiscretion

Oh love, what is it in this world of ours
Which makes it fatal to be loved? Ah why
With cypress branches hast thou wreathed thy bowers
And made thy best interpreter a sigh?
As those who dote on odours pluck the flowers
And place them on their breast – but place to die;
Thus the frail beings we would fondly cherish
Are laid within our bosoms but to perish.

DON JUAN, CANTO III

"**WHAT DO** you mean, you're *tired* of her?" Hobhouse peered at Byron over the creamy froth of his ale. "Moore, what do you think of this revelation?"

Thomas Moore, all five-and-a-quarter feet of him, barely looked up from his broth. "This is news? I hardly think so." Moore's English accent, painstakingly acquired at Samuel Whyte's English Grammar School for Boys, occasionally slipped to reveal traces of Moore's childhood in Dublin. Particularly when he sang, his voice deep and resonant. "Only the Irish can do justice to the dirge," he would insist when in his cups. Lifting his glass, he would raise a toast "to the suffering Irish!" and burst into tears.

The tavern was crowded and noisy, clattering dishes and flatware competing gamely with voices raised to be heard over the din. The Golden Grommet, it was called, though no one knew why, since neither gold nor grommets were much in evidence. "Someone must have liked the sound of the word, to embroider so mundane a fabric," Byron had observed when he and Moore first discovered the place.

"Maybe so," Moore replied, tucking into a steaming hot meat pie, "but the food's simple and the ale's sweet."

Byron had surveyed the tradesmen and stock jobbers who stood at the counter and occupied most of the rough tables, "Even better," he said, "the peerage gives the place a wide berth. Increasingly, I consider this a virtue."

He had spent the holidays at Newstead, hosting a series of parties – they tended to merge as he tried to recall them – at which he and his guests had depleted stores of caviar, *foie gras*, roast duck and *Dubois Père & Fils* champagne. In what had become a post-New Year's habit he was now watching his weight, which to Byron's way of thinking involved imbibing to the point of nausea and then foregoing meals for two days running.

It was the afternoon of the first day and, as he nursed a cup of tea and nibbled on a soda cracker, he was thankful that the pounding in his head had subsided. He had been out late with Moore and Hobhouse, awaking to find a girl he did not remember curled up like a cat in his bed. She yawned as Fletcher helped him dress but, thankfully, did not offer her name. She was young – no more than twenty to his eye – and as he watched her sit up in bed holding his sheet carelessly against her chest, he was relieved to find her fetching. He nodded to her politely; she yawned, rolled over and returned to sleep. Fletcher would see her off and make sure she didn't help herself to any of Byron's things. Caroline had an annoying habit of dropping by unannounced; he hoped for the girl's sake they didn't run into one another on her way out.

Hobhouse looked at Byron with mock pity. "How could Caroline not be impressed by how fluidly our friend combines the predatory instincts of a raptor with the inconstancy of a hummingbird." He raised his glass. "Inspired choice, Byron, to take up with a maniacally possessive mistress, and a well-connected one at that!"

Moore nodded in agreement. "If she were only *quietly* maniacal, things could be managed. But Byron's *diva* is spectacular! A lifetime spent in the theatre, I should know. The lass sees herself as the leading lady in a Drury Lane melodrama, with Byron the hero or, should he disappoint, the villain." He pushed his empty bowl to the side, dabbing his pursed lips with a cloth. "Maybe another drink to sort this out for the poor lad?"

"Even taking into account his aggravating tendency to prefer the dangerous over the sensible, disillusionment was inevitable." Hobhouse drained the rest of his ale. "He doesn't mind provoking outrage among his peers; in fact, that's often his objective. But disdain – or worse, amused pity – that's another matter. I just didn't expect him to see reason quite so fast. He usually displays greater commitment to his mistakes."

"You know I'm here, right? That I can hear you?"

They ignored him. "Give the lass some credit," Moore observed as he scanned the room for the serving girl. "She knows what she's about. She places herself strategically, attracts his attention, gets him interested. Then, when he nibbles at the bait and asks an acquaintance to introduce him, she refuses, lets slip her disdain for his bevy of female admirers, and implies that while *they* may be charmed, *she* is less impressed. What's that she said – that Byron's 'mad, bad and dangerous to know?' Have you ever heard a more flattering insult? Can you imagine *anything* better-calculated to draw him in?"

Trundling his fingers across the table, Moore flicked at an unlit candle, which toppled over and rolled to the table's edge, perilously coming to rest only inches from the abyss. "She set him up like a bowling pin, then knocked him flat at Almack's."

"Byron imagined himself the spider," agreed Hobhouse, "when any fool could see he was the fly."

"If this was all so clear to you – which I very much doubt – why did you not warn me? Raise an alarm? Have me restrained?"

Hobhouse rolled his eyes. "I did warn you, several times. Including when you were sober. I swear, I feel like Cassandra – since when do you listen? Besides, Caroline was a known quantity; half of London heard of her hysterics with Webster, and the other half witnessed them directly. You knew her character, enough of it anyway. If you chose to be charmed, you've no one to blame but yourself."

Confronted with such inconvenient facts, Byron chose not to debate the point. "Let's not quibble about who killed who. The question is, how to end it? She may be indecorous, obstinate, and absurdly melo-dramatic, but –"

"Sound like anyone we know?" Moore, who had had his own romantic difficulties, was enjoying this.

"–she is in equal parts charming, clever and brave, though as dangerous and unpredictable as a volcano." Byron stared moodily into his tea. "So long as she loves me, her grip will be fierce, and an eruption is never far." He sighed glumly, resting his chin in his hands, his elbows propped on the table. "I've tried to break it off, have been unmistakable in my intent. In response, her letters either contradict or ignore – I seem unable to extricate myself."

"So, what do you intend to do?" Hobhouse gestured towards Moore, who was craning his neck in search of someone – anyone – who might bring them more ale. "Perhaps Moore might agree to sweep her off her feet? He can cast her in one of his plays, she'll love the attention."

"Be serious," scolded Byron. "Even Moore deserves a measure of happiness. Besides, it wouldn't work; Caroline is incapable of taking direction." He picked up the candle, set it firmly in its wax base, and struck a match. "No, other than death or banishment –"

"Yours or hers?"

"If this continues much longer, I'm indifferent. Anyway, there's really only one solution." He angled the match to envelop the wick, which caught and briefly sputtered. "There's nothing to do but make her hate me." He snuffed out the flame between his thumb and index finger.

"Shouldn't be too difficult," offered Moore. "Just be yourself."

He couldn't help but laugh – Moore amused him, even mostly sober. "One would think so. But who can say how Caroline will respond to anything? At times she's faithful to the script in her head, but sometimes not – although who knows, maybe even her departures are scripted." He shrugged. "There are rules that govern the flouting of convention. The Italians understand this well; the choreography of their indiscretions is elaborate, and executed with style. The English too, though our restraint comes less from urbanity than from repressed emotion, which we pretend is a virtue and like to call manners."

He pushed away his tea, which had gone cold. "Caroline exults in Feelings, nurtures them like flowers, arranges them for display, the more profuse and public the arrangement the better. She doesn't care that eventually the petals all fall off and make quite a mess." Seeking confirmation, he turned to Hobhouse, who had helped him clean up his fair share of messes. Hobhouse merely shook his head.

Byron's attention wandered as a dark-haired barmaid carrying pints of ale swept by, her figure shapely and pleasing. He met her eye and smiled, taking note of the coy arch of her brow. He ran his fingers through his thick black locks, smoothed his jacket and pushed back his chair. Dirty work, he told himself, this business of driving away one's lover.

CHAPTER 21
Betrayal

WHEN THEY awoke, the setting sun had painted shadows on the rocky teeth concealing the mouth of their shallow cave. Byron slept fitfully, the pain in his flank throbbing and incessant. Polidori had done his best to clean and bind the wound, but his efforts were hampered by a lack of a clean dressing or effective antiseptic. Panos carried a small *boda* of red wine, a portion of which Polidori used to wash the wound in the hope that the alcohol might act as a disinfectant. Ultimately, the doctor decided that drinking the wine would likely be just as therapeutic, and so he did.

Panos estimated his village to be five or six hours distant, and that even stopping frequently to allow Byron to rest, they could reach it well before morning. Polidori didn't like it – he wasn't convinced a weakening Byron could manage the journey. "I'll remain here with Byron while you and Hobhouse get help," he suggested.

"I cannot for sure to say that anyone from the village will return to here," Panos said hesitantly. "Maybe yes but maybe also no; at these times, to travel is dangerous."

"I can make it," Byron protested, "and I'll be damned if I'm going to sit in this cave all night." He coughed violently, the pain like a knife in his side. He bent over and took a few deep breaths, trying to calm the spasms.

"What if we get halfway there and you can't walk further, Byron?

We'd be as helpless as baby deer on the Crown's hunting grounds in Richmond Park."

"I'll make it. If I've learned anything from long-distance swims, it's that you can do more than you think when you have no choice." He shot a glance at Panos, who was busily scattering leaves and dirt over the soil where they had slept. "And if we encounter trouble, we can deal with it; isn't that so, Panos?"

The partisan nodded. "If I cannot save me by giving you to the Turks, then yes, we will fight." He looked skeptically at Polidori. "He can fight?"

Byron started to laugh, then clutched his side. "Well, Hobhouse here can fight," he assured Panos. "I'm afraid the doctor isn't much of a fighter, but if there's trouble we'll use him as bait." Polidori bristled, muttering something about field surgery.

They walked in silence for several hours, the only sound their labored breathing as the rough dirt track climbed through patchy strands of scrub oak and manzanilla. In the faint glow of a pale half-moon they could make out trees and boulders, but not much else. Panos was sure-footed and had no trouble negotiating the familiar trail, but the Englishmen stumbled now and then over unseen rocks and hidden ruts. Polidori tripped over a root and fell to his knees. He scrambled to his feet, anxiously examining his trousers for damage.

Byron rolled his eyes. "You needn't worry, doctor. Before they lop off your head, the Turks will doubtless appropriate your suit, which will almost certainly survive you." Polidori frowned, leaving Byron to wonder which horrified his physician more; the prospect of decapitation or the loss of an expensive Christie & Son suit.

They came to a clearing and paused for a rest under an oak tree whose branches drooped so low they had to stoop to get inside its canopy. The leaves and branches obscured the moonlight, so they sat on the rocky ground in near darkness. Byron lay on his back and closed his eyes; his head was spinning and he felt nauseous. Polidori slid over and crouched low, pressing two fingers against Byron's wound. It yielded to the pressure, soft and spongey, and Byron winced. Polidori pressed his palm against Byron's forehead, which was clammy and warm to the touch.

The doctor turned to Hobhouse. "The wound may be infected." He shrugged helplessly. "If we were in London I could do more–"

Byron didn't open his eyes. "Excellent idea. Let's get champagne and oysters at Wiltons."

Panos, suddenly alert, cocked his head and motioned them to be still. "Horses," he whispered. "Make no sound." He scuttled over to Byron, his back to the others. Whispers were exchanged, and Panos passed him something dark. Without another word the young partisan shouldered his pack and slipped away into the darkness.

Polidori removed his jacket and laid it over Byron like a blanket, instructing Hobhouse to elevate his feet. "Are you thirsty?" he asked Byron. When Byron nodded, Polidori held the *boda* bag to his lips, helping him take a few shallow swallows. Byron wiped his mouth with the back of his hand and touched Hobhouse's arm. "Sorry to have dragged you into this, Hobby; never meant for you and Polidori–"

Hobhouse cut him off. "We're grown men, Byron. Anyway, my money says you'll not die here. Not dramatic enough."

"Strange, isn't it? The most important thing we ever do, and the one thing we can never practice." Byron suppressed another cough. "You need to do something for me."

"I haven't done enough?"

"No, something important."

"Keeping you alive isn't –"

"Listen. When you get back to England, you'll find my memoirs – minus the volume that was stolen when Lyon was killed – in a wooden box beneath my bed. Don't let them see the light of day."

"Burn your papers?" Hobhouse rubbed his jaw, conscious of the stubbly growth of his beard. "Why on earth would you want me to do that?

"You know why, Hobby. What's done is done, but maybe it's possible to avoid doing any further damage." He offered Hobhouse a weak grin. "It will please you to know that, posthumously, I intend to lead an exemplary existence – I imagine it's much easier to resist temptation in the afterlife." He coughed, grimacing at the sharp pain in his side. "A memoir," he whispered, shaking his head, "is either an apology or an attack. I'm not much good at the former, and have no further use for the latter."

Before Hobhouse could reply, they heard voices, indistinct but drawing nearer in the darkness. Hobhouse and Polidori waited in silence. Byron exhaled and closed his eyes.

Four men emerged from the woods into the moonlit clearing. One was the partisan, who was followed closely by three Turks. By their billowy yellow pants and blue tunics, as well as the curved short swords they carried in sashes that encircled their waists, Hobhouse saw that they were part of an Ottoman cavalry unit, though their horses were nowhere in evidence.

They stopped, twenty paces distant, as Panos pointed to the oak tree beneath which the Englishmen were sheltered. Laughing, the Turks drew their swords. One, whose sharp voice and bantam strut marked him as an officer, spoke in Turkish to the partisan, who stepped a few paces forward. "Come out," Panos called in a loud voice, "and the writer bring out with you."

Hobhouse had a dagger but knew he would be no match for three armed soldiers, and Polidori would be of little help in a fight. Byron was in no condition to fight. Hobhouse hesitated; had Panos betrayed them to the Turks? Was there a way out? A whisper from Byron settled the question: "Pull me out by my feet. And don't do anything stupid." Hobhouse gave him a sharp look, then seized Byron's legs by the ankles and, with Polidori following behind, backed out under the branches, pulling Byron into the clearing. Gently, he set Byron's feet on the ground and turned to face the Turks.

The officer strode forward, his sword loose in his hand. Motioning toward Hobhouse and Polidori, he barked a command. Hobhouse and Polidori looked at one another; neither understood the language.

Panos took a step forward and nodded towards the Turk. "He wants for that your weapons are no longer with you."

Hobhouse reached into his jacket pocket – the Turk angled his sword in a subtle but unmistakable warning – and carefully extracted his dagger, which he tossed to the ground at the officer's feet. The Turk turned to Polidori, who shrugged, spreading his jacket to show that he carried no weapon. The Turk smiled and, reaching forward with his sword, lifted Polidori's jacket to expose his trouser pockets. Polidori turned them inside out. Satisfied, the Turk murmured something to his men, who laughed. Polidori glanced at Panos, who shrugged. "They say women only carry not the weapons. As a – a – what do you call it, a politeness?"

"Courtesy."

"Courtesy. As courtesy, you they will kill last."

The Turkish officer pointed his sword at Byron who, draped by Polidori's jacket, hadn't moved. Without looking away the janissary said something to Panos, who responded in a low voice. Moving closer, the officer studied Byron's face. His eyes widened, and he spit a command to one of his men, who reached into his tunic and extracted a worn and folded paper, which he passed over. The officer examined it, then Byron, then the paper once more. He turned toward Panos to ask a question; Panos responded with uplifted palms.

At a signal from the officer, his men drew their swords. Lacking swords, Hobhouse and Polidori drew their breaths. Before anyone could move, Panos whispered something to the janissary officer, gesturing from time to time at Polidori. The janissary nodded, his features contorted in an ugly sneer. Speaking rapidly, he issued another order to his men, who stepped in to flank Hobhouse. Their swords at the ready, they forced him to his knees.

The janissary commander motioned to Polidori to approach. Tentatively, the doctor took a step and paused, afraid to move closer. The Turk motioned again, this time more insistently. Convinced that he had only moments to live, Polidori took a deep breath and stepped forward. With a rattlesnake smile, the Turk struck the Englishman in the belly with the handle of his sword, knocking the wind out of him and driving him to his knees. The two janissaries behind Hobhouse snickered.

The cavalryman looked down with contempt at the gasping Polidori, then stepped behind him. He slid his short sword into a loop on the back of his sash and, raising one booted foot in the air, pushed the doctor hard from behind, sending him sprawling on his face in the rocky soil.

The Turk growled, his voice harsh and guttural. He untied the drawstrings that held up his pantaloons and let them drop to the dirt. Reaching down, he fondled himself. Then, putting the lie to Byron's earlier prediction he grasped Polidori's trousers and ripped them straight down the backseam, exposing the thin undergarment beneath. Polidori, who was still trying to catch his breath, felt a stab of panic and tried desperately to rise, but the Turk seized him by the throat, jerked his head straight back and struck him sharply on the side of his head. Polidori groaned and fell once more to the dirt.

Hobhouse, who had been watching the unfolding assault helplessly, was stunned by the suddenness of what followed. Panos yelled "Nuni!" and from behind him Hobhouse heard the concussive roar of a pistol blast. He felt something warm and wet splatter his head and neck. As he turned toward the sound, he saw the Turk to his left collapse, his cry gurgling through a gaping hole in his throat. There was another booming report and the second Turk dropped his sword to the ground, his dying eyes wide with surprise and his chest slick with blood. Hobhouse looked wildly over at Byron, who was sitting up and surveying the scene, Panos' smoking two-barrel pistol in his hand.

Polidori had closed his eyes; he understood his likely fate. When Panos yelled, he jerked them open just in time to see the partisan fly past him through the clearing. As he twisted around, he saw the young Greek slash at the neck of the partially disrobed Ottoman cavalryman. It was over in an instant; blood spurted in convulsive spasms from the Turk's severed throat and, with a shudder, the janissary officer collapsed and fell forward in the dirt, his blood pooling beneath him.

Hobhouse scrambled to his feet. "Jesus bloody Christ! Byron, why the hell didn't you tell me you were going to shoot a man standing less than a foot from my back? You scared the living hell out of me!"

Panos, wiping the blood from his knife with what remained of Polidori's pants, didn't look up. "I tell him no to tell you and doctor. I did want that you not by mistake ..." he struggled for the words, "that you not act funny."

"Act funny? Why, you crazy Greek, would I act funny?" Hobhouse took a deep breath, struggling to control his pounding heart. Brushing past the partisan, he knelt down next to the doctor, who sat in the dirt looking dazed. "Are you alright, John?"

Polidori wiped his eyes with the palms of both hands. "I'm fine," he said, his voice quavering. He took a deep breath, steadying himself. "But if Panos and Byron hadn't acted when they did, I might not have been able to show my face in some of the better London clubs this season."

Hobhouse extended a hand and, taking it, Polidori struggled shakily to his feet. He turned to the young partisan. "Thank you Panos," he said unsteadily. "I owe you a debt." He shuddered, his face a pale white. "I knew they were going to kill us – but I wasn't expecting, you know."

Panos gazed evenly at the doctor. "I did to them say that they should – in Greek is gamó, how say in English?" Panos lewdly rocked his hips forward and back.

"Fuck!" Polidori stared at Panos, his mouth open.

"Yes," agreed Panos, "I did to them say they should – *fuck* – you in the ..." He looked to Byron, uncertain of the word in English. Byron nodded back equably but said nothing, figuring further clarification was unnecessary. Panos turned back to the doctor. "They thought to *fuck* you was good idea, disgrace to you and good time to them."

Polidori was incredulous. "Let me get this right," he sputtered. "You thought it might be a good idea to suggest that before they killed me, they should sodomize me. *That* was your idea?"

Panos didn't know the word sodomize, but he got the gist of Polidori's grievance. "Yes. I think it when I find them and said I lead them to three Englishmen." He paused to light another one of his little cigars, the wooden match flaring. "Not easy for Turk to make the fight when he has pants around his ankles; yes?"

Hobhouse ran his hand through his hair, which Byron recognized as a Hobhousian gesture of exasperation. "Forget that for a moment. Tell us why, Panos," Hobhouse asked slowly, anger darkening his features, "you would want to lead three bloody janissaries to where we were bloody hiding? And why would they trust you anyway? You people *are* at war with them," he observed acidly. "Or have I been misinformed?"

Panos held up his hand as he took a long draw and held it. After a few moments he exhaled, the smoke sweet in the pine-scented night. "I hear them and know they have horses. I think we need them to get By-roon to village – he looks sick. So, I bring them here, with no horses for quiet. Before, I tell By-roon to be ready and give him my gun." He pointed to Hobhouse. "The Turks see only you as danger, they believe By-roon too sick, and I tell them doctor is like woman." He looked apologetically at Polidori. "And when filthy one –" he paused and spit on the dead Turk – "pulls down pants, I yell and By-roon shoots them." He shrugged at Polidori, once again apologetic. "Sorry I was to wait, but was necessary. Now we have horses."

"Panos. It's Byron, not By-roon. But to Hobby's point, why did the Turks trust a young Greek partisan?"

Panos lowered his eyes, hesitating. "My mitéra, ago twenty years … was gamó … forced … by janissary. I was born. My mitéra made me for to learn Turkish, how to speak like a Turk, act like a Turk. Things that a Turk only will say." Panos drew again from his little cigar. Byron could see that the boy's hands were shaking.

"She said that she, and me, and our village, would rest not before we kill as many Turks as we can and Greece is free." He ground out his smoke on the side of his boot and carefully put the stub into his pocket. "I tell them I am Turk, that I hate Greeks who are dirty and foolish, that I hate English who help Greeks. They very interested in English, think you have gold and silver and much money that they will steal." He shrugged again and lifted his palms in the universal gesture of *what-can-you-do?* "We needed the horses."

Polidori took a deep breath and in two strides crossed the clearing to the startled Panos, whom he seized with both hands and fiercely embraced. Byron was already limping towards the edge of the clearing. He stopped for a moment at the body of the slain Turk officer and, reaching down, retrieved a sheet of paper from the dead man's vest. Glancing at it briefly, he slipped it into his pocket. Suddenly bone-weary, he was amused to see Panos delicately trying to extricate himself from Polidori's clutches. "This is all very gratifying," he announced, "and will make a grand verse. But perhaps we should retrieve the horses before I bleed to death?"

CHAPTER 22
Dame Fortune

IF, AS Juan had heard it said, the sea was a vast and limitless desert, then the pirates that roamed its waters were its nomadic tribesmen. Outcast from the society of ordinary men, they were led by the strongest and most ruthless among them, and were truly at ease only amidst the desolation of their chartless realm. Juan had no experience with pirates first-hand, and only little with the sea, but as a boy he'd read stories of their cruelty. He'd once met an old man who claimed to have sailed with Cabeza de Perro who, like the vicious dog for which he was named, had been caught and put down for his crimes.

Now, rescued and captive all at once, Juan sat on a rough wooden bench in the fo'c'sle of the pirate ship Panagia. His soft muslin trousers hung loosely on his slender waist, his hands nested in the pockets of the rough white jacket he had worn since he was carried aboard more than a week ago. Starved, burned by the sun and more dead than alive, he had been tended to by a brigand he knew only as Ali, who had given him small sips of water and slices of salt pork and rubbed aloe on his lips and skin. "Don't mistake these ministrations for kindness, boy," Ali had grumbled. "If you weren't worth more to us alive than dead, we'd have left you to rot for the gulls and I'd be putting my valuable time to better use."

As Juan grew stronger, he thought of the Angelica's passengers and crew, none of whom he knew well but all of whom he mourned. He was ashamed at how his sorrow at the loss of so many souls was mixed with guilty relief at his own survival. As a child, hearing his mother speak sorrowfully of his drowned sister Luna, he'd felt shame at living a life that rightfully should have been hers. Now, with the naiveté of youth, he vowed that so long as he should live, he would try to be worthy of the unknowable purposes for which Providence had spared him. Whatever pains he might suffer he pledged to accept as payments on a debt. To acknowledge this obligation, the extent of which he could not yet comprehend, he made the sign of the cross, as Dona Inez had taught him as a child.

"A good Catholic, are ye?" Juan turned to face a large, ruddy man, a good two meters in height, with a full beard and mustache that were of an erubescent hue particular to the English and Scots. His eyes were sharp, with crinkled lines at the corners that suggested both laughter and experience. Juan was not yet adept at estimating age, but guessed him to be old, perhaps forty or more, though stronger and more fit than most men of so many years.

There were six of them in the hold, all dressed alike. Juan was the youngest and, at least by his countenance and bearing, of the highest birth. Two, who sat in sullen silence at the far end of the bench, seemed from their mustaches and stocky build to be Albanians or Serbs. Another, his skin as black as night and his eyes bloodshot and heavy, rocked forward and back as though swaying to some internal melody.

To the black man's left sat a thin, emaciated husk. From the twin anchors tattooed on his forearm it was apparent that this man had once been a sailor. His lips were thin and colorless, his parchment skin wrinkled and pale. His face was haggard, and in his hollow eyes Juan saw hardship that seemed to have choked off the spirit inside. The man's hands trembled in his lap, and his breathing came in shallow, jagged gasps. Although it was impossible to guess his age, to Juan the more urgent question was how he drew breath at all.

The Englishman was waiting patiently for an answer. "Yes," Juan replied. "I was raised as a Catholic in Seville, though I am perhaps less devout than some."

"Our upbringing and early devotionals give us a start on the road to faith, my friend, but circumstances create countless detours, and not all of us find our way." The Englishman smiled at Juan, an open, friendly grin. His eyes swept the cramped hold. "This here would be one of those circumstances, made all the more vexing, wouldn't you agree, by being not of our making."

He ran his hands through his thick red hair and looked Juan up and down. "Unlikely you volunteered for this duty, am I right lad? I once knew a silversmith who, in penance for his sins – which, mind, were not inconsiderable – chose to confess them not to the priest but to the sheriff." He rolled his eyes "He did not live long to regret that decision, the misguided sod."

Juan, who still had a guileless tendency to confuse actual and rhetorical questions, shook his head. "I was sailing from Seville to London on the Angelica when we ran into a terrible storm. The ship was lost with all hands, but I survived." Juan described the ferocity of the storm, the unsuccessful efforts of the captain and crew to save the ship, and the final moments of the passengers and crew. "After days at sea, when I was weak and parched with thirst, could barely sit up and thought my death certain, I was rescued and put aboard this ship. I came on board willingly, it is true, but only because the alternative was even worse. I had no more choice than any of us."

The big man laughed again. "No, I suppose not." He extended his rough, calloused hand to Juan, who grasped it firmly but saw his own simply disappear into its weathered maw. "I'm Harry, Harry Dryden, no relation to the poet. Born and raised on Ellan – what outsiders call Mann. Small speck in the middle of the Irish Sea, wind-swept green and pretty as a picture, but hardly a place where one can see much of the world. Left when I was younger than you and never looked back."

Juan tried to imagine what it must be like to live on a small island, isolated from the cross-currents of art, politics, music and commerce that swirl constantly in cities such as Seville. For a man of intelligence and curiosity like this Harry, sailing from home to see the world must have been a great adventure.

"If I may presume, sir, what brought you here?" Juan, to whom the value of good manners had been introduced by Dona Inez and his tutors at an early age, hesitated to ask so direct a question, but his brush with death had made him bold.

Dryden did not seem to take offense. "I'm a soldier. Started out as a foot soldier, just one more man in the ranks. I was young then, Juan – about your age – and foolish enough to be thought brave. I kept my mouth shut, learned my trade, and was smart enough to outlive both the foolish and the brave – so they made me an officer. For a time, I rode with the Hessians in Austria and Sweden; good soldiers, though not a one of 'em has any sense of humor. After peace broke out – only a temporary thing, obviously, but one never knows how long hard times will last – Gudovich hired me as a sort of consultant to help with his campaign against the Turks." Juan gave him a blank look.

"You don't know Gudovich?" Harry was appalled. "With a force of less than eight thousand Russians and one hundred cases of motivational vodka, men led by Marshal Ivan Vasilyevich Gudovich defeated a Turkish army three times their number at Arpachai. Damnedest thing I ever saw – even the horses were too drunk to fear death." Harry shrugged. "It all went well until the last moments, when it didn't. Here I am."

"I don't understand. If this Gudovich was victorious ...?"

"Bad luck, mostly. Gudovich's blood was up – he wanted to pursue the Turks, maybe finish 'em off. But he's too smart to be drawn into a trap, so he sent me and a dozen men to scout out a dry river canyon on his left flank, just in case the bloody janissaries were looking to circle back and catch us by surprise. I told him that anyone running that fast has nothing else on his mind, but no matter, I follow orders, most of 'em anyway. Especially when they come from Gudovich, whose staff I'd rejoin tomorrow if given the chance. Well, there were no janissaries to be found. What we did find was a company of Circassian slave traders whose strategy at the time was to lie in wait at the margin of battle to collect runaways and survivors. Clever, actually."

Juan had thought his own adventures stirring, but next to Harry's they seemed as nothing. Even more impressive to the boy – only the first of many lessons learned at Dryden's elbow – Harry's accounting was matter-of-fact and understated. Juan had never met an Englishman before.

"Anyway, they examined us closely, slit the throats of some, and took others, yours truly among them. They sold us to a slaver in the Crimea, who sold me in turn to these fine fellows in Cyprus." Harry gave Juan a broad grin. "It would seem I'm worth more than I look."

Harry had his own questions. "What is your tale, young Juan? Prior to your ill-fated voyage, I mean. While the stories of young men tend either to be dull or invented, I expect yours might be of greater interest, and perhaps less fictional than most."

Juan drew a breath. What and how much to say? "My name is Juan Pedro Calderón de Castilla–"

"As I'm confident you know that to simplify is not to insult, I shall call you Juan."

"–and I am from Seville, one of the most beautiful cities in Spain. An … awkward situation arose in Seville, and I, I decided to embark to Genoa to see more of the world, about which I have read much in books but have little experience."

Juan told Harry about Dona Inez, his life in Seville, his studies in everything from the arts and literature to horsemanship and swordplay, and his "friendship" with Julia. Harry didn't interrupt, but Juan thought he detected in the older man's eyes a gentle amusement, as though he understood that there might be more to the story. Julia often teased that Juan was incapable of artifice, and on several occasions had admonished her young lover to leave any required duplicity to her. Juan had a sudden, confessional impulse to tell Dryden of his affair with Julia and its aftermath but, remembering Harry's story about the silversmith, suppressed the urge.

"Who are these pirates?" Juan shivered in the chill dampness of the hold. "Where do you think they're taking us?"

"As I'm not sure where we are," Dryden replied with a shrug, "I can't say for sure where we're going. I was put aboard this ship in Cyprus, so it's likely these are Gramvousan pirates. If that's so, the closest slave market that matters would be in Constantinople. The Turks look the other way where the pirates are concerned; their victims are most often European merchant ships or, when taken on land, captives of war." For a second time Harry ran his hands through his hair, this time extracting a squiggling sort of insect which he nonchalantly flicked away. Suddenly, Juan's scalp itched. *"Through commercial interests and relationships too Byzantine to track"* – at this Dryden laughed out loud, pleased at his pun – *"the Sultan himself profits nicely from the slave trade."*

Horrified at the thought that he might soon be sold at auction as a slave, Juan was nevertheless impressed with his older companion's sang-froid; he seemed to deem their appointment with the slave market no worse a fate than any other thing, and perhaps less dire than some.

Reading Juan's thoughts, Harry clapped the boy on the shoulder. *"Dame Fortune has served me as poor as you,"* he said with a wink, *"but never despair. The bitch shifts as quickly as the wind, and carries you as easily away from sorrow as to it."*

"I reckon you'll fetch a pretty price on the block, boy." The words were as thin and jagged as the wreck who uttered them. Juan had not thought him capable of speaking at all. The withered tar regarded Juan with undisguised malice, as though the boy's youth and vitality were treasures flaunted by the thief himself. *"The bloody infidels like nothing more than to bugger a pretty young lad like yourself; I've seen 'em do it."* He hawked, green bile splattering on the bulkhead. *"I'd wager you won't survive more n' a few months of that service."*

Scowling, Harry fixed the gaunt ruin with a withering look. *"You'd best keep your filthy thoughts to yourself, old man. It's plain to me, as it should to any man with eyes and ears, that young Juan has more than his fair share of courage."*

The sailor glared at Dryden. *"Why so quick to befriend the lad, English?"* he asked in a sullen growl. *"Mayhap you think he can be of use to you in the market? Offer, say, to broker a ransom kind o' deal with the boy's relations? Or bugger the lad yourself if you get a chance? They say that's a common pleasure in the Tsar's ranks."*

"Not likely I'll be doing much negotiating in the slave market, scabby. And even if I was inclined to such evils, I'm pretty sure the management here would frown on anything that might damage the merchandise." His expression hardened. "Although in your case – since there's not much value there to begin with – I imagine they might not mind too much."

"I can take care of myself, Senor Dryden." Juan wasn't frightened by the old sailor. The prospect of slavery, however, he found more daunting. "But how are you able to face our fate so calmly? It is a prospect to frighten any man, is it not?"

Harry considered the question. "Think on it," he suggested. "What is our present state? Most men are slaves; indeed, none more so than the great. To silver, or drink; to rank, or power; to hatred, or love; to fear, whether of God or Man; or to a thousand other whims, sins and passions."

Juan frowned – he'd never thought of it that way. "That may be true. But must we merely submit, like sheep?"

"The arrows of destiny were launched at our birth – we cannot stop them. But it takes only the slightest deflection to alter their course, if we only have the courage to act."

They were interrupted by a piercing cry from above. "Arazi! Arazi!" Juan glanced at Dryden, but there was no need to ask. The old tar answered the unstated question anyway. "Land, boy, they've sighted land. By this time tomorrow you'll be standing on the block while A-rab camel drivers and Turk rug merchants check your teeth and privates like you was a mule. Trust to luck or fate if you want to, boy," he said, lifting a bony, trembling finger to his temple. "But if I was you, I'd keep my wits about me. You'll not survive long wit 'out 'em."

CHAPTER 23
Only a Mortal Sin

Temperate I am, yet never had a temper;
Modest I am, yet with some slight assurance;
Changeable too, yet somehow idem semper;
Patient, but not enamoured of endurance;
Cheerful, but sometimes rather apt to whimper;
Mild, but at times a sort of Hercules furens;
So that I almost think that the same skin
For one without has two or three within.

Don Juan, Canto XVII

AS HE dried himself with a towel, Byron watched with amusement as Hobhouse dragged himself from the grey-green Thames to collapse, chest heaving, on the grassy bank. He reached into a satchel and tossed a towel to Hobhouse. "Don't pretend exhaustion, Hobby. What you're experiencing is exhilaration."

Hobhouse sat up and shook his head. Byron threw up his arms in mock exasperation. "No? You just swam more than a mile – you are becoming a bloody fish!"

Hobby shook his head again, hurling droplets of the Thames into the slanting afternoon sunlight. The weather had been glorious for more than a week, the warmest March that anyone could recall, and Byron had insisted that though the river might be "bracing," they would be warmed by their exertions. Hobhouse thought the whole thing madness but, in what he recognized as a metaphor for their entire relationship, had followed Byron into the river nevertheless. He angled his head and thumped it with his palm. "Half the river and at least one or two fish – fishes? – seem to have filled the hole in my head where a brain is supposed to be."

"Well, Hobby, *horror vacui*."

Hobhouse fought amusement. "Tell me, Byron – you've made no effort to recruit me to versifying, or to boxing, or to any number of your various hedonistic or self-destructive pursuits. Why do you insist that I swim?"

Byron laughed. "I see no reason to try the public's patience with yet another poet, Hobby, nor do the critics require fresh meat. You're a strong man, but boxing requires more quickness than strength, and while you are certainly quick of mind, I fear that your strength is not quickness." He reached into the satchel and extracted two apples, which he regarded critically for size, firmness and color. Making his selection, he tossed the reject to Hobhouse. "I encourage you to swim, Hobby, because you are a friend who has done me such honor and service that I am inextricably in your debt. But on one of our swims you will founder. I will rescue you, and my debt will be extinguished."

Hobhouse felt that he should be appalled, but instead found himself more or less resigned. "Of course, that's your plan, Byron – what else could it be? But your calculations are off – you'd have to fish me out of the river three or four times to even our accounts."

They sat on the bank and ate as an endless variety of boats slowly passed by. There were wide, flat river barges running low in the water and piled high with coal; weathered fishing boats returning from the sea with their netted catch sparkling silver in the late-day sun; two-oared *wherries* shuttling their busy clientele to destinations up and down the river, their long, extended bows making them look like a praying mantis; and 60-ton *hoys* that ferried passengers and cargo up the Thames from East India Company ships too large to navigate the river.

Byron waved an arm at the water. "You know, don't you Hobby, that when I was nineteen, I swam from Lambeth through both the Westminster and Blackfriar Bridges, all the way to where the Fleet empties into the Thames? With twists and turns to accommodate current and the odd boat or two, it was a little more than three miles. Not bad for a boy with a club foot, wouldn't you say?"

Hobhouse had heard the story before, but – particularly after a one-mile swim which he felt fortunate to have survived – was still impressed. He could hardly say so, of course, lest Byron become altogether insufferable. "And who was witness to this feat, Byron? Without a witness, *braggadocio* is no more achievement than masturbation is sex."

"Augusta – with Elizabeth Pigot by her side – saw me into the river, and Frank Hodgson saw me out." Byron took a final bite and threw the remains of his apple into the river where, borne by the current, it headed resolutely for the sea. "She's here in London, you know. Arrived several days ago."

"Who, Elizabeth Pigot?"

"No, haven't seen Liz in years. Augusta." Reaching for a nearby stick, he poked at a passing column of ants. Vexed, they detoured to the south. "I had strong feelings for Augusta when I was fourteen or fifteen. She was five years my elder and, even then, had this – this – extraordinary sexual energy. I swear it, Hobby, she was kind and innocent and pure, and she practically smelled of sex." He took a deep breath, as though summoning the scent. "In fact, my mother noticed something and did what she could to keep us from being alone together."

Hobhouse regarded his friend with an all-too-familiar foreboding. God knows, Byron could be impulsive and reckless, particularly where women were concerned. His affair with Caroline Lamb had become a disaster, and London society was officially appalled – though privately titillated – by the couple's public indiscretions. Byron's friends, Hobhouse included, attributed most of the fault to the manic and insecure Caroline. He'd tried to warn Byron that she was trouble, but in matters of sex and romance his friend listened to his heart, not his head, and certainly not to his friends.

Still, even he had been surprised by the ferocity with which this elf of a woman sought to establish dominion over Byron's affections. Did she understand him at all? Did she not recognize that his compulsion to challenge convention and defy authority – the characteristics that attracted her most – made it impossible for any of his romantic attachments to last? If, as she claimed, Byron was "mad, bad and dangerous to know," how could she now claim surprise or betrayal? More than once, Hobhouse had urged Byron to put an end to it, and quickly. "This may be difficult for you, Byron," he had practically shouted, his exasperation palpable, "but consider its effect on me. I swear, it's like watching a driverless carriage careen toward the abyss while its unheeding passengers alternately couple and quarrel in the cab!"

Hobhouse returned to the subject at hand. "That was a boyhood infatuation," he suggested hopefully, "which came to nothing. And Augusta now has – what – fifteen children?"

"Five – don't exaggerate." Byron tossed the stick past Hobhouse's head, and was rewarded with a scowl. "It isn't my intention to bed my sister, if that's what you're thinking, you perverted wretch. Anyway, Caroline is trouble enough right now, and it's all I can do to sever those ties without it leading to even greater agitation on her part."

"Well, Byron, that's a great re–"

"Still, Hobby, she – Augusta – stirs such opposing sentiments! She makes me feel both comfortable and aroused at the same time. It is a novel combination – I have always found the two to be mutually exclusive."

"As I was saying," said Hobhouse, pressing on, "that's a relief. Bedding one's sister is common enough among the gods, but I'm pretty sure it would be frowned upon here. I suppose that's why it's called a 'mortal' sin."

Byron opened his mouth but got no further – Hobby was on a roll.

"Fine, half-sister. The distinction might be of interest to the lawyers, but would have little influence on the periodicals and none at all on the public. My advice to you – which I always give you freely in the knowledge that you rarely heed it – is to greet Augusta with a chaste kiss on the cheek, make your excuses, and send her on her way."

Byron, amused, waved his hands in surrender. "Your advice, which I concede is always well-intended, is in this limited instance – and do not take this as a more general endorsement – sensible. But it isn't necessary. Whatever liberties I may sometimes take, I recognize the grim dictates of convention. I would never intentionally compromise Augusta. We'll spend a few harmless days reminiscing about our childhood. When her business is concluded she'll return to children, home and husband."

Temporarily mollified, Hobhouse changed the subject. "How do you intend to resolve things with Caroline?"

Byron sighed. "I'm working at it, Hobby; the woman is like a crab. Once her pincers have attached, they aren't easily dislodged. I've employed all my usual tactics – bedding others chief among them – but she either pretends indifference or throws tantrums that make me fear both for her safety and mine. You would not believe our correspondence – two ships, crashing in the night!"

"While you have your charms, Byron, such behavior cannot be entirely on your account. Her family is self-destructively eccentric – though I will admit, the same can be said of half the peerage. What about her husband? What has he to do with Caroline's excesses?"

"I don't know. We haven't spoken, but he is a handsome man and, according to Caroline, clever enough. More often than not, the price of bedding a man's wife includes the obligation to endure an endless recounting of his cruelties; yet I've heard little of that from Caroline. As far as I can tell, his good qualities seem to be his own. His misfortune is having her."

"He's done nothing to keep Caroline close to home and hearth? Or, more to the point, away from you?"

"He's done what he can, I think – he took her away to Dublin for a time, and she admits that he has been as attentive as can reasonably be expected. For the most part, he appears to feel secure as regards her affections – he is not entirely wrong about that, by the way – and believes that this storm will simply blow itself out." Byron's voice rose. "If the woman could be quiet, like the rest of the amatory world, things might be managed. But no! – everything she says, does or imagines must be public, which in the end is exceedingly inconvenient, however piquant it may have seemed in the beginning."

They stood and gathered their things. As they headed back towards Byron's rooms, both men shielded their eyes in twin salutes to the setting sun.

"What you need," Hobhouse scolded, a twinkle in his eye, "is a good woman, faithful and kind, waiting for you at home."

"No good woman would have me," Byron snorted. "Besides, they'd have to agree to take you in the bargain, and what are the chances of that?"

"I mean it. I know you think it surrender, or even worse, dull. But you have it wrong. Just imagine the scandal! 'Lord Byron, the voluptuary lover and poet, whose notorious affairs with wives and daughters of high birth and low have enflamed his critics and thrilled his admirers, marries at last!' You would be condemned as insincere by those priggish enough to loathe you, and as an apostate by those misguided enough to envy you. It's just what you like – all of London would wonder what you're up to!"

"Jest all you want, Hobhouse, but at heart you're an irredeemable monogamist. And, like so many of your sad lot, you wish the envied free to surrender to your unnatural conceptions of virtue." They had reached the Strand, at whose cobbled curb they waited while a stylish barouche chattered past. "Wake up, Hobby! This is *England*. Here, the only homage paid to virtue is hypocrisy." Without waiting for a reply, Byron launched himself from the curb like a newly-christened ship, sailing across the cobbled boulevard with the winds of fortune at his back.

CHAPTER 24
Varasova

THEY'D RIDDEN for several hours along a trail dotted with thin stands of oak, cedar and black pine, Byron and Hobhouse on two of the Turks' horses, Panos and Polidori doubled up on a third. Here and there they passed through olive groves whose leaves seemed to cast their own silver light, the rows of gnarled trunks hunched like trolls beneath the thin moon. Byron felt sick to his stomach, and Polidori insisted that they stop from time to time to rest. Despite Polidori's efforts, blood continued to seep through the saturated bandages.

"How are you feeling, Byron?" Hobhouse called as they mounted a rise, the smell of the pines mixing with that of the sea. They could not yet see the water, but the scent told them it was close.

Byron focused on his breathing, trying to suppress the nausea. "Reminds me of when I sailed from Lisbon to Cadiz in a storm. I'm not sure which heaved more – the ship or my innards."

"My village is not now so far," Panos assured them. He pointed to a vague form that loomed above them in the distance, and whose outline they could just make out in the waning darkness. "The big rock, we go around; then maybe one hour more to village." With a gentle nudge, he urged his horse forward. "We should moving keep. Even here, not so close to all the towns, it is risk to ride in the day."

As they drew closer, they could see that the formation was a huge limestone rock at least a thousand meters in height. On its northern side it rose, at first gradually and then precipitously, from the coastal plain. On its southern and western sides, vertical cliffs dropped into the Gulf of Corinth, which separated the Greek mainland from the Peloponnesian Peninsula and Patras. Hobhouse pointed and asked Panos whether it had a name. "Varasova is a name," Panos replied in a soft voice, "but it is called also 'Sanctuary Mountain' because of the holy places inside." Byron saw pain in the young partisan's eyes that he hadn't seen before. He looked up at the rock looming above them, indistinct and shadowy in the darkness, and felt a foreboding that seemed to amplify his exhaustion. "Something happened here," he said, his voice flat.

They stopped for a brief rest, releasing the horses to graze. At the base of the rock the trail was only a few feet wide, so they would need to lead their mounts. Setting his pack down on a rock, Panos took a drink from his gourd and passed it to Byron. They could hear the muffled crash of the waves against the cliff, and could smell the salt spray.

Panos wiped his mouth with his sleeve and raised his eyes once more to Varasova. "There was a town, near to this on the edge of the water, what is the word ..."

"Coast."

"Yes, coast. The Turks tried over to take the town for long time, but the Greeks killed them. More came, and more they killed. Finally, it fell the town after many months. The men first they tortured, then they killed. But the women and children – what is the word? – they decided – no, they *choose* – to die and be not raped or made as slaves." He paused, taking another swallow. "More than 50 women and of the children, the same number there were."

"They jumped off the rock?" whispered Hobhouse.

"No." Panos' eyes were fierce. "They *danced* off the rock. With their babies holding in their arms, they danced the *hasapiko* and one after one leaped to the death. It was ago two years."

No one said a word. Finally, Byron asked the question on all of their minds. "You knew them, Panos? They were to you?" Byron's voice was edged with exhaustion, but his eyes were steady. He knew the answer.

"My older sister Antonia. Her baby, Athanasios. It means – to live forever, what is word in the English?"

"Immortal."

"Yes, it is that. Immortal." Regaining his feet, he slung his pack over his shoulder and led his horse along the narrow trail that skirted Varasova's flank and then tracked northward, away from the churning sea. The rock obscured the waning moon. In the darkness, Byron was unable to see the young partisan's eyes, but felt the sting in his own.

CHAPTER 25
Augusta

But she was a soft landscape of mild earth,
Where all was harmony and calm and quiet,
Luxuriant, budding, cheerful without mirth,
Which if not happiness is much more nigh it
Than are your mighty passions and so forth,
Which some call 'the sublime'. I wish they'd try it;
I've seen your stormy seas and stormy women
And pity lovers rather more than seamen.

DON JUAN, CANTO VI

THERE IS something calming, Byron reflected, in the sound of music heard over still water. In passing over the lake's moonlit silver surface, the waves of sound seemed to conjoin with those of water, amplifying each note. The night was warm, the fine weather holding longer than the greyest beards could remember, and his wine glowed an incandescent red in the reflected candlelight.

Closing his eyes, he listened as the strains of Handel's *Suite No. 1 in F* wafted across the water to his lakeside table. No wonder Handel called this piece *Water Music*. Not for the first time, he wondered how the Muse visited Handel, or Haydn, or the incomparable Mozart? Did they spend hours in laborious composition, introducing and then modifying each element of pitch, timbre, tone and tempo? By what alchemy were bare notes shaped to form chords, concatenated to stately progressions, regulated by meter and suffused with melody and rhythm, ultimately to burst like butterflies from their chrysalis as animate concerti, suites and symphonies? He had never learned to play an instrument, but had always loved music. He thought about a concert he'd attended recently, a stirring symphony by a young Austrian named Schubert. Perhaps, he mused as he swirled the claret in his glass, he would send the composer a letter proposing that they collaborate on an opera. Schubert could provide the music, Byron the words. He had never written for music, but how hard could it be?

The restaurant, which was attached to a fashionable inn on the outskirts of London, featured a rectangular stone terrace that fronted a pretty lake whose cool waters lapped like a cat at the smooth green edge of the stone. A series of torches provided a muted illumination, sufficient for sight but too meager for critique. A stone's throw from the water's edge, a string quartet played from a circular platform built from the same stone. No boat was in evidence, so the musicians must have been ferried out earlier. They played with a gentle grace, enhancing the genius of the composer. Byron thought of Orpheus, whose playing charmed the Gods and induced concessions even from Hades and Persephone, though these he squandered. It occurred to him that perhaps Hades failed to recognize an opportunity; had music such as this wafted over the River Styx, the passengers Charon ferried to their fate might have welcomed the crossing. On second thought, no – their pale dread was no doubt intended.

Byron's thoughts were interrupted by Caroline's laughter, whose rising trill reminded him of children on break from school. "I dare say, Byron, your sister is as soft and sweet as a melon, and every bit as ripe!" Out of the corner of his eye, Byron noted the raised eyebrows of a couple at an adjoining table.

"Augusta," Caroline continued, "are your children framed as fully? Robust health in a child must be such a relief! As a child I was always thin

– our cook insisted I eat not three but five times daily, and still I couldn't keep on any weight. Even today I weigh just under eight stone." She took Augusta's arm in hers. "Your brother has promised to fatten me up, and does his very best to keep me filled." She smiled sweetly at Byron, who shifted uncomfortably.

Augusta laughed. Byron's half-sister – the daughter of Jack Byron's first wife Amelia, who died shortly after Augusta's birth – was neither as voluble nor as striking in appearance as Caroline, whose wild curls and quick eyes well-matched their tempestuous owner. Where Caroline was slight and almost boyish, Augusta's body was full, the curves of her hips and breasts pronounced. Her brown eyes were sleepy and heavy-lidded, her cheeks rosy, her lips full and erubescent. To Byron, Augusta possessed a fecund abundance that stirred something elemental. As the guest of the Albanian warlord Ali Pasha during his Grand Tour of the continent, Byron had been intrigued by Ali's harem, which the Pasha proudly boasted was greater in number and quality than even that of the Ottoman potentate. As he watched his sister return to the table with Caroline, Byron was reminded of Haisha, Ali's third and youngest wife, whose shy smile and full, sensuous figure promised limitless depths of sexual potency.

Rising to his feet, Byron pulled out Augusta's chair, bowing slightly as his sister smiled and slipped into place. He glanced at Caroline and hesitated – just for an instant – before continuing around the table to help her into her chair. She gave him a withering glance as she took her seat, and Byron wondered how he would survive the evening.

"So, tell us, Augusta; how long will you be able to stay in London?" Caroline furrowed her brow. "You have – how many? – five children? Who is taking care of the dears while you visit your doting brother? Perhaps Lt. Col. Leigh is in residence for a time?"

"In fact," Byron interjected, "Augusta hasn't come to London to visit me, though I have invited her on many occasions." He reached for the wine and refilled Augusta's glass. "She is here on matters relating to her affairs, and will be in town only for a few days."

"Your affairs, Augusta?" Caroline leaned forward, elbows on table and chin in hand. "Byron makes it sound so mysterious! Are these affairs of the purse, or of the heart?"

Byron made no effort to hide his irritation. "Given your experience, it isn't surprising that you might confound the two. Augusta's business here is just that."

If she noted the tension between Byron and Caroline, Augusta chose not to show it. "My brother," she confided to Caroline in a throaty stage-whisper, "is very protective of my privacy." Affectionately, she stroked Byron's cheek.

Turning back to Caroline, Augusta shrugged. "My husband invests far more time and money on gaming than he does on his family. While we have resources, they have been depleted faster than I ever thought possible." She shook her head in disbelief. "How is it possible that they *always* lose? The tables are like a fire; they teach no lessons, just consume what's fed them until there's nothing left to burn."

"The trick," said Byron, "is to stow in a sufficient supply of wood. At least, that was Mad Jack's angle. First your mother Amelia, then – when she died and he was cut off – my mother's inheritance. Your husband is no different; he just wields his ax in a smaller wood."

"Oh, you poor thing!" Caroline refilled her own glass. "How terrible it is when, like King George's madness, ancient family characteristics reappear to plague present generations." She paused, as though parsing her thoughts. "I suppose such dangers may be multiplied when matches are made within families." Lt. Col. Leigh, she knew full well, was second cousin to Augusta. She turned to Byron. "What do you think, m'lord?"

"Our wills are free, Caroline. We can choose our own path." He sat back and crossed his arms. Both his smile and tone were cold. "If our characters were preordained by blood, yours would be the life of a cory-bantic slattern, and none who know you could ever think that so."

Caroline reddened, but before she could respond, Augusta lifted her glass. "Family," she declared firmly, "should be neither the subject nor the occasion for disputation; don't you agree? Let's toast to London, to this extraordinary weather, and to my handsome brother's continued successes, both literary and intimate." Smiling sweetly at Byron and Caroline, she tapped each of their glasses in turn before drinking deeply from her own.

CHAPTER 26
Sultanahmet Square

ROPED LIKE goats and their wrists bound with cord, Juan and Dryden waited on the pier at the Port of Azaymah while one of the pirates – scurvy had cost him most of his teeth, so Dryden called him Smiley – doled out the required bribes and obtained the necessary permits. A sum to anchor the ship in the crowded harbor, another to bring men ashore, still another to obtain a seller's permit for the slave market in Sultanahmet Square. Harry nudged Juan, gesturing as gold coins changed hands. "Takes capital to ply this trade," he whispered. "That's why they fed us well and salved our wounds. There'll be little profit in't if we don't fetch a good price."

One of the young scabs who'd been left to watch them scowled, giving Dryden a sharp poke in the ribs with the metal hilt of his dagger. "Kapa çeneni," he muttered – "Shut up." The dawn had arrived only an hour ago and the day was already hot; even down by the water the air was heavy, and a weak breeze only stirred the heat. Dryden laughed. "Careful, lad – the captain will have your liver if you damage the merchandise."

They didn't know why they had been separated from the others, though Dryden suggested with a wink that they were simply a higher class of slave. Whatever the reason, their fellow captives had been led away to the south, leaving Harry and Juan in Smiley's toothless custody.

Bribes paid, they left the pier and entered the narrow streets, Smiley in front, the two younger pirates at the rear. Juan almost forgot their predicament as he took in the sights, sounds and smells of the ancient city. Buildings of all styles rubbed shoulders, reflecting the means and tastes of toppled empires – Byzantine, Roman, Greek – and of empires whose turn to fall had not yet come. Juan had expected the city to be strange and exotic, but was surprised to see blocks of imposing buildings that wouldn't have looked out of place in Madrid or Milan. All of the major European powers had embassies here, each reflecting the architectural fashion of its day. For the French, a rococo swirl of undulating lines and graceful fountains; for the British, chiseled steps rising to imposing stone columns of sober grey; for the Russians, a revivalist confusion of Byzantine vaults and Greek Orthodox domes, with a few filigreed columns thrown in for good measure.

As they passed into what seemed to be an older district, government buildings gave way to narrow private residences made of wood. Although these were not grandiose, many were fronted by iron gates and verdant gardens with crocus, tulip and lilies shaded by flowering almond and apricot trees. Some of the houses featured pergolas windowed on the front and side with latticed screens. Behind several of these, Juan detected movement as they passed.

"Women," Dryden murmured in a low voice. "The ones you see on the street? Mostly low-rank slaves, or so poor they might as well be. With no reputation to lose, why not? But the rich ones – the wives of merchants, clerics, important officials and the like – they can't be parading about the streets, now can they?" Juan supposed not, although in Seville they did so largely without incident.

Dryden cast a sharp eye on a latticed screen at the rear of a wrought-iron balcony two floors up. "They're as curious about things as you and me. I'd wager that more than a few lovelies have their eyes on you right now." Looking up, Juan stumbled over an uneven cobble. Harry chuckled. "Best keep your eyes forward lad, before you fall and earn yourself a poke in the ribs."

As they climbed from the harbor to the city above, the smell of grilled onions and goat sausage made Juan's mouth water. Iron braziers glowed like serpents' eyes in the shadowed alleys, the fragrant smoke spiraling skyward. Old men crouched in clusters, smoking something sweet and sipping coffee so strong it stained their tongues black. They appraised Juan shrewdly as he passed by; here's a young one, said a gap-toothed ancient in a blue hirka, the short robe faded and frayed at the edges. He's better looking than most of these sad Europeans; displayed well, he might be worth 150 piastres. Even more, cackled his companion, if he's already had his balls cut off. Never too late! suggested blue robe, to laughter all around. Juan had no idea what they were laughing about, but he didn't like their looks.

At length the light before them changed, brightening like a forest giving way to meadow. They blinked as they emerged from the shadowed street into a grand square. Arranged in a rough oval, Sultanahmet Square was built on the ruins of the ancient Hippodrome commissioned by the Roman Emperor Constantine in the 4th century to celebrate the transfer of his capital city from Rome. He'd named it New Rome, but the name never stuck, and it quickly became known as 'Constantine's City' – Constantinople. In its day, the Hippodrome seated tens of thousands; the weekly chariot races held there enlivened the city's social life and were one of the few events attended by members of every social class. On race days, thousands lined up at dawn in anticipation, and the line snaked around the arena, its tendrils trailing down adjacent streets.

The Hippodrome was destroyed long ago, a victim of the carnage of the Fourth Crusade, but the Square remained. On its western terminus several ancient monuments survived, including the Serpent Column, whose brass spirals coiled towards the sun to commemorate the victory of the Greeks over the Persians at the Battle of Plataea almost five hundred years before the birth of Christ. When the sky was clear, the early sunlight caught the polished spirals just so, suffusing them with a fiery glow. It was said that Theodosius the Great believed this to be a highly favorable omen; when contemplating military campaigns, Theodosius would rise before dawn to follow the tunnel that led from the Grand Palace to the Kathisma, or emperor's loge, at the eastern end of the arena. There, facing west, he would await the sunrise to judge for himself the intensity of the column's illumination, and whether conditions were favorable for battle.

As they entered the bustling square, Constantinople burst to life. There were high-ranking janissary officers grown rich from bribes and confiscated property, strutting about like militant peacocks, their short, curved swords dull from disuse. The Sultan planned to weaken their power but, from their bearing and sneering contempt, it seemed they did not yet feel much threatened. There were merchants and guild men of every stripe: stocky builders, stonemasons and carpenters; elegantly-dressed spinners of silk, weavers, tailors and shoemakers; fire-blackened blacksmiths and molders of metal; rosy, sweetened bakers, faintly dusted with flour; wrinkled tanners, stinking of lime and urine; milliners in brightly-colored turbans and European-style hats; butchers, their rough hands stained pink and scarred by a thousand cuts; sellers of vegetables, sellers of fruit, sellers of rugs and sellers of men.

The city's variety was not limited to trade. As befit the breadth and scope of the empire, peoples of every ethnicity and description crossed paths in the vast square. There were Kurds, their long hair braided and wrapped around their heads like turbans, ornamented with tassels and bits of silver that sparkled as they caught the morning sun; Berbers, their djellabas scraping the ground and their dark skin offset by bright red fez that rested precariously upon their heads like overturned cups; Mameluke warrior-slaves with red-belted outer jackets over decorative inner gowns; Crimean Tatars, who swaggered as though the empire were theirs, with two daggers tucked into their tunics and a third in the brilliant yellow sash that girdled the top of their billowing trousers; Souliote clansmen resplendent in white pleated fustanella and tight-fitting triq pants; Orthodox Christian clerics in long black robes, heavy medallions looped over their necks on thick chains of gold or silver; mustachioed Albanians in pleated kilts and matching ornamental vests and leggings; and assorted Bulgarians, Slavs, Greeks, Armenians, Jews and Copts.

Then there were the Moslem Turks themselves. In addition to the guildsmen and merchants who made up the commercial infrastructure of any significant city – and in the first decades of the 19th century, Constantinople was still one of the leading cities in the world – the empire's leading military, clerical and administrative officials were a conspicuous presence in its capital. This was especially so in Sultanahmet Square, which was flanked on three sides by palaces, mosques and military headquarters housing the leaders of all three realms. There were kazis, who had completed rigorous training at the higher medressehs and acted as judges to resolve ordinary disputes according to the dictates of Sharia and the supplemental kanuns promulgated by the Sultanate; venerable white-bearded mufti's in sober robes, whose decisions on weighty matters governed by Sharia were final and binding, even on the Sultan himself; the Sultan's elite sipahi palace guard, expert cavalrymen who had earned their place in Constantinople by surviving suicide missions designed to identify the bravest and most able horsemen in the empire; and, occasionally, borne on litters crafted from ebony and cushioned with silken pillows of the deepest magenta, members of the ruling Divan who, under the leadership of the grand vizier, second only to the Sultan, were responsible for oversight of the administrative and military affairs of the empire.

"Look around you, Juan. The military's general staff? The treasury men who collect the taxes? The bureaucrats who run the harbor? Even the court officials who mete out punishment to those unfortunate enough to deserve it? Many of them are Christians; or at least, they used to be. And they're all slaves."

"Do not mock me, Senor Dryden."

"Harry. Slaves shouldn't stand on ceremony."

With a tilt of his head, Juan gestured towards a group of men sitting at a neat café near the edge of the square. They were well-dressed and relaxed, laughing as they sipped their coffee. Compared to the Turks they were light-skinned, and one had light hair. "Those men? They are slaves?"

"Don't be so surprised. You think the bloody Turks could run an operation of this scale? Sultans have recruited—"

"*Recruited?*"

"*Nice word, isn't it? Makes the whole thing sound so bloody cooperative. They've relied on slaves captured in the Crimea or on the seas for hundreds of years. They pick out the best of the lot, teach 'em the language, train 'em to do the Sultan's bidding. Even as a slave – maybe especially as a slave – you can rise according to your merit. It's confounding – a slave can wield power and be an honored guest at one of the Sultan's feasts. But he's still a slave, and must answer to his master.*" Harry shook his head. "*Meanwhile, the Turks become scholars, clerics, soldiers, judges or the like.*" Dryden glanced to his right, motioning with his chin. "*Seems you've caught someone's eye.*"

Juan followed Dryden's gaze to a group of sipahi who surrounded a magnificent gold and jewel-encrusted litter. The sipahi were relaxed but alert, their swords ready at hand. Behind them, an enormous black man stood beside the litter. His head was shaved and oiled, reflecting the angled sunlight like polished silver. He wore pointed blue sandals, matching blue şalvar that billowed like sails around the thick twin masts of his legs, and a sleeveless white vest cut high to expose his taut midriff. His arms were thickly-muscled, and each bicep was encircled by a jeweled yellow band. His left ear was adorned by a bright green emerald, his right by a thick gold loop. He reminded Juan of one of Scheherazade's genii from *The Arabian Nights.*

Juan's gaze shifted to the litter's occupant. She – itself a surprise – reclined on the deep-cushioned pallet, her head supported by her hand, her elbow resting on a silk pillow of the brightest blue Juan had ever seen. Though Juan and Dryden were twenty meters from the litter, Juan's eyesight was sharp, and he could see the dark ovals of her eyes through a slit in her gauzy veil.

Not entirely concealed by the veil, her hair was thick and dark. She wore a light-blue gömlek that extended to the middle of her calf, and above it a purple entari, the silk of the jacket shimmering as though spun from threads of diamond. It was buttoned only to her breast-bone, and Juan could see the swell of her hips and the curve of her breasts. She was speaking to the massive Nubian, who listened intently, but her expressionless gaze was locked on Juan. For a brief moment their eyes met, until a passing horseman in a magnificent black uniform and high, shining boots rode between them. Juan wondered who she was, and why she chose to squander her gaze on a slave.

The moment was broken by the sound of shouting. "Seems we've arrived," said Dryden.

They had reached a far corner of the square. On a platform erected in the shadow of the outer wall of an ancient mosque Juan saw a man on his knees, his head bowed and his hands bound. Behind him was a sinewy Berber in a tasseled red fez whom Juan took to be the auctioneer. At a call from a thin Arab in a white keffiyeh, the Berber shook his head and, pulling the kneeling slave to his feet, thrust his hand into his crotch, clutching the wretched man's balls and scrotum tightly enough to make him wince.

To the left of the platform was a latticed wooden screen, behind which were half a dozen rough stools. Smiley gestured towards the stools, and when Juan and Dryden did not immediately respond, shoved them forward. They sat.

A young boy of no more than nine or ten approached, a small bottle in his hand. Smiley pantomimed to Juan and Harry, indicating that they should remove their shirts. The boy removed the stopper from the bottle, poured some of its contents into his cupped palm, and rubbed it onto Juan's bare chest and shoulders. The oil was warm, reminding Juan of the olive groves in which he and his friends played as boys, pelting each other until their skin was pocked with the rich dark stain of the fruit. The boy kept his eyes downcast and, after finishing with Juan, moved on to Dryden. Juan wondered whether he too was a slave.

The bidding had reached a climax, and the auctioneer scanned the crowd from front to back, hoping to solicit further bids. The thin man in the keffiyeh had offered several bids and appeared eager to bid again. But he hesitated, glancing over at a man of tremendous girth who sat *on a wide chair at the rear of the crowd, smiling placidly and sweating in the heat. He was attended by several retainers, who looked like the kind of hard men to whom Juan had learned to give a wide berth in the seamier districts of Seville. One of the fat man's retainers removed a dagger from his tunic and honed its blade with a flat stone. He didn't take his eyes off the Arab, and the message was clear. The Arab swallowed hard and nodded to the fat man, who nodded back. There were no further bids.*

Disappointed, the auctioneer closed the bidding and the newly-purchased slave was guided to the far side of the platform, where one of the fat man's retainers led him away. The fat man did not move but merely mopped his face with a damp kerchief, awaiting the next lot.

"It's like the fair," said Harry. "Some of the dogs will be groomed for exhibition, some will be trained for the hunt, some will be bred for pups, some will make good companions and lead contented lives." Harry could see the fat man and his entourage through the latticework. He shrugged. "Some won't be so lucky, and will be ill-used, to fight or kill or worse."

It was time. Glistening with oil and stripped to the waist, Harry and Juan were led up a short set of steps to the platform, where the auctioneer awaited. They were no longer roped together, but their wrists remained trussed.

The Berber looked them over with a critical eye and seemed pleased. He had a few words with Smiley, who made sure that his captain's expectations were understood. Nodding, the Berber surveyed the crowd, thinking about who would be most likely to bid and how to heighten their interest. These two, he knew, would fetch a good price, although for different reasons. Even a foolish woman could see the value in the big one – he was strong, and looked like a man who'd seen the world. From the scars on his chest and arms it was plain he'd seen battle; he'd be wanted for the military, or the palace guard, or to defend private mercantile or tribal interests.

He stepped close, leaning in to examine Juan closely. This one is too pretty for hard use, he thought, though he could see that the boy was deceptively strong and, from the way he stood and held his head high, uncommonly sure of himself for one so young. The boy's eyes were clear, his black hair thick and lustrous, his nose and lips finely-formed. The Berber leaned in close, and was pleased to see that the boy's olive skin bore no sign of pox.

He gave Juan a broad smile; when the boy didn't smile back, he reached out with a practiced hand and squeezed Juan's cheeks, forcing his mouth open. The teeth were white and all in place – this boy would make some lucky man a pretty toy. He looked out to the crowd and saw that the sweating fat man was admiring Juan with obvious interest. The fat son-of-a-whore, he's practically licking his lips, and is more than rich enough to afford such a fine bauble.

Releasing his hold on Juan's cheeks, the Berber turned to the crowd, which had pushed forward to get a closer look at Harry and Juan. Motioning for silence, he spread his arms and, half-turning, beckoned towards the blue, stepped-back domes of the Sultan Ahmet Mosque, whose balconied minarets rose high above the square.

"This is a wondrous day," he declared, "for Allah has smiled on this market and on the fortunates who gather here in the shadow of his house." Turning back to the crowd, he swept his arm toward the auction block, directing all eyes to Juan and Harry. "How else to explain the bounty that you see before you? True, they may be infidels. But Allah makes all men – believers and infidels alike – and endows them with a purpose." He lifted his eyes to the heavens, giving thanks for its cloudless benediction. "Perhaps it is the destiny of one of you to help these unbelievers find theirs."

A grizzled Albanian snorted. "Berber, you scabrous cheat, your purpose should be to get on with it! You waste our time with invocations to Allah, in whose name you'd fuck a goat." The crowd laughed, but the auctioneer didn't miss a beat.

"If I waste any time, my tiny-membered friend, it isn't yours – you haven't the means to buy the goats I fuck, much less slaves as fine as these."

Over the ensuing guffaws he stepped behind Juan and Harry and, with a hand in the small of his back, urged Harry forward. "We'll start with power, and then move on to beauty." He turned his palms up to Harry in mock apology, then gestured at the big Englishman. "This man is a soldier, captured from Gudovich's forces following the Sultan's brilliant victory at Arpachai. As you can plainly see, he's strong and battle-hardened, in excellent health, and in the prime of his—"

"Praise be to Allah," called an Egyptian whom the Berber knew was ever on the alert for a bargain. "He must be forty years old! My grandfather is younger than this wizened relic. Thirty piastres."

"Thirty piastres wouldn't buy your grandfather, Ibrahim, I don't care how syphilitic he is!" Raising his arm theatrically, the auctioneer slapped Harry flush across the face with the flat of his palm, the crack resounding across the slave market. Harry didn't flinch, but merely stared mildly at the auctioneer, as he might a particularly annoying dog.

"Do you see, my friends, what this broad fellow is made of? He's strong as a bull and tough as a bear." The auctioneer searched the crowd for the janissary buyer and found him towards the side. "Who can doubt that this is the kind of man – the kind of soldier – the Sultan himself will wish to see in the sipahi." As the auctioneer had anticipated, the janissary scowled; the animosity between the Sultan's elite palace guard and the janissaries who served the Sultan in theory but rather more themselves in practice was common knowledge. The Berber looked at the Egyptian and sniffed dismissively. "Now, who will start the bidding in earnest?"

"First let's see the pretty one," shouted a turbaned bey whom the auctioneer recognized as a senior functionary responsible for administering tax collections someplace or the other. His robes were expensive and his beard was neat and well-kept; not likely he could win the young European, but with some encouragement he might help drive up the bidding. The auctioneer knew his trade – men would pay well for a slave who is useful,

but when stirred in the loins they would move heaven and earth and turn their pockets inside out.

"Your tastes are refined indeed," he flattered the bey, adding an unctuous bow. "In ancient Greece, may her children serve the Sultan, a creature like this would pleasure only the gods." Taking Juan by the arm, the Berber led him past Dryden towards the front of the platform. "By Allah's grace, and the Sultan's most enlightened rule, one of you can be a god!!" Gently, lasciviously, he stroked Juan's cheek. Juan smiled and, with as much force as he could muster, slammed his heel down hard onto the arch of the auctioneer's foot. The auctioneer yelped in pain and hobbled on one leg in a small circle, like a boat with a broken rudder. The crowd broke out in raucous laughter.

Furious, the Berber pulled an ivory-handled dagger from his tunic, its thin blade curved and menacing. "This one has not yet been readied for service," he hissed, his eyes wet with tears of pain and rage. "I say now is as good a time as any."

One of the fat man's retainers pulled his own blade and leaned forward; his master might choose to unman the boy himself, but had no wish to purchase damaged goods. With a sharp look and a shake of his bulbous head, the fat man held him back. Wait.

Seizing a handful of Juan's hair, the auctioneer pulled his head back and forced him to his knees. He moved behind the boy and, sliding his dagger into the yellow sash that encircled his waist, grabbed the waist of Juan's trousers with his free hand.

He did not expect Dryden's reaction. Moving with an agility surprising in a big man, Dryden spun swiftly to his right, bringing him behind the auctioneer. As he stepped in close, he raised his bound wrists and extended them over the Berber's head and around his neck. Simultaneously, he drew his right knee up hard into the man's groin, driving him to his knees. Leaning forward, the big soldier used his size and weight to force the auctioneer's head and upper body forward until, bent almost double, he was able to reach the handle of the dagger protruding *from the Berber's sash. He grasped the knife and leaned back, the Berber rising with him, until the blade hovered an inch from the auctioneer's exposed jugular.*

"Shall I slit your throat, my friend," Harry asked pleasantly, "or shall we start further down?"

CHAPTER 27
A Waning Tempest

In her first passion woman loves her lover,
In all the others all she loves is love,
Which grows a habit she can ne'er get over
And fits her loosely like an easy glove,
As you may find when'er you like to prove her.
One man alone at first her heart can move;
She then prefers him in the plural number,
Not finding that the additions much encumber.

DON JUAN, CANTO III

9 December
To Lady Caroline Lamb

It is altogether strange, don't you think, that as the
third Act opens I should be cast as a scold? The Playwright,
apparently fond of irony, has me – me! – begging you to observe
a species of social convention that is close cousin to rules I have
conscientiously flouted for most of my life. How poorly I play
the part; how utterly miscast is the Actor! If I have defied
convention – if you have worn your feelings more openly than
is fashionable – the fault is traceable to a passion so elemental
that we have been stained crimson, as if painted with that
violet substance – 'iodine' they call it – discovered last year by
the Frenchman Courtois. I should have a pendant made for
you from its crystals, so appropriate is it to our present posture.
Not only as respects its color – the rich red blood of martyrs!

*– but its discovery as well, which I am told was made in the
process of developing an alternative source of the saltpeter used to
manufacture gunpowder.*

*We have been warmed by previous fires, Caro, and know
that this one, however long it may burn, generates heat of a
greater intensity. Still, it is wise to keep in mind the maxim of
Rochefoucault: 'Few are unashamed of having loved, when they
love no longer.' I cannot bear to see you unhappy, a pain made
worse by knowing that I am so much the cause. We must – both
of us – enforce at least a public restraint, revealing ourselves
only in private. Otherwise, gossip shall become embarrassment,
which shall become scandal, which shall beget shame and loss of
reputation. My character and reputation are such that, like rain
washing over a struggling swimmer, little of consequence is added
by merely incremental opprobrium. But though you may have
been wet by scandal Caro, you have yet to be soaked by it – and
not merely for the sake of your husband and family, but for your
own – must take care not to be drowned.*

Ever yours,
Byron

❧   ❧

20 December
To Lord Byron

*When I saw that a letter in your hand had arrived, my
heart as always beat faster, as though responding to 'un timoniere
di amore.' When I read it, I regret to say, the only quickening
I felt was not that of love but of anger. Why, now, do you care
what people say, or profess concern for my 'reputation'? When*

*you urged me, in the carriage that first night, to kiss your lips
and I demurred, you urged me again, with your hands, and eyes,
and with words that flowed like honey from your silver tongue.
And when I could no longer resist, but felt my need for you to
be overpowering and wrapped myself in your arms, and then in
your bed, did you not exult in your conquest, and share the glad
tidings with Hobhouse, Moore and God knows who else? Have you
not declared that you love me, both in the flesh and in amatory
writings of the highest order? So, now you have me, and should
not be heard to complain that the passions you have so carefully
kindled sometimes break out into unseemly flame!*

*I am not disconsolate and will not be made so; not by you,
not by William, not by my elegant witch of a mother-in-law or
by my despairingly hysteric mother. My B, we are, you and I,
the same. More than once you have declared to me, as you have
to Murray and Kinnaird, Hobhouse and Moore, that you care
not a whit for the approbation of the public, or of society or the
political classes, that – how did you put it last? – you 'will never
flatter the Millions' canting in any shape, nor sit on a degraded
throne.' Do you think that I was drawn to you only because of
your beauty? No! – though you are beautiful. What attracted me
and attracts me still is your reckless courage, and your willingness
to describe the world and contend both with its vices and yours
without pretense. If I am not as gifted, I am at least as honest;
and I care not what is thought of me nor how I am regarded by a
class of hypocrites who pretend that by concealing their poisonous
thoughts and salacious deeds, they render them less sensible or
their consequences less awful.*

Everlastingly,
Caroline

᠅   ᠅

13 January
To Lady Caroline Lamb

If I may be so bold, Caroline – what were you thinking? Fletcher came to me this morning, embarrassed on my behalf. Even my manservant pities me, Caroline! And well he might – outside of a Shakespearean comedy, it cannot be often that a man's mistress is caught in his private rooms, disguised as a page and rifling through his desk and papers. While Fletcher may have limited formal education, he is no fool and certainly isn't blind – did you think he would believe that you served Lady Caroline Lamb and that I had sent you for some papers? And what did you expect to find? Letters to other lovers? Pages of heartsick verse? A map, its edges singed by flame and its amatory treasure marked with an X, cartographically revealing the secret path to the inner sanctum of my heart? In its stalking, predatory aspects, this latest episode is even more disturbing than your blustering intrusion of a few weeks ago, when – despite Fletcher's delicate warning that I was engaged with a visitor – you insisted on being admitted at once. The ensuing debacle ruined the evenings of all concerned but Fletcher, who cheerfully insists that his own was greatly enlivened.

It is clear to me, Caroline, as it must be clear even to you, that this cannot continue. I intend to leave London for a time, both to create the space that distance provides and to attend to several small renovations at Newstead. I need time to think and to be clear of the increasingly public humiliation that now seems always to swirl about us and to make fools talk, friends grieve and the wise pity. I shall write you from Newstead, but until then leave you,

With affection
Byron

28 January
To Lord Byron

Forgive me, my love! When I see you with other women or hear that you have charmed this one or that, it is difficult – one in your position has no idea how much – to pretend disinterest, or to act with the detachment I too seldom manage to affect. Indeed, of late it is only with the aid of laudanum or claret that I manage to sleep, so consumed am I with what has become a constant fear of losing you.

I know that I have acted badly these last two months, that I have placed you in one difficult position after another, and that I have failed to act with the 'decorum' expected of mistresses, women of high birth and, as I have the misfortune to be, both. I am sorry if I have troubled or offended you – – in particular, I apologize for my rather appalling display the other night at Scrope Davies' party. It was bad enough that you didn't invite me to attend, worse that I could see through the window that your considerable charms were having quite the impression on the busty strumpet who clung so tenaciously to your arm. Had the bushes not given way I can assure you I would not have made such a scene, but I challenge anyone to maintain both silence and composure while flailing about in three feet of juniper. I hope you understood that my urgent cries were calculated not to embarrass you but to enlist your assistance.

There will come a time, perhaps not so very distant, when these days will seem as nothing, and you and I shall never leave one another's company or yearn for that of any other. I will read your verse, and critique it in ways that make you laugh. You will bring me books – always more books! – and we will read by the fire and gaze into the flames and be content. You are wise to spend

*some time away, and I shall ride, and walk, and make good use
of the days and nights until your return. Be well, and know that
until the arrival of your next letter, I remain,*

*Yours with everlasting love,
Caroline*

*17 February
To Lady Caroline Lamb*

*Those who know me well – and is there one who knows me
better than you, Caroline? – know that whatever my faults – and
I have as many as the stars – deceit and duplicity are not among
them. As is true of most 'virtues,' there is invariably a price that
must be paid for candor, especially where matters of the heart
are involved, and if only I alone could bear the burden of the
accounting! The truth – as cruel and cutting as the winter wind,
but just as blameless – is that our love, always a tempest, has blown
itself out. As much as I love you – will always love you – it is clear
to me that the love you have for William, if not as swift a craft as
ours, is better fitted to ride out even the most violent of storms. You
have graced me with your wit – your laughter – your passion – not
one of which finds a worthy rival anywhere in this grey and somber
isle. I know, as do you, that we have drunk deep from a chalice that
has touched the lips of only a fevered few. Never shall its taste fade
from my memory but shall remain – as you remain – part of me
forever. Therefore, with affection and respect, I remain,*

*Your friend and confidant,
Byron*

✳   ✳

3 March
To LB

*Your letter reached me in Dublin, to which we have retired –
or perhaps it would be more accurate to say, I have been removed.
William and his mother have expressed concern over what they
ungenerously refer to as my 'histrionics,' and are of the opinion
that my 'nerves' will be more at ease away from London. I have
no illusions as to their true meaning; it is they, not I, who will be
more 'at ease' away from London. And so I find myself at rest
(bored!) in this drear and stony city, waiting I suppose for the
fever I am thought to have contracted, a kind of pox of the heart,
to pass.*

*My B, lovers often quarrel, and the volatility of passion is
proportionate to its intensity. I know that you love me as you know
I love you, and my feelings for my husband, which I cannot with
honor deny, have never for a moment reduced those I feel for you.
When I am returned to London – which I expect will be within
a fortnight – I shall behave, and we will dine, and love, and love
some more. Until then, and with you in all ways that matter but
one, I remain,*

Yours forever,
Caroline

CHAPTER 28
The Judgment of Milton

But words are things, and a small drop of ink,
Falling like dew upon a thought, produces
That which makes thousands, perhaps millions, think.
'Tis strange, the shortest letter which man uses
Instead of speech, may form a lasting link
Of ages. To what straits old Time reduces
Frail man, when paper, even a rag like this,
Survives himself, his tomb, and all that's his.

DON JUAN, CANTO III

THREE O'CLOCK on an early April morning – an hour fit only for insomniacs, criminals and writers. Tendrils of fog hung in weightless suspense above the silent streets. A solitary guttersnipe shuffled by – his shabby clothes were loose on his gaunt frame, and he stank of fish. As he passed, ruminating on the declining quality of the scraps he had been able to draw from the veins of this so-called exclusive district, he looked up, his attention drawn by a faint light in a second-story window. Even the rich, he supposed, don't sleep. His mum, who cleaned rooms in a house like this before she got sick, used to say that money was like medicine – a little might help, but too much only makes things worse. Poor mum. He scratched at a scab on his cheek and wondered what it must be like, having money.

As he faded off into the fog, the light in the second-floor rooms flickered fitfully, casting faint, uneven shadows on the wall above the satinwood library table that Byron used as a writing desk. The desk was illuminated by three candles, which Byron insisted were neither more nor less than needed.

"One candle," he would explain both to those who cared and those who did not, "casts insufficient light, while two create opposing and contradictory shadows that obscure sight as effectively as Southey's twists obscure whatever might remain of that lost soul's principles. It requires *three* candles," he would conclude with the air of a man overcome by the brilliance of his deduction, "to produce a steady and properly distributed illumination."

Although the study's other walls were papered, Byron had insisted on painting the wall behind his desk an egret white, which reflected the candlelight and amplified its reach. Bottles of ink and vinegar rested on the right margin of the desk; Byron used the vinegar to dilute the ink. He found it amusing that his freshest work was always infused with the smell of vinegar – "verse gone bad," he liked to joke.

Neatly arranged in the middle of the desk sat three stacks of paper. The left-hand stack consisted of empty sheets, while the sheets to the right were lined with stanzas, each one made up of eight lines in *ottava rima* format: *a-b-a-b-a-b-c-c*. In the center – a stack unto itself and at the moment the only thing in the universe that mattered – rested a single sheet, Byron's hovering quill poised to plunge into the unsullied cream of the paper's rich surface. He frowned – touched quill to paper – retreated – girded himself for a renewed assault. *Nothing.*

He glanced at a bottle of wine that whispered to him from a side table. *Almost empty, but enough for one more glass.* He stood, stretched, poured and drank, sighing softly as he returned the empty glass to the table. Slowly, almost resentfully, he headed back to his desk, the sympathetic floorboards adding their own soft sigh to his.

Lyon, Byron's massive black Newfoundland, lifted his head, disturbed by his master's agitation. Detouring to Lyon's corner, Byron squatted down to stroke the dog's heavy head and rub his chest. Satisfied that nothing was amiss, Lyon offered a half-hearted lick and returned to sleep.

Back at his desk, Byron glared at the unblemished page which, as though jealous of its maidenhood, continued prudishly to resist his advances. *Why the hell is this so hard tonight?* He tapped his quill against the edge of the inkwell, knowing that it was not the flow of the ink that was wanting. *There's no getting around it – there are times when composition is a pain. I suppose it's like giving birth; no one in their right mind enjoys the process, but occasionally the outcome is satisfactory.*

"The need to write," he had once explained to Hobhouse, "arrives in a rage, and if denied leads to a roiling, capped-volcano kind of madness." Hobhouse had looked skeptical, but Byron was insistent. "No, I mean it. Venting the pressure is much like sex, but with a more durable emotional attachment."

He stared at the blank sheet on the desk before him. *It's true, the verse often comes easily, in a torrent. But the empty page is an imaginative void – it can be filled, but too quickly requires replenishment. It's the literary equivalent of the bloody Aegean stables. Still, for me, all convulsions end in rhyme. Why now only the dry heaves?*

He opened the desk's shallow middle drawer and, pushing aside his journal, withdrew a letter from John Murray which he regarded with distaste, began to re-read, then lowered once more. *It's the same thing with every canto – 'tremendously entertaining, Byron, genius. But are Juan's adventures in the Sultan's harem too licentious? Your passages on Castlereagh and the Regent too provocative?'* At one point, Murray had even implied that in criticizing Byron, Moore and others for their supposed blasphemy, Southey – Southey! – might be expressing a more widely-held sentiment.

Byron thought his publisher's fears – which Murray preferred to characterize as 'concerns' – were ridiculous. *The poem's a bleeding satire, and meant to amuse. Does it misstate the facts? As for being "licentious,"*

Ariosto, Smollett and Fielding were all far worse; and anyway, who truly believes the reading or non-reading of a book will provoke or deter the unbuttoning of a single corset!

Byron shook his head, his eyes red from fatigue, his head swimming from the claret. *Hypocrisy and venality are my targets, not a particular party or cause. Can I help it if the bloody Tories have made the sinner synonymous with the sin?*

Resisting the urge to throw Murray's letter on the fire, Byron compromised by tossing it on the floor. *How can Murray defend Southey's rantings? I could demand satisfaction – Moore at least thinks so – but where's the fun in that? Better the pen than the pistol with Southey; the wound's deeper and more permanent.*

He leaned on the desk, his pen poised. He was weary to the bone. As he stared at the empty page his eyes lost focus, his mind wandered and he imagined himself removed to an ethereal realm. Fog in knee-high drifts; an unearthly, diffuse light; no discernable furniture. Time and Death were temporarily set aside but not Judgment, which appeared, characteristically severe, in the form of John Milton. The blind poet – dead these last 150 years but apparently not much the worse for it – was silent, but the question he posed was plain; if called to account, where in the balance stood Byron?

The living poet, confronted by the dead one, considered the question. *On one side of the ledger, some clever words, a fine handful of friends, the well-earned enmity of those whose friendship would be damning. A name. And on the other? Drink, dissipation and degeneracy, a revolving cycle of boredom, hunger, engorgement, nausea and disgust.*

He waited as Milton, grave and unsparing, scrutinized the balance. But when the dead poet failed to respond, Byron pressed the point. *Surely you, of all men, do not believe that Poet's Corner should be reserved solely for the timid and the compliant? For rascals like Southey who, as Blake put it, 'publish doubt and call it knowledge?' If you believed that probity and restraint are the stars by which we must chart our course, how to explain the magnificence of your Lucifer?*

Milton was unmoved – even in death his blind eyes missed nothing. Byron bristled – he was accustomed to being judged, but not to caring. *You accuse me of having lived life too fully? Of crossing lines drawn by the priggish, and meant to constrain all but the conniving draftsmen? You, who wrote to condemn the King, and in favor of his regicide? Who embraced Cromwell as savior, only to find that he was simply a less profligate tyrant? Whose first wife was a girl of sixteen, and whose third – you rogue! – was more than thirty years your junior?* Unaccustomed to being challenged, or perhaps in mute response, the blind prophet said not a word.

Byron sulked in the accusatory silence. He took a new tack. *What about the verse? Whatever you may think of the poet, what is your measure of the poem?*

Silence.

You needn't say it. What does it matter if a certain reputation does nothing to diminish sales? That's a by-product, not a strategy. Byron paused, aware that he sounded defensive.

The truth? I admit to seducing that harlot, Fame, or at least of having been seduced. Why? Perhaps from ambition, or for the money, or simply because I could. Still, say what you will of the poet, the verse speaks for itself. And is Orthodoxy not a graven idol? Did you not abandon a career in Divinity, and refuse to teach from well-worn texts, in order to create from first principles your own?

He waited, his imagination roiled, but still Milton remained silent. It reminded Byron of being called before the headmaster at Harrow.

John Milton, I leave it to you to elevate men's minds. Frankly, I've not the heart for it and, for the most part, don't believe them to be worth the trouble. Between you and the Italian, Heaven and Hell have been adequately chronicled. But my purpose – for I suppose I must have one, or what's the point? – is to chronicle Life. Surely, someone must? The verse may be bawdy – but is it not good English? It may be profligate – but is it not Life, is it not the Thing?

At this the apparition seemed to soften, and Byron thought that he detected the most grudging of nods. Milton drew a breath – at last, he seemed ready to speak.

The wind rose, a loose shutter banged, and the moment passed. Byron was suddenly aware of an ache in his writing hand, which had remained poised, the loaded quill cocked like a pistol. He shook his hand and felt his fingers tingle as the flow of blood resumed. Lyon, troubled in his sleep, twitched and whimpered. "It's alright, boy," Byron said softly. "Just a dream."

Checking to be sure his ink hadn't clumped, Byron brought quill to paper:

> *Well – well, the world must turn upon its axis,*
> *And all mankind turn with it, heads or tails,*
> *And live and die, make love and pay our taxes,*
> *And as the veering wind shifts, shift our sails.*
> *The king commands us, and the doctor quacks us,*
> *The priest instructs, and so our life exhales,*
> *A little breath, love, wine, ambition, fame,*
> *Fighting, devotion, dust – perhaps a name.*

CHAPTER 29
A Shiver in the Cold

The heart is like the sky, a part of heaven,
But changes night and day too, like the sky.
Now o'er it clouds and thunder must be driven,
And darkness and destruction as on high,
But when it hath been scorched and pierced and riven,
Its storms expire in water drops. The eye
Pours forth at last the heart's blood turned to tears,
Which make the English climate of our years.

DON JUAN, CANTO I

CAROLINE HAD no friends – no close ones anyway – and could hardly cry on her husband's shoulder. Not about the loss of any lover, and certainly not about Byron. She'd known it was over, could feel it in the distance between them, in the rows that came more frequently, even in their lovemaking, which had become more frenzied on her part and more desultory on his. But she'd hoped some time apart might heal things, that he loved her enough to overlook the occasional ferocity of her attachment. She saw no need to be forgiven.

"I love you – will always love you ...." She crumpled the letter, threw it in a fury into the bin; then retrieved it, flattening the paper against her chest. *"You shall remain ... part of me forever ...."* And in what part of him

did she remain? None that she could detect, judging from the last time they'd seen one another.

She had come to his rooms unannounced, just before noon. The weather had turned cold and a chill wind scoured the drear London sky. She longed for the days when, meeting in a rush of arms, legs and lips, they jealously hoarded every precious moment. But he'd failed to answer her most recent letters, leaving her no choice but to go to him. She thought she detected a smirk when Fletcher answered the door, though she supposed she could have been mistaken. He asked her to wait in the parlor, drawing the doors closed behind him. When Byron finally appeared, dressed in only a cotton nightshirt and soft satin robe, his eyes were bloodshot and his face unshaven. She guessed he'd been out drinking.

"What are you doing here, Caroline?"

"Good morning to you too, Byron. I'm fine, thank you for asking."

"Yes, sorry, I feel like hell. Kinnaird's birthday. Lazarus no doubt looked better four days in the ground." He collapsed into one of the armchairs and ran his fingers through his thick, unruly hair, which looked like it might harbor a mouse, or perhaps a small bird. "How are you?"

"I'm fine, as I just said." She paused to allow Fletcher, who'd reentered with a pot of tea, to pour them both a cup. Byron glanced at him as he withdrew, but she couldn't decipher his expression. "Byron, what have you been doing? I haven't seen you in weeks."

"Working, mostly. Augusta was here for a few more days but had to get back to her children." The tea was very hot, and he sipped at it slowly. She noticed that his hands were unsteady.

"You two seem to get on very well." She hesitated, reaching up to twist a wayward curl around her finger. "Does ... being with her make you happy?"

"Being with her? Of course, she's my sister, we've always been comfortable together."

Caroline hesitated again, then sighed. "Sometimes," she said sadly, "I think it might have been nice to have a sister."

Byron was hunched over, his elbows on his knees and his teacup in both hands. The steam rose in gentle tendrils, which he sniffed at like a dog on a scent. "Caroline, really, I don't wish to be rude, but what *are* you doing here?"

She'd been uncertain what to say. *I came to see my lover? I've missed you terribly? You bastard, why haven't you answered my letters?* She drew a breath, held it to a three count and gently exhaled; her grandmother had taught her how to calm herself when she was a child, and sometimes it helped.

"I – we – need to talk."

"There's nothing to talk about, Caroline. The talking's done – it's all done."

"You don't mean that –"

"I mean *exactly* that, Caroline!" Byron almost shouted. He groaned and, putting aside his tea, pressed both palms against his temples. He looked like he might throw up. "We've been through this already," he said more gently, "there's nothing more to say. It couldn't last – almost none of my relationships last."

"What do you mean, *almost*?"

He sighed, ignoring the question. "You should count your blessings – you've a husband who's got money, connections and a bright future. That's more than most women can say these days."

"Is that what you think I want, Byron? Do you know me so little?"

"I don't know what you want, Caroline, and half the time I don't think you do either. Honestly, I don't think it's me – it's more your *idea* of me, someone more devoted and, I don't know, emotionally consumptive." With an effort, he stifled a belch. "And, at the moment, someone far less bilious."

"There was no need to *invent* you, Byron – you invented yourself! Have you never wondered why you fly from this thing to that, never alighting for long? Or why, beneath the gaiety of your manner and the brilliance of your wit, melancholy so often overwhelms you?"

"I do not," he muttered wearily, "though I fear you intend to tell me."

"You're afraid to *see* yourself, afraid of what you might find, of who you might be! So, you fabricate a – a – *persona*, the brilliant and charming poet and seducer, the man of letters and of action. The rogue! But the coat doesn't quite fit, and you're forced constantly to make alterations." The words jumbled out in a torrent, and she had to pause to catch her breath. "You say I don't know what I want? Perhaps, but at least I know who I am!"

He stared at her for a moment, and when he responded his voice was flat. "As do I, Caroline. You are mad and malignant, and your ... absurdity ... masks a spirit of meanness that delights in the infliction of misery." He frowned, checking himself. "You have talent, and spirit, and passion that flows molten through your veins. At times, you can light up a room. But your eruptions are toxic, and all too frequent. You don't know –" Stopping in mid-sentence, he exhaled and put down his tea.

"Enough. It's over." He rose, pulling his robe more closely around him. "Caroline," he said firmly, "you need to go."

She'd felt tears welling in her eyes and a lump in her throat that made it hard to speak. "Byron," she managed to say, choking out the words, "you swore that you loved me."

"I did very well, Caroline – until you took abundant pains to cure me of it."

She had felt small and helpless and hated it and hated Byron, hated him as much as she loved him. She would have killed him had she a knife, and then taken her own life. They would find them there on the floor of his parlor in a pool of blood, united forever. She looked up as he extended his arm, and she took his hand and slowly made her way to the door, his fingers gentle on her back. Even at that moment she was ashamed to realize how much she still needed to feel his touch, and how desperately she wanted him to take her in his arms. But when he opened the front door and bade her farewell, she didn't look at him or say a word.

The sun was cold in the grey London sky, and the wind stung her face. She shivered, and walked away.

CHAPTER 30
An Unpleasant Business

When we have made our love and gamed our gaming,
Drest, voted, shone, and maybe something more;
With dandies dined, heard senators declaiming,
Seen beauties brought to market by the score,
Sad rakes to sadder husbands chastely taming,
There's little left but to be bored or bore.

Don Juan, Canto XIV

LORD CASTLEREAGH couldn't walk past the Admiralty buildings without being struck by their resemblance to a prison. How else to regard a massive grey portico, flanked on both sides by an even row of bar-like columns and fronted by an imposing wall and heavy iron gate? Pretty typical, he supposed, of old Viscount Howe, Admiral of the Fleet, who had always seemed more interested in appearances than results. Of course, Castlereagh had thought the same of the rigidly formal Washington, only to discover that there was far more to the General than first appeared. It was a sobering reminder, he reminded himself as he crossed Horse Guards Road into St. James Park, of the wages of over-confidence.

It was still early, less than an hour after dawn, and Castlereagh turned his collar up against the chill as he approached the lake that occupied the center of the park. In an hour or two the paths and meadows would be alive with government officials on their way to Whitehall, young mothers and nannies with energetic children in tow, and Irish street-vendors, their bulging wicker baskets draped by a cloth, selling warm slices of apple dotted with sugar and baked to a golden brown.

It was only two days after Easter, and signs of the well-attended celebrations in the park were still in evidence – discarded palms; brightly colored fragments of painted eggs; and the last remains of hot cross buns and simnel cake that the birds hadn't yet found. But at this hour Castlereagh had the park almost to himself, and he passed not a soul as he turned onto a gravel path that skirted the edge of the lake. Stopping at a small bench that faced the water, he reached into his pocket, emerging with a handful of bread crumbs which he tossed to an idle group of ducks. To the Foreign Secretary's delight, there ensued a lively scuffle of webbed feet and a flapping frenzy of wings.

The strutting ducks, full of agitated scuffle and squawk, reminded him of that pompous ass Southey – *"The poet laureate,"* he marveled. *Imagine that!* He'd known Southey for several years, as their respective Tory social circles occasionally intersected at party functions, but only well enough to say hello or engage in superficial pleasantries. *He's intelligent*, Castlereagh conceded, *and has been cunning enough to curry favor with those who might advance his interests. But he's pedantic, and even worse, interminably so – it's no mean feat to disengage from the man once his conversational claws find purchase.*

Still, Castlereagh reflected as he watched a particularly aggressive mallard snatch a crust from one of the smaller birds, his most recent conversation with the *poet laureate* had proven far more interesting than he could have expected. They had run into one another at a political dinner sponsored by the Tory-leaning *Quarterly Review*, and Southey managed to corner him in an anteroom outside what wags – in mock tribute to Wellington's decisive victory over Napoleon – had taken to calling "the 'loo.'" Rarely relaxed, Southey had been even more intense than usual.

"Has your Lordship had the dubious pleasure of reading Byron's latest excretion?"

Castlereagh had pursed his lips at Southey's indelicacy, but merely nodded. "I have, Mr. Southey. Indeed, I've never read anything quite like it."

"Nor have I, your Lordship. If I may be so bold, I am outraged, nor merely as poet laureate, but as a citizen and a patriot."

Castlereagh chuckled. "I suppose, Mr. Southey, you and I both find ourselves on the wrong side of Byron's pen."

"In truth we do, your Lordship, exactly." He inclined his head. "But at least Byron's attacks on me are for the most part private libels. His vilification of you is a direct assault on the dignity of the state, as well as the honor of His Majesty's minister."

With an effort, Castlereagh stifled a laugh. "Those of us who've stumbled into politics are well used to it, Mr. Southey – we have thick hides." He glanced past Southey to the hall beyond, where his dinner was getting cold. "As a writer, I imagine you're used to it as well."

"It's one thing to express literary differences, my Lordship. I've been on both sides of such debates and try to neither give offense nor take it. But Byron's blasphemies suffer not merely from a lack of literary merit. They are intended to discredit the government and the Church – and even more than that, the Christian virtues that make the English God's chosen people."

Castlereagh considered reminding Southey that he, Castlereagh, was Irish. But before he could reply, Southey stepped close and lowered his voice. "My Lordship, if the government wishes to, um, have recourse against Lord Byron, or to make an example of him to discourage further libels ...." He hesitated, the unfinished question hanging in the air like a cloud of noxious fumes.

"What are you suggesting?"

"Only that my sources tell me that Byron's known malefactions are but the tip of an iceberg of scurrilous activity; and that his misconduct extends to behavior that even his most fervent supporters would find appalling."

"Unspecified offenses, reported by unnamed sources? Come now Southey – if that's all you've got, my dinner is getting cold."

"My Lordship, Byron has a sister, Augusta. She's married to a Grenadier, a certain Captain Leigh. They live out in Cambridgeshire, have four or five children."

"So, what of it?"

"I am told that Lord Byron's affections towards his sister are not of the sort a brother naturally harbors towards his sister. That they are ... sexual in nature."

Castlereagh had been in power too long, and had seen too much of the world, to be shocked. Still, if this was true it was a serious matter. "Do you mean to tell me that Lord Byron is fucking his own sister?"

Southey reddened. "Well, technically she's his half-sister, the daughter of his father and his father's first wife. But subject to that qualification, yes, that is exactly what I'm saying."

Castlereagh paused to consider the matter. *Southey's antipathy to Byron is well-known, and any information that he might provide would need to be verified from one or more independent sources. As one of Byron's most recent targets, my own motives and credibility could also be questioned, and any reasonably competent lawyer would position Byron as the innocent victim of a government stung by his very public criticism. I'm too old, and have neither the time nor the patience, to get into a spitting match with Byron, no matter how satisfying it might be to put the preening cad in his place.*

Still, he recalled the King's note regarding Byron's satirical savaging of his father – "Have you seen this?" he had scrawled – and the conversation they'd had the following week. George Augustus had issued no directives but had made his irritation plain enough.

"Is it possible, Lord Castlereagh, that subjects of this realm are free to accuse the King's ministers of the foulest of crimes, and the King's father of gross incompetence and self-aggrandizing abuses of power, and the government is powerless to act?"

Inclining his head, Castlereagh had asked his sovereign whether he wished the government to prefer a Bill of Libel against a peer of the realm, and a popular one at that? The King grumbled something inaudible and changed the subject.

But what if we could direct Byron to our own purposes? What if incriminating information could be leveraged, not to disgrace Byron, but to manipulate him? Might it be possible both to be rid of Byron and to use him to achieve more important ends? He wasn't sure precisely how it could be managed, but he'd been chewing on the kernel of an idea ever since his most recent correspondence with Metternich concerning the situation in the Levant.

"What evidence do you have to support this accusation?" he had asked, returning his attention to Southey. "It's one thing to accuse Byron of being intemperate, or of harboring radical political views, or of involving himself in romantic liaisons with other men's wives. Of these sins the Magistrate might well take judicial notice." Castlereagh, who stood a good five or six inches taller than Southey, looked down on him sternly. "It is quite another to accuse him of an incestuous sexual relationship with his sister – excuse me, his *half-sister*."

Having gone so far, Southey wasn't about to turn back. "I have no direct proof, my Lordship – this isn't the type of offense one commits in public. But my information comes from one close to Byron, and in a position to know. Further, my source has reviewed a journal in which Byron apparently records his impressions on matters both within and outside the public eye. The journal apparently contains one or more entries which, though not quite literal admissions of incestuous conduct, are damning nonetheless."

"Do you have the journal? Or any of these entries?"

"No. But it is possible they might be obtained."

Castlereagh sighed. "This is an unpleasant business, Mr. Southey, very unpleasant indeed." He frowned, rubbing the bridge of his nose. "Alright, listen to me carefully. For the moment do nothing, and for God's sake say nothing of this to anyone. Or have you done so already?"

"No, my Lordship – only my source."

"Who is?"

Southey looked pained. "I gave my word, my Lordship, that I would not reveal that information. As a gentleman, I cannot renege on such a promise."

Castlereagh considered reminding Southey that this was hardly a matter for gentlemen. "Very well," he said instead. "I'll look into the matter. In the meantime, keep this to yourself. And Southey?"

"Yes, my Lord?"

"While His Majesty is no doubt grateful for your ardent defense of his departed father, for whom you so thoughtfully arranged a celestial vindication, I'd ask that in future you stick to your knitting and avoid weighing in on political matters."

"My Lord?"

"For God's sake, Southey! Your latest poem, the Vision of something or other I think you called it? You invoked angels, archangels, cherubim and God knows what else in a ridiculous attempt to vindicate a sovereign who would best be put behind us. Not only was it ridiculous, it gave Byron the opportunity to deliver a hilariously devastating response which is being reprinted and recirculated by every Whig back-bencher between London and Liverpool!"

Southey blanched. "I ... I certainly did not intend –"

"Of course not. No one ever does." Castlereagh had nodded his head. "I'll be in touch," he said as he strode off, hoping to salvage the cold remains of his supper.

"Lord Castlereagh, m'lord."

Without turning his head, Castlereagh reached into his pocket and tossed another handful of crumbs to the churning ducks. "Yes, good morning Turner, have a seat."

Turner sat, waiting patiently while Castlereagh continued to feed the ducks, who by now had been joined by two geese and a scrawny pelican. After a few minutes, his bread crumbs exhausted, Castlereagh raised his arms, his palms open. Disappointed, the birds trundled off. Castlereagh brushed a few stray crumbs from his coat and turned to face the man – who was of medium height, had thinning black hair, and except for a full, lustrous beard, features that were generally unremarkable – sitting beside him on the bench.

"How are Henrietta and your beautiful girls?"

"Why, thanks for inquire'n, m'lord, they're fine, all fine they are." Turner had removed his wool cap, which he twisted in his hands, his eyes fixed on the lake. The surface rippled as the ducks and geese reentered the water. The pelican chose to remain on the bank, where he scratched in the mud for worms.

"Good, good, I'm glad to hear it." Castlereagh cleared his throat, wishing he'd taken the time to make himself a hot cup of tea before leaving home. His joints ached and his throat felt swollen. "Well, Turner, I've got a small job if you've the time for it."

CHAPTER 31
Brother Sunshine and Sister Wind

She walks in beauty, like the night
Of cloudless climes and starry skies;
And all that's best of dark and bright
Meet in her aspect and her eyes:
Thus mellow'd to that tender light
Which heaven to gaudy day denies.

LORD BYRON, SHE WALKS IN BEAUTY

SIX WEEKS after her dinner with Byron and Caroline, Augusta returned to London. Although her business there could easily have been conducted by mail, she had leaped at the opportunity to see her brother again.

Augusta let a set of rooms in Belgravia, not far from Westminster and just on the other side of St. James' Park from Byron's flat in Mayfair. She napped in the afternoon while Byron wrote but, as the dusk faded into night, hunger overpowered indolence and routed inertia. They dined at Tom Rules' new restaurant in Covent Garden, sharing roasted pheasant stuffed with apples and prunes, wild rice with Arborio mushrooms, and a golden, rum-infused *Gugelhupf* which Augusta first considered, then declined, soon relented, and ultimately devoured. Byron declined dessert but, just as Augusta popped the last delicate bite into her mouth, wondered if he might have just a wee taste. Her mouth full, his sister gave him a regretful smile but extended a rum-soaked finger, from which he nibbled the few remaining crumbs.

The evening was pleasant and their bellies full, so they dismissed the coachman, choosing to walk the two miles to Augusta's rooms. Taking Byron's arm, she and her brother strolled through Leicester Square and along Piccadilly. They paused at Fortnum & Mason, peering through the window to admire raspberry jams, pomegranate preserves, and exotic black teas brought all the way from the Orient.

At the northern edge of Green Park, Augusta paused to take in the herbal scent of the damp grass, rising on her toes and breathing deep. When they reached Chapel Street, Byron kissed his sister's hand and turned to go. "But Byron," Augusta protested, "it's not often that I have the chance to enjoy your company. Surely you've time for a glass of wine?"

Byron glanced up and down the street. Except for a black carriage that stood at the edge of the park, its bearded coachman smoking idly on the driver's bench, all was still. "The evening has been so fine and the company so charming, I didn't wish to ruin it by taking uninvited liberties. But, seeing as how you've now *invited* me, and I *have* worked up a bit of a thirst ...."

The first-floor flat was small, but its mullioned windows looked out on the street and the park beyond. A small fire crackled in the sitting room, which featured a low marble table in a well-turned wrought iron frame. Surrounding the table were two armchairs and a comfortable loveseat, all upholstered in a textured beige silk that Byron remembered admiring in the lobby of Mivart's Hotel. Augusta, who had exchanged her more elaborate evening dress for a soft linen chemise and a long jade-green bed jacket, settled in on the loveseat, tucking her legs and bare feet beneath her. Byron brought over two glasses of claret, setting the bottle on the table.

"The *Lynch-Bages* is good," Byron pronounced, swirling the wine in his glass. He took another sip and sat back in one of the armchairs, across the table from his sister.

"Yes, can you believe it came with the rooms?" She started to say something more, then seemed to think better of it.

"What?"

"Well, I don't mean to be ungrateful ... but the wine *is* more – um – more drinkable than the bottle we had at Mr. Hobhouse's."

"You must forgive Hobby," Byron said with a laugh, "he's quite frugal, and no doubt got it at a very good price. I've told him more than once that he should have become an accountant."

"Any chance he could help balance my accounts?"

"No. He will have nothing to do with finance or accounting, whose procedures he finds dull and whose rectitude he thinks dubious. Why he thinks a political career more honourable is beyond my understanding."

Augusta laughed and made a face – whether in reference to accounting, politics or Hobhouse himself, Byron couldn't say. "I can picture John in the Commons," she replied, sipping at her wine. "He's honest, disciplined, and so very earnest."

Byron nodded in agreement. "His father was an MP and, if I'm any judge of men, his son will surpass him in the family business. Hobby's smart and, while principled and honest to a fault, flexible enough to be effective."

Augusta sipped her wine. "Byron," she asked, "do you think talents run in families? You know, like disease?"

"Well, given our ancestry, I certainly hope not." He leaned his hand on his chin, his finger extended below his nose, looking for all the world like Michelangelo's statue of a pensive Lorenzo de Medici. "Although I suppose murder and drunkenness aren't so much talents as vices."

"No. Yes. Oh, I don't know, it's not the point. I was watching you this afternoon as you worked. Your pen fairly flew across the page with scarcely a pause. I wish the words came to me so easily, even for something as mundane as an entry in my silly little journal."

"You don't give yourself enough credit. Remember when we were small, and we played the rhyming game? You were better at it than me!"

"Nonsense," she scoffed. A pause. "You really think so?"

"I do, without question! I've improved a bit since then, but it wouldn't surprise me if you were good at it still." Noticing that her glass was empty, he reached for the bottle and refilled both their glasses.

"Let's have a go at it, shall we?"

She glanced at him archly. "Um, I beg your pardon?"

"You know, the rhyming game. Remember the rules? I'll start with a couplet, you follow, *et cetera*."

"Yes, I do remember, though I can't recall how one wins."

"Oh, no one wins – enough wine and everyone loses, no one more than Poesy herself, who inevitably turns away in dismay to see her measures so ill-used."

"I don't know, Byron ... how can I be sure you won't humiliate me, as I'm told you did poor Southey?"

"Southey deserved it. But you? My own sister, flesh of my flesh, blood of my blood? I put the chances of it at less than ten percent. I'll start ... sharpen your wits!"

The summer wind blows gentle, warm,
In swaying branches shows her hand ...

Augusta squinched up her face in concentration. After a few moments, she was ready.

Her brother, sunshine, brooks no storm,
The clouds recede at his command.

"Oh, this is good, Augusta; you're as clever as a child!" Augusta stuck out her tongue. Now it was Byron's turn to think, but before he could offer another couplet, Augusta continued her own.

As tides respond to lunar pull,
So too does sun disperse the rain ...

Byron didn't miss a beat.

Revealing vistas broad and bright
The birthright of his noble reign.

Augusta paused, a look of mock dismay on her face. "Just four stanzas in and already you've assumed the mantle of the Sun King? Is there no limit to your presumption?"

Byron grinned. "Le Poeme, c'est moi!" He leaped to his feet, tucked his right hand into his jacket in Napoleonic fashion, and began to pace across the room, his pivots sharp and regimental. He recited his next lines while on the march.

Napoleonic empire pales,
So too, do Alexander's spoils ...

Augusta thought on it a few moments and then gave her brother a sly smile.

Disfigured are these puny males,
By Ra – the greatest of the moils!

Byron, whose pacing had taken him around the table and behind the loveseat, laughed. Leaning over the back of the couch, he kissed Augusta on the forehead and then, fleetingly, on the lips. "An inspired rhyme!" he declared. "To think it took this long for circumspection to give way to circumcision!"

Augusta, her head turned over her shoulder, watched her brother intently. Then, flushed from the wine and the heat of the fire, she unhooked the stay that fastened her bed jacket and undid the top button of her chemise. Without taking her eyes from Byron, she offered a new couplet.

Like lovers, sun and wind unite
Their issue, an unblemished sky ...

Still standing behind her, Byron gazed intently at his sister and at the visible swell of her breasts, which she made no effort to conceal. As he recited a following stanza, his voice was choked.

The laws of Man have taken flight,
Forbidden love been banished by;
Disregarding consequences,
Solar wind and heat entwined.

Augusta's breathing had become shallow. As she paused to consider her options, she dipped her finger into her wine and sucked it gently.

A summer storm, a sudden flood,
Her passion careless of his fame ...

Byron circled back around the couch and table. His legs suddenly a bit weak, he more toppled than sat back in his chair.

Sun and wind, conjoined by blood,
Engulfed in swirling, frenzied flame!

Augusta was breathing heavily; Byron could see her dilated pupils, could smell her sex. Slowly, deliberately, she pressed her wine-wet finger to her breast, her tumid nipple visible through the damp fabric. Byron's face was flushed, and he was conscious of his own labored breathing.

"Augusta," he croaked, like a boy nervously poised on the precipice of his first tryst. Lurching awkwardly from his chair, he reached for her. His elbow struck the half-empty bottle of wine, which careened across the table and onto the floor, the wine cascading everywhere.

"Bloody hell!" Byron quickly bent to retrieve the bottle, but his foot slipped on the wet floor and it skittered away, unburdening itself of the little wine that remained.

For an instant, Augusta seemed astonished. Then, her hand flying to her mouth, she began to giggle. Byron looked like a little boy trying to decide if his feelings had been hurt, but – the absurdity of the situation overwhelming any remaining vestiges of pride – he too broke out in laughter. Together, they giggled until their sides were sore and tears rolled down their cheeks. "Where," she implored, blotting her eyes with her sleeve, "is *Don Juan* when you really need him?"

Outside, the bearded coachman turned away from the lighted window. Taking the reins in hand, he gently urged his horses forward. A cold front had begun to move in off the Channel and, as the carriage clattered slowly down the dark cobbled street, the horses' breath condensed and floated like smoke in the chill night air.

CHAPTER 32
Iphigeneia

THE VILLAGE of Pentias wasn't a place one stumbles upon. Ten kilometers from the nearest town, the village was shielded on the south by olive groves that Panos claimed were more than a thousand years old, and on the west by a rocky creek bed that was bone-dry in the summer but ran cold and fast in the winter when the hard rains fell. Oak trees lined the narrow track along which they rode, their leaves green no matter how searing the heat.

The village was home to twenty families, most of whom had lived there for generations, tending to the olive groves, raising goats for cheese and milk, or – depending on family tradition and the shifting caprice of consumer demand – selling carved "relics" in the monthly market in Pelosia, ten kilometers to the northeast.

Hobhouse and Panos had dragged the bodies of the dead Turks into the woods, covering them with branches, leaves and dirt. They made good time once they had the horses, and it took them just a few hours to reach Panos' village. The ride was uneventful, the only people they saw on their way a few farmers who leaned on their hoes and stared as they slowly rode by.

The horses pricked up their ears as they approached the village, alert to the smell of horses and goats carried on the dry summer wind. Panos too was alert but, after cautiously scanning the surrounding rocks and trees, he whistled and made a circling motion with his right hand, index finger extended. When Byron raised a brow, Panos explained that the villagers took turns standing watch on the approach to the village. "They will to this place bring the village elder."

Byron was pale as the moon and swaying in his saddle. "Panos," urged Polidori, "we need to get him somewhere I can properly clean and bind his wound. Now."

Panos shrugged. "Before you can go in the village elder must decide. Are you danger? Pentias has women, children, old men. For as long as any remember, no strangers enter the village until the elder says yes, is safe."

They had stopped in a small clearing at the edge of the olive grove. The fruit on the trees was green and hard; once the olives were harvested, they would be soaked in brine to remove their bitterness, then allowed to ferment for several months. When they were ready the olives would be pressed into fragrant oil or bottled in brine, to be sold when the winter settled in and the fields turned pale and sharp with frost.

"Your mother," asked Polidori. "I assume she'll accept your assurances?"

"Sometimes yes, sometimes no. She trusts me, yes, but her feelings – what is your word?"

"Instincts."

"Yes, her instincts. Those she trusts more."

Before Polidori could respond, a man and a woman materialized out of the grove at the far side of the clearing. Silent as deer in their approach, they now advanced with purpose. Both carried pistols in their belts and daggers on their hips.

"And for good reason," declared the woman, who apparently had excellent hearing. "Panos, what stray cats have you brought with you this time, to eat our bread and drink our wine?"

Her English was good, much better than her son's. She was short, just a shade over five feet by Byron's reckoning. Her thick black hair, troubled with soft streaks of grey, was tied behind her in a simple braid, and her skin was hard and weathered. She wore a peasant smock over black cotton leggings and worn sandals whose straps were tied loosely around her sinewy calves. Byron guessed she was at least forty, maybe older, but her teeth were even and her blue eyes sharp. Byron noted the deep creases at their corners and supposed she owed them more to sorrow than to laughter.

Panos gestured towards Polidori and Hobhouse. "These men fight the Turks, Mána." He turned to face Byron, who nodded respectfully. "This one killed two janissaries, whose horses now we ride." Remembering his manners, he made introductions. "This is the elder of our village, my mother Iphigeneia." He introduced each of the Englishmen, noting that Polidori was a doctor, that Hobhouse was strong and brave, and that Byron – whose name he continued to pronounce as "By-roon" – was a poet and a warrior.

Byron, who was having a hard time remaining upright in the saddle, smiled at Panos' description. "I am no warrior, and had the misfortune of being on the field of battle only because the Turks surprised us in our camp." Grimacing with the pain, he raised his arm so she could see the blood-soaked bandage on his flank. "A true warrior would have avoided the Turk's blade and saved you and Panos much trouble."

The man who accompanied Iphigeneia frowned, his unsmiling eyes narrow and distrustful. He was strong, that much could be seen at a glance, and along with the dagger at his side he carried a scar on his cheek that charted a jagged path from aquiline nose to stubbled chin. His hair revealed not a trace of grey, but his olive skin belonged to one who spent his days in the orchards and the fields. He carried himself with a sullen swagger, and Byron sensed the impatience that strong men sometimes feel when they must defer to someone stronger still. His age was hard to guess, but his sentiments were transparent.

"No trouble to let you die, English," he said, his manner dismissive. He extended his chin towards Polidori and Hobhouse. "Those two may need a little push."

Without diverting her eyes from Byron, Iphigeneia shook her head. "Is it not enough that we must kill the Turks, Nikolaus? Must we kill the English too?"

Hobhouse cleared his throat. "Byron is very well-known in England, and has provided money and supplies to the Greek partisans, for whose struggle he has great sympathy. We are no threat to you; to the contrary, we support your cause."

Nikolaus snorted. "The partisans," he spat, "are nothing but local warlords who pretend to champion the cause of Greece. They care for nothing but power, and can be trusted only to steal the bread from honest men."

Byron nodded. "What you say is true," he acknowledged. "Corruption is rampant, and many of those who claim to champion Greece champion only themselves. This much I have learned," he added ruefully, "at great personal expense." He turned back to Iphigeneia. "Still, I must give them credit; they swindle with the cleverness of foxes."

"A talent," Iphigeneia replied with the barest hint of a grin, "that has both served and plagued our people since the days of Menelaus and Odysseus." She motioned to Nikolaus. "But not all who fight the Turks are cowards and dogs, and our submission has lasted too long. At some point subjugation becomes a habit, and a great people are lost." She turned back to Byron and met his eyes. "That you have given your treasure and your blood for a cause that is not your own – this is something to respect, no matter how foolish it may be."

Iphigeneia turned to Polidori and pointed at Byron. "You, the doctor. Will he live? And if no, how long until he dies?"

Polidori was startled by Iphigeneia's directness, but Byron laughed. "Yes, Polidori, I was wondering about that myself."

"I can keep him alive for now, if I can get him off that damn horse and into a proper bed where I can clean and bind his wound." He shrugged. "After that, it's hard to say."

Iphigeneia glanced at Panos, who nodded almost imperceptibly. Nikolaus scowled, but offered no protest. "You are welcome in our village," Iphigeneia said to Hobhouse, who had dismounted and was standing beside Byron's horse, "but only for so long as this one needs to heal or die. Then you must leave."

Byron lifted his hand to his pocket, fingering the sheet of paper taken from the dead janissary. He hesitated for a moment, uncertain, then returned his hand to his side. "We are grateful for your generosity," he whispered, as the pine boughs swirled and the hawks traced circles in the washed-out sky. His shirt was soaked with sweat and caked with blood. The last thing he remembered was Hobhouse reaching out to catch him as he swayed at the edge of his saddle and fell off into blackness.

CHAPTER 33
Confrontation in the Slave Market

"WHAT IN *the name of the Prophet is going on here?" The booming voice carried across the open square and above the raucous shouting in the slave market. Dryden, who had no problem recognizing a voice well-used to command, slid to his left so that he could face its source, the Berber bent under his weight and the auctioneer's knife still pressed to its owner's throat.*

A small contingent of sipahi, on regular duty in the square, had been alerted by the commotion and had arrived to find Dryden, Juan and the Berber on the auction platform and a roiling crowd, many with their weapons raised, in the plaza below it. From the shouting, it appeared that a portion of the crowd favored an immediate assault on the platform and the dismemberment of the upstart slaves. Others seemed more amused than angry, pleased at the unexpected entertainment and eager to see it to what they hoped might be a bloody conclusion. Still others could be heard to counsel caution; these slaves are valuable, they admonished. Killing the soldier would be a shameful waste of initiative and talent, and don't forget about that pretty young boy!

The fat man had risen and, with a handful of his retainers, was advancing on the platform, his eyes fixed not on Dryden but on Juan. Even amidst the uproar men hurried to get out of his way, responding not merely to his wealth and girth but to a placid menace that made the hair on the back of their necks stand up.

At the other side of the platform, Smiley and the two young pirates who brought Dryden and Juan to the slave market had leaped to their feet when Dryden seized the Berber, and now stood on the steps of platform a few feet away, their swords drawn. The two young pirates seemed eager to hurl themselves at Dryden, but Smiley – aware that his Captain, who wasn't a man to be trifled with, expected these slaves to fetch a nice profit – restrained them with a snarl.

The sipahi officer surveyed the situation. He was neither young nor old – Dryden estimated him to be in his mid-thirties or so – and his features tagged him as a descendant of the Mongol horsemen that swept in from the Asian steppes in the thirteenth century to put an end to the short-lived Seljuk Empire. His long, straight black hair was gathered in a pony tail at his back. He wore billowing purple şalvar, a red, high-collared undercoat bound at the waist by a wide band of jade-green silk, and an outer jacket, open at the front, with five ornamental brass buttons arranged vertically on each side. On his left hip he carried a curved dagger in a sheath, and on his head sat a cylindrical black hat that looked to Dryden like a ribbed drum.

Making up his mind, the officer issued a command. In an instant, three of his men leaped onto the auction block. Drawing their swords, they pushed past the pirates to surround Dryden and the Berber. Three more sipahi took up positions at the front of the crowd, their backs to the block, their legs spread and their arms crossed in a stance calculated to discourage any challenge. Despite some grumbling, the restive crowd remained in place. So too the fat man's retainers, although to Dryden, who had appraised the situation at a glance, they appeared more calculating than cowed.

Taking his time, the sipahi officer climbed the steps to the block and nodded to Dryden. "So, English, what's your name?"

"Dryden." He motioned to Juan, who had seized a wooden staff that lay at the rear of the platform and now gripped it, hands spread evenly along its length. "And this young man is Juan. From Seville, in Spain. Your accent is excellent – how'd you know I was a Brit?"

The sipahi shrugged. "Red hair, light skin. You don't look Russian, and

Constantinople doesn't see too many Irishmen. As for your tongue, I fought with the Hessians for a time in the New World. My name is Tokaskh."

The Berber, bent almost double under Dryden's weight, managed to spit out a curse. *"Could we dispense with idle talk, sipahi? Or do the sipahi hesitate to safeguard the Sultan's interests?"* He had more to say but Dryden didn't wish to hear it, silencing him with a little pressure on the blade.

Tokaskh ignored the interruption. *"You've seen battle, Dryden?"*

"More than my share, I'd wager. Perhaps even more than you."

"You know, then, that I take no pleasure in killing you and the boy."

"Don't kill us then." Dryden's voice was soft, his tone conversational. He lifted his free hand and gestured broadly at the magnificent square, which was now bathed in sunlight. *"It's a lovely day, Tokaskh. It'd be a shame to ruin it."*

"No doubt. I wouldn't think of it to save this flea-ridden dog," he said with disdain, gesturing at the Berber. *"His fez is worth more than his miserable life. Personally, I don't care whether you kill him. But … I don't get to decide such things."* He sighed. *"This empire is built on the slave trade, and the Sultan earns a pretty sum on every slave bought and sold. Your resistance? Brave, but very bad for business."*

The Berber raised his head, at least as much as possible with the big man leaning on him. *"Your sympathy and good wishes warm my heart, sipahi. But I am misunderstood. I see no gain in killing the English – far better that we put this incident behind us."*

The fat man, who had approached within a few feet of the platform, belched, a deep, abdominal eruption whose sound and odor were vaguely sickening. Tokaskh regarded him without expression, though Dryden thought that just for an instant he detected fear. *"You have views on this, Engin?"* Dryden had to smile at the Turkic name, which meant vast.

"So good of you to inquire, Tokaskh – it is not by accident that you have risen to a position of leadership. It is good to have power – yes? – no matter how limited." The fat man's voice was high and surprisingly thin, reminding Dryden of the eunuchs he once encountered when dispatched

by Gudovich to Ali Pasha's court in Tirana. Despite his reputation for brutality, Dryden had found the Albanian warlord to be charming in person. He detected no similar qualities in this fat fellow.

"To my astonishment," continued Engin, "I find myself in agreement with the Berber. A first time for everything." He emitted another gaseous, susurrating belch. "I do not question the Sultan's prerogatives with respect to matters of civil discipline. Still, the insult here has been not to the Sultan, but to a private enterprise. Whose principal, I might add, has been known to understate the revenues owed to my most esteemed cousin the Sultan."

The Berber's objection emerged only as a strangled groan, as Dryden cut it off with a renewed tilt of the dagger. The conversation had become interesting – best to see how it played out.

"What are you suggesting?" Tokaskh asked carefully.

Engin gestured towards the crowd. "The slave market teems with buyers and the Empire with slaves, many in positions of influence. Their cooperation and loyalty is an asset that has, over many years, been purchased with restraint. An officer as perceptive as you will recognize that the merits of executing the infidels – which, by the way, I do not underestimate – must be weighed against the uncertain consequences of wielding too heavy a hand."

"There are consequences to all things." Tokaskh gestured towards Dryden and Juan. "This, even these slaves must understand."

The fat man inclined his massive head. "True, Tokaskh; but there are sensitivities to consider. That the big slave is English complicates matters; I know I do not need to elaborate on this point." He shook his head, as though sympathetic over the immense difficulties confronting the sipahi officer. His jowls quivered, droplets of sweat flying from the overlapping folds of his chins. "If I might be so bold," he suggested softly – Dryden was impressed by how smoothly the fat man worked to reel in his catch – "perhaps I am in a position to help bring this dangerous episode to a satisfactory resolution."

Tokaskh knew a hook when he saw one, but had little choice but to nibble. Engin was both well-connected and, based on stories whispered among sipahi officers in the still of the night, capable of unspeakable violence. "Your solution?"

"Order must be maintained, and an example made. I will purchase them both, at a generous price." He cast a sharp glance at the Berber. *"But not an extortionate one."* He shifted his attention to Dryden, who remained impassive, waiting for the true deal points to emerge. *"The big one I will castrate, here in the market, as a warning. He can still be of use to me, and will be easier to manage."*

"And the boy?" Tokaskh already knew the answer, though in truth, he had no business caring and, within the limits adhered to by men of decency, didn't.

"He'll be a fine addition to my house and will serve me well, at least for a time." Delicately, he licked his lips. *"Such beauty is rare, is it not? I am fortunate to have the means to possess such things, and by doing so to help you solve your problem."*

Tokaskh considered his options. He could kill Dryden and Juan, although probably not before the soldier cut the auctioneer's throat, which wouldn't be a problem except that the Berber was extraordinarily skilled at his profession, produced consistent profits for the Sultan, and was a distant cousin to Gulbayez, the Sultan's seventh wife and current favorite. She was not a woman to cross, that one; he'd heard that, incensed by one of the Sultan's flirtations, she'd had the girl stuffed in a weighted bag and thrown into the Bosporus. Yes, he'd told Dryden it was fine to kill the Berber, but that had been nothing but a ploy.

On the other hand, the fat man's proposal had its merits. Handled properly, no one had to die and no revenue had to be sacrificed. Castrating the soldier would indeed set an example. As for the boy, he didn't see this ending well under any scenario. There was no chance that he would allow Dryden and the Spaniard to escape; were he to do so, he might as well slice his own throat and save the Kiaya-bey – the Grand Vizier's lieutenant, and the man responsible for the administration of discipline within the sipahi officer corps – the trouble.

Dryden, who had been listening attentively, decided it might be time to participate in the negotiations more directly. "An attractive offer, Tokaskh

– I can understand why you'd find it tempting." He leaned back, the Berber arching with him to avoid the rising knife. "The Sultan gets his gold, the Berber keeps his life, the fat man satisfies the perversities of his appetites, and the crowd gets a little blood. What could be neater?"

"Except?"

"Except that you aren't that kind of man. Except that the British government won't take less offense to my public castration than to my death. And except that this arrangement isn't acceptable to me or to Juan. If you or any of your men take a step in our direction, I'll kill the Berber and we'll both slit our throats. Which will leave the Sultan without profit and you with quite a mess to clean up."

Without taking his eyes from Tokaskh, Dryden called to Juan. "What do you say, young Juan?"

Juan swallowed hard; the notion of slitting his own throat held no appeal. Still, neither did any of the alternatives. "As you have spoken, Senor Dryden." He shrugged. "By all rights I should be dead already anyway."

To Juan's surprise, the fat man laughed, his chins and jowls rippling in gelatinous waves. "English, you have courage!" he shouted, clapping his soft, pudgy hands in delight. "To die takes nothing, any fool can do it. But to die with courage? That is more difficult, and – I can tell you this from my own observations – occurs only rarely. Indeed, to watch a man meet his death with courage is a gift, and were you and the boy less valuable, I would take great pleasure in seeing you die so well."

The fat man sighed. "But there will be time for that, won't there? For today, you seem to have forgotten that you have only the one knife." He motioned to his men, who slowly mounted the auction platform, their hands light on the hilts of their daggers. "You may kill the Berber – I don't care much either way – but my men will seize you before you can draw the blade across your own throat." He glanced at Juan. "As for the boy, unless he plans to bludgeon himself to death with that staff – a project that may take some time – we'll have him in hand quickly enough."

Wary of the approach of the fat man's retainers, the sipahi on the platform looked to Tokaskh, who hesitated for a moment and then twirled a finger in the air. His men immediately shifted their stance, turning so that they could see Dryden to the one side and Engin's retainers to the other.

"You may enjoy the confidence of the Sultan, Engin," Tokaskh admitted, "but I am in command here, not you. Tell your men to fall back. No one will die today unless I say so."

Engin's eyes narrowed, his amusement vanished. "You are correct, Tokaskh," he hissed. "I do enjoy the confidence of the Sultan. If you wish to remain in your present position, humble as it is, you will not interfere with me on this." He motioned to his men, who drew their daggers and slowly moved toward Dryden and the encircling sipahi.

The pirate Smiley, who had become increasingly concerned over where the situation was heading, muttered something under his breath as he and his two shipmates slowly spread out, their swords pointed at the fat man's retainers.

"The soldier and the boy don't be your property, fat man. nor are they yours, sipahi. Right now, they be mine; and if this market can't manage a simple consignment sale, we'll take 'em to a market that can." He glared at Engin. "You may be a big fish here, you steaming, maggot-ridden heap of camel dung, but that means nothing to my captain and even less to me!"

Dryden, who by this time was beginning to get tired of leaning on the Berber, glanced over at Juan and rolled his eyes. Juan took in the scene unfolding around them – the sipahi on the platform, edgy and tight, their attention divided between the fat man's retainers and Dryden; their brothers at its front, facing down a snarling, well-armed crowd; Tokaskh in front of them, uncertain whom he should kill and whom he should merely offend; the pirates to one side, demanding the return of their property in the hopes of salvaging something from their investment; and the fat man's retainers on the other, daggers in their hands and debauchery on their master's mind. He had a mind to laugh, and might have were their situation not quite so dire. Instead, he merely looked back at Dryden and shrugged, both resigned and curious to see what might happen next.

Which no one anticipated, least of all Juan. From the side of the platform closest to the square a voice rose above the tumult, its resonance so deep and arresting that, even though it arrived not as a shout but as a proclamation, the slave market fell silent. "All bow," intoned the massive Nubian whom Juan and Dryden had seen in the square earlier that morning, "and make yourselves lowly! In the name of Sultan Mahmud Han, Sovereign of The Sublime House of Osman, Sultan of Sultans, Khan of Khans, Commander of the Faithful, and Successor to the Prophet of the Lord of the Universe, I command you, and each of you, to pay heed to the Word and prostrate yourselves to the Wishes of Her Most Esteemed Sultana, the Lady Gulbayez, Seventh Wife and Consort to the Sultan!"

CHAPTER 34
A Delicate Matter

Roll on, thou deep and dark blue ocean – roll!
Ten thousand fleets sweep over thee in vain;
Man marks the earth with ruin – his control
Stops with the shore; – upon the watery plain
The wrecks are all they deed, nor does remain
A shadow of man's ravage, save his own,
When for a moment, like a drop of rain,
He sinks into thy depths with bubbling groan,
Without a grave, unknell'd, uncoffin'd, and unknown.

CHILDE HAROLD'S PILGRIMAGE, CANTO II

AFTER HIS meeting with Castlereagh, Lord Strangford finished his business in London and arranged passage on HMS Weymouth – an aging forty-four gun fifth-rate that had been recommissioned as a storeship in 1806 – for the long journey back to Constantinople. Bad weather forced the ship to harbor for a time in Malta, and it wasn't until mid-March that he finally got back to his office in the Ottoman capital.

During the voyage he'd had ample time to consider his options and, upon arriving in Constantinople, he set out to implement the instructions he'd received from the Foreign Secretary in late

November. There was little time to waste, as the violence had only escalated in intensity.

Within days of his return, Strangford arranged a meeting with Count Vasili Makarov, the Tsar's minister in Constantinople. The meeting did not go well. In response to Strangford's 'hope' that the Tsar might exercise restraint, Makarov affected indignation.

"Come now, Lord Strangford – as you well know, the Tsar has a solemn obligation as Protector of the Orthodox Church. Does your government expect him to stand idle as the Sultan's janissaries loot and pillage Christian churches and shrines? That he do nothing to address the *Porte's* violation of its treaty obligations in the Danubian Provinces? That he turn the other cheek to its interference with Russian shipping in the Straits?"

"No. My government recognizes the Tsar's legitimate interests in these matters. But military force will not produce an accommodation – it will lead only to further violence." He paused, choosing his words carefully. "The British government believes that confrontations – whether between ethnic groups or nations – are best avoided."

"Sage advice," Makarov sneered. "How disappointed the Irish must be that your Lord Castlereagh hasn't taken it more to heart."

Strangford shrugged – there was little to be gained by prolonging this debate. "Has the *Porte* responded to Alexander's ultimatum?"

"In its own way." Makarov struck a match, twirling the tip of his cigar through the flame. "The *reis effendi* never addressed the Tsar's specific demands, choosing instead to deliver a lecture on imperial sovereignty and the Sultan's right to put down internal rebellion."

"I suppose that's not altogether surprising. Would Alexander countenance rebellion in the Crimea? Or in Georgia? Or among his new vassals, the Azerbaijani's?"

"It is one thing to maintain order, Lord Strangford. It is quite another to use the preservation of authority – and a dubious and disintegrating authority at that – as a pretext for religious persecution. Or are you English as indifferent to the survival of the Russian Orthodox community in this rotting empire as you are to the rights of the Papists in your own?"

If his meeting with the Tsar's envoy was unproductive, Strangford at least understood the Russians' calculus. He was unable to say the same for his meeting with the *reis effendi*. It took him almost a month merely to arrange an audience and, when he was finally ushered into Hamid Bey's richly-furnished office overlooking Sultanahmet Square, the *Porte's* foreign minister was uncharacteristically terse.

"Lord Strangford," he greeted the British envoy, his eyes red with fatigue, "it is good to see you again. Come, sit with me by the window; if there isn't time to take the air, I can at least enjoy the view." As they settled themselves, the *reis effendi* glanced at an intricately filigreed timepiece on his desk. "Please accept my apologies, Lord Strangford, I have but a few minutes. The Sultan is expecting me."

"Of course, *reis effendi*," Strangford replied with a sinking feeling. "I will get right to the point. My government is concerned about the continuing violence, as well as the danger of a broader conflict if relations with the Russian Empire cannot be repaired."

"We too are concerned, and have exercised considerable restraint. But there are indignities that the Sultan simply will not tolerate. The Tsar's presumptuous ultimatum is one of them."

"The preservation of dignity is of paramount importance," Strangford replied with a nod. "Indeed, it is an objective that is second only to the preservation of imperial identity itself."

The *reis effendi* chose to misinterpret the point. "I am gratified, Lord Strangford, to understand that your government recognizes the Sultan's right to put down a rebellion within his borders."

"It does, *reis effendi*. All governments have such right. But Alexander has over half a million men at his immediate disposal, and his ears are filled with cries for war – and a holy war at that."

Strangford met Bey's eyes and spoke with grim conviction. "The *Porte* can survive an accommodation with the Greeks, who may be satisfied with something short of independence. As you know better than I, the Sultan's predecessors have survived similar concessions in the Balkans." He lowered his voice so that the *reis effendi* had to lean forward to hear him. "My government believes that neither the Sultan nor his empire can survive an open military conflict with the Tsar."

The *reis effendi* leaned back and crossed his arms, sweeping aside the billowing red sleeves of his robe. "Sovereign dignity, Lord Strangford, is not like the feathers of a goose, which may here and there be plucked without lasting harm. It is the heart of the goose itself. Once it has been pierced, death is inevitable." He offered a tired smile. "Of course, if your government is correct and the Russians succeed in bringing down an empire that has stood as a bulwark against Russian ambitions in Europe and in the Mediterranean since the 15th century, none but Alexander will rejoice; will they?"

After dispatching his meeting summaries to Castlereagh, Strangford was called away to Cairo, where a legation of European trade ministers was meeting to discuss issues pertaining to shipping, import duties and trade. The meetings dragged on for almost a week, accomplishing little, and Strangford was relieved when the discussions collapsed entirely and he was free to return to Constantinople.

Upon his arrival, a coded dispatch was waiting for him. It was from the Foreign Secretary. Hanging up his outer coat, he locked the door, retrieved the most recent code keys from his safe, and sat down at his desk to decipher the message. It didn't take him long – it was short and to the point.

Disbelieving, Strangford read Castlereagh's instructions a second time, then a third. At last he rose and crossed the room to a cabinet in which he kept a few bottles of whiskey. Wishing for at least the thousandth time that he could procure a block of ice, he poured himself a drink.

In his rise through the foreign service, Strangford had achieved success at every step and had believed himself prepared for any challenge. This, however, was a different thing. He recalled, at the conclusion of their meeting in London, Castlereagh's parting words: *"You have a bright future, Strangford – you have my trust, which is more than can be said for some of your colleagues. Be sure that you do nothing to make me regret it."*

Downing his drink, he returned to his desk. Darkness was falling. He lit a candle and, taking Castlereagh's message in hand, fed it to the flame. As he dropped it into his empty glass and glumly watched it blacken into ash, it seemed a fitting metaphor for his career.

Within a few days he arranged a third meeting. This one took place not in a diplomatic or government office but in the back room of a dingy café situated in the Janissary Quarter, at the terminus of a narrow, sunless street that ran up to the crumbling banks of the Lycus River. Strangford was very careful in his arrangements, and the janissary officer with whom he met – an elegant staff officer named Demir with thinning hair and greying beard – was no less cautious. Neither wished their meeting to be known, or their conversation overheard.

Strangford took a sip of his coffee, the tiny cup still awkward in hands more used to the size and heft of a pint of stout. With some effort, he managed not to purse his lips at the burnt, bitter taste.

"You are a brave man, envoy," Demir noted, his English nearly perfect. The janissary waited, stroking his thin beard as he sipped at his own coffee.

"Why? Is meeting with you more dangerous than I thought?"

"Not at all." Demir laughed and gestured at Strangford's coffee. "But to drink strong Turkish coffee without sugar? For a European, *that* is dangerous!" He laughed as Strangford sheepishly added several teaspoons of sugar to his *demitasse.*

"Your translator," Demir continued, "contacted his cousin who, as you know, works for me. He said you wished to discuss a matter of some sensitivity?"

"Yes. I appreciate your taking the time. Indeed, the matter is quite delicate. As a consequence, I require assurances that you will keep what we discuss to yourself. Is this understood?"

The janissary nodded. "Yes, for now. But depending on what it is you require, confiding in a few of my men may at some point be unavoidable. If I can assist you at all."

"Of course." Although they had the room to themselves, he lowered his voice. "Suppose it was determined that a British subject – a man of some reputation – constituted a threat to the *Porte's* interests, particularly as respects the current rebellion of the Sultan's Greek subjects?"

"That is not beyond understanding; yes."

"And suppose further that, in connection with such matters, interested third parties sympathetic to the Sultan's interests – and to those of his esteemed janissary corps – felt it necessary to remove such a threat. And, of course, to appropriately compensate the agents responsible for doing so."

The janissary thought for a moment. "What you describe is not unknown, nor is it proscribed by the Qur'an – this man, he's not a follower of the Prophet, I take it?"

"No, I don't believe he is."

"But he is a British citizen, and there might be consequences were his – 'removal' – to be traced to his own government; yes?"

"Yes. Hence the need for your absolute discretion."

"When? Is he here now?"

"No, no. At the moment this is hypothetical, and it may remain so. But if circumstances change, it will be imperative that we move with dispatch."

The janissary nodded. "I can see, Lord Strangford, that you are a careful and thorough man, and one who likes always to be prepared. It is a virtue, is it not? What did your poet say?" Demir stroked his beard. "Ah yes. 'All things are ready, if our minds be so.'"

"You've read Shakespeare? Good. Then you're familiar with Macbeth – "If it t'were done when 'tis done, t'is well it t'were done quickly."

Both men rose and inclined their heads, their right fists tight to their chests. "I will contact you again," said Strangford, "when – and if – there is a need for your services."

"Peace be with you," said the janissary, turning toward the door that led from the back of the café to a narrow alley.

"And with you," Strangford replied, wondering, like Macbeth, whether he would know peace again.

CHAPTER 35
Rivers of Blood

But now being lifted into high society
And having picked up several odds and ends
Of free thoughts in his travels, for variety,
He deemed, being in a lone isle among friends,
That without any danger of a riot, he
Might for long lying make himself amends
And singing as he sung in his warm youth,
Agree to a short armistice with truth.

DON JUAN, CANTO III

SEVERAL WEEKS after Southey cornered Castlereagh at the *Quarterly Review's* annual dinner, Fletcher interrupted Byron's reading to announce the arrival of visitors. Byron's second-story rooms in Mayfair weren't sumptuous, but they were comfortable; a small entry chamber gave way to a narrow hallway, the dark hardwood floors contrasting with white wainscoting and a patterned-fabric wall covering of grey and blue. To the right was Byron's office, to the left, a comfortable parlor.

Byron entertained most of his guests in the parlor, which was furnished with a formal couch and two armchairs, both upholstered in a delicate plum-colored fabric. One end of the room was commanded by a severe bronze eagle standing upon a scarlet and black pillar as tall as a schoolboy; the other by a mantle and large fireplace whose bricks were so charred with ancient soot the black paint underneath had long become redundant.

Byron rose from the parlor couch, tossing onto a side table a letter and pamphlet. He wore elegant black trousers of a fine Scottish wool, a brilliant white shirt whose subtle pleats ran from midriff to collar, and a fitted black waistcoat of Chinese silk. As Fletcher ushered Byron's two guests into the room, Byron nodded and gestured to the armchairs. "Fletcher, would you please bring us some tea – unless either of you gentlemen would like something stronger?"

The two visitors declined – or, more accurately, the smaller man declined while the larger one acquiesced – and seated themselves in the two armchairs. In their early fifties, both were dressed similarly in utilitarian tweed trousers, white muslin shirts, and somber black long-coats that Byron reckoned would make an undertaker proud. In a surprising concession to style they wore black top hats, which had recently come into fashion. Byron found them ridiculous – the top hats, not his guests – and was always delighted when towering 19th century top hats met cramped 18th century doorways.

"Mr. Blaquiere, Mr. Bowring, thank you for your letter and pamphlet. I read both with great interest. Hobby – John Hobhouse, whom you both know – has been very complimentary regarding your committee, although obviously, you are still in the early stages of its organization." He paused for a moment as Fletcher entered with a pot of black tea and three cream-colored saucers and matching cups, a finely-rendered landscape etched in red and black on the side of each cup. These he placed on a sideboard before withdrawing.

Inclining his head, John Bowring signaled his agreement. He was a short, energetic man with black hair and dark eyes that seemed out of sorts with his fair complexion. For more than a decade Bowring had served as secretary and collaborator to Jeremy Bentham, whose progressive ideas were anathema to the Tories. Among the many liberal causes to which

Bowring applied his efforts was the cause of Greek independence. The murder and defiling of the Greek Orthodox Patriarch, Bowring had predicted in the pamphlet he'd sent to Byron, was just the beginning; without assistance many more would perish, and he begged his readers "to lend succor, and their robust financial support, to the Greeks' fledgling democracy."

"Thank you, my Lord," Bowring replied, "you are far too kind. Mr. Hobhouse has made us generally aware of your sympathies. But I became aware of the *depth* of your feelings on this issue only when I read Canto III of *Don Juan* – which, I must say, is an extraordinary achievement even in – how did you put it? – 'so early a stage of its organization.'"

Byron grinned. "One must be careful, Mr. Bowring, in attributing to the scribe sympathies expressed by his creations."

With a Hindustani flourish – palms together, fingers splayed, head inclined – Bowring acknowledged the point. "Of course, I should not be so bold, particularly with respect to a work so varied and expressive. Still, *The Isles of Greece*, your poem-within-a-poem, reflects such a deep sympathy with the glories of Greece's past and with its present sad state that I cannot believe it to be mere artifice."

Reaching into his inside jacket pocket, Bowring extracted a copy of *Don Juan* – Byron could see that portions had been underlined and annotated in a neatly slanted hand – and began to read aloud:

> *A king sat on the rocky brow*
> *Which looks o'er sea-born Salamis;*
> *And ships by thousands lay below.*
> *And men in nations – all were his!*
> *He counted them at break of day,*
> *And when the sun set where were they?*
>
> *And where are they? And where art thou,*
> *My country? On thy voiceless shore*

The heroic lay is tuneless now,
The heroic bosom beats no more!
And must thy lyre, so long divine,

Degenerate into hands like mine?
'Tis something in the dearth of fame,
Though linked among a fettered race,
To feel at least a patriot's shame,
Even as I sing, suffuse my face.
For what is left the poet here?

For Greeks a blush, for Greece a tear.
Must we but weep o'er days more blest?
Must we but blush? Our fathers bled.
Earth! Render back from out thy breast
A remnant of our Spartan dead!
Of the three hundred grant but three,
To make a new Thermopylae!

Normally, Byron disliked hearing his poems read aloud; as he complained to his friend Sheridan, had he wished to hear his work performed he would have written bloody plays. But as Bowring lowered his pages and fell silent, the tingling at the back of Byron's neck and the sudden weight in his chest made him feel as if he were hearing his own words for the first time.

"The Greek whose words you find so moving," he said at last , his voice soft, "trades in Hope, and for his fee, tells men they can be more. But what is Hope? Nothing but paint on the face of Existence. The least touch of Truth rubs it off, and then – too late – we see what a hollow-cheeked harlot we have got."

Blaquiere hadn't said a word. He was a big man, broad in the chest and military in his bearing, as befit his prior service as a Captain in the

Royal Navy. He had a full mane of red hair touched with grey at the temples, and a seafarer's rich beard and mustache. It seemed to Byron that while Bowring's top hat might be consonant with his skills and character, a sailor's cap would have suited Blaquiere best. As Byron's words hung in the air, Blaquiere took a deep breath, cleared his throat and spoke in a soft Irish lilt.

"My ancestors were Huguenots, my Lord. They were slaughtered, along with thousands more, on St. Bartholomew's Day, and those who survived migrated to Ireland to practice their faith. We have long been loyal subjects of His Majesty, in whose government my father served, and for whom I fought against the Buonaparte."

Blaquiere drew another deep breath, steadying himself – Byron imagined that, like many soldiers, the Irishman was more comfortable in action than in discourse. "There are today only a handful of us left, and our culture, our religion, even our language, is only a tattered remnant." He gestured at the copy of *Don Juan*. "My Lord, I have traveled to Greece, have met the leaders of their rebellion and of their church, have seen with my own eyes the hatred they carry for the Turks. Better than anyone, you have captured the plight of a proud people, much like my own. For more than four hundred years – four hundred! – they have been subjected to the indignities of conquest, occupation and enslavement. And now, in defiance of an empire, they seek to rise up, throw off their shackles, and fly a flag of their own choosing."

He glanced at Bowring, who nodded his encouragement. "My good friend Mr. Bowring has been blessed with the manners of a diplomat and the deference of a politician. I am only a soldier, and an aging one at that. But I can recognize a cause that is just, and in you, a man capable of acting as its champion. We've come to ask you, my Lord, to join the Committee, to represent it on an organizing mission to the Peloponnese, and to take a leading role in advancing its cause."

Byron did not immediately respond, but slowly sipped his tea. He had anticipated a request for a small financial contribution, nothing

more. But if he were to take a leadership role, his name would be tied
to an enterprise in whose prospects he was doubtful. Worse, his ability
to influence events on the ground in the rebellious provinces would be
limited; he possessed no rank, commanded no troops, and had as weapons
only an inkwell and a quill. He doubted these would impress the Turks.

"You do not speak like a soldier, Mr. Blaquiere. You speak with the
passion of a patriot."

"The ideals of democracy," responded Bowring, "often require the
patriot's fervor, my Lord."

"Yes, Mr. Bowring, you'll get no argument on that from me. But
oratory, passion and even courage go only so far, particularly in that part
of the world."

Half-turning, Byron gestured towards the bronze eagle perched
on its stand behind Bowring and Blaquiere. "Do you see that eagle,
gentlemen? It was presented to me by Muhammad Ali Pasha, of
whom I am sure you have heard. As the Ottoman Sultan's Governor
of Albania, Egypt and Sudan, Ali has ruled without challenge for
more than a decade. As a young man I traveled through the Balkans
and arrived in Albania with a letter of introduction. Ali greeted me
warmly and, on the third and final night of my visit, hosted a dinner
in my honor."

"During the feast, Ali described how, in consolidating his power in
Egypt, he had eliminated the Mamluks as a threat to his authority." Byron
spread his arms wide. "As a gesture of peace and respect, he had invited
the Mamluk leadership to a feast at the Cairo Citadel in honor of his son
Torun, who was to lead a military expedition into Arabia." He stood up,
circled behind the couch, and stopped directly behind Bowring. "When
all were seated, his men surrounded the table. On Ali's signal, they slit the
throat of every Mamluk present from ear to ear." Byron softly drew his
finger across Bowring's throat. "With the gentlest smile I think I've ever
seen, Ali told me that their blood collected in thick pools on the tables
and mixed as one with the wine."

As Byron returned to his seat on the couch, no one said a word. Finally, Bowring broke the silence.

"We do not expect your Lordship to assemble a force, nor take an active role in military operations." He placed his hand on Blaquiere's arm. "We might as well ask Edward to write an ode, or myself to sail a ship. But your Lordship has the ability to stir men's passions, and to energize support for our cause."

"As it happens," Blaquiere interjected archly, "I have written several odes, as well as a modest treatise on the economics of naval operations." Byron was indifferent to the latter and prayed he would not be subjected to the former. "But I agree with Mr. Bowring – while your Lordship's involvement will be welcomed in any capacity, it is through raising the British people's awareness of the present conflict that it will be most valuable."

Placing his hand on his heart, Byron thanked them for their kind words and "misplaced confidence." He shook his head. "Gentlemen, I may have an audience, and perhaps even some influence, in certain political circles and with portions of the public – although with respect to the latter, I suspect I am read more for entertainment than policy. But the Tories hold the reins of power, and it is only recently that I kicked their lead horse in the teeth."

Blaquiere laughed. "My father knew Castlereagh in Ireland, when he was Chief Secretary. He's a ruthless sod, no doubt – as he showed the Irish Catholics in '98."

"It's doubtful that he will be favorably impressed by my involvement," Byron said, nodding. "Indeed, it's likely to have the opposite effect."

"My Lord may read correctly the foreign secretary's personal preferences," Bowring responded, "but it must be kept in mind that he is above all a politician. And politicians respond to popular pressures, however catalyzed." He leaned forward. "The enterprise hangs in the balance. The Ottoman is rotten at its core, and requires only a shove to collapse. For all their faults, the Greeks are in rebellion, and want only a champion and some foreign support. Your Lordship need only help tip the scale."

Byron rose. "I want to thank you gentlemen for your visit," he said, ushering Blaquiere and Bowring to the door. "I'm flattered by your proposal, though far less sure that I am what the situation requires. But I'll think on it and respond in due course." As he called to Fletcher to see his guests out, he framed a final question.

"Mr. Bowring. Insofar as the major powers are concerned, do you think this is all just the usual power politics? Or do we have a religious war brewing in the Levant, with the Europeans itching to launch the next Crusade?"

To his surprise, it was not Bowring who answered, but Blaquiere. "Religious resentments have fueled atrocities among the people, but among the powers they are more an excuse than a motivating force. The Greeks may be Christians, but the British government would doubtless prefer that they remain compliant; and if that requires them to be ground under the heel of the infidel, so be it. The Turks are an important buffer against the Russians."

"What about the Turks? Are they as cynical?"

"Without question – they cannot afford the luxury of principle. The Sultan's game is to play one side off against the other, using whatever tools he has at hand." He chuckled. "The Turk foreign minister – the *reis effendi* – apparently called the Greek Orthodox Patriarch 'the Sultan's Cardinal Wolsey,' on the theory, I suppose, that the Patriarch's fealty might insulate the Sultan against accusations of religious animus, as Henry VIII hoped might be true of the Cardinal." He snorted. "Seems it worked out for the Patriarch about as well as it did for Wolsey."

Byron nodded, wondering whether there might be more to Blaquiere than had first appeared.

Bowring spoke up. "I doubt Castlereagh wants to intervene, but he'll do so if it's the only way to keep the Russians out of the Mediterranean.

You know as well as I do, my Lordship, that there aren't sufficient votes in Parliament at present. But Parliament will respond to a concerted outcry from the public and the Church. Those cries will grow louder and more strident with each village raped and each cleric gutted."

Blaquiere looked Byron square in the eye. "You've said it yourself, your Lordship – or at least, your Greek lyricist has. The freedom of the Greeks will be won only with rivers of their blood."

CHAPTER 36
The Calculation of the Cuckold

[Love] mak'st the chaste connubial state precarious
And jestest with the brows of mightiest men,
Caesar and Pompey, Mahomet, Belisarius
Have much employed the Muse of history's pen.
Their lives and fortunes were extremely various;
Such worthies Time will never see again.
Yet to these four in three things the same luck holds;
They all were heroes, conquerors, and cuckolds.

DON JUAN, CANTO II

"LORD MELBOURNE is here to see you, sir." Reilly glanced at the Foreign Secretary's appointments list for the day. "He's six minutes early – shall I have him wait?"

"No, Reilly – see to it that he's flogged." As Reilly nodded and turned to go, Castlereagh decided to take no chances. "Bring him in," he called, "and see if he'd like some tea. I know I would."

As he waited for Lord Melbourne, Castlereagh considered the delicate nature of this morning's conversation. Melbourne did not have much experience in foreign affairs, but neither was he a fool. Overt manipulation – Castlereagh's stock-in-trade – would not do, as Melbourne would detect it quickly and resent it just as fast. No, the best approach for this sort of thing, with this sort of man, was to bring him inside, align his interests with Castlereagh's, and ensure that Melbourne had something to gain.

The door opened and Melbourne stepped past Reilly into Castlereagh's office. "Viscount Castlereagh," he said in greeting, inclining his head. They knew each other – they ran in the same social circles, after all – and on several occasions had shared dinner and drink in a larger group. Castlereagh recognized in Melbourne a man not dissimilar to himself, several decades past. Smart and ambitious; patient, but not excessively so. He was in his thirties and, after a decade in the Commons, had taken his hereditary seat in the House of Lords the previous year. When, in preparation for this meeting, Castlereagh had asked Henry Addington his opinion of Melbourne, he'd had to smile at his old friend's neat summation – "He's too clever to fool but too honest to bribe. If you want something from him, I'm afraid you may have to resort to extreme measures – apparently, he's susceptible to reason."

"Lord Melbourne, it's a pleasure to see you again. Did Reilly offer you some tea?"

"He did, and I'm told it's on the way." Melbourne was dressed in grey woolen trousers with a narrow fall, a white muslin shirt with high starched collar, a grey waistcoat and black tailcoat, and a maroon cravat, elegantly tied at the throat. As Castlereagh waved him over to the twin armchairs that faced the hearth, it occurred to him that he'd never seen Melbourne dress in anything other than high style, with never a hair out of place. He wondered if this was effortless, or the mark of an outsized vanity.

"You are acquainted with Percy Smythe – now Lord Strangford?"

"Of course, though I don't know him well – he's spent so much time abroad."

"Yes, well, he's proven himself a valuable man. You know he's envoy to the *Porte*?"

"Someone has to be." Melbourne paused as Reilly brought in a pot of tea and two cups and saucers. "I imagine he must be busy – it's quite a bloody mess."

Castlereagh nodded. "Nor is the situation improving. The Greeks are strong enough to rebel but too weak to win, while the Turks view matters through a 12th century glass. Rather than co-opting the Orthodox Christian Patriarch, whose cooperation was there for the asking, the Sultan thought it a good idea to make him a martyr. Meanwhile, sensing an opportunity, the Russians are likely to intervene in the Spring, which will almost surely lead to Constantinople's collapse and the likelihood of a broader conflict." He snorted, gazing into the fire.

"So – Strangford?"

"Yes, right. He was here in London to provide a report which, as I've described, was bleak." He poured Melbourne a cup of tea and another for himself. "If the European powers do not intervene, this is unlikely to end well."

"Intervene?" Melbourne leaned back and sipped his tea. "In what manner?"

"Well, ideally it would be through a limited naval engagement. The *Porte* has quite a large navy, you know, in which – or so I'm told – the Sultan takes no small measure of pride. But their guns are small, mostly 12 and 16-pound cannon. They'd be no match for our 24 and 32-pounders."

Melbourne nodded. "If only the political issues were equally straight forward."

"Yes, well, isn't that usually the case?" Castlereagh stared into his tea. "You spent, what, eight years –"

"Seven."

"– *seven* years in the Commons. What do you think it would take to persuade the lower house to support a more – oh, how should I put this – a more *active* policy with respect to the Eastern Question?"

Melbourne paused, considering the question. Not that he had to think too long on the answer; he'd spent enough time in the Commons, and had had enough recent conversations with his former back-bench colleagues, to know that such support in Parliament was likely to be thin. No, what had him thinking was *why* Castlereagh – whose sources of information were surely better than his own – was asking him for his assessment.

"I suppose it would require greater enthusiasm on the part of the public than currently exists."

"Precisely." Rising, Castlereagh wandered over to the hearth to poke at the dwindling fire, which grudgingly flared to life. "Forgive my lack of manners, Lord Melbourne; how is your lovely wife? I haven't had the pleasure of seeing Lady Caroline for quite some time."

"Caroline is well, thank you for asking."

Continuing to poke at the fire, Castlereagh did not reply. Eventually, Melbourne broke the silence. "We spent a few weeks in Dublin and returned to London early last week. She's very busy with her dancing and her writing – she loves to write, you know." Feeling like he'd blathered on too long, he broke off.

Setting the poker aside, Castlereagh turned back to his visitor. "Hmmm, yes, Caroline is so energetic and creative – it doesn't surprise me that she might have literary talent." He paused, trying to look sympathetic. "She's quite interested in poetry, I'm told."

Melbourne did not allow his expression to change, but his mind raced. "Viscount, if you are referring to Caroline's *dalliance* with the redoubtable Lord Byron, I am well aware of it, thank you." He set his jaw. "If I might ask, what is your interest in such matters?"

"Byron. It won't surprise you to learn that not everyone finds him amusing. In fact, he's made some powerful enemies."

"With you among them?"

Castlereagh waved. "I imagine Byron thinks so. Clearly, he doesn't think much of me or, for that matter, His Majesty's government generally. He's even savaged our friend Strangford's verse," he added with a chuckle, "though I expect a jury would find that particular assault to have been justifiable." With a weary grin, he leaned back in his chair. "As hard as I try, I can't seem to summon much indignation these days. Byron is an annoyance, nothing more."

"I wish I could say the same. But Caroline –" He stopped, not exactly comfortable with the notion of unburdening himself to the Foreign Secretary. "Let's just say I'm not an admirer. Though I must concede, he's an extraordinary talent. For a poet, his popularity is astounding."

"Quite right. Extraordinary." Castlereagh set his cup down on the saucer, finally getting to the point. "Melbourne, what if I were to suggest that Byron might be *persuaded* to leave England. Permanently. Would such a development be welcome to you?"

Melbourne sat back, hiding his surprise at this unexpected turn. "I don't suppose I'd shed a tear," he said carefully, "though my wife would be disconsolate."

"I'm not so certain. It seems she and Byron have had a break, and that she feels the wrath of a woman scorned." Anticipating Melbourne's question, Castlereagh added, "I don't think it's pertinent how I came by this information – what matters is how it can be put to good use."

Feeling his cheeks flush, Melbourne made an effort to control his emotions. It was bad enough that Castlereagh had interested himself in Caroline's affair with Byron; even worse that he seemed to know more about it than he did.

"I certainly have reasons to wish Byron gone. But what are yours?"

"Byron has expressed what appears to be heartfelt support for the cause of Greek independence. To my mind, he's one of the few Whigs who actually gives a fig, although most of that lot like to use the issue as a talking point."

A nod. "Go on."

"As you've pointed out, he's talented and extraordinarily popular. If – *if* – England were to become inhospitable to Byron, and an opportunity arose for him in Greece ... well, he might become less of a thorn in our side, and rather more of one in the *Porte's*."

As the son of a woman seasoned in the art of manipulation, Melbourne was no stranger to intrigue. Still, as he considered how to respond, he looked at Castlereagh with new eyes. Finally, he leaned back and crossed his legs. "I must say, Viscount; when I received your invitation, I did not see this coming." He allowed himself a grim little smile. "What do you need from me?"

CHAPTER 37
The Seeds of Exile

I have brought this world about my ears, and eke
The other; that's to say, the clergy, who
Upon my head have bid their thunders break
In pious libels by no means a few.
And yet I can't help scribbling once a week,
Tiring old readers, nor discovering new.
In youth I wrote because my mind was full,
And now because I feel it growing dull.

DON JUAN, CANTO XIV

"STILL FEEDING the ducks, Robert?" Henry Addington, Home Secretary of England, shook his head. "Is that government bread?"

Castlereagh reached into his pocket and, scattering the last of his breadcrumbs, brushed off his hands. "These may look like ordinary ducks to you, Henry, but in fact they are agents of His Majesty's Government. At the snap of my fingers, they'll speed my commands to the furthest reaches of England, or across the Channel to the Continent." He snapped his fingers to demonstrate his powers – the birds paid not the slightest attention. He shrugged. "It's a work in progress."

Addington laughed. "So, Robert," he asked, settling down on the bench next to Castlereagh, "what can I do for you on such a fine May day?" It was early afternoon and balmy, warm enough to require neither hats nor gloves. Only a cotton cloud or two floated in the pale blue sky, the sun warmed the fresh spring grass, and a mild breeze sketched ripples on the pond's shimmering canvas.

"Sometimes, Henry, I think about how nice it would be to sit here all day, feeding the birds, watching the shadows shift on the pond, and listening to the sound of nothing at all." He sighed. "There's never a good time to step down, always one or another crisis. I wonder what would happen if we ignored them? Would the world turn no longer?"

"I don't know, I've been in this bloody job so long I don't remember having time to myself. I suppose I'd like to think we're indispensable. You know, full of silver-haired wisdom?"

Castlereagh snorted. "Well, I suppose we've made enough mistakes along the way that we'd be fools to have learned nothing." His expression clouded and he winced, his latest headache throbbing in time to the incessant metronome of his pulse. "It would all go easier," he muttered, half to himself, "if so many of those claiming to champion the interests of the realm didn't work against me in secret."

Addington arched his brow but made no response. After a few moments, the Foreign Secretary turned to business. "Do you recall my asking about Melbourne?"

"Of course. Did you meet with him?"

"I did. I've chatted with him at parties and functions, but it was the first time we've discussed matters of substance. He was just as you said; ambitious and, oh, how should I put it? Calculating."

Addington nodded. "He has the top job in mind, and I can't say he's wrong in thinking it might eventually be within his reach."

"Yes. Well, he has both the connections and the talent. But I think he's come to realize that his wife is doing him no favors. In fact, this thing with Byron has become a rather public embarrassment for him."

"Byron's a thorn in more substantial sides than Melbourne's. Our sovereign monarch – bless his profligate heart! – expressed dismay just the other day over Byron's send-up of Southey's ridiculous poem – what was it called?"

"*A Vision of Judgment.* Yes, the King sent me Byron's satire – which I have to admit, had me in tears – with a stern note, and we talked about it the following week. It seems he was unamused at the treatment of his father, though we both know he thought the old man a relic of the last century, and daft as a hatter besides!"

Addington rolled his eyes. "He can declare his wife to be ugly as a bulldog, but let another man say the same and he'll soon find himself on the outside looking in." He patted Castlereagh on the arm. "Byron's taken a particular liking to you, hasn't he?"

"Just one more in the queue," Castlereagh said with a shrug. "But he does have a more prominent platform than most, and his vituperation is of a superior quality."

"I'm relieved that you can be so diffident about it – a lesser man might be incensed."

"Henry, you know me better than that. What you see is the detachment that comes with age. Don't mistake it for indifference. In fact, I think Byron's gone too far, not just in his criticism of me but in his conduct more generally. Keep this to yourself – I really mean that, Henry – but I've been told that in addition to fucking Melbourne's wife, Harley's wife, and God knows who else's, he's also been fucking his sister. Excuse me, his *half*-sister." He paused, and then added thoughtfully, "She's someone else's wife as well, come to think of it."

Addington whistled softly. "Unbelievable. But from what I know of Byron, it could actually be true. He's quite the rake – at Almack's last year, Liz Foster said that Byron 'was the topic of almost every conversation – the men jealous of him, the women of each other.'" He sat back and thought for a moment. "Incest, you say? You're aware, I suppose, that technically it isn't a criminal offense. Except in Cromwell's day, when it earned you a date with the hangman, incest has been handled by the canonical courts, and as grounds for divorce or annulment."

"Does that really matter? Consider it, Henry – if this were to become public, I'd think Byron would be ostracized. It's one thing to cut a broad swath through the wives of the peerage; it's quite another to fornicate with one's blood relations."

"I suppose that's right – incest might give pause even to the French." Addington smiled ruefully. "Although I doubt it would damage Byron's sales."

Castlereagh laughed. "No, quite the opposite!" He shifted in his seat, half-turning to face Addington. "Henry, for a variety of reasons, it would be best if Byron were to leave England. I want to put pressure on him, including legal pressure. You know Leigh Hunt?"

Addington nodded. "Quite the radical, that one. Didn't he publish Byron's – what was the bloody name again, *The Vision* or something? Not sure why I can't keep that in mind. Anyway, didn't he publish that?"

"*The Vision of Judgment*. Same as Southey's, almost, damned confusing. Indeed, he did, as John Murray seems to have been wise enough to turn it down. Anyway, it's pretty clearly libelous and seditious both, and George Augustus wants something done about it. The courts fall under your authority – do you agree that a case against Hunt is well-founded legally?"

Addington thought for a moment. "On the face of it, I'd say yes, though I'd like to get my deputy's opinion, as he's been more deeply involved in these prosecutions than anyone."

"I'd be quite grateful if you could do that, Henry. Though bear in mind, the purpose here isn't to bring a case against Hunt, much less win it. What's needed is pressure on Byron, and putting his friends and collaborators at risk is one way to apply it."

"I can see that. And the other ways?"

"I've spoken about it with Melbourne. He needs to discuss the matter with Caroline, but I believe he's prepared to retain counsel and to threaten an action against Byron for criminal conversation. He'd seek damages exceeding £20,000, which would hit Byron where it hurts."

Addington looked at Castlereagh with surprise. "Criminal conversation? Really? Melbourne is prepared to hear testimony in open court that will paint him as a cuckold? And his wife as a trollop?"

"Those flags have already been run up the pole, Henry, and have long been fluttering in plain sight. And he wants Byron gone. Besides, the intent isn't actually to file an action, but merely to threaten one. If Byron has any sense, he'll choose exile over disgrace, prosecution and bankruptcy. If not for his own sake, then for that of his friends."

"If Byron had any sense, he'd have conducted his affairs with more discretion." A late-arriving duck wandered over, hoping for some bread; Addington glared, and the bird wisely chose to seek its fortunes elsewhere. "But who's to say? Perhaps he's already plucked the choicest fruit from England's tree, and would welcome an opportunity to forage in foreign orchards."

Castlereagh shrugged. "We'll see. I want Melbourne to hire Bob Gifford as his attorney – he's aggressive, but subtle enough to understand the distinction between legal and political objectives."

"Gifford's a good man," Addington agreed. "Would you like me to talk to him?"

"Yes, thank you Henry, tell him Melbourne will contact him."

Shading his eyes, Castlereagh looked out on the water. "Henry," he said, his voice soft but firm, "I need to stress how important it is that you keep these matters to yourself. Particularly this thing between Byron and his sister. Our objective here is to drive Byron out of England, not destroy his reputation – such as it is – with the British public."

"What are you up to, Robert? Why do you care whether Byron retains his reputation, 'such as it is?' Seems to me you could force him abroad with his name intact or in disgrace, as you choose."

"I have my reasons and, for now, it's better that they remain hidden even from you. It's hard to be sure," he confided, leaning close, "who we can trust." Castlereagh rose and, extending a hand to Addington, helped the older man to his feet. "Henry, thank you for your help on this, and as always, for your discretion."

Addington nodded, keeping hold of Castlereagh's hand. "Robert, you understand that banishing Byron won't silence him? In fact, free from the risk of a sedition action, he's likely to feel more at liberty than ever to say, write and do what he pleases."

Lord Castlereagh squeezed the Home Secretary's hand and, extending his free arm, clapped him on the shoulder. "Quite aware, Henry. In fact, I'm counting on it."

CHAPTER 38
Some Measure of Satisfaction

Alas, the love of women! It is known
To be a lovely and a fearful thing,
For all of theirs upon that die is thrown,
And if 'tis lost, life hath no more to bring
To them but mockeries of the past alone,
And their revenge is as the tiger's spring,
Deadly and quick and crushing; yet as real
Torture is theirs, what they inflict they feel.

DON JUAN, CANTO II

IN THE first few days following the outright break with Byron, Caroline had mourned, flagellating herself with barbed remembrances of their vanished passion. Dante was right, she had sniffed as she stood in the rain, staring out at the Thames: *There is no greater sorrow/Than to remember happiness in times of grief.*

But she soon grew weary of grief – by nature, she despised the role of victim – and began methodically to revisit every aspect of their relationship, from their initial courtship and seduction to Byron's final damning judgment that she was "heartless and malignant." She examined her conduct and his and, after a time, concluded that though she might not be entirely blameless, it was Byron – who pretended to love, but truly knew it only as a diversion from himself – on whom the greater measure of blame should fall. And so, convinced that he had it coming, she had acted.

Now, almost a month later, she heard the coachman call to slow the horses, and clutched at the strap as the carriage jerked to a stop. "Sorry, m'lady," the man mumbled as he opened the door and helped Caroline down from the cab. "D'you want me wait'n here, or come back f'you after a time?"

"Wait here. I won't be long."

She crossed the road and looked up at the wooden sign hanging above the entrance to the inn – *The Spotted Owl*. It was an old tavern, set back from the road, and Caroline had been there only once, not intending to return. Aside from a few tradesmen drinking away the noon hour the place was almost empty, but she paused at the door to make sure there was no one there she knew. When she was satisfied, she found a dark corner booth and settled in to wait.

She didn't have to wait long. After taking his own quick look about, Robert Southey crossed the room and slid into the booth across from Caroline. He wore brown woolen trousers, a white shirt gathered at the sleeves, and a black waistcoat with silver buttons. In protest against the recent fashion of leaving one's waistcoat open, which he considered ungentlemanly, he kept all of his buttons tightly fastened, and Caroline could see the fabric straining against his belly. He signaled to the barmaid and, when she sidled over, looked to Caroline.

"Nothing for me. Let's make this brief."

Southey shrugged. "I'll have a pint," he ordered peremptorily, "and a couple of those sausages I saw as I came in. And for the love of God, don't forget the mustard."

When the barmaid left, Caroline frowned and folded her hands in front of her on the table. "Why did you insist on meeting me again? Have I not already provided sufficiently pertinent information?"

"You have indeed, Lady Caroline. For which I am very much in your debt. But without proof ... well, it would be your word against Byron's."

"My word? Was I not quite clear, Mr. Southey? I have no intention of providing any kind of testimony against Byron, in any forum." She clasped and unclasped her fingers, hoping that Southey wouldn't notice that her palms were damp. "I have given you valuable information. What you do with it is up to you."

"You made yourself well understood, La–"

He broke off as the barmaid returned with his sausages and ale, which she set down with a clatter, some of the ale sloshing onto the table. "Careful there, missy!" he barked.

She gave him a withering look. "Sorry, *gent.*"

Southey glared at the girl but let it drop. "As I was saying, Lady Caroline," he continued, tucking into his meal, "we need proof, especially if you would prefer to remain hidden in connection with this matter. You spoke of a journal entry – can you obtain the journal, or any of the relevant pages?"

"As I told you, I am no longer involved with Lord Byron. Under the circumstances, I don't see how." She paused, torn between her fury at Byron and her own self-loathing at having betrayed him to Southey. "But Augusta was here for almost a week – why did you not take advantage of my information to catch them in the act?"

"While that is not as easily done as you might think, m'lady, certain intelligence has in fact been gathered. Still, more is required. Tell me again – where, exactly, does Byron keep his journal?"

"It's in the middle drawer of his writing desk. He takes it out from time to time to make an entry, or to consult prior entries."

"You've read the entry on Augusta?"

"I read an entry, yes, but there may have been others, I don't know."

Caroline leaned forward, her voice low. "Look, Mr. Southey. I am taking a risk. My mother-in-law no doubt wished my affair with Byron to end, but I think that was as much for Byron's benefit as for William's. Were she to learn that I was the source of any public revelations with respect to this matter she would be furious, and could make my life even more unpleasant than it is already."

Southey popped the last of the sausage into his mouth, washing it down with a swallow of ale. He wiped his mouth with his napkin, staring calculatedly at Caroline. "Does your husband know?"

"Does he know what?"

"You know, about Byron and his sister?"

Caroline paused. She hadn't told William of her suspicions directly – she seldom discussed her lovers with her husband, any more than he discussed his mistresses with her. But Augusta's name had come up, as by coincidence Augusta's lawyer shared an office with William's, who had mentioned seeing her.

Caught off guard, Caroline had been rudely dismissive. "She's a bit of a cow, and I simply can't understand what Byron sees in her." William had raised his brow, seemingly surprised, not at the criticism, but that it had been couched in the language of rivalry. She doubted he'd thought much more on it, but William was clever, and she had learned that it was never wise to underestimate him.

"I don't think so. I certainly haven't told him."

"Alright. I will see whether we can establish the facts of Byron's unholy tryst without your further involvement. Byron is reckless, and always over-confident; if given enough rope, I expect he'll hang himself."

As Caroline started to rise, he reached out and pressed her hand to the table. "For the moment, Lady Caroline, this matter is private. But you must understand that it could become public, and of a legal character." He looked her hard in the eyes, and she fought off the urge to look away. "In such circumstances, it may no longer be possible for you to remain aloof. This is why I asked about your husband, whose connections and political ambitions are well-known."

"Leave my husband out of this, Mr. Southey. This has nothing to do with him. And if you involve me in this matter directly or reveal my name, it will not go well for you."

"I have no desire to involve him and, at present, no reason. But, if Lord Melbourne's influence were directed to resolving this matter in a way that avoided embarrassment to you both, that might be something to consider, wouldn't you agree?"

He eased his pressure on Caroline's hand, and she pulled it free and slid out of the booth. She stared at him coldly. "I trust we shall have no further reason to meet, Mr. Southey."

Southey raised his glass and finished off the last of his ale. "It must give you some measure of satisfaction," he said slowly, "to know that, however corrupt and morally repugnant your relationship with Byron may have been, your sins pale in comparison to the incestuous degeneracy of his present course." Without getting up, he inclined his head. "Good day, m'lady."

CHAPTER 39
'By Your Bloody Side'

WHEN BYRON passed out at the edge of the olive grove just outside the village, Polidori quickly checked his pulse, then directed that he be taken someplace clean and dry. Iphigeneia offered her own house, and when they arrived a place was cleared and Byron was laid on a straw-stuffed mat in a sort of living room just off of the cooking area.

Polidori asked for honey, vinegar and boiling water – Nikolaus, shaking his head, wondered aloud if he was a doctor or a cook. Panos brought him the water and, when it had cooled a bit, the doctor applied it to dissolve the crusted blood. As he carefully peeled back the sheet that they'd used as a bandage, Byron drifted in and out of consciousness.

Polidori soaked a cloth in the hot water and cleaned the area around the wound. The Turk's sword had slashed Byron's right flank from the edge of the ribcage to just above the hip, and when Polidori cleared away the clotted blood he could see that the blade had been very sharp; the incision, though deep, was narrow and well-defined. "It could have been worse, Byron," he said more cheerfully than his patient thought warranted. "If a fever doesn't kill you and you can stand a good deal of pain for a few weeks, this may heal up nicely."

"Don't sugar-coat it, Polidori," Byron muttered, his jaw clenched.

"In fact, that is exactly what I'm going to do." At the doctor's request, Iphigeneia built a small fire in the cooking hearth, and she and Nikolaus watched while Hobhouse paced outside – he'd been banished for asking too many questions, offering too many suggestions, and generally making everybody nervous.

Polidori poured vinegar from a jug into the pot and, after bringing it almost to a boil, added honey to fashion a golden, viscous poultice. "The sugar seems to promote healing," he explained to Iphigeneia as he applied the warm poultice to Byron's side, "as does the vinegar. No one is quite sure why." He poured a little more of the vinegar into the poulticed incision, frowning as Byron flinched and gritted his teeth. "Stings a bit, I know. Sorry, can't be helped."

He used the rest of the cloth to bandage the wound and, when he was done, nodded to Iphigeneia in thanks. Washing his hands in the warm water, Polidori instructed Byron to take a nap – an instruction with which, to his astonishment, Byron promptly complied – and went out to find Hobhouse.

He found him sitting on a wooden cart whose four slotted wheels appeared to have been designed to ride along a set of tracks. Near the cart stood several dozen stout wooden barrels that were sheltered within a sort of storage shed, its sides open under a low, peaked roof of interlaced pine boughs. As Polidori approached, the sharp, pungent scent of olive brine filled his nostrils, and he realized he was hungry.

Hobhouse had other things on his mind. "How is he?" he asked, easing himself off the barrel. "Will he live?"

"I have no idea. But I've done what I can, so now we wait. I'll change his bandages regularly and, with luck, maybe he'll survive." He glanced right and left, taking in the village for the first time; he'd been focused entirely on Byron when they'd entered, and hadn't taken the time to look around.

There wasn't much to see. Pentias was a tiny village, no more than a cluster of perhaps twenty rough houses, some made of wood, others of what seemed to be dried, packed clay. All the houses had shallow-peaked roofs that were covered by rounded clay tiles, much like those the doctor had seen on his travels in Spain. There were no paved roads or streets, just packed dirt. But it must have been someone's job to keep them clean, for Polidori saw no debris, and despite an occasional gust of wind, the air was mostly free of dust.

There were only a few people in sight; two old men sitting on a log smoking, a small child struggling with a basket of pine needles, a woman in a black skirt and yoked white top nursing a baby. "The men, and some many of the women, are in the olive trees," Panos had explained, immediately conjuring in Polidori's mind an image of grown men and women crouched high in the branches. "Or away to Pelosia to sell the oil."

Many of the houses in the village stood on flat ground, but to the north the village rose into oak-studded hills and the houses were a little bigger, with a view beyond the village onto the surrounding olive groves. Iphigeneia's house was one of these, and Polidori saw that a pair of wooden tracks led down the hill from the storage shed where he and Hobhouse stood. Heavy, waist-high railings lined both sides of the tracks. He strained his eyes to see where they ended, but as best he could tell they simply disappeared into an olive grove. They had passed a river as they approached the village; Panos had called it the *Evinos*, and said that it emptied into the Gulf of Patras. "Sometimes the river is not much, and only the small boats can go." He'd grinned, and made a whooshing noise, wiggling ten fingers. "But when the rains are strong, and the *Evinos* has much water, then the fun is so much too!" Polidori could hear the relief in Panos' voice as they'd neared his home, and was reminded that the partisan was still very young.

Hobhouse slumped to the ground, his back against one of the barrels. It didn't budge as he leaned against it, and Polidori – who weighed 150 lbs. on a good day – figured it probably weighed more than he did. Hobhouse had a round, soft face and a receding hairline, and Byron often joked that his friend had never looked younger than twenty nor older than thirty. But Polidori thought he looked older than that now, and could see the tension in his face and the fatigue in his eyes.

"How long before he can travel?" Hobhouse asked, his arms resting on his drawn-up knees, his head back and eyes closed.

"Hard to say, but we'll know better in a day or two. In the meantime, we all need to rest, get some sleep, and eat something." He spread his palms, gesturing at his slight frame. "I tell you, Hobhouse, I'm wasting away to nothing!"

Hobhouse snorted. "I swear, Polidori, you eat like most men breathe, and still weigh less than Byron's dog!" Polidori was about to make the opposite point when Panos leaned out from the front doorway. "My mother and Nikolaus would see you here, if now is time for good." Polidori found it amusing that no matter how Panos might garble their native tongue, he usually understood what the boy was trying to say. He would have to chide Byron, who was always prattling on about clarity of expression.

Hobhouse struggled to his feet. "We'll be right there, Panos," he said, brushing the dirt from his trousers as he and Polidori headed back to the house.

As they stepped inside, they saw that both Iphigeneia and Nikolaus were waiting for them, sitting around a simple wooden table in the cooking area. Iphigeneia looked grim, thought Polidori, and Nikolaus angry, though he had the impression that Nikolaus was angry much of the time. Hobhouse shot a questioning glance at Polidori, who merely shrugged.

"Sit down," Iphigeneia said, nodding toward the two remaining chairs.

"Is something wrong?" asked Hobhouse. Nikolaus crossed his arms, his jaw tight.

"Have you told us everything we need to know about you and your friend?" She glanced towards the back of the house, where Byron was sleeping, a blanket thrown over him and an embroidered cushion beneath his head.

"I'm not sure what you're getting at. What more do you want to know?"

"Why are the Turks so interested in this Byron? And why did you not tell us that there is a price at his head?" Iphigeneia looked from Hobhouse to Polidori. "Did you not think that might be important information?"

Polidori felt his heart beginning to pound. Hobhouse glanced at him, and Polidori arched his brow – he had no idea what Iphigeneia was talking about.

"A pri – you mean a reward? For Byron? Offered by whom? And for how much?" He paused, and Polidori could almost see his mind racing. "Where do you get this information?"

Iphigeneia glanced at Nikolaus, who reached into his pocket and extracted a worn scrap of paper. With a sudden, furious motion, he slammed it flat on the table. Polidori flinched, but it was nothing compared to the shock he felt when he looked down at the table and saw Byron's face staring up at him.

The writing was in Turkish, but the name at the top of the page needed no translation. "George Gordon, Lord Byron" it read in large, black letters. Below it was a surprisingly good sketch of Byron, apparently reproduced from a portrait by Thomas Phillips that had been exhibited at the Royal Academy in 1814. It was in three-quarter profile, and Byron – whose full white collar protruded on both sides from what looked like a black velvet gown of the type worn by university dons – seemed pensive, his right arm extending across his lap from the high sleeve of the gown. He looked young and contemplative, as though life was a puzzle he was determined to master.

Hobhouse frowned as he studied the paper. "This must be what the Turk who –" He stopped in mid-sentence, but Polidori finished it for him.

"...who almost raped me was looking at when he first saw Byron." Hobhouse nodded and turned to Iphigeneia and Nikolaus. "This was never shown to us, but it was in the possession of the Turks that Panos and Byron killed."

"You lie." Nikolaus did not raise his voice, which to Polidori made him seem all the more menacing. "This was in the poet's pocket. He knew and said nothing."

He turned to Iphigeneia. "They have exposed us to great risk

– the dead janissaries will be found and the Turks will follow the trail of the horses."

Panos, who had been standing in the front doorway, said something to Nikolaus, weaving his hand first left, then right. Nikolaus shook his head. "Your path may have been winding, but still it can be followed. If they pick it up from where the Turks left the horses, it won't take them long."

He scowled at Hobhouse and Polidori. "You need to leave. Tonight."

Iphigeneia shook her head. "Nikolaus," she said softly, "you're fierce as a lion, and I trust you with my life." She reached out and tapped the paper bearing Byron's likeness. "But think on it. Why do the Turks want this Byron dead? Why would they offer ten thousand kuruş for his head? That's enough money to feed this village for six months!"

"Why do we care how he's angered the Turks? Does it matter? All I know is that a wounded stag has taken refuge here, and the dogs have his scent. Soon they'll be here, baying at his heels."

"They are enemy to us, Nikolaus. If they want him dead, there must be a reason."

"Why do they want him dead?" Hobhouse asked, his voice rising. "I'll tell you why. He's spent a bloody fortune outfitting and organizing Souliote fighters to oppose the Turks. He's provided invaluable leadership – you said it yourself, Nikolaus, it is sorely needed – at the risk of his own life. And, if given the chance, he has the ability to move public opinion in England in favor of your cause." He glared at Nikolaus. "If the Turks *didn't* see him as a threat, well, now *that* would be surprising."

No one spoke. After a time, Iphigeneia put her hand on Nikolaus' arm. "Nikolaus?"

"Why did they lie to us? Why not tell us the truth, and let us offer them shelter, or turn them away, with full knowledge of the risk?"

"I should have done." They looked up to see Byron standing in the doorway to the back room, wrapped in a blanket. His face was pale, he was unsteady on his feet, and Polidori could see a thin sheen of sweat glistening on his forehead.

"Why did you not?" Iphigeneia spoke softly but her voice was hard, and it was clear to Polidori – as he knew it must be to Byron – that further deceptions or omissions would not be tolerated.

"I'm sorry," he said. "I should have told you. I almost did, but was afraid you'd turn us away." He nearly lost his balance but caught himself on the doorframe, leaning against it for support.

"I took that paper off the Turk that Panos killed. If I'd told you, and you'd turned us away ...." His voice trailed off. He nodded, indicating Hobhouse and Polidori. "They are here because of me. I'll be damned for all time before I see them die here."

Polidori didn't know whether to be angry or touched, but Hobhouse seemed to feel no such ambivalence. "Damn you, Byron!" he shouted. "Do we look like children to you?" He jabbed the paper with his finger. "Did it even occur to you that Polidori and I had a right to know about this? Not that it would have made any difference – and you seem blind even to that!"

Hobhouse took a deep breath, trying to control his emotions. Byron hadn't seen him this angry since a terrible night in London he would have liked to forget.

"I'll speak for myself," said Hobhouse, "as Polidori may feel differently. Yes, Byron, I'm here because of you, just like I've slept in caves, and with whores; drank more in a night than five men should in a week; swam in frigid waters, and in company no decent man should keep; cleaned up your vomit, and worse, the shambles of your affairs; and defended your honor even when your honor was indefensible! All this and more, I've done for you." He glared at Byron, who stood motionless, his jaw agape.

"What, no words? That's a first." Hobhouse turned from Byron to Iphigeneia. "All this and more, I have done for Byron," he repeated, shaking his head. "Why? Because of all the men I've known, he is the most generous – and the most selfish; the most brilliant – and the most obtuse; the bravest – and the least willing to confront his demons; the most disciplined – and, much too often, the most reckless."

He turned back to Byron. "I'm here risking my bloody life in part because the cause is noble; in part because, having lost my seat because of you, I had nothing better to do; and in part because I can't imagine being anyplace other than here, by your bloody side –" He stopped, staring at Byron's bloody side. Suddenly, unaccountably, he burst into laughter.

Byron, whom Polidori thought looked more astonished than he'd ever seen him, opened his mouth as if to speak, closed it again, and then he too began to laugh. The room was spinning, the pain in his side cut him like a knife, and he tried to compose himself, but his stifled laughter leaked out in a helpless, gasping wheeze. Though he really didn't think it all that funny, Polidori felt his nervous grin degenerate into a smothered giggle. Within seconds, he was crying with laughter, tears rolling from his eyes as the accumulated strain of the past week spilled out of him, out of all of them.

As the Englishmen tried unsuccessfully to bring themselves under control, Iphigeneia and Nikolaus looked first at one another, then at Panos. The boy merely shrugged. "English peoples," he offered tentatively, "I think are – *trelós*?"

"Crazy." As Nikolaus glowered beside her, Iphigeneia allowed herself a smile. "Yes," she said. "They are crazy."

CHAPTER 40
The Sultan's Palace

"*THAT WAS* a close one," breathed Dryden, seated next to Juan on the bench of a small boat.

Juan nodded, still astounded by the morning's events. They'd been surrounded by every manner of threat, and without even the leverage of self-annihilation. He'd put up a brave front: before Dryden, whose valor he already held in awe, he could do no less. But he'd expected to die, and had been steeling himself to meet his end when the Nubian had intervened. Or, more accurately, the Sultan's wife, or one of them anyway.

It was as though Allah himself had reached down and plucked them out from Belial's slavering maw. The Nubian – Babarassian was his name, he told them later, but they might call him Baba – had named his price for Juan and Dryden, and no one had dared to challenge it, though one glance at the glint in the Berber's eyes told him that it exceeded all expectations. The transaction was quickly consummated, their manacles were removed, and the Nubian led them away, staring at the fat man with imperious contempt. As they moved off, Juan looked back to see Smiley, dagger in hand, collecting the pirates' share from the Berber. He didn't see Tokaskh and his men as they withdrew to resume their patrol duties in the square, but imagined that the Sipahi captain might be wearing a relieved smile, to have the matter resolved so neatly. As for the fat man, it was Juan who felt relief, and despite the fact that *their present fate was far from certain, he felt grateful to have escaped Engin's libidinous clutches.*

The boat in which they now found themselves had two benches and a small, elevated platform for the oarsman. The front of the craft was patterned in black and gold scales like a snake, curling upward to form the shining green head of a serpent, its red wooden tongue fixed in undulating menace. Juan and Dryden sat on the front bench, with Baba on the bench behind them.

Silently they glided into the pitch black of a tunnel, emerging to find themselves inside what Juan assumed, from the size of the scimitar-shaped dock and the vastness of the arched ceilings above their heads, must be some kind of palace. Torches suspended in enormous sconces on the walls cast a flickering light that lit the dark water orange. Dryden nudged him. "It looks like Charon's rowed us 'cross the River Styx," he whispered, "and we're here at last in Hades." Harry craned his neck, taking note of how they'd come in and how they might, if Fortune smiled, go out.

After tying up at the dock they followed Baba along a series of narrow tunnels and up three winding stairways cut into the cold grey stone. At the top of the last set of steps was a heavy iron door, its plating attached by rivets the size of a man's palm. Two sentries, their bald heads glistening with oil, stood guard, but at Baba's approach they moved quickly to open the door, stepping aside to let him pass.

Their breath caught as they entered the palace. They were standing on a polished floor of rose-hued marble. Raising his eyes, Juan found himself gazing down what seemed to be an endless corridor, defined on either side by twin rows of white stone columns. Outside of the columns were open spaces, or 'rooms,' of every description; and as they followed Baba down the corridor they marveled at the diversity of the palace's inner life. In one room young maidens washed and arranged an elegant matron's hair; in another, two men sat on jade green pillows with gold tassels dangling from each corner, engaged in a game of chess, a handful of spectators behind them. In still another room, three bearded men were tethered, or so it seemed to Juan, to some kind of pipe, which made a bubbling noise as a white, cherry-scented smoke drifted languidly above their heads.

The corridor stretched on and on, and as they advanced Juan saw a dozen men reclined on pillows watching a young woman, her face covered by a veil but her midriff bare, sensuously dancing to the music of a lute. On the other side was a library, the walls lined with cedar shelves of ancient leather-bound texts, the center occupied by two long tables inset with rich red leather. Around the table were matching armchairs, and in the center a row of heavy yellow candles. In an adjoining space that smelled strongly of soap and oil, men sat on elevated couches, their heads back and their eyes closed, while barbers used a variety of delicate gold and silver scissors to snip their hair and trim their beards. One of the men opened his eyes as Baba, Dryden and Juan walked by. He stared at them for a moment, his face expressionless, until the barber tilted his head and he closed his eyes once more.

At last they came to a narrow door that was painted a brilliant blue. Passing through the portal, they found themselves in what appeared to be a dressing room. In the center were four pleated ottomans as blue as the door, and along three of the walls were racks on which hung clothing of every description. On the fourth wall were several long mirrors, and as Juan gazed at his reflection, he realized that he was badly in need of a bath and some clean clothes.

Baba reached up and, running his hands through the soft wools, delicate silks and rich furs, selected blue pantaloons, a spotless white tunic with a rounded collar and delicate buttons of milky pearl, a crisp yellow vest with black stitching along the pockets and seams, and a pair of black slippers. He handed these to Dryden, who accepted them with a skeptical grin. "Quite the dandy, I am," he said to no one in particular.

Baba crossed the room and, after regarding his options with a critical eye, selected some clothing for Juan. A delicate chemise of golden amber, its long sleeves filigreed at the cuffs with colored threads of blue and yellow; red silk şalvar, loose on the legs and snug at the rear, which reached to and were banded at the ankles; a blue and yellow kaftan of brocaded silk, its buttons as black as a hawk's eyes; and matching slippers, each one decorated with cut glass that glittered in the torchlight. For his face and head, a thin black scarf of Egyptian cotton, which covered the head and hung down to the shoulders, and, finally, a black silk veil that fastened behind the head and concealed everything but the eyes.

Confused, Juan held the clothes at arms-length, as though they smelled of skunk. "I am no lady," he protested. "Why do you ask me to wear things which befit only women, and which on a man serve little purpose other than to make him look foolish?"

"I have no time for this," Baba replied, crossing his arms. "After you have bathed you shall put them on, or I shall summon those in whose hands you will soon have no sex at all." Dismayed, Juan regarded the outfit in his arms with a look of pitiful resignation. Softening, Baba laughed. "There is a cause for this charade that will become clear in time. Trust me – in this place it is best that your manhood remains concealed."

They removed their clothing, which Baba kicked away to a corner. He rapped twice on the door and a boy entered, gathered up the discarded clothing and, lowering his eyes, withdrew. "They will be washed and mended," Baba assured them, "but you will not much need them here." He pushed at the edge of one of the mirrors and the wall gave way, pivoting to reveal an opening to an adjoining room. With a small bow and grand sweep of his arm, Baba indicated the way and, naked but for the clothes in their arms, Juan and Dryden stepped through the passageway.

They had entered a spacious, blue-and-yellow-tiled bath. Water gurgled from elevated granite fountains, each carved to resemble a creature of the wild – a lion, a bear, an eagle, a silver fox. These overflowed to fill perhaps a dozen baths, each separated from the next by beaded curtains, and each large enough to accommodate several bathers.

Four young women stood waiting, each dressed identically in soft cotton robes. At the sight of the women Juan hurried to cover his privates, while Dryden merely broke into a broad grin. At a nod from Baba, two of the young women took Dryden by the arms and, with shy smiles, led him away through one of the curtains. The other two guided a hesitant Juan through a separate curtain to another bath. Baba smiled beatifically as he watched them go, his teeth a sparkling white against the midnight black of his skin.

It took almost an hour, but when Juan emerged, dressed as Baba had directed, he felt clean for the first time since he left Seville. His thick black hair, which the girls had washed, brushed and scented with exotic oil, shone with a lustre that would have made any woman jealous. However uncomfortable they may have been to Juan's self-esteem, his garments fit him well; evaluating the product of his efforts, Baba pronounced himself pleased.

"In my youth," he complimented Juan, "before the advent of my present service, I bedded women less attractive than you." Reaching into a cedar chest banded with silver, he extracted a shining tress of long dark curls, which he fit to Juan's head, stuffing the real hair inside the fake. Once it was arranged the way he wanted he stood back, nodding with satisfaction. "That's better. I think you're ready now – it is time."

Baba led Juan down a broad corridor lined by an elaborate Chinese runner which, as far as Juan could see, had not a single seam along its entire length. Mounting a curved staircase, they turned first right then left – a design element intended to enhance the palace's defense – and then navigated still another corridor. Juan noticed that there were more guards on this level, all well-armed and alert. Each wore the silver breastplate and leather leggings of the sipahi. As he passed the soldiers, Juan wondered what rigors they'd endured to earn their present position.

At last they came to an ornate set of double doors. Baba turned and, placing his hand on Juan's shoulder, gave him his final instructions.

"If anyone asks you, your name is Juanna – you should be able to remember that – and you have been brought here to serve Her Most Esteemed Sultana, the Lady Gulbayez, Seventh Wife and Consort to the Sultan." Baba offered up a grim smile. "I suggest that you say as little as possible to anyone but the Lady Gulbayez, who among all you may meet is the only one who knows who and what you are."

As he reached to open the door, he offered one final word of advice. "If you please the Sultana, you may just live. If you fail, well, the sea will welcome you, as it has welcomed others who have displeased her."

CHAPTER 41
The Sultana's Pride

THE SULTAN Mahmud II had seven wives, each unique in her own way. Akasma, his first, was the plainest, but she was adept at managing the requirements of the harem, from the retention of slaves to the sleeping arrangements in their opulent apartments. Halime, his third, was gentle and shy; it was to Halime that Mahmud would turn for comfort when the responsibilities of leadership weighed heavy. To Pinar, the Sultan's fourth wife, laughter came as easily as breath, while Sibel, wife number six, possessed wisdom beyond her years and – for those few issues within the purview of women – sometimes acted as a sounding board for Mahmud.

Gulbayez, the Sultan's seventh wife, was his youngest. To call her lovely – to aver that she possessed the delicate beauty of a flower or the soft radiance of the maiden sunrise – would borrow from Homer to no good end, obscuring with well-worn platitudes what words are ill-suited to convey. Gulbayez possessed beauty beyond description, and in form was so nearly perfect that men wept to know she could not be theirs, and women to see what they could never be.

Her features – her dark, thick hair, high cheekbones, delicately rounded nose, soft sensuous lips and oval eyes – were as fine as had ever been rendered by the sculptor's genius or revealed through the painter's skill. But hidden in their perfection, like a subtle blemish in the most exquisite diamond, was a flaw – a haughty arrogance that could not entreat but only demand, and which posed as a smile on the lips but revealed itself in the eyes. As Juan stood in the Sultana's presence while Baba bowed and withdrew, he felt as if he was standing in a shadow.

She was the only child of an Albanian warlord whose loyalties had been available for purchase. From the beginning, Gulbayez had wanted for nothing, and her every whim, however capricious, was indulged. As a consequence, she never learned to tolerate disappointment, nor even to conceal it. Her friends she treated as servants, and her servants as fungible instruments of her will. She basked in the love of her father, for whom she shone like the sun, but of her mother she knew nothing. Raised to mistake riches for comfort and power for virtue, she rarely asked and saw no reason to mourn.

Word of her beauty passed beyond the borders of her father's fief and ultimately reached the royal court in Constantinople. "Gulbayez," her father had proudly informed her as she approached her sixteenth year, handing her a bridal veil given to him by the Sultan himself, "you are to be the seventh wife to the Supreme Khan!"

She'd leaped to her feet and thrown down the veil. "You would marry me off to an old man, and a weak one at that? Never – I'd sooner die!"

There were limits even to the most doting father's indulgence. "My sweet Gulbayez, light of my life," her father had responded, his face turned to stone. "You will obey me and marry the Sultan – he is younger than me, praise Allah! – or I will grant you your wish and spend the rest of my days mourning your passing!"

Juan heard the click of the latch as Baba pulled the doors shut behind him. He stood before Gulbayez, feeling ridiculous in his women's clothing, long dark tresses and concealing veil. Gulbayez, who reclined on a divan of plush red velvet trimmed in gold, slowly rose to her feet. Taking her time, she circled Juan, removing his veil and wig and examining him like a stallion. Returning to her seat, she stretched out on the chaise, idly dipping her fingers into a crystal bowl of lemon water that sat on a table beside her.

"Do you know why you are here, Christian?" she asked.

"I have no idea, nor why I have been required to pose as a woman." Juan recognized that he probably should have used an honorific – Sultana, or Exalted One, or some such thing – but he was angry and in no mood to pander.

Gulbayez sought out his eyes and, when he did not look away, seemed satisfied. *"Christian,"* she asked imperiously, *"canst thou love?"*

A thousand thoughts flashed through Juan's mind, a thousand warnings, a thousand intimations of peril. He ignored them all, and with an impetuous disregard that can often be found in the young – and is usually at odds with the attainment of greater years – answered the Sultana with a directness to which she was unaccustomed.

"Yes, I can love, and though I am young, may have loved too much already." He took a breath. *"If you mean to ask, 'can I love thee,' then my answer is that I cannot, for my heart still yearns for another."* It wasn't exactly true, which he found a little shameful, but it was the least objectionable basis for refusing the advances of a Sultana he could think of.

Gulbayez opened her mouth to speak; then, too astonished to form words, closed it. She furrowed her brow and clenched her fists, her cheeks flushed crimson – and still she did not speak. To her, it was as if the night had come, but not the darkness; or that the rains had fallen, but the grass remained dry. Never had she been refused, nor felt the bitter sting of humiliation.

Aware of the likely consequences of refusing a Sultana, Juan steeled himself, expecting that Baba would be summoned to exact retribution for his disrespect. Instead, Gulbayez rose and, padding softly across the room, reached out to stroke Juan's cheek. She looked him in the eye, searching for any sign of the adoration that was her due.

Grasping her perfect hand in his, Juan brought it to his heart. *"Here, Sultana; can you feel it beating? For all your beauty, wealth and power, do you think it beats for you? Or that, like the Sultana's falcon, it responds to your command?"*

He took her hand from his chest and, with as much kindness as he could muster, lowered it. *"Love is not love that can be commanded. If I am a slave*

– and putting a price on my head hardly makes it so – then at least my thoughts and heart are free, and entirely my own!"

"You? Free?" Her voice rose, brittle with fury. "What freedom you have – that I choose to allow you – is nothing but an illusion! Had I not seen you in the square today and thought you a pretty Christian, the lowest worm would not envy your fate. Certain, it would have been far worse than what I have offered, and you have so foolishly scorned."

She spun away, took three furious strides, then turned back. To Juan's amazement, her eyes were wet, and he could see that she trembled with frustration. "She to whom your heart is given," she asked, "is she lovelier than the moon, and more radiant than the sun?"

"She is lovely," Juan replied, "or so my mind remembers. But love beguiles more than the heart; it both entices and deludes all the senses. Julia's dark eyes and gentle aspect; her birdsong laughter; her scent, like jasmine carried on a warm wind; the way her mouth and lips taste like sweet papaya; how her body yields to my touch – to me, she is indeed as close to perfection as God allows. She claims that I am the same to her." He felt guilty, speaking this way of Julia for his own selfish purposes, but he wished to live.

Gulbayez took a step closer to Juan. "Am I not pleasing to you?" She reached up and, one by one, undid the ivory and jade loops that fastened her blouse. With a shrug of her shoulders, it fell away. She took another step. "Has your Christian beauty such as mine?"

"No, I mean, yes, um, no – Sultana, you're missing the point!"

A mirror hung on the wall near the divan. Turning, Juan crossed the room to stand before it and gestured.

"Look at me – I am far from perfect in form, and less worthy still in character. My legs are too long, my nose too large, my cheeks too drawn. At the slave market my pride nearly got us killed, and I stand before you now dressed as a woman!"

Returning to where Gulbayez stood silently, Juan gently lifted his hand to the Sultana's cheek, using his palm to wipe away her tears. "But even if our senses are deceived, and our lovers are less perfect than we foolishly imagine, it doesn't matter: we love, and our flaws themselves become beautiful. And, even in my youth, I know one thing more; love can neither be banished nor summoned by any mortal power. It recognizes no sovereign, and owes fealty only to the heart."

Gulbayez stared at Juan like he was a madman. "Oh, you foolish boy. Do you not see? You confuse what should be for what is."

She looked down at her blouse, then at Juan, who – deciding that adding insult to injury might not be the surest way to remain among the living – retrieved it from the floor and wrapped it around Gulbayez' shoulders.

Gulbayez shook her head. "Love is not an eagle, proud and free to fly wherever it chooses. No, it is like a flower, which may flourish if the soil is rich, the water pure and the weather fine. But if conditions are unfavorable, or it is poorly matched to the climate, it will wither and die." She swept her arm wide. "I have been planted in this garden, and though it is magnificent, still it is a prison, and the Sultana a prisoner."

Juan did not respond, in part for fear of saying something that might make his situation even more precarious, in part because he had lost track of the metaphors and similes of love. For the ten thousandth time, he wished his sister had lived – perhaps then he might have better understood women.

He was saved by a brisk knocking at the door, which yielded as Baba reentered. "Sister of the Moon and Bride of the Sun," he exclaimed, bowing low in apology, "forgive my intrusion!" Raising his eyes, he saw that Gulbayez and Juan were still – mostly – dressed. "I hope my return is not ill-timed," he continued cautiously, "but I am sent by the Sultan, who bids me to say that he is on his way."

When Gulbayez did not move, he spoke again. "On his way. Here. Now."

Gulbayez refocused. "Delay him for a moment, if you can." Turning back to Juan, she sighed. "Christian, in good time you will discover the cost of your naïveté, and of love's tight chains." She handed him his black tresses. "For now, mix in with my servant girls and try not to give yourself away. If you do, you and I shall be as united in death as you have chosen to remain apart in life."

CHAPTER 42
Cut Glass

I say, in my slight way I may proceed
To play upon the surface of humanity.
I write the world nor care if the world read;
At least for this I cannot spare its vanity.
My Muse hath bred and still perhaps may breed
More foes by this same scroll. When I began it, I
Thought that it might turn out so; now I know it,
But still I am, or was, a pretty poet.

DON JUAN, CANTO XV

TWO DAYS after his meeting with Lord Melbourne, Castlereagh reluctantly summoned Southey to his office. Dispensing with the pleasantries, he got right to the point. "If we are to use your information effectively, Southey, we need proof. I am aware of the source of your information – can Lady Caroline obtain Byron's journal?"

Southey shrugged. "I pushed her on it but she claims she cannot, that she sees him no longer."

"Oh? Were you clear as to the alternative?" Castlereagh labored to keep the irritation from his voice. He was a seasoned politician and statesman, and ordinarily had great control, not merely of his emotions, but of his bearing and expressions. But he seemed to have less patience these days, and to be far more irritable. The headaches didn't help, but there was something about Southey – even when they pursued an objective of mutual interest – that set him on edge. In fact, he found the man obnoxious, and wondered how he'd managed to achieve even a small measure of fame.

"I was quite clear, my Lord, to the point of being brusque. She has no wish to involve herself in any legal proceedings, or in any public proceedings of any kind. And she understands that Byron's journal entries could be used to great effect. When she says she cannot obtain them, I think she is to be believed."

Castlereagh sighed. "We must have them – Byron mustn't have a choice, or think it possible to escape disgrace through any expedient other than exile." He eyed Southey, who sat in a stiff-backed wing chair on the opposite side of the Foreign Secretary's massive desk, one leg crossed tightly over the other. Castlereagh thought he looked like a prig. "His journal's in his writing desk?"

"Yes, middle drawer. Unless he's moved it."

"I'll see what can be arranged." Castlereagh reached for his tea and leaned back in his chair, the cup to his lips. "Tell me, Mr. Southey," he asked, "what do you gain from Byron's exile? Other than the elimination of a more talented rival?"

Southey flushed. "It is not my interests that concern me here, my Lord, but those of my country." He offered an ingratiating smile. "Just as your motives, my Lord, arise not from any personal *animus* towards a vocal and calumniating critic, but from your perception of what is best for England."

"*Touché*, Mr. Southey. Nevertheless, it is rather important that you understand the end-game here. While I cannot say much on the subject, you need to know that I have – *that England has*– some use for Byron once he is no longer resident here. And that use depends on his reputation remaining, if not spotless, then at least reasonably intact." Castlereagh returned the cup to its saucer and leaned forward. "We want to exile the man, not destroy him. Do you understand, Mr. Southey?"

Southey returned the Foreign Secretary's gaze without blinking. "I do, my Lord. But I think you misapprehend Lord Byron."

"Do I? Enlighten me."

"No one needs to act affirmatively to destroy Byron, though I concede that actions might be taken to accelerate the process. But despite his talent – or, who knows, perhaps because of it – Byron is profoundly self-destructive. Given enough time and freedom, he will destroy himself."

Castlereagh shrugged. "Perhaps. So long as he doesn't immolate himself in the near term, I couldn't care less."

He rose, as did Southey, and together they moved towards the door. As he pulled it open to call for Reilly, Castlereagh put a final question to the *poet laureate*. "Does it bother you, Mr. Southey? You know, that despite Byron's devastatingly poor judgment, not to mention his rather scandalous personal proclivities, he's achieved such an astonishing degree of critical and popular acclaim?"

"Not at all, my Lord," Southey answered with a self-satisfied smirk that made Castlereagh want to slap him. "One writes for the ages, not the current fashion. In time, Byron's work will be seen for what it is; clever, but soulless at its core. He's like a piece of cut glass tumbling through the air – pretty as it catches the light, but too fragile to withstand the fall."

Surprised by a soft tapping at the door, Henrietta Turner straightened her back and pushed her stool away from the hand-loom that took up most of the utility room off of the kitchen. It was too early in the day for her clients to come by with the piecework that she took in to supplement her husband's modest income, and the Turners didn't get many social callers, certainly not at 7:00 am. Quentin wasn't up yet, and the girls were still asleep – it was scandalous how late they slept in the bed they shared. She'd have to get them to work straight away, or they'd grow up to be lazy as a pair of old dogs. And no good man – or at least, none with the wit to earn an honest living – would want to spend his days supporting such, not unless they were a good ways prettier than her girls.

"Good morning to you, ma'am." The young man at the door had taken off his hat, and by the color of his hair Henrietta figured him to be Irish. "I hope I didn't wake you?"

"Not likely, with all there is to do around here." She waited and, when he just stood there, huffed impatiently. "Something I can do for you?"

"Yes ma'am," he said, reaching into a satchel he had slung over his shoulder. Pretty official-looking, she thought, wondering how long he'd keep hold of it in this neighborhood. Not that they lived in a slum; the houses were modest but sturdy, and most folks worked steady. "My name is Reilly," the young man continued, "and I have a letter here for your husband."

Henrietta looked at this Reilly, and at the envelope in his hand. "My husband isn't in," she lied, not wanting to say he was still sleeping. "Do you want to come back later?"

He glanced around, thinking it over. "You're Mrs. Turner?"

"No, the Lady Turner's upstairs in the bath. I'm her lady-in-waiting." With a flourish, she whipped the loose flannel of her tattered robe around her hips.

Having spent several months in Lord Castlereagh's employ, Reilly was beginning to develop a better ear for sarcasm. "Yes ma'am." He handed her the sealed envelope. "If you could see that Mr. Turner receives it, ma'am, I'd be very grateful."

As Henrietta closed the door, she heard her husband coming down the hall, and looked up to see him rubbing the sleep from his eyes. "Quentin, some lad's brought a letter for you. From Castlereagh, I'm thinkin'."

Turner yawned as Henrietta handed him the letter. Tearing it open, he read it once quickly, then a second time. When he was done, he handed it over to his wife. "Burn it, would you Hen?"

She nodded, waiting to see if he wanted to tell her what it was about.

Sometimes he did, and sometimes he didn't. This time, it seemed, he didn't.

Quentin Turner yawned again and ran his fingers through his thick black beard. Turning towards the kitchen, he called back over his shoulder. "Hen, what's a man got to do around here for a hot cup of tea?"

CHAPTER 43
Approach of the Janissaries

FOR SEVERAL days he had burned with fever, and what little sleep he'd managed had been uneasy and pocked with nightmares. In the worst of them he dreamed of a twisted Augusta who, lacking the gentle sweetness of his sister, reminded him instead of one of Ali Pasha's many wives. In his dream they coupled, but she was displeased with his attentions. "Place him in a weighted bag," she commanded in a fury, "and then in the Bosphorus."

"Augusta," he begged as they bound his wrists, "have you no mercy, even for your brother?"

"What mercy did you expect, brother? The mercy of a sibling? My name is Cain. Of a disciple? I am Judah. Of a wife?" She'd laughed, her voice poisonous. "Are you joking?" She nibbled at a fig as Byron felt the scratch of burlap on his arms and neck. "Perhaps your God will show you mercy. Or have you scorned Him as well?"

"Scorned Him? No!" he'd screamed as the burlap closed over his head and her retainers tied it with a length of rope. In a panic he kicked against the sack, but his struggling only exhausted him. "Augusta!" he pleaded. "I loved you!"

"Loved me? Yes, you did, many times." This time, her laugh was bitter. "And then left me alone to face the guilt and shame. I assure you, my brother, the waves will treat you with more kindness than I received, or you deserve!"

They'd lifted the sack and heaved him into the sea, and he felt the wet and the cold and the tightening fist of death and shrieked ... awakening in a sweat with Hobhouse's hand on his shoulder.

"It's just a dream, Byron – a dream."

He was breathing fast, his heart pounding. He sat up, struggling to separate nightmare from reality. Sunlight streamed in through the narrow window next to his mat and, confused, he struggled to calm himself. "Where – no – have I been – how long?"

"It's been three days. You don't remember any of it?"

Byron pulled himself up so that he sat propped against the wall, his knees drawn up. He felt agitated and dazed, but the panicked fear of his nightmare was dissipating. He took a deep breath. "I – I'm not really sure. I remember talking to Iphigeneia and to you and Polidori ... not much after that."

"You almost died; or at least, that's what Polidori said. You had quite a fever, we all took turns putting cold cloths on your face and chest." Hobhouse leaned over and felt Byron's forehead. "Well, I'm no doctor, but you seem better to me. How do you feel?"

"Tired. Weak." He paused, taking stock. "Hungry."

They heard a step, and looked up to see Polidori, a smile on his face. "You're hungry? Really? That's a good sign, as is the fact that you aren't, well, you know, dead."

Byron cocked a tired eye. "That's your clinical analysis? Where exactly did you study medicine again?"

"The University of Edinburgh, as you well know. If you wanted a *qualified* physician, you should have reached a little deeper into your purse and engaged an Oxford man." Although Polidori did his best to look disapproving, he was unable to conceal his obvious relief.

"To the contrary, doctor, I think that the return on my investment has already been extraordinary." He took another deep breath, fighting a sudden, enervating fatigue. "Polidori, I don't know what you did but, as I'm alive, thank you for doing it well."

"Actually, Byron, I didn't do much at all." Polidori shrugged. "You may be annoying, but you're stronger than you look." He clapped his hands, as though to dismiss further expressions of gratitude. "Let's get you something to eat."

Panos fixed him a light meal – Polidori insisted he go easy – and Byron ate it slowly, savoring each bite. "What is this," he asked Panos, "it's delicious."

"What do you name the eggs, when they are ... around the stuff?"

"Omelet?"

"Yes, this has the *feta* and some *spanáki* that has my mother's garden. Also, I put again the medicine inside." When Byron paused, his fork hovering before him, Panos started laughing. "No, I am to make the joke. No medicine in the food, but if later you need, I can help."

After he'd eaten, Iphigeneia looked in. "It's good to see you up, Mr. Byron," she said. "For a time, we had our doubts."

"You have my thanks, m'lady." Byron tilted his head towards Panos. "First, your son collects us like lost lambs and leads us from danger. Then you offer us shelter in your village at great risk to yourselves." He gestured at Polidori. "And if you've fed the doctor here for three days, no doubt the villagers are running short of food."

Polidori indulged himself in an obscene gesture, which Byron acknowledged with a weak grin. "If I had my pen and ink, I would do my best to immortalize you in verse!"

Iphigeneia smiled, and Byron saw a shadow of Panos in the curve of her mouth and the brightness of her eye. He wasn't much for odes, and an elegy would be inappropriate, or at best, premature. "I've at least a dozen cantos to add to Donny Jonny – perhaps a place of honor for you there, if you don't mind sharing the page with characters less noble than yourself."

Before Iphigeneia could ask who or what Donny Jonny might be, they heard the thump of an approaching horse. Through the open doorway they saw Nikolaus swinging down from the saddle.

Iphigeneia was on her feet. "What is it, Nikolaus?"

"Janissaries, a dozen or so. We saw them at the river, and it seemed they'd turn away to the east." He was breathing hard, and paused to catch his breath. "But for some reason they changed their minds. They'll be here in ten, maybe fifteen minutes!" He motioned toward Byron, Hobhouse and Polidori. "These need to leave. Now."

They heard another rider, and saw an older man pull up his horse and gesture to Panos as the animal, its nostrils flaring, side-stepped nervously in the dirt outside the door. "It's Demetrios," Panos said, as he rushed out the door. "My brother," explained Iphigeneia as she hurried to follow. They listened as Demetrios described the janissaries' approach, gesturing first west, then east and north. Iphigeneia nodded grimly and said something to her brother, who wheeled his horse and rode off.

"They come from several sides," Iphigeneia said as she returned to the kitchen. "It's too late for the Englishmen to get out." She turned to Nikolaus. "Perhaps we can kill them all?"

"If they remained in a single group, it might have been possible. Or if we had more time. But now?" He shook his head. "I warned you, Iphigeneia. We should kill the English ourselves, and hand their bodies to the Turks."

"Nikolaus, always with the killing."

"Don't be weak, Iphigeneia. Better they die than –"

"No, Nikolaus! I have another idea. Maybe a good one, maybe not, but we're not going to kill these men, or give them to the Turks, not so long as the responsibility is mine."

Nikolaus set his jaw, and Byron could see his body tense. Iphigeneia saw it too. Brushing a loose strand of hair from her eyes, she softened her voice. "Nikolaus," she asked, taking his hand, "do you remember what you said when Antonia and Athanasios died?"

Nikolaus hesitated, as though he didn't want to answer. "You know that I do."

"What did you promise me?"

"I said that my life was yours, and that I would follow you to hell if you asked it." He glared at the Englishmen, and then, with a small shrug of resignation, squeezed Iphigeneia's hand. "You're not really going to hold me to that, are you?"

Iphigeneia smiled. To Byron, she seemed as full of grace as anyone he'd ever known. "We needn't travel that far, dear Nikolaus." She glanced out the door and squared her shoulders. "Alright," she said firmly, "this is what we will do."

CHAPTER 44
The Pain of New Life

THE JANISSARIES approached with caution, alert to the danger of an ambush. Five advanced through the olive groves, riding slowly as they peered down rows of gnarled, lichen-ruckled trunks. Four more rode in two-by-two on either side of the dry creek bed that bordered the village to the west. Two of these held swords at the ready, their tips pointed skyward; the other two held loaded cross-bows, with a dozen two-foot metal bolts in quivers on their backs. A remaining group entered the village from the east, walking their horses along the rutted track that led in and out of Pentias. Behind the village to the north stood a line of rugged cliffs, and beyond these loomed the mountains of the Pindos range. Fleeing the village to the north, the janissaries knew, was unlikely; even if the cliffs could be surmounted, the closest pass through the mountains was twenty miles distant.

They converged at the edge of the olive groves where Demetrios, still astride his horse, awaited them. He carried a dagger in a sheath on his hip but was otherwise unarmed. As the janissaries approached, he raised his arm in greeting.

"It must be a slow day," he said jovially to a mounted Turkish officer who detached himself from the main body of janissaries, "to bring so many of the great Khan's finest warriors to our sleepy village. I am Demetrios."

The janissary officer simply stared. "I don't care if your name is Tamerlane – by any name, you are goats, nothing more." He prodded his horse, which danced forward, bringing the Turk within only a foot or two of Demetrius. "And if you do not wish to be staked like a goat and fed to the beasts, you will give us what we've come for."

Demetrios remained where he was, gazing evenly at the officer. "*Effendi*," he said, bowing his head, "we have nothing here of great value, save for the olives we take to market, a few bony goats, and a sway-backed horse or two."

"Do not lie to me, peasant." Reaching into his tunic, he held up a copy of the poster bearing Byron's name and image. "This man has committed crimes against the Sultan. We believe you may be hiding him." He handed the paper to Demetrios, who studied it carefully. Finally, he shook his head.

"*Effendi*, of all the humble villages that have the misfortune to squat in the harsh shadow of the Pindos, this one may be the poorest and most meagre. Why would this –" he squinted at the writing on the poster – "this *Lord Byron*, shelter here?"

Chuckling, he handed the paper back to the Turk. "And why would we protect him if he did? With a price like this on his head, we'd hand him to you faster than you can count to ten!"

The janissary officer stared coldly at Demetrios. "Who can understand the logic of fools? I no longer try." He raised his sword, and turning the blade side away, struck Demetrios a backhand blow across the head. Staggered, Demetrios somehow remained in the saddle, ignoring the blood that trickled from a gash above his eye.

"I'll ask you again, goat man. Where is he?"

"I haven't seen him, *effendi*," Demetrios repeated. "But if I do, I will demand that he turn himself over to you at once!"

The Turk wheeled his horse and barked a series of commands to his men, who formed into three groups and began to move northward through the village, their swords held before them. The janissary officer turned back to Demetrios. "If we find this man in this dung-heap of a village, goat man, we will put your people to the sword. Starting with you." He pointed toward the village. "We ride together, so that I do not have to search you out to kill you."

✦ ✦

They went house to house, searching every room. The villagers watched them, sullen and silent, but knew better than to interfere. They knew as well that anything of value that could easily be carried would be taken, and they'd hidden what they could. The janissaries made no pretense of civility, roughly pushing the men and boys aside and leering at the women, but – perhaps because they seemed in a hurry – did nothing worse, and stole only a silver hand-mirror, a carved ivory pipe, and a few other small items. A little girl, her brown eyes wide, stood in the dirt and clutched a soiled rag doll as the janissaries swept past. One of the riders pointed and, to general laughter, shouted something obscene.

When they reached the upper village, they paused at the open-sided storage shed where Hobhouse had rested on the day he and the others had arrived in Pentias. Panos was there, hammering a wooden stopper into one of two barrels that had been loaded onto the wooden cart that rested on the tracks. He looked up as the janissaries approached, exchanging a brief look with Demetrios.

"You there, boy. What's in the barrels?" demanded the janissary officer, pointing his sword at the dozen barrels in the shed and the two on the cart.

"Olives." Panos lifted his mallet and gave the stopper another good whack.

"Show me."

Panos sighed and, putting down his mallet, jumped down from the cart and stepped over to the side of the shed, where two barrels stood off by themselves. He began to remove the stopper from one of the barrels.

"No." The janissary pointed to the two barrels on the cart. "Those."

Panos shot a quick glance at Demetrios. "They're all the same, but those are full and very heavy. It will be faster to open these."

"Do you want trouble, boy? Now open the barrels on the cart before I lose my patience."

Panos sighed once more. "Like I told you, they're heavy. I'll need a hand to get them down."

The Turk motioned to Demetrios. "Go help him, and be quick about it." He waved his *kilij* towards Panos. "Be careful, old man – do anything I don't like and this boy will lose his left hand." He looked at his men and snickered. "I'd cut off his right, but this one probably uses his left to eat!"

Together, Panos and Demetrios heaved the barrels down from the cart, setting them in the dirt in front of a large iron trough. Lifting an iron screw that could be turned by a wooden cross-bar, Panos loosened the stoppers and then removed them by hand. Grunting with the effort, he and Demetrios tipped first one barrel and then the other into the trough, and the air became heavy with the pungent smell of the fruit as the olives poured out in a purple and black slurry. Panos stood aside as Demetrios turned to face the janissary officer.

"*Effendi*, there are no better olives north of the Peloponnese. As we've gone to the trouble to unload them, can we offer you a bag full to take with you on your travels?"

Scowling, the officer spat in the direction of Demetrios and Panos. "Your crops are as filthy as the goats that tend them. I'd sooner eat dirt." He turned in his saddle and motioned to his men, and together they rode up the hill towards Iphigeneia's house.

The janissaries heard the screams as they approached the house. As the Turks reined in their horses and their commander dismounted, Iphigeneia stepped outside the house to meet them, her hands red with blood.

She wore a soft cloth across her nose and mouth, reaching back to untie it as the soldiers approached. The janissary officer leveled his *kilij*. "Do not take another step, woman," he barked. "What is that blood on your hands, and who is that screaming?"

"Life does not wait for war to end," she said, fatigue in her voice. "If God wills it, a new soul is coming into the world."

The Turk looked past her to the open door of the house. "We are looking for an Englishman," he said roughly, "and will see the inside of your house."

"A woman is giving birth," she began to protest, but was interrupted by a piercing scream that made the hair stand up on the back of her neck. "Giving birth," she continued. "You must wait."

"And who are you to issue orders, woman? We will search the house *now*. Interfere, and it will be you who screams to wake the dead."

She started to argue further but stopped herself, seeming to think better of it. "I cannot stop you," she admitted, "but you should be warned – the woman inside is sick with the pox. This is why the birth is so difficult. But if Allah goes with you, perhaps –" another blood-curdling cry – "perhaps all will be well."

The janissary hesitated, then turned to one of his men. "Ayaz, check it out. Every room."

Ayaz, who was younger than his fellows and seemed no more than seventeen or eighteen, blanched. He stared at his commander for a moment and then, resigned, started forward. "Wait," said Iphigeneia. Reaching into her pocket, she pulled out a clean cloth. "Wear this – it may keep you safe, although with the pox, who can really say?"

Ayaz looked to his officer, who nodded impatiently, gesturing toward the house. Iphigeneia handed Ayaz the cloth, which he tied over his nose and mouth. The screaming continued, even louder than before, and Iphigeneia saw that most of the janissaries had taken a few steps back, away from the doorway. She re-tied her own cloth and, motioning Ayaz to follow, reentered the house. His weapon ready, the janissary followed close behind her.

As his eyes adjusted to the darkness, Ayaz surveyed the kitchen, which was spotless save for a tub of hot water that rested on the embers of a cooking fire. He nodded to Iphigeneia, who led him through the doorway to the back.

On a sturdy table covered by a straw mat lay a dark-haired woman of uncertain age. She wore a simple peasant blouse and skirt, with the latter pushed up and bunched about her belly. On her head she wore a black cotton shawl, and across her face a dark veil, so that only her eyes – grey and wide with fear – were visible. Both her legs were bent, her knees drawn almost to her ample bosom, and a blanket extended over them like a tent.

At her feet, reaching between her knees with both hands, stood an old woman as stout as a tree trunk. Her hands were obscured by the blanket, but Ayaz could see a copious amount of blood on both her wide forearms and on the mat below. She ignored Iphigeneia and Ayaz, concentrating on the figure on the table. "Push, Aspasia! It won't be long, now. Push!"

Aspasia grunted, straining with the effort, then screamed with a ferocity that caused Ayaz to retreat with alarm. The scream cut off abruptly, replaced by a series of rapid pants. Iphigeneia turned to the janissary. "Have you never seen a birth before?" She needed no answer – the boy had turned white as a sheet and his weapon, which had been raised and ready, hung limply at his side.

She stepped close and gestured towards the table. "It's been more than six hours ... I fear the pox may have consumed the child." She shook her head. "I pray that it hasn't – the flesh will be putrid and will ooze with rot. Can you not smell it?" She broke off, choking back a sob. "So much sickness in this house, so much death." With an effort, she composed herself. "Do you wish to examine her more closely?"

Ayaz shook his head and staggered away, his hand at his mouth. Bursting through the doorway, he ripped the cloth away from his face, bent over, and vomited in the dirt. The janissary officer looked at him with disgust, while the other janissaries laughed nervously.

"Ayaz, you are no braver than a woman, and judging from this one –" he pointed to Iphigeneia – "a good deal less." He gestured toward the house. "No Englishmen?"

Ayaz shook his head, wiping the vomit from his lips with his sleeve. "Only women, and the stinking rot ..." He bent over and was sick again.

There was a sudden rumble from the area of the storage shed, and the officer jerked his head around just in time to see the wooden cart, loaded with two barrels, roll out of the shed and down the hill along the wooden tracks. Demetrios and Panos stood on either side of the tracks, their gloved hands tightly gripping a thick rope that stretched taut before them, controlling the descent of the cart.

"Stop!" the janissary officer shouted. Panos turned and lifted his arms. "What?" Demetrios, left to hold on to the rope alone, uttered a curse and yelled "Panos!" But it was too late. The cart was too heavy for one man and, despite Demetrios' efforts to hold on, the rope slid through his hands and jerked free, snaking along the tracks as the runaway cart quickly picked up speed.

The officer glanced at the trough, which was still full of olives, and saw that the two barrels that had previously stood at the side of the shed were gone. He cursed at Demetrios and, without waiting for any further explanation, barked out an order to his men. Screaming at Ayaz to follow, the officer and his men wheeled their horses and rode off down the hill in pursuit of the cart and its cargo.

They rode hard to the western end of the village, then south along the creek bed until they saw the olive groves to their left. Spurring their horses, they galloped through the grove and saw the cart, its cargo careening wildly against its sides, hurtle past. The restraining rope, now useless, trailed in its wake, whipping against the rails at either side of the track like the tail of an angry serpent. The janissaries wheeled their horses to follow but had no need to go much further.

The cart had come to a curve, which at its normal speed it could have managed without difficulty. But without the braking effect of the rope even a small curve was too much, and the cart wobbled for a moment, jumped the track, and broke through the rails. With an impact that could be heard across the grove, the cart slammed into the solid trunk of an olive tree that – if Panos was to be believed – had been a sapling when Charlemagne was crowned as Holy Roman Emperor. It was no sapling now, and the cart splintered in a burst of slats, boards and wheels. The barrels were thrown clear, and when they hit ground more than twenty feet past the site of impact, they cartwheeled and bounced off a tree or two before finally coming to rest in the shadow of the grove.

The officer signaled to two of his men. "Bring a hatchet," he ordered, and together they dismounted and made their way through the grove toward the two barrels. Neither barrel stirred, and the officer motioned to one of his men. "Break it open. By the Sword of Allah, a man inside will surely be broken open already."

It took only three or four hard blows to split the metal banding and crack the first barrel open at a seam. Once more the janissary sniffed the rich, musty scent of the olives, which spilled out to form a spreading purple-black puddle. Angered, the officer seized the hatchet and with as much force as he could muster, buckled the side of the remaining barrel. Uttering a curse that devout Muslims had long disdained as bringing dishonor to the One True Faith, he jumped clear as a glistening torrent of olives sloshed from the broken barrel, accumulating in a viscous mound at his feet.

As they headed east, skirting the road in favor of a narrow goat track that he had traveled since he was a young boy, Panos reached into the satchel that he carried in a sling across his back and tossed a bundle of clothing – pants, a rough shirt, a woolen jacket – to Byron. "Please you not to be the insult, By-roon," he said, his face deadly serious, "but as the woman you are very ugly." He stared at Byron for a long moment, then cracked a wide grin.

"No offense taken, Panos." He reached into the peasant blouse and pulled out two wads of stuffing. "Still, I suppose I was pretty enough to fool the young Turk, who I concede may have been distracted by the pig's blood and your mother's graphic invocation of the pox." He shook his head appreciatively. "Iphigeneia is a remarkable woman."

Walking alongside Byron, Hobhouse looked back over his shoulder every few moments to make sure the janissaries hadn't followed. "Remarkable she is, Panos, and as cool under pressure as a tigress. But holy Christ, Byron," he marveled, "even from the roof, your wails were loud enough to be heard in Constantinople!"

Polidori nodded in agreement. "I've delivered a few babies in my time, and I must say, your ability to pretend such pain was astounding. How on earth did you do it?"

Byron, who'd paused to discard his skirt and don the trousers Panos had given him, looked up with a pained expression. "Pretend? Bloody hell, there was no need to pretend! The mountainous woman that attended me?"

"Yes?"

"The wench shoved a bloody candle up my arse!"

CHAPTER 45
A Christian Girl

WHILE GULBAYEZ *was grateful for the advance notice, it wasn't like the Sultan could sneak up on anyone. For one thing, his approach was at all times heralded by the bright ring of trumpets and the low rumble of drums, which could be heard even by the wizened ancients whose job it was to read the Sultan's fortune and to find it full of promise. For another, he was invariably proceeded by a train of retainers – eunuchs, footmen, musicians, clerics, armed sipahi, healers, concubines and the like – the advance elements of which arrived at the Sultan's destination well before he did.*

The Sultana too had a retinue, which consisted of serving girls, handmaidens and an astonishing variety of household slaves responsible for everything from washing and cutting the Sultana's hair to preparing her meals. It was into this sizable company that Juan, disguised as Juanna, was hastily escorted as the Sultan approached. Several of the handmaidens smiled or giggled as he slipped past them but, if they suspected this new Christian slave girl was not as she seemed, they showed no sign. Seeing the retinue lining up to bow to the Sultan's approach, he did the same, hoping for the best as he checked to ensure that his head covering and veil remained in place.

"Sister of the Moon and Daughter of the Sun," Mahmud said jovially as he greeted Gulbayez, "it makes one feel young again just to see you!" He lowered his hand to the inclined head of his seventh wife and then to her cheek. "Rise, so that I may see the light in your eyes."

Gulbayez lifted her head to meet her husband's gaze. "Leader of the Faithful and Emperor of the Earth, it is I who am grateful, and desire only to be worthy." She stood, kissed his extended hand, and then, without lowering her eyes, took the Sultan's middle finger into her mouth, caressing it with the firm rolling pressure of her tongue.

His desire rising – Gulbayez could arouse him with the merest touch – Mahmud withdrew his hand and turned to the gathered assembly of slaves, retainers, servants and court officials. "Leave us," the Sultan ordered with a peremptory wave of his hand. He paid no attention to the knowing smiles, but as the traveling court unraveled itself to disperse down myriad passages and through dozens of doors and curtains, Mahmud – whose eyes were sharp – noticed a face he hadn't seen before.

As more than a dozen heads turned to look at him, Juan felt rather than saw the Sultan approach. Sure that his masquerade was about to be exposed, he blushed and bowed his head.

"So, Gulbayez, you've found yourself a Christian girl," he said slyly, examining the new slave. "She's a slender young thing, and tall, but worth no more than a half-measure of silver – I hope you didn't pay too much."

"That one?" Gulbayez flicked a well-formed wrist in Juan's direction. "The price was fairer than the girl."

"Still," responded Mahmud, "I find these Christian girls curious. Does she speak?" The room hushed as he stared expectantly at Juan, who hadn't the slightest clue what was required of him.

"My poor, famished husband," Gulbayez pouted, sliding over to Mahmud and pressing her breasts against his chest, "have I become so common a dish, that you crave more exotic fare?" With the back of her hand, she lightly brushed his cheek. "If I bore you, perhaps you'd like to take a Christian for your next wife?" She sniffed dismissively at Juan. "Or perhaps you would prefer to couple with this one?" With a toss of her head, she turned her back and crossed her arms.

Conciliatory, the Sultan turned away from Juan to place his hands on his seventh wife's waist. Pressing his lips to her hair, he breathed her in

– she smelled like lemons. "Do you know what I told your father when our marriage arrangement was struck, Gulbayez?"

"That you'd like – what do the French call it? – a *garantie*, should I prove deficient in my duties?"

"No," Mahmud laughed, "though that's not a bad idea." He signaled to the grand vizier's first assistant, who nodded and scribbled a note. "No, I told him that of all the fathers whom Allah has blessed with daughters, he is the most blessed, to have had a daughter as clever and as lovely as you." He raised his hands and brushed them across Gulbayez's breasts. "Why are you still here?" he demanded of the remaining stragglers. "I said, leave us!"

Juan, who had stood there dumbly, uncertain whether he was free to leave, felt a hand on his shoulder and turned to see the frowning face of a girl only two or three years older than he. She wore flowing white şalvar that were gathered at the calf, a blue inner kaftan that fell to her thigh, and an outer, raw silk kaftan of similar length. Her long black hair was gathered atop her head and held with crossed ebony rods. On each side, a narrow braid dangled almost to her shoulder, dancing lightly as she walked. Her eyes were unusual – a pale, piercing blue – and were quick and sharp. It seemed to Juan that she moved less with grace than with a sort of brisk efficiency.

The girl was staring at him. "Do you have no more sense than a turtle?" she asked quietly. She leaned close, whispering in his ear. "You may have fooled the Sultan, but you have not fooled Caria. Now, pull your empty head from the sand and come – quickly – or you may find that the Prophet himself cannot save you."

"I don't know what you mean," he whispered, panic competing with astonishment. "I –I'm –"

"Hush, Christian! Now is not the time, and this is most certainly not the place." She turned on her heel and stalked out the open door, angling to the right along a broad marble corridor that, to Juan's amazement, was divided down the center by a stream.

Juan glanced back in time to see the Sultan, his hand on his seventh wife's bottom, usher her past two bare-chested and unsmiling eunuchs and through a gilded doorway. Thinking that every hour seemed to yield surprises stranger than the last, he hurried to catch up to the slave girl – Caria, she had called herself – following a factitious indoor river that, for all he knew, emptied into a broad palatial sea.

CHAPTER 46
Brave as a Lyon

Near this Spot
Are deposited the Remains of one
Who possessed Beauty without Vanity,
Strength without Insolence,
Courage without Ferocity,
And all the virtues of Man without his Vices

INTRODUCTION, EPITAPH TO A DOG
JOHN CAM HOBHOUSE

FLETCHER HAD Thursday nights off – what he did with his time Byron had no idea – so Byron invariably made a point of going out. Although Augusta had promised to visit, she had written to say that one of her daughters had come down with the croup and that she couldn't get away. She'd begged him to make the trip out to Cambridge, but the idea of spending a lovely June weekend in so domestic an environment held no attraction.

So, after dashing off a note suggesting that she come to London when her little girl was feeling better, he and Hobhouse had dined at an expensive restaurant in Mayfair that was owned by one of their friends. As was often the case, Byron's celebrity threatened to make it difficult to eat without interruption, but the owner had given them a table in a semi-private alcove that was separated by a low wall from the other patrons.

Weary of Byron's continued musings about Augusta, Hobhouse had launched into a lecture. "Byron," he remonstrated, helping himself to what remained of their third bottle of claret, "even apart from the fact that she's your sister, which I'd have thought reason enough to forebear, she's not the sort you favor. In everything from discourse to disputation, you require an unholy degree of stimulation, and grow bored in less time than it takes for a leaf to fall from a tree."

"Then how to explain *our* long friendship?" Byron had snapped, irritated by his friend's stubborn refusal to let him be. He wasn't a fool, and his mistakes were usually due less to a lack of awareness than of discipline, a weakness he detested but to which he had become resigned.

"My point, Byron, is that Augusta's interests – her way of speaking – her daily pursuits – all the things that are most important to her – don't much intersect with yours. She may be the proverbial apple, but once you've had a bite I'm pretty sure you'll find her too bland for your taste."

"Don't mistake what is diverting for what is important. Even were I to concede what you say – and I don't – it wouldn't matter."

"No?" Hobhouse took a deep breath, his head spinning. He'd had more to drink than he'd intended. "Why the bloody hell not?"

Byron set his jaw. "Hobhouse, this isn't something I wish to discuss. I know her better than you do, understand?" His head felt light and the room seemed to tilt.

"No, I do not bloody understand, Byron. Explain it to me. Use small words!"

Byron glared at Hobhouse, who glared right back. "Let it be. We're friends, but this is none of your damned business."

"How is it that it's not my business until you've made a mess of things and need someone to help you out of a scrape? Or have you already forgotten your catastrophic liaison with Caroline Lamb?"

Byron slammed his fist on the table, toppling his empty wine glass.

"What do you want from me?" he demanded, his voice loud enough to be heard across the room. "Who made you the judge of whom I might love? Whatever authority you pretend to have, it surely isn't based on your vast experience!"

Seeing that heads had turned toward their table, he lowered his voice, which was cold with fury. "Friendship – love – means nothing unless it's unconditional. I learned that from my sainted mother, who loved or spurned according to her mood!"

"Oh? Is that how you love, Byron? Unconditionally?" Hobhouse gestured at the empty bottle of wine. "You've shown greater commitment to the claret than to any of your lovers!"

"You dare lecture me on constancy? On commitment? Do you truly contend that a willingness to endure for years what should naturally expire in months is love's proper measure? Look at the lifeless couples that surround us!" he said, sweeping his arm across the room. "The maintenance of a pale shadow of affection is nothing to celebrate – it is the intensity of affection that matters, however long it might last."

Hobhouse snorted, throwing back his head and crossing his arms. "Which is it, Byron? First you claim that love must be unconditional; then, within seconds, that the intensity of one's passion excuses its swift exhaustion. Is this the 'unconditional' love you offer to Augusta?"

"I have loved Augusta since I was a boy – in fact, when I reflect upon it, she may be the *only* woman I have ever truly loved. Certain, she is the only woman who asks nothing of me; who accepts me for who I am, rather than who I have become; and whose trust and affection are given without question or condition." Reaching over, he retrieved the fallen wine glass and set it upright, glowering throughout. "Indeed, I sometimes believe she's the only person of whom that can be said."

Hobhouse could feel his heart pounding. He had been friends with Byron since their university days at Cambridge, and they'd argued – about politics, and poets, and yes, about women – more times than he could count. Still, they had never had a row like this, and he couldn't remember being this angry. He was just so tired of Byron's recklessness, tired of how careless he was of his name, tired of worrying about him. How absurd, he thought bitterly, that a man renowned as a lover understands nothing of love.

"I don't know what you think you're doing, Byron, but whatever the meaning of this, this *duel* you're having with life, I've no appetite for continuing as your second. Bloody Christ, I'd rather just shoot you myself!"

Cutting the evening short they parted coldly, each of them regretful but too stubborn to admit fault. As he stamped gloomily along the darkened streets, his eyes cast down and his hands buried in his pockets, Byron thought about Augusta. Hobhouse's observation that she lacked most of the characteristics he found most interesting in a woman wasn't entirely off the mark. In her company he sometimes struggled to make conversation, a skill at which he ordinarily excelled. Still, she had a way of putting him at ease, and of letting him lay down the burden of meeting the absurd expectations engendered by his reputation.

He hadn't meant to bed her. Hadn't meant even to flirt, or to engage in the coy give-and-take that so often leads to seduction. It wasn't that she was unattractive; though she wasn't a classic beauty, she was soft and full in all the right places, and possessed of a fecund sensuality that stirred something elemental. No, it was that she was his sister – *half-sister* – and he understood that if discovered, such a liaison could have serious consequences.

But from the moment she'd arrived in London there had been an unmistakable sexual tension between them. How she had looked at him through those heavy-lidded eyes, and smiled, and touched his arm. Caroline had sensed it as well, he was sure of it, and it had been all he could do to maintain a façade of mere brotherly affection during an interminable dinner that he still winced to recall.

Yet, Hobhouse's views to the contrary notwithstanding, he was not *entirely* without discipline, and had resolved to avoid allowing the unthinkable to become the inevitable. He had been surprised when, rejecting his chaste kiss goodnight, Augusta invited him up to her rooms, and been more surprised still at how their childhood rhyming game had become erotic. When she unbuttoned her blouse, sucked on her finger and wet her nipple – well, no jury of twelve good men could reach any conclusion other than that he had been not the seducer but the seduced. Even more to the point – though it was not one he meant to debate with Hobhouse or with anyone else – should blame attach to the mere intent, or only to the deed?

He reached his rooms and, fumbling with his key at the door, managed to let himself in. He braced himself as he entered, for although Lyon was no longer a pup he usually rose to greet his master's return, an endearingly annoying habit in a dog that weighed more than a hundred pounds. On this occasion, however, there was no onslaught of affection; the flat was dark and still.

Setting his keys on a small table by the door, Byron called to his dog. When Lyon failed to come running, Byron turned to head up the staircase, figuring he was fast asleep in his place in the study. He took no more than two or three steps when he thought he heard a sound, soft and indistinct. He stopped to listen more closely, but heard nothing more. "Lyon?" he called again, louder than before.

Thinking about it later, Byron realized that he should have retreated to the kitchen to arm himself with a knife or mallet, just as a precaution. But, still feeling the effects of the wine, he headed up the stairs without further hesitation.

At the top of the stairs he turned to his left, toward his study. It was then that he sensed movement from the corner of his eye and, as he shifted his weight, felt the blow coming. It landed on his left shoulder, just below his neck. The pain hit him like a hammer, and he cried out as he raised his arm and twisted, protecting himself. Pivoting, he came face-to-face with his attacker, who raised a stout walking stick, ready to strike again. The man was wearing dark clothing – Byron hadn't time to take a proper inventory, but thought he saw heavy boots, grey trousers and a black wool coat. Some kind of satchel was looped around his neck and across his chest, and he had a thick, full beard that was as black as soot.

Byron didn't think, just reacted. As his attacker stepped forward, his right arm accelerating to deliver a second blow, Byron moved not away from the blow but toward it. Jabbing with his left arm, palm open, he struck the bearded man's right shoulder, pushing it backward. The combined effect was to shorten the arc of the descending club and pull it a few critical inches to Byron's left, where it landed – painfully but without anything close to the force of the previous strike – at the edge of Byron's left shoulder.

Surprised by Byron's quickness, the bearded man swept his weapon up and across, hoping to connect with a backhanded blow. Byron saw it coming and ducked under the heavy stick. The miss left his assailant exposed, and Byron drove his fist into the man's side, eliciting a groan. With his left hand he seized the intruder's wrist, and together they lurched across the hall and slammed into the wall. Byron felt the man's breath on his cheek and heard him panting with the effort. Widening his stance as he had learned in the boxing ring, he managed to deliver several hard punches to the bearded man's side, aiming for his kidney.

The series of body blows had the desired effect. Grunting in pain, Byron's assailant changed his tactics, abandoning his attempts to strike Byron with the walking stick. Dropping the stick, he lowered his shoulder, pushing Byron toward the stairs. The tactic was only partially successful, for as Byron felt himself about to fall he dropped his shoulder and rolled, bringing the bearded man beneath him. Locked together, they toppled into space and half-slid, half-bounced down to the landing below. When they hit the hardwood steps, both men lost their grip, flailing at one another as they fell.

They lay dazed for a moment on the landing. The bearded man gained his feet first, clinging to the bannister for support. He stared at Byron, who had struggled to his knees, and then limped awkwardly down the remaining stairs and through the entry alcove to the front door. Pausing, he patted first his coat pocket and then the bag he carried. As Byron got to his feet the man hesitated and, to Byron's utter astonishment, called out to him. "I'm bloody sorry 'bout your dog, I am." Then he pulled the door open and stumbled off. Byron reached the front landing just in time to see him turn the corner, heading towards Green Park.

Breathing hard, Byron struggled to catch his breath. He was too tired for a chase and doubted he could catch the man anyway. He reached up and felt for the spot where the walking stick had struck him. His neck was tender and sore, but nothing seemed to be broken. His side ached where he'd landed on the stairs. Weary to the bone, he turned, headed for the study.

Lyon lay on his side, close to the door. If not for the clotted blood that covered the side of his head, Byron would have thought he was sleeping. He knelt and pressed his hand to Lyon's flank, feeling for the rise and fall of his breathing. When he realized that his dog was dead, he felt a cold shock. Leaning over, he wrapped his arms around Lyon's massive head and hugged him close.

When he rose, blotting his tears with his arm, he saw that the drawer of his desk was open, its interior dimly illuminated by a single flickering candle. Even before he reached the desk he knew what was missing. Where his journal always lay, he now saw nothing but bare wood.

The intruder had come with a specific purpose in mind; he'd known of Byron's journal. But who would go to the trouble to break into his rooms for a journal? And why?

As he reached to close the drawer, he realized that his journal wasn't the only thing that had been disturbed. His serialized novel of *Don Juan* – which wasn't yet complete and, based on his misgivings with respect to the enterprise, might *never* be completed – was missing as well. It couldn't have been the thief's intended target – no one but Kinnaird and Murray even knew he was considering the project, and they thought he had abandoned it – and he wondered why the thief would have bothered with it.

His thoughts were interrupted by a rapping on the front door. Descending the stairs, he took a deep breath, gathering himself. When he opened the door Hobhouse was there, his hand poised to knock a second time. Hobhouse lowered his arm to his side, and he and Byron stood for a long moment, looking at one another in silence.

"I'm sorry, Byron," Hobhouse finally mumbled, though he looked Byron square in the eyes. "I drank too much and said too much as well. You're a grown man, and entitled to ruin your life however you see fit."

Byron held his friend's gaze and felt a lump in his throat. He nodded, pulling Hobhouse into an embrace. They held each other for a moment, then broke off, pretending embarrassment the way men sometimes do. Only then did Hobhouse notice the bruise at the base of Byron's neck, and the distress in his eyes. "Good God, Byron – what's happened? Are you all right?"

Byron paused, taking the measure of his own emotions. He felt the sorrow in his chest like a weight but realized that now – after the initial shock – it was accompanied by a mounting rage. He looked at Hobhouse, his jaw clenched. "I'm fine. Someone broke in and I interrupted him." He struggled to compose himself. "It's Lyon, Hobby. He's dead."

Hobhouse's face fell. "Bloody hell," he said softly. "I'm so sorry, Byron. Fucking bloody hell. Knowing Lyon, he died trying to protect you."

Byron nodded, and the men stood for a time in silence. Finally, Hobhouse spoke. "Do you know what he was after?"

"Yes, I think so. He took my personal journal. Much of it is candid, some of it embarrassing, to myself or others." He forced himself to meet his friend's eyes. "Hobby, one entry concerns Augusta."

CHAPTER 47
The Cost of Conscience

When all is past, it is humbling to tread
O'er the weltering field of the tombless dead,
And see worms of the earth, and fowls of the air,
Beasts of the forest, all gathering there;
All regarding man as their prey,
All rejoicing in his decay.

LORD BYRON, THE SIEGE OF CORINTH

MOST PEOPLE like dogs, even if they lack the wit to train them properly. Quentin Turner was no exception; he'd had dogs as a boy and, much like Byron, considered them vastly superior to people. He and Henrietta always talked about getting a dog for the girls, though Turner knew that it would really be more for him.

As he stood by the bench in St. James' Park two days after breaking into Byron's rooms, he felt as low as he could recall, lower even than when he hadn't a guinea to his name and no prospects to speak of. If he hadn't met Lord Castlereagh, who'd seen something in the unshaven hand working for a few schillings a day in the Crescent Mews stables, he reckoned he'd prob'ly be dead by now, and could never have dreamed of having a good woman like Henrietta, two healthy daughters, and a roof over his head that didn't leak too bad.

Henrietta called Castlereagh "the Fixer," and Turner couldn't find fault with the handle. Ever since his Lordship had bought him a square meal, then given him a little job and then another and then another, he'd seen how carefully the Foreign Secretary arranged things and how little he left to chance. "Turner," Castlereagh had said to him not long after they'd met, "while you've not much education, you have more sense than half the men I knew at school. From time to time I'm going to ask you to take on various projects. I expect you to complete them well and say not a word to anyone. Do that, and you will earn a comfortable living, and I'll make sure your girls are taken care of. Do we have a bargain?"

He'd hesitated. "Mean'n no disrespect, my Lord, but wot sort of *projects*?" His da' had always said that, even if he never had much, he could look any man in the eye and not be ashamed. Turner desperately needed work, but he'd spend his days in the stables before he'd shame his da'.

Castlereagh had smiled, clapping him on the shoulder. "You're a good man, Turner. Let me tell you straight: I won't ask you to do anything that's not in the best interests of our country, nor anything that will keep you lying awake in the wee hours of the morning." He squeezed Turner's shoulder, looking him straight in the eye. "You have my word on it."

Well, thought Turner, pulling his cap down a little further against the morning chill, *it 'adn't turned out quite that way, 'ad it?* In the almost ten years he'd handled *projects* for the Foreign Secretary, he'd done things he wasn't proud of. He'd stolen items from some men's quarters and placed papers, maps and money in others. He'd followed men – and sometimes women – and reported on who they met and where. He'd handed sealed envelopes to shadowed figures in dark alleys, and accepted them from others. He'd arranged things for men with foreign accents and even more foreign ways, men whose carnal requirements could not be satisfied in the usual manner. And several times he'd delivered messages in ways calculated to make sure they were fully understood. Henrietta knew of some of this, though only in the vaguest way; but he assured her that he knew what he was doing.

But he'd never killed a man, or worse, a dog. His instructions had been plain. "No one is likely to be there between 7:00 pm and 10:00 pm on a Thursday night. Find a way into Byron's rooms. Locate his journal, which you will find in the center drawer of his writing desk. Take it and get out quick as you can. And if you see any letters to or from his sister Augusta Leigh, take them as well."

Simple. He'd brought tools, which he carried in a cloth bag looped across his chest, in case he needed to force a window or break a lock, but they weren't needed – a window in the servants' quarters had been ajar. Nor had it been difficult to locate Byron's study.

But he didn't expect the dog and, in the darkness, didn't seen him until he was frozen by a low growl. "Easy boy," he'd murmured, extending his hand to give the giant a good sniff. What he got instead was another growl and a frightening baring of teeth. He'd grabbed the first thing that came to hand – a walking stick that rested against the wall by the door – and, as the dog lunged, used it to defend himself. He hadn't meant to kill him, but he'd heard the crack as the heavy stick struck bone. The dog collapsed at the blow, jerked spasmodically for a few moments, then lay still.

He was shaken, but the damage was done. He found the journal, which shared the drawer with what looked to be a manuscript bound at the side with sturdy, double-stitched thread. It was then he heard the sound of the front door opening. Moving fast, he tucked the journal into his bag and, on an impulse, took the manuscript as well. Grabbing the stick and moving as silently as he could, he edged down the hall past the staircase, concealing himself just inside the bedroom door. When Byron paused at the top of the stairs he'd struck, hoping to render him senseless.

He was stunned at how quickly Byron reacted, and at how capable he was in a fight. He figured a poet wouldn't put up much of a struggle, but Byron had put the lie to that and it had been all he could do to get out in one piece. His flank was tender where Byron had punched him, and his hip was still bruised from the fall he took on the stairs. He wondered whether Byron was feeling the effects of their struggle. He hoped not – he'd already killed the man's dog.

The sun was rising and Castlereagh still hadn't arrived. Using his glove, he wiped the dew off the bench and eased himself down. "It's still dark, Quentin," Henrietta had called after him as he slipped away, her voice muffled by blankets and pillows. "Can't the Fixer meet you at a decent hour? Or is 'e one of them who can'a expose himself to the sunlight?" She knew he was upset; it was clear enough when he returned home that night. But she didn't ask him about it, just got him a pint and leaned against him as he slowly drank. He sighed. She was better than he deserved.

He'd seen no letters to or from Byron's sister, but Turner had reviewed the journal and figured he knew which entry Castlereagh would find most interesting. Opening the volume, he turned to Byron's entry of 2 November, which by now he knew almost by heart.

> *How close the line between love and sin – how blurred the distinction between drama and farce! Last night's scene with Augusta was nothing short of catastrophic, yet – particularly in the retelling, if I ever have the courage and can disguise the actors – it could have been played to ribald approval as Commedia Dell'Arte! That passion exists between us there can no longer be any doubt; and excepting the consummation, blazing desire has obliterated the fainter glow of mere familial bonds. Still, how strange to feel relief at passion's thwarting – is this the cost of conscience, or its saving grace? She's gone tomorrow, back to her loving children and feckless husband. For the life of me, I don't know whether to grieve, rejoice or follow.*

Turner slipped the note back into his pocket. That the poet lusted for his sister was clear enough – but had he fucked her? Turner wasn't certain from the journal entry, and he'd seen nothing to resolve the question the night he'd watched Byron and his sister from the street outside her rented flat. He sighed – it wasn't his business, and anyway, he was more concerned with the fate of his own soul.

He considered the manuscript – he still wasn't sure why he'd taken it, and had read only the first few chapters. It was an adventure story of sorts and more than a little entertaining, though there were portions he wasn't sure he understood. But it didn't seem to have anything to do with Byron and his sister, and he decided not to mention it to the Fixer – at least not until he finished reading it. He knew Castlereagh well enough to understand that withholding the manuscript – withholding anything, for that matter – wouldn't serve him well if he was found out. But he didn't care – he'd done enough for the bloody Foreign Secretary. Too much.

He heard the scuff of shoes on gravel. As he started to rise, he felt a firm hand on his shoulder. "Morning, Turner, don't get up." The Fixer sat down next to him and dug his hands deep into his coat pockets, hoping to ward off the dawn's grey chill. Half-turning, he gave Turner a vacant smile. "How are Henrietta and your lovely girls?"

CHAPTER 48
Enemies Visible and Invisible

THEY'D STOPPED to rest and to eat some of the bread, cheese and olives Iphigeneia pressed on them as they hurried out of Pentias. "Get them to Antirrio, Panos," she'd directed. "To Nico. He'll know how to get them across the gulf."

"Yes, Mana," Panos said, stuffing the provisions into his bag. "My uncle," he explained to Byron and the others. "Always to have the good food and drink, and to laugh."

Iphigeneia wasn't done. "Panos, take care not to let his shrew of a second wife Zehra learn who they are or what they might be worth to the Turks. I tried to warn Nico; it's bad enough she's *Ahıska Türkleri*, but she's false and stupid in equal parts as well." Iphigeneia shook her head. "The woman would sell her eyes for a house with a view!"

She embraced each of them in turn and then, looking every part the worried mother, hugged her son fiercely. "Be careful, Panos," she admonished, brushing a few stray locks off his forehead. "I'll expect you back here in no more than four days' time, so don't you keep me waiting!"

As the others ate, Byron sat quietly, his knees drawn up to his chest. Although he felt a little stronger, he was still weak from the ravages of the fever. But more than that, he felt strange in a way he did not quite understand.

As long as he could remember, he'd harbored a detachment that bordered on alienation. He felt, at times, less an actor in Life than a critic, and a bloody contemptuous one at that. Even in the company of friends, to whom he appeared a model of gaiety, he felt a loneliness that reached deep into his core, and which he had come both to abhor and to fear. This was why, with Dionysian determination, he so often and so recklessly plunged into the river of Life, extracting its pleasures and enduring its pains. Better to be carried away by the current, he had long ago resolved, than to stand numbly on the bank.

In the way that some people learn to live with depression, or with the pangs of a nervous anxiety, he'd grown accustomed to a constant, low-grade agitation, a creeping despair that, having acknowledged the world's folly, it was useless – or worse, fraudulent –to adhere to its conventions. He was revolted by the seeming triumph of sentiment and hypocrisy, which he despised in equal measure, expressing his revulsion through a vehement intemperance and an almost reflexive defiance of authority. If Pope's scathing verse was the product of a dwarf's resentments, what of his?

But now, altogether unexpectedly and for reasons he did not yet understand, he felt the familiar detachment but none of the customary agitation. While he could not claim to be *content* – given the state of things, that would make him no better than the charlatans and fools he despised – he felt an unaccustomed acceptance. Could it be that, having felt Death's panting breath so close, a slate had somehow been swept clean? Certain he was that no man salvaged by the valor of Panos, or graced by the generosity and courage of Iphigeneia, could walk away unchanged.

He felt as though a headache that had pressed on the back of his skull for decades had unaccountably relented. It was disconcerting, this feeling that his frenzies were past, that he had outgrown the role he had taken on so long ago. He allowed himself a wry smile. It also seemed rather at odds with the customary urgency with which one flees for one's life.

"Byron – are you listening? What do you think?" Hobhouse tossed an olive pit, which struck him in the chest. "And what the bloody hell are you smiling about? Are you feeling alright?"

"Um, sorry, lost in my own head." He grinned. "An unsavory neighborhood, that – best not to wander there too long. Think about what?"

"Why the Turks want you dead, for starters."

"I thought you put it pretty well to Iphigeneia – I'm supplying the rebels and might galvanize support for their cause in England."

Hobhouse snorted. "Please, Byron – be serious. I was just trying to save our lives. While your efforts are unselfish and heroic, they seem unlikely to have more than a passing impact on events. Killing you, on the other hand, might outrage popular sentiment among the English, who are more than willing to mistreat you themselves but damn well don't want to see the bloody infidels take a turn."

"I can't say you're wrong. The Souliotes – damn their vulpine eyes! – can squander my expenditures far more quickly than I can replenish them."

"Which takes us back to where we started," Polidori noted grimly. "The Turks aren't fools, and are likely see the situation in much the same way. So, why have they put a price on your head?"

Panos, who'd been occupied drawing the outline of daggers in the dirt with a stick, looked up. "The Turks, to understand is not hard." Reaching for a hunk of bread, he added a slice of cheese. He extended his arm, offering it to the others. Getting no takers, he shrugged and tore off a bite.

Hobhouse made a rolling motion with his hand. "What do you mean, 'easy to understand?'"

Panos took his time, savoring the bread and cheese while Hobhouse waited. "For the Turks," he said at last, "or some of them, in the true – two things are that matter. Allah is one, but why he will smile if By-roon be killed I cannot say." Polishing off the bread and cheese, he brushed the crumbs from his shirt.

"And what's the other?" Hobhouse asked impatiently.

"Money. If to kill By-roon brings silver to the Turks, they will kill him, even if it the trouble brings." He looked at the Englishmen and shrugged. "It is so."

Hobhouse frowned. "So … you think someone else is paying the Turks to kill Byron?"

Once again, Panos shrugged. "To say, I don't know. But if no reason there is seeming that the Turks want him to be dead –"

"… then someone else wants me dead, someone with means." Byron scratched at his head, suspecting lice. "But who would want me dead? Besides Caroline, that is?" He smirked, amused at the idea. "She had opportunity enough to do away with me in England – and nearly succeeded!"

"The better question," interjected Hobhouse, "is why? Who would gain from your death – in Greece – in pursuit of Greek independence – at the hands of the janissaries?"

The question hung in the air. In the silence, Byron could hear the call of a woodpecker – *kiu–kiu–kiu* – and the soft rustle of wind in the trees. He closed his eyes, savoring the warmth of the sun on his face and the herbal, piney scent of the woods. And suddenly, he remembered something – something that he hadn't focused on at the time, but that, like a tiny splinter, had been bothering him nonetheless.

"Blaquiere – you remember him, don't you Hobby?"

"Sure, big guy, former naval captain – he and Bowring founded the Greek Committee in London. They were odd bedfellows, I thought, but quite persistent." He looked quizzically at Byron. "What about him?"

"Well, when we were finishing up our initial meeting in my rooms in London, I asked Bowring a question about how the *Porte* viewed matters. Blaquiere answered – quite cogently, I thought. But it was interesting; he said that the Ottoman's *reis effendi* had referred to Gregory – you know, the murdered Greek Orthodox Patriarch? – as 'the Sultan's Wolsey.'"

"So?"

"So, how would he have known that? I've been following events here closely for quite some time, and I don't recall seeing any such comment in the papers. Blaquiere said he'd visited the region to survey the situation and had talked to some of the rebels. But he wouldn't have had access to a high official of the *Porte*."

Hobhouse stared at Byron. "You think ... you don't think ... what are you saying?"

"I'm not sure, but there's something more. When Blaquiere first started talking he gave this little speech about the Huguenots, and how they'd fled persecution in France to settle in Ireland. Anyway, he said that his father had served in the government–"

"The British government?"

"Yes, the British government. That he'd served in the government, had been in Ireland at the time of the Irish Rebellion in 1798, and knew Castlereagh." He struggled to his feet, his side still tender, and began to pace, thinking it through. "If his father knew Castlereagh, and he – Blaquiere, I mean – described himself as 'a loyal subject' of the Crown, well, maybe he did as well."

"If anyone in England would have known that the Sultan thought the Patriarch his Wolsey," Hobhouse interrupted, connecting the dots, "it would be Castlereagh. He'd have people in Constantinople, and no doubt get regular dispatches containing all sorts of information."

"Blaquiere did everything he could to sell me on the Greek Committee. To convince me that I could make a difference here. If Blaquiere knew Castlereagh – if he might even have been working for him – that suggests that Castlereagh himself wanted me here."

Polidori seemed skeptical. "Why would Castlereagh want Byron to take on this cause? Why would he want him in Greece? And most pertinent of all, why the bloody hell would he want him murdered by the Turks?"

Panos had been following the conversation with the alertness that comes from having to understand not merely the matter under discussion but the language itself. "The Patriarch, Gregory? His name – what is the word, for to make the name on metal?"

"Engrave?" guessed Polidori.

"His name is – engravered – on the swords of many who fight against the Turks. In his life, he did not much do for to help the rebellion. But in death ...."

Byron stopped in his tracks, staring at Panos. He looked at Hobhouse, then at Polidori, turning it over in his mind. "It's almost too cynical," he said so softly that the others had to strain to hear him, "even for Castlereagh."

"What?" urged Hobhouse and Polidori in unison.

"Well, Panos' point about Gregory got me thinking about martyrs. What if Castlereagh wants to intervene in this conflict, but knows he lacks sufficient popular support in England?" He squinted, trying to coax a logic from the tangled facts. "If I were murdered by the Turks – an Englishman, a peer, and, if I may be forgiven some immodesty, a celebrity with a public following – might that not put some wind in the sails of a more assertive policy in the region?" He paused and offered a grim smile. "And if such a scheme incidentally removed a thorn from the wily bastard's side, so much the better, don't you think?"

"Come on, Byron – do you really believe that the British government conspired to have you murdered, here in Greece, as an element of its foreign policy?" Polidori shook his head. "You left England of your own accord, though admittedly, under legal and financial duress. Was that Castlereagh's doing as well?"

Byron scowled – as far as he knew, Castlereagh had had no direct involvement in the matters that compelled him to leave England. Still, if Castlereagh was anything at all he was an opportunist. He would have been aware of the storm clouds of scandal that had gathered around Byron, and of Byron's views on the legitimacy of the Greeks' struggle for independence. Maybe he saw an opportunity and took it? Or maybe his hands had turned the wheel from the start?

He had another thought. "Hobhouse, think back to your time in the Commons."

"Before you cost me my seat?"

"Yes, and ruined your life, I know. Sorry. Who was Castlereagh close to? Particularly among the King's ministers?"

Hobhouse scratched at his temple. "Addington, I'd say, was closest to him. They were both efficient, both ruthless – kindred spirits."

"As Home Secretary, doesn't Addington have jurisdiction over prosecutions under the sedition statutes?"

"He does. But to my amazement, you were never charged with sedition."

"No, but Leigh Hunt was. Over his publication of *The Vision of Judgment*." Noting Polidori's blank look, Byron briefly described Southey's celestial vindication of George III, a fawning abomination of a poem that left even Tory critics aghast.

"And to top it all off, Southey included an introduction to his poem in which he condemned my verse as immoral and perverse, and yours truly as 'Satanic.' I couldn't leave such rot unchallenged, so I wrote and Leigh published my own *Vision*, which satirized Southey and George both." Byron frowned. "Anyway, Castlereagh and Addington would have known that Leigh and I are good friends."

"I don't know, Byron." Polidori remained unconvinced. "So, they went after Hunt. How does that prove they sought to force you into exile?"

"Prove it? That's a high bar. But it's another piece of a puzzle that is starting to look like a picture. And I've still another piece for you." Byron, who had resumed his pacing, strode over to the seated Hobhouse. "Get up, Hobby – the brain works better when you move."

As Hobby lumbered to his feet, Byron put his hand on his friend's arm. "When Melbourne raised the issue of an action for – what's it called, 'criminal conversation'?"

"Yes. Makes it sound more sinister than amatory, doesn't it?"

"Hmmm. Anyway, the attorney he hired, Robert Gifford – you know him, right?"

"Not well. We overlapped in Commons for a short time, when I represented Westminster and he represented Eye. We didn't agree on much; he was born a Tory, and apparently nothing in his experience led him to question it."

"Well, as I'm sure I told you, he wrote me a letter laying out Melbourne's grievances and demanding redress. Just a few nods to the details of my affair with his client's wife, but lots of legal hitherto's, aforesaids and therefore's, including a fair number in Latin. All intended to intimidate, I assume."

"Right. I think you told me you tossed it on the fire."

Byron grinned. "I may have said that for effect. In fact, I gave it to my attorney. But that's beside the point. The interesting thing is that the letter contained a rather queer paragraph, right at the end. I don't remember it precisely, but the thrust of it was that, so long as my land and properties continued to be held in my name and I remained in England and subject to legal service there, I would be in legal jeopardy."

Hobhouse, who had embarked on some half-hearted pacing of his own, stopped short. "Really? That *is* unusual – it's not something I'd put in a letter to a potential target of litigation."

"Why not?" asked Polidori. "Sounds pretty bellicose to me."

"It seems that way on the face of it," Hobhouse agreed. "But it rather clearly apprises the target – Byron – that were he to sell off his holdings and retire to the Continent, he would no longer be subject to legal process, and his wealth and reputation would no longer be at risk. At least not from Gifford's client."

"Exactly." Byron shook his head. "It struck me as strange at the time, but other matters demanded my attention and I didn't dwell on it. Now it's beginning to make sense, as does Gifford's involvement."

"Gifford? What about him?" Polidori still looked confused.

Byron started to respond but Hobhouse beat him to it. "Gifford's a couple of decades younger than Addington. After he was called to the Bar, he practiced law in Addington's shop for several years. Learned his trade from Sir Henry, and I'm pretty sure they've remained close."

"So, let me get this straight," Polidori said slowly, getting to his feet. "You two believe that the British Foreign Secretary conspired with the British Home Secretary to put pressure on Byron to leave England.

That the scheme included the institution of an action for sedition against Byron's friend; a threatened lawsuit for criminal conversation against Byron himself; and a suggestion – communicated through an Addington protégé who not-so-coincidentally was selected to represent Lord Melbourne, the potential plaintiff – that by selling his property and fleeing to the Continent, Byron could avoid the unpleasantness and potential financial ruin of litigation."

Byron and Hobhouse both nodded. "Not bad for a doctor," Byron said grudgingly. "Go on."

"You further believe that Castlereagh, recognizing your genuine sympathy for the cause of Greek independence and operating through this Mr. Blaquiere, whose father was one of his contemporaries, created an opportunity for you to become more directly involved in the cause. That he recognized that, exiled from England, you would seek adventure – or fulfillment – where you found it; and that were an opportunity in Greece to present itself, you might well take it."

Again, nods from Byron and Hobhouse. "*I have enemies both visible and invisible,*" Byron murmured. In answer to a blank stare from Hobhouse, he offered a grim smile. "Cervantes."

Polidori remained focused on the matter at hand. "Finally," he continued, "and surely this is the most perverse aspect of the plot, you believe that once in Greece, Castlereagh arranged to pay off the Turks to have you murdered."

"Yes," Byron confirmed. "Presumably, in a manner that could not be traced back to Castlereagh or to the British government."

"And he did this so that, by serving you up as a martyr to the cause of Greek independence, he could rally support in the Commons to intervene on behalf of the Greeks against the Turks."

"Precisely." Byron, now deadly serious, laid his hand on Polidori's shoulder. "I'm sorry, John. Hobby. If this is even partly true, it seems I've been nothing more than a pawn, and through my gullibility and vanity–"

"Oh, shut up, Byron." Hobhouse broke into a broad grin. "First of all, we're here because we want to be, and for a cause whose lustre is dimmed by none of this." He held up his palm, forestalling argument.

"Second, how could you have known, or even suspected anything like this? I can hardly make sense of it myself."

"Third – and this is the important thing – if this becomes known in England, if it can be proven, it could very well lead to the fall of the present government. Think of the headline: 'Tory Government Plot to Murder Famed Poet!'"

Rising to his feet, Panos shouldered the pack containing their provisions and some extra clothes. "There will not to be returning to England," he said, "unless first we are to Nico's in Antirrio. If the Turks will find By-roon, him and us too they will kill. So, we walk, and now to make no noise."

As they turned to go, heading east towards Antirrio, he muttered, almost to himself but so all could hear. "The Greeks, I always think, are very smart, but to trust not much. But compare to you English? We are only the babies!"

CHAPTER 49
Caria

THE CORRIDOR *seemed to go on forever, and as he hurried to catch up to the slave girl – Caria, she'd called herself – Juan's mind raced through likely scenarios. It seemed inevitable that she would expose him to curry favor. But whose favor? Would she see this as an opportunity to insinuate herself into the Sultan's retinue? Or would she perceive her duty to lie with her current mistress, whose hand in Juan's appearance so far remained hidden? Was she alone in having seen through Juan's disguise; and if so, could he save himself by removing the threat? Could he kill her even to save himself?*

A hand emerged from a doorway so closely cut to the corridor wall as to be almost invisible. The hand gestured impatiently, and an urgent voice whispered "Come! Quickly!" Juan stepped through the door, which closed behind him with a muffled thump. Before him stood Caria, her arms crossed. Juan didn't think she seemed angry, exactly, but neither did she seem pleased, an impression that was promptly confirmed.

"Who are you – and don't you dare lie to me!" Seizing Juan's veil and head scarf, she pulled them away to expose his hair and face. Unaccountably, Juan felt violated and, for the first time in his young life, had a visceral sense of what it might feel like to be a woman.

"My name is Juan Pedro Calderón de Castilla, and I am from Seville." She looked at him blankly. "Seville. In Spain. It's a city."

Caria flushed. "Yes, I know of Seville – do you think me uneducated, or stupid?"

"Well," Juan stammered, "the way you looked at me, I thought maybe –"

"I looked at you that way because you're a Christian man, hiding within the Sultana's quarters, pretending to be a woman!" She reached out and fingered Juan's blouse. "And wearing the Sultana's own clothes, though I have to tell you, I'd have chosen a different color."

Turning her back to him, she walked over to a circular table of polished rosewood, whose outer circumference encircled a raised inner core on which rested an enormous bowl of fruit. Plucking a couple of figs from the bowl, she tossed one to Juan.

"So?" she asked, popping the fig into her mouth.

"So, what?"

Caria rolled her eyes skyward, as tutors sometimes do when confronted with an uncommonly dim-witted pupil. "So, what are you doing here, in the Sultan's harem, disguised as a woman?" She raised her hand to her mouth, her eyes widening. "Are you an assassin, here to murder the Sultan? An agent of the janissaries, perhaps?"

"No, no! Nothing like that. I'm a slave, purchased just today by the Sultana."

In as few words as he could, Juan described how he'd been captured by pirates, brought to the slave market to be sold, almost lost his life after precipitating a near riot, and then been saved by the Sultana's intervention. He told how he'd been directed to disguise himself, and to let no one know him to be a man. Out of a sense of gentlemanly honor he said nothing of the Sultana's desire for him, or that he had spurned her advances.

"So, you see," he concluded, "I'm hardly an assassin. It's been a very strange few weeks. At this point, who I am seems increasingly fluid."

Caria, who'd been listening closely, began to pace. The room was small – just the table, some overstuffed pillows on which to sit, and a strange, backless chair. Affixed to the wall above the chair was a small cistern, from which dangled a rope and porcelain handle.

Curious, Juan approached the chair and, seizing the handle, gave it a sharp tug. He jumped back in surprise as a torrent of water gushed out of a newly-opened hole at the rear of the cistern and swept down the wall and into a cavity beneath the chair.

"Have you never seen a commode before? They don't have them in Seville?"

This time it was Juan who reddened. "Oh, sure, we have them – they just don't look quite like this one." He peered into the cavity under the chair but couldn't see where it led. "Where does the water go?"

Caria shrugged. "I don't know. Baba– have you met him? – says there's a river beneath the palace that empties into the Bosporus, and ultimately into the Sea of Marmara."

"I thought so. When we were brought here –"

"We? There's more of you?"

"Not of me, no. But Harry Dryden – you know, the soldier I told you about who took such bold action at the slave auction – the Sultana purchased him as well, and we were brought here together. Anyway, as we approached the dock under the palace, I thought I heard a faint rushing sound. Maybe it was the river?"

"Maybe. Or maybe someone finished their business and pulled the rope, just like you did. It doesn't matter anyway," she huffed with annoyance. "Why are we even talking about this?"

"I don't know, you brought it up."

"I did not bring it up, you did."

Juan was placid. "No, I merely asked where the water goes; it was you who mentioned an underground river and the Bosporus and the Sea of Marmara. Also, who are you, what are you doing here, and what do you want of me?"

Caria hesitated, surprised at this young Spaniard's composure. "I don't have to justify myself, Christian – it is you who has disguised himself and has the most to lose if discovered."

Juan inclined his head. "It is not my intention that you justify yourself, Caria – may I call you by your name?" He didn't wait for her consent. "To the contrary, I find myself at your mercy, and wonder only that you have not exposed me already." Idly, he reached out and tapped the dangling knob, which swung back and forth like a pendulum. "Since you've chosen not to do so – at least not yet – it occurs to me that perhaps you think I might be useful, though for what I cannot say. So – to ask you again – who are you, what are you doing here, and what do you want of me?"

Caria stilled the swinging cord. "Don't touch anything!" she grumbled. Turning on her heel, she crossed the room and settled down on a large purple and white pillow, gracefully folding her legs beneath her. Juan couldn't help but admire both her spirit and the fine shape of her calf.

"I too am a Christian," Caria began, "or at least I was. I am from Batumi, on the shores of the Black Sea. For four hundred years Batumi was the jewel of the Kingdom of Georgia, but after a century or two in which it was taken and then retaken by the Turks and the Georgians in turn, the Turks consolidated their hold a century ago. Batumi's people were reduced to vassals of the Sultan."

"Like the Greeks?"

"Yes, like the Greeks. Anyway, during the last Russo-Turkish war, Ottoman cavalrymen overran Batumi, and though they were beaten back I was taken from my family and, like you, sold at auction as a slave." Caria tossed her head, her braids dancing. "The Sultan liked my blue eyes – he has a weakness for the exotic, and said he'd never had a Georgian with blue eyes – and no doubt intended to bed me when I came of age."

"How old were you when you were taken?" Juan asked gently, then regretted it as Caria glared at him. Clearly, she neither expected nor welcomed pity.

"I was ten. When they came for me I fought, but that was just stupid. My mother knew as much, asking only that they treat me with respect. Which – mostly – they did."

Juan nodded. He felt the hairs rising on the back of his neck, and a knot in his gut. "Sometimes, I think that it is important to be stupid."

He approached and, glancing at the pillows, asked with his eyes. Caria nodded and he eased himself down beside her, folding his legs as she had. He felt awkward, sitting on pillows this way, but pretended it was second nature.

"How did you come to the Sultana's service?" he asked.

"I was sixteen, and the Sultan made it known that he wished to bed me. He'd taken Gulbayez as a wife only a few months earlier, and when she learned that the Sultan wanted me, she had a fit." She giggled – it was the first time Juan heard her laugh, and strangely, it made him want to kiss her. "Is that how you say it, to have a fit?"

"Anyway, she was very angry and wanted to have me put in a sack and dropped into the Bosporus. She would have, too, but Baba advised her that the Sultan would be displeased. He still wanted to bed me, and besides, he'd paid 200 piastres for me at the auction."

Juan leaned forward, almost falling off the cushion. "That's terrible," he muttered, rearranging himself in what he hoped might be a more stable position.

"What's terrible?"

"That you commanded a price of 200 piastres," he responded gravely. "Gulbayez paid only 300 for both Senor Dryden and me!" He was rewarded with another laugh, and noticed that the knot in his stomach had dissolved into butterflies.

"I'm sorry," he told her, "I shouldn't joke about such things. What happened?"

"She struck a deal with the Sultan. She told him she needed someone good with numbers, and that with my assistance she could reduce her expenditures by a quarter. The Sultan is most pragmatic – he has no difficulty finding a place for his seed, but to find someone who might curb this most profligate of his wives?" She smirked. "It was impossible for him to say no. So, for the last four years I have served the Sultana, and am responsible for ensuring that she spends no more than twice what the Sultan allows her."

Juan grinned. "A good arrangement for the Sultan and for Gulbayez as well. But I'm afraid it's likely I'll soon complicate your ledger."

"What do you mean?"

Juan swallowed. "The Sultana is quite displeased. I expect you'll need to write off her entire investment in me, and soon."

Caria angled her head, her eyes sharp. "You've only been here a few hours! You're annoying, yes – but already she wishes you dead?"

Juan decided that honor did not truly require that he shield Gulbayez. "Apparently – do not laugh, I beg you – the Sultana wished to, to couple with me. When I declined, she–"

"What?" Caria was incredulous. "You declined to couple with the Sultana? By Allah's grace, what is the matter with you?" She looked him up and down. "Does this garb signify something more than a disguise?"

"No! I am quite capable of loving, thank you!" After a moment's pause, he added hastily, "With women!"

"Was she not pretty enough for you then? Search day and night, and you will not find anyone who thinks her unattractive."

"That's not it." Juan sighed. "It's just that ... well ... I'm not a stud horse, to be bred as my master chooses!"

"You – not a stud horse? Your pretty chemise, slippers, scarf and veil say otherwise!" She laughed, but composed her face when she saw that Juan was blushing.

"Juan – if I might call you by your name as well – you have courage, though in this case I think perhaps your principles betray you." She folded her hands in her lap. "You were right, you know."

"Right about what?"

"That I thought you might be of use to me. But now, it seems that we may be of use to each other." She extended her hand, resting it on Juan's folded knee. Her touch would have been thrilling had both his legs not fallen asleep. "I can remain here as a slave no longer – it is not a bad life, but neither is it the life I choose."

"What are you suggesting?"

"That I help you escape the palace, and you help me get back home."

Juan broke into a broad grin. "Nothing would please me more. Particularly when I consider the alternative. But we need to find Senor Dryden. He is my friend; I cannot leave him here."

Caria started to object, but Juan was insistent. "It is necessary. Besides, Harry is very resourceful. If we escape, we are more likely to survive with him than without him."

Caria hesitated, then nodded. "It will be difficult, but perhaps there is a way." She withdrew her hand and rose gracefully to her feet. Juan moved to do the same and, his legs tingling electrically, almost fell down. If she noticed, Caria made no sign of it, handing him his scarf and veil. "Put these on and I'll take you to your quarters. I need to make some arrangements; I will return as soon as I can."

As she reached for the door, she had a final question. "Juan," she asked delicately, "do you happen to know, um, exactly when Gulbayez intends to do away with you?"

CHAPTER 50
The Turning of the Screws

For 'tis a low, newspaper, humdrum, lawsuit
Country, where a young couple of the same ages
Can't form a friendship but the world o'erawes it.
Then there's the vulgar trick of those damned damages.
A verdict, grievous foe to those who cause it,
Forms a sad climax to romantic homages,
Besides those soothing speeches of the pleaders
And evidences which regale all readers.

DON JUAN, CANTO XII

AS THE snows in the Lesser Caucasus began to melt and the door to invasion slowly opened, the cascading violence between ethnic Turks and Greeks continued to intensify. In a dispatch marked *Urgent – Foreign Secretary's Eyes Only*, Lord Strangford reported on the spiraling tensions between St. Petersburg and the Porte, venturing that, in the absence of a credible threat of major power intervention in the Greek rebellion, Alexander could move by late June or early July.

Castlereagh felt that he'd made progress towards convincing Parliament to authorize at least a limited intervention, but he still lacked the necessary votes. What was wanted, he told his staff, was a catalyzing event – something to rally the popular support required to convince timid backbenchers to cast a vote that would send men into battle. Various ideas were bandied about, but they were either impractical or likely to take too much time. It didn't matter, as the discussion was a sideshow – Castlereagh had foreseen this moment and the groundwork had been carefully laid.

Only a few days after receiving Strangford's dispatch, a peculiar message appeared in the classified section of *The Times*. *"Wanted,"* the classified announced, *"a hero worthy of the name. If interested, reply by no later than 30 June, 1821."* The ad provided no further information, nor any way to reply. But no reply was necessary – the ad was nothing more than a signal, understood only by those for whom it was intended. The signal was received, and over the next several weeks a series of seemingly unconnected actions combined to turn the screws on Byron.

It started with the formal delivery of a letter. "My Lordship," a cherubic young man greeted him one morning as Byron left his flat, handing him an envelope sealed with red wax and bearing what he recognized as the Melbourne family seal. He tipped his cap. "Sorry to have bothered you, sir."

Byron broke the seal and, extracting the letter, scanned it quickly. "What is it, Byron?" inquired Jane Harley, Countess of Oxford, wife of the 5th Earl of Oxford and Byron's occasional and blessedly undemanding lover.

Byron paused. It will be a delicate thing, he thought, to explain to one married lover – no matter how relaxed she might be – that he might soon be sued by the husband of another. "It's nothing, Jane," he said dismissively, sliding the envelope into the pocket of his grey tailcoat. "The King perseveres for naught; he can beg all he wants, but I shall never serve in his bloody government!"

Only a few days later, Byron's friend Leigh Hunt called at his flat. Hunt, who was well known for his radical politics, had published Byron's scathing reply to Southey, *The Vision of Judgment*, in the inaugural issue of *The Liberal*. Byron greeted him warmly and, when they were seated in Byron's study, asked how the new literary periodical was faring.

"Not well," Hunt replied gloomily. "My brother and I misapprehended the costs of printing and distribution. We shall have to sell twice what we might reasonably expect just to break even."

He fixed Byron with a baleful look. "Worse, Addington's apparently decided to make an example of me – I received notice last week that I am to be prosecuted for 'seditious libel,' the evident consequence of having criticized the government's enthusiasm for the flogging of its soldiers and sailors."

Byron shook his head. "A great honor, Leigh – a man should rightly be judged by the quality of his enemies, and Addington is a scoundrel of the highest order. But are your views on flogging the sole accusation? You're not the first critic to question whether whipping the poor sods is the best way to ensure their loyalty."

Hunt's eyes were downcast, and his answer was so soft Byron had to strain to hear it. "Well, that's why I've come. The government has also taken issue with *The Vision of Judgment*, which they contend dishonors the memory of the late King and impugns the dignity of the Crown."

Byron sighed – Murray had anticipated this, had warned him. "Leigh, I'm sorry, this is an outrage."

Hunt nodded. "We both know it to be nonsense. I suppose it's a sign of the times."

"Well, it cannot go unchallenged. We shall engage Henry Brougham, who's had some success defending these cases."

"Byron, I can't afford Henry Brougham. I can't afford his cat."

Byron was firm. "Nevertheless, you shall have to. You shall pay the cat's fee, and I shall pay Brougham's."

Hunt reached out and took Byron's hand in his. "You have always owned my respect, Byron; you now own my gratitude as well."

He let go, lacing his fingers together nervously. "But there is something you should know. Addington's man – Geoffrey Godfrey is his name – met with me to 'represent' the Crown's position. While he promised nothing, he implied that were I to withdraw the first volume of *The Liberal*, and undertake never again to publish any of your verse, the Crown might 'be inclined to leniency.'"

Stunned, Byron was silent for a few moments, thinking it through. "Leigh," he said at length, "if you can get a solid commitment from this Godfrey, you should agree to his terms."

"No, Byron. I don't intend to be bullied."

"Nor does the lamb intend to be eaten. But that's just what the wolf will do."

The following day, Byron rose early and, after sending the letter from Melbourne's lawyer to his own, spent the morning in his study working on *Don Juan*. A few minutes after noon, Fletcher knocked as the echoes of the mid-day church bells faded. "Fletcher!" he exclaimed, setting his pen on the narrow wooden tray he'd had made for that purpose, "how thoughtful of you to synchronize your arrival with that of the infernal bells. I tell you – Papist, Methodist, Lutheran, Calvinist, it makes no difference in whose name they peal – they are all a cacophonous plague!"

Fletcher nodded, more or less inured to Byron's rants. "Quite so, sir. If only these churches would emulate the Jews, who take care not to draw undue attention to their devotionals." He handed his employer a letter. "This arrived a few minutes ago, my lord. I thought you might wish to see it right away." Fletcher bowed and took his leave.

It was a letter from Kinnaird. *"As you know too well,"* his banker wrote,

> *it has become increasingly difficult to put off your creditors, whose patience can no longer be purchased with token payments. Still, I was surprised yesterday to receive a letter from a solicitor in Nottinghamshire who purports to speak for the largest of your*

creditors, including the money-lenders in London and Leeds; the refitters, upholsterers, carpenters and other tradesmen involved in your extensive renovations to Newstead; your erstwhile bookseller Mr. Miller; Goodall & Sons, the London coachmaker; and Dr. Marsden, whom you will recall as the long-serving physician to your long-ailing mother. For some reason, they have chosen this moment to issue a collective ultimatum.

On behalf of his clients, the solicitor professes a willingness to make one final attempt to resolve your debts over a limited period of time – he suggested no more than thirty days – and at what he characterized as a 'modest' discount. Failing that, he intends to take legal action against you, including by way of a reference of these matters to the sheriff.

Byron, the sale of Newstead can be delayed no longer. This has become a serious matter, and I beg you to give me your authorization to proceed post haste.

Awaiting your prompt reply, I remain, most urgently,
Kinnaird

Byron groaned, tossing the letter aside. Sales of *Don Juan* were still brisk, and had stoked demand for his other verse as well – income wasn't the problem. But Newstead was nothing more than a hole into which limitless monies could be shoveled and, as Kinnaird had pointed out many times, his expenses were and had forever been extravagant. He felt hemmed in, and knew it to be a predicament largely of his own making. Taking his pen in hand, he composed a reply to Kinnaird:

Douglas,

Were it not for your advice, and the value that I place on our friendship, I might prefer to hold out indefinitely, content in the knowledge that – whatever misfortune such a course might entail – my creditors too would be sorely inconvenienced. However, as I am unwilling to embarrass you, and reject self-destruction as a stratagem, I will agree to the sale of the Newstead property and furnishings, on the condition that, having spent so much time, effort and money on the project, they be sold as a package. Get what you can, as quickly as you can, and if a portion remains after the voracious appetites of my creditors have been sated, perhaps we'll spend it on dinner, or a modest claret.

"With warm regards and sober resignation, I remain, your friend and client,

Byron

⁂   ⁂

Surprisingly enough, the final blow – or, as Byron later referred to it, the *coup de grâce* – was delivered by Caroline Lamb. He had not spoken with Caroline since he ushered her from his flat in April, and though his friends had warned that she had embarked on a campaign of slander against him, he had done his best to ignore it. But over the past few weeks he had been met rather coldly at dinners and parties, and there were others to which he wasn't invited at all. It was a marked departure from the fawning attention to which he'd become accustomed. Despite his breezy dismissals – "These events are a frightening bore and a staggering waste of time," he assured Moore and Hobhouse, "it would be a relief to be done with them!" – he felt cut to the quick.

In mid-June, Augusta spent the weekend in London. On a balmy weekend evening, she and Byron attended a party at Holland House, the grand mansion that Lady Holland shared with her prominent Whig husband Henry Fox. Heads turned as he and Augusta entered the grand salon, and Byron saw ears bend to lips and disdain color disapproving faces. Glancing at Augusta, he could see that she felt it too, so rigidly did she hold herself.

As they drifted like ghosts through the salon, he squeezed her arm. "A sorry lot, these," he whispered as a servant passed by holding a silver tray laden with champagne. Securing two glasses, he and Augusta drank together in silence as the party swirled about them.

"Byron, Augusta! How good to see you!" They turned to see Caroline Lamb threading her way through the crowd. Bursting with her usual nervous energy, Caroline seized Augusta's hands and pulled them to her chest. "It is *such* a relief to see you here together – I feared that with so much salacious gossip about, you might choose to keep to yourselves!" Releasing Augusta, she offered a gloved hand to Byron, who dutifully pressed it to his lips, half-expecting the poisonous taste of bitter almonds.

"Gossip, Caroline?" Byron's voice was cold. "I never knew you to trade in such nonsense."

"Oh, I don't, Byron," she said brightly, winking at Augusta, "except when it's me that it's about." She glared at a couple who had sidled close, perhaps hoping to eavesdrop on their conversation – they glared right back but moved off. "Still, these rumors are more vicious than most, though far less credible, particularly to those who know you both."

"What are you talking about, Caroline?"

"I make it a practice not to repeat such tripe, Byron. But I suppose that you and Augusta have a right to be informed." Caroline glanced about and lowered her voice to a whisper. "It is said – I do not know the source – that your love for Augusta, and hers for you, goes beyond that which is proper for siblings." As she spoke, Caroline's eyes were fixed on Augusta's, but if she expected Byron's sister to gasp or faint, she must have been disappointed. Augusta remained composed, her expression impassive.

"I do not believe it for a moment," Caroline continued, "you both must know this to be so! Still, even the most scurrilous of rumors may be credited by the gullible, or by those whose existing opinions require validation."

Augusta smiled. "My brother has a talent for speaking truly, Caroline, which, however noble, earns him the enmity of the powerful. As for me, my reputation is of no consequence to those who seek to use one Byron to wound or silence another." She reached for Byron's arm, and moved close. "I have nothing to hide, and no reason to be ashamed. Let them talk."

As Byron listened to his sister's bravado, he felt a cold clutch of ice in his gut. He had said nothing of the break-in; he hadn't wanted to worry her. But he recognized that his journal had been stolen for a reason, by someone who knew what they were looking for. And if they knew what to look for, and where, such information had to have been provided by someone close to him. Or who had been close to him once. While there were many who might wish him harm, he could think of only a very few who might play Brutus to his Caesar.

"Caroline, from whom did you hear these rumors? For when I find out, I shall call them to account for their lies in an action for slander. And you shall have an opportunity to prove your friendship by testifying on our behalf. After all, as a friend and intimate to us both your testimony would be powerful evidence of the unsullied nature of the relationship that exists between Augusta and myself."

Caroline hesitated, and in the silence the sounds of the room – the pianist softly playing a Bach concerto; the rise and fall of a score of murmured conversations; the laughter of men courting women, and of women flattering men – seemed suddenly to have been amplified. In a gesture Byron recognized, she reached up to bother a ringlet of curls, absently twirling it with a finger.

"As I said, Byron, the source of these rumors is unknown to me." The lightness with which she had previously spoken was absent, and she leaned in, her voice low and grave. "But you mustn't create a forum in which these accusations can achieve broader exposure. You know that William has retained counsel, that he is prepared to bring an action against you for damages arising from our affair. I tried to talk him out of it but there is no reasoning with him on this – it's most unlike him."

"Yes, quite aware – I received a letter from his attorney. But what has that to do with this?"

"He ... we argued, it was awful. In a rage, he said that you have sinned, not merely against him under the laws of the realm, but against decency and the laws of God. And that he has proof, which he intends to use against you if you contest the suit." She shuddered, and Byron was reminded once more of her talents as an actress.

Augusta looked at Byron, waiting for a rejoinder which never came. Her eyes widened, the color draining from her face. "What does he want, Caroline? What will satisfy him?"

"He wants Byron out of his life, and mine." She swallowed, and tears welled in her eyes. *If she's acting,* Byron thought, *she's doing it exceedingly well.* "He suspects that I still love your brother," she whispered, her voice catching, "and that I always will. He told me that he will stay his hand, and that of his lawyer, only if Byron leaves England. And does not return."

Augusta started to respond, but Byron cut her off. "Caroline," he said in a firm voice, "thank you for your candor. I shall reply to Gifford's letter in due course. In the meantime, you can tell your husband this; if I choose to leave this gloomy isle, I shall do so when it suits me, and for my own reasons." Inclining his head, he took Augusta's arm and led her through the crowded room, heading for the door.

"Byron," Augusta whispered, "what was she talking about? What 'proof?'"

As they strode past Lady Holland, who peered at them curiously over a pair of long-handled spectacles, Byron nodded but did not pause to pay his respects. *She's a skillful hostess indeed. By opening her salon to the objects of so juicy a scandal, she's thoughtfully provided grist for a dozen prurient conversations.* "It's been a bad week, Augusta," he muttered in response, "truly, a very bad week." As they passed through the door into the cool night air, he pulled his coat more closely around him. "But just out of curiosity – *Come è il tuo Italiano?*"

CHAPTER 51
No Need to Bluff

He was a cold, good, honourable man,
Proud of his birth and proud of everything,
A goodly spirit for a state divan,
A figure fit to walk before a king,
Tall, stately, formed to lead the courtly van
On birthdays, glorious with a star and string,
The very model of a chamberlain,
And such I mean to make him when I reign.

DON JUAN, CANTO XIV

WHEN CAROLINE came downstairs, William was seated at the breakfast table reading *The Times*. A servant brought her tea, which she welcomed, and a bowl of oatmeal topped with molasses, which she pushed to the side. They sat in silence for several minutes. Finally, William set down the paper. "So, Caroline, how did it go at Lady Holland's last night?"

Caroline wanted to scream at him, to denounce him as Castlereagh's bloody pawn and tell him to bugger off. But she understood that that would be pointless; and besides, it had been she who had initiated this chain of events by lashing out at Byron through Southey. It was too late for regrets, and she had done her husband's bidding. "They were there, as you said they would be. Did Lady Holland require much persuasion?"

"None – I think she would have invited them anyway, you know, to spice things up a bit." He gestured at her oatmeal. "You should eat something, Caroline, you're too thin."

"Perhaps you'll understand if I'm not hungry."

Lord Melbourne shrugged. "Did you manage to deliver the message?"

"Yes, I *managed* it well enough. You gave me little choice, did you? What was it you said? 'Do this for me, Caroline, and perhaps both our marriage and your present annual income can be preserved.' For God's sake, William; I knew you to be ambitious and capable of cruelty, but I had no idea you'd ruin me or make me a supplicant solely to curry favor with that weasel Castlereagh!"

"Your pique is presumptuous, Caroline – was your catastrophically public affair with Byron my doing? Besides, simply because Castlereagh wishes to exile Byron for reasons of his own does not mean that I do not wish it as well." He stared at her with a contempt that chilled her to the bone. "Do you think I've relished the role of a cuckold?" He did not wait for a reply. "How did Byron respond?"

She no longer had the stomach for a fight. "He said he'd respond to your lawyer in good time, and that if he chooses to leave England it will be his own decision and made at a time of his own choosing." She was silent for a moment, recalling the details of her conversation with Byron and Augusta. "I think Augusta may have been a bit shaken when I said you had proof. Is it true, or are you bluffing?"

"You know me better than that," Melbourne reminded her as he rose from the table. "Why would I bluff when I hold all the cards?"

CHAPTER 52
An Accidental Encounter

When a man hath no freedom to fight for at home,
Let him combat for that of his neighbours;
Let him think of the glories of Greece and of Rome,
And get knock'd on the head for his labours.
To do good to mankind is the chivalrous plan,
And is always as nobly requited;
Then battle for freedom wherever you can,
And, if not shot or hang'd, you'll get knighted.

BYRON, STANZAS

NO MATTER how foul his mood, Byron made it a point never to slam a door. Always at extremes, his mother had slammed doors so regularly that, based on the volume and vibration, Byron could take the measure of her temper with barometric precision. As he left Murray's Albemarle Street office on an oppressively humid afternoon in early June, however, he was sorely tempted to rattle the windows on his way out.

"Look Murray," he had pressed his publisher, careful to keep the desperation from his voice, "there's little risk in it for you. The twelve cantos you've printed thus far have sold out three printings apiece, and I'm still just getting started."

"I know, Byron, and believe me, I have no concerns on that account." Murray tapped a ledger that sat before him on the desk. "But I publish dozens of authors, and if I pre-pay your royalties every single one of them will demand that I pre-pay theirs. I can't sustain that kind of cash outlay for long, and not all of my titles will sell as reliably as *Don Juan*."

"They don't have to know, Murray – and even if they did, have I not earned more favorable terms?"

Murray sighed. "You have been a tremendous asset to this house, Byron, and a good friend in the bargain. And I understand your financial predicament, though I agree with Kinnaird that the sale of Newstead Abbey should produce a significant sum. But that will take some time and, if Melbourne follows through on this legal action his attorney has threatened, those proceeds may themselves be at risk." Murray hesitated, torn between viewing the situation as a friend or as a businessman. The former won out, though not without a struggle. "Would you accept a personal loan?"

Byron shook his head. "I have already borrowed more than I should, and while I have no difficulty avoiding many of my creditors, I don't see how I can avoid my publisher. But be warned, Murray – in future, I shall demand an enormous bloody advance."

Albemarle Street was still on such a warm afternoon, and those who ventured out moved sluggishly, unaccustomed to the heat. Turning south toward Piccadilly, Byron had taken only a few steps when he heard someone call his name. He glanced up to see John Blaquiere striding across the street, his hand raised in greeting. Blaquiere was sweating and, in a modest concession to the heat, had exchanged his somber black waistcoat for one of white linen. He wore no hat, squinting into the afternoon sun as he approached.

"Lord Byron, what an unanticipated pleasure to see you. I pray all is well?"

"Quite well, thank you Mr. Blaquiere." Byron repositioned himself to put the sun at his side and gestured at the empty streets. "What brings you out in weather better suited for Spain or North Africa than our gloomy isle? Exhibiting more sense than usual, our countrymen seem to have taken refuge from the heat."

"Perhaps you underestimate them. It has been my observation that the English are capable of great perspicacity when given no other choice." Reaching into his pocket, he extracted a handkerchief and mopped his brow. "I suppose we should follow their example. But still, my lord, I'm pleased to have run into you. Have you given further thought to the proposal Mr. Bowring and I made to you a few months ago?"

"I have been following events closely – it is a sad thing to see the tender shoots of liberty so violently uprooted. I fear the rebels may be overmatched."

Blaquiere shook his head. "The thing is, the Turks are weak, and spread quite thin. Insurrection suppressed in the Morea springs to life again in the Peloponnese, and *vice versa*. Did you see that the Sultan, seeking reinforcements, has had to appeal to the Egyptian Pasha Mehmet Ali, who, if the rumors are to believed, has agreed to send his son Ibrahim to help suppress the rebellion. One can only imagine what the Turks must have agreed to give up in return."

"You make my point, Mr. Blaquiere. I do not see how I can make a meaningful contribution."

"We look at the same facts, my lord, but reach different conclusions. The Ottoman is an ancient tree whose roots have been rotted by incompetence and corruption. The appeal to the Egyptians proves it. Were any of the major powers to intervene, Ibrahim would turn tail and run, and the Porte lacks the means to put down the rebellion on its own. Your appearance alone – and perhaps a few brave and inspiring words, for which we know you to have a gift – is all that it would take to uproot the whole thing, root and branch."

"Come now, Mr. Blaquiere, you don't believe that. If that rogue Castlereagh can't muster the necessary support in Parliament, it seems unlikely that I can do so." Byron snorted. "He may be a tyrant, but he's not without political skills."

"My information, which Mr. Bowring can confirm, is that the Foreign Secretary has indeed made progress. It would take only the changing of a few votes – and mostly Whig votes at that – to tip the balance. As a student of history, my lord, you know better than most that a sudden change in the wind can alter the course of nations. But for a sudden typhoon at the eleventh hour, Genghis Khan would have overrun Japan; but for the unforeseeable heroics of Charles Martel, all Frenchmen might bow to Mecca."

Byron laughed. "I'm neither Khan nor Hammer, Mr. Blaquiere, though I appreciate the comparison!"

"It is not your military prowess that matters, but your reputation and your pen." Blaquiere lowered his voice. "What if I were to tell you that a force of over six hundred Albanian Souliote warriors is currently available for hire, and wants only outfitting and leadership to enter the fray on the side of the rebels? The committee has raised some funds and, if animated by leadership and some additional funding, this force could be in the field within a few months."

Byron pursed his lips. Since Bowring and Blaquiere's visit, he'd followed the situation in the Levant with even greater interest and had wondered – as he had for much of his life – whether he might not achieve something more important than scribbling. Yes, he was good at it, and felt ... unburdened ... each time he completed a poem. But could he not say the same after using the privy? From the start he had understood that writing was an escape; like drinking, or sex, it allowed him for a time to withdraw *himself* from *himself*. Still, the emptiness always returned, and he yearned to accomplish something more meaningful. And yes, if he was honest with himself, more *glorious*.

He was tired of England, tired of a viciously self-satisfied rectitude that rested on unearned pillars of lineage, title and property. Tired of shouting uselessly into the regressive wind of Regency politics. Tired of the damp and dreary fog, whose constancy made it seem as if the affairs of Nature were guided by Castlereagh himself. Tired of England's coldly calculating women, who so concerned themselves with the pedigree of the *terroir* that they paid scant attention to the qualities of the grape. In England – "this tight little island," as he put it to Moore – he was beset with financial, legal and social difficulties; and if these were largely of his own making, they were no less inconvenient. Blaquiere and Bowring believed that in the Levant he might contribute to the cause of liberty. Such an opportunity is not afforded to every man – had he the right to squander it?

Reaching into the pocket of his waistcoat, Byron extracted a card. "Douglas Kinnaird is my banker, and he has my trust. If you will provide him with an accounting of what you have raised to date and what you believe may still be needed, I will be in a better position to consider your proposal."

He handed the card to Blaquiere. "As you know, I spent time among the Albanians in my youth, and had occasion to meet several Souliote chieftains who had allied themselves with Ali Pasha. They were fierce in aspect, canny in their dealings, and, as best I could tell, armed to the teeth even as they slept." He grinned at Blaquiere. "If – *if*, mind you – I were to undertake a project such as this, the trick will be to allow the Souliotes to steal slowly enough to get good use from them before the money, provisions and equipment disappear or are entirely depleted."

Blaquiere broke into a broad smile; Byron had the impression that, were it not for the differences in their standing, the man might have hugged him. "Of course, my lord, I will turn to it at once. I am enormously pleased – and the cause we support is enormously fortunate – that you would consider involving yourself so directly. John – Mr. Bowring – will be beside himself."

Byron nodded as they shook hands. "Good day, Mr. Blaquiere. Probably best that you get out of the sun," he added, surprised to feel himself flush with the kind of optimistic excitement he often felt in the early stages of a seduction. "You Irish are better-adapted to the rain and clouds of your island."

"I have seen Phillips' handsome portrait of you in Albanian uniform, my lord. I hope you still have it, as the head-dress and shawl would protect you from the Ionian sun."

Byron laughed. "I do, Mr. Blaquiere, though I have had little occasion to wear it. Indeed, I suspect the shawl would receive far more use than the purple-hilted *yatagan* I held for Phillips."

Blaquiere smiled. "No doubt, my lord. Without detracting from the importance of what we hope you can achieve, it is unlikely that you will find yourself in need of a personal weapon – other than your pen, of course."

Blaquiere watched Byron turn the corner onto Piccadilly. Turning away to the east, the Irishman walked the few blocks to Castlereagh's office. After waiting for a few minutes under Reilly's watchful eye, the Foreign Secretary emerged from his office. "Come in Blaquiere, and let's be quick about it, I've much to do."

As Blaquiere followed Castlereagh into his office, he tried not to display his shock at the dramatic change in the Foreign Secretary's appearance. Normally elegant and refined, Castlereagh was disheveled, his auburn hair in a tangle and his waistcoat wrinkled and spotted at the hem with soot. There were circles under his eyes, and Blaquiere thought he detected a faint sheen of sweat on his brow. In the nine years he'd worked for Castlereagh, never had Blaquiere seen him like this. "How are you, your lordship?" he asked as Castlereagh circled around his desk and settled into his chair.

"Tired, Mr. Blaquiere. Tired." He waved at one of the chairs opposite his desk, but Blaquiere raised a palm.

"No need, your lordship, I'll not take up much of your time. I just wanted to let you know that I was able to engineer an encounter with Byron outside Murray's office."

"Good. How did he seem?"

"No different in affect – he's a charming one, isn't he? No wonder the ladies flock to him like bees to honey." Blaquiere wiped at his brow, which remained damp from the heat. "As you directed, I renewed our proposal, and flattered him that he might make a contribution commensurate with his self-regard."

"How did he react?"

"The hook's taken, I think. All that's left is to reel him in."

"Excellent. Did you mention the Souliotes?"

"Aye. You were right, he was intrigued. He fancies himself knowledgeable as regards the Albanians, and the idea of leading Souliote warriors into battle seemed to capture his imagination. Although to his credit, he expressed concerns over whether they were more likely to fight or steal."

"Very good. How did you leave it?"

"He gave me his banker's card and asked that I fill him in on the likely financial requirements." Blaquiere fingered Kinnaird's card. "Your lordship, I'm not sure what the budget is for this operation, but I believe we may need to provide some seed money if we wish to convince Byron that this endeavor is practicable from a financial standpoint."

Castlereagh waved dismissively. "That will not be a problem. I want you to prepare the document Byron requested and get it to his banker – Kinnaird, right? – within a day or two. Indicate that £7,500 has been raised to outfit and equip the Souliotes, and that an equal amount will be needed over the next six months."

Blaquiere whistled. "That's not an insubstantial sum, your lordship. You're aware of Byron's financial difficulties – indeed, you've played a role in exacerbating them. What if he can't manage it?"

"How did you know of my involvement in such matters?" Castlereagh demanded, suddenly agitated. "Who told you that?"

"Why, you did, your lordship." Blaquiere gestured to the chairs by the hearth. "We sat right over there and discussed every aspect of your plan. Do you not remember?"

Castlereagh leaned back and closed his eyes. "Yes, of course. As I said, I'm tired, the press of work hasn't – yes, I remember." He opened his eyes, and for a second, his stare was vacant.

"No matter," sighed Castlereagh, willing himself to refocus. "He's put Newstead Abbey up for sale, which should yield enough to pay off his creditors, complete the provisioning of the Souliotes, and support our Lord Byron in the extravagant manner to which he is accustomed. Especially in the Levant," he added sarcastically, "which, as I understand it, is less dear than Mayfair."

"Everyone knows that Newstead is a bit of a project," Blaquiere cautioned. "It may take some time for Byron to find a buyer, and I know you want him in place as quickly as possible. I worry that it may take him six months or more to sell the place."

Castlereagh shook his head. "No, he'll sell it – and at a good price – within the week."

"Oh? How can you be so sure?"

"Because, Mr. Blaquiere," responded Castlereagh, standing up to escort his visitor to the door, "I will arrange for a buyer."

CHAPTER 53
One Hell of a Woman

AS IT turned out, despite the not inconsiderable danger of being discovered, there were certain mitigating benefits to being a man disguised and hid in the midst of a Sultan's harem.

For one thing, the harem enjoyed in abundance the most exotic foods Juan had ever tasted. On one table stood plates of creamy roasted eggplant, rich with garlic; nutty hummus sprinkled with paprika; a golden spread of roasted breadcrumbs, crushed walnuts, cumin, red pepper and olive oil they called hihammara; tender grape leaves stuffed with rice, tomato and parsley; and tiny, three-cornered spinach tarts that disappeared in a single bite.

On another were roasted meats – lamb flavored with rosemary, the edges crisp from the grill; thin slices of chicken served with fragrant caramelized onion; minced beef with mint, baked apple and a spicy yoghurt; and flakey fish, served sizzling hot on cast iron skillets with fried shallots and spiced with tamarind and pink Himalayan salt.

On still another table were sweet breads and cakes topped with molasses and almonds; rich Kunafeh, a phyllo and semolina cake stuffed with some kind of soft white cheese and soaked in a sweet syrup; Baklava, a layered phyllo pastry filled with chopped nuts and drizzled with a golden honey; and bowls of red, yellow and orange confections sweetened with honey and molasses and dotted with fine powdered sugar.

There were other benefits as well. In the inner chambers that no man but the Sultan was permitted to enter, the Sultanas and their attendants wore what they wished – and often, very little at all. Despite his youth, Juan was no stranger to the female form, and had seen such things before. But in such proximity, and in such variety! Because he was a gentleman, and because he did not wish to give himself away, he tried hard not to stare, but every averting of his eyes simply brought a different wonder into view. Hoping that it might prevent his manhood from betraying him, he tried to think of unpleasant things.

After placing him in the care of a sober matron who introduced herself without so much as a smile as 'Mother of the Maids,' Caria had drawn Juan to the side. "If all goes well, I will return tonight, when all are asleep. Be ready." She looked past Juan's shoulder to the tables of food and the half-clad women who lounged on chaises or sat in pairs, whispering and laughing as they gazed with curiosity at the new slave girl. "Remember who you are," she admonished him, "and be sure to temper your appetites, as a woman would."

Juan gestured imprecisely at the pleasures behind him. "May I help myself?" he asked innocently. "One needs sustenance from time to time."

At sunset he heard the muezzin's call and joined the others in prayer. He ate as much as he could without being indelicate, though he saw that several serving girls laughed when he filled his plate for a third time. They prayed again upon the muezzin's call to Isha'a, and, yawning with fatigue, Juan collapsed onto the sleeping mat the 'mother of maids' assigned him, pulling a blue, satin-lined quilt to his chin. The last thing he remembered before falling into slumber was hoping that he wouldn't snore.

He was awakened by a booted toe. "Get up," a voice whispered harshly, "and make no sound, lest I kill you here and now!" Juan opened his eyes and looked up to see Baba standing above him. The eunuch stared at him impatiently, his arms crossed. Juan sat up, hoping to see Caria and that Baba might be part of her plan. But there was no sign of her, and when Baba drew his leg back a second time, Juan scrambled to his feet. "No need to kick me again, Baba – where are we going?"

Baba didn't answer, but turned and strode from the harem chamber with Juan at his heels. For a moment Juan considered trying to overpower the eunuch, but he had no weapon and the Nubian was so massive that even Dryden might be no match for him. He followed Baba down first one corridor then another until they came to the portal through which he and Harry had first entered the palace. No guards were in evidence and, opening the door, Baba gestured to Juan to proceed. Together, by the flickering light of the torches whose glow had greeted their arrival less than a day before, they descended the stone steps until they reached the half-moon dock at the edge of the water.

Juan's heart sank. On the dock, their wrists trussed behind their backs, stood Caria and Dryden. Two stone-faced sentries were posted at either end of the dock, perhaps fifty feet from where Gulbayez stood waiting. She wore a black, high-collared gömlek, a matching entari that fell to her knees, and şalvar of a blue so dark it might as well have been black. She's dressed like an executioner, Juan realized with a shiver.

As he and Baba approached, Harry offered a wan smile. Juan met Caria's eyes and had no difficulty understanding their message – Sorry, I did the best I could. He shrugged, and as he drew near saw a small boat, its oars docked, bobbing in the water behind them. Three burlap bags lay on the footboards and a coil of rope hung off one of the oarlocks. Juan understood this to be a very bad sign.

"Christian," Gulbayez demanded accusingly, "has your disrespect no limit? First you spurn me; then, when I show you the mercy of allowing you to live for a time, you conspire to flee."

"My disrespect?" Juan shot back, his anger quicker than his fear. "Does the Sultana command respect by threats of drowning or dismemberment?" His eyes flew to Caria and Harry. "Will the murder of innocents – neither of them complicit in the encounter that seems to have wounded the Sultana's pride – earn her the respect of others, or restore her own?"

"How dare you speak to me in this way, slave! Remember who I am!"

Juan did not flinch. He lowered his voice to ensure the attending guards could not hear. "I do remember, Sultana. I remember that, for a few moments, you discarded the robes of arrogance your position seems to require you to wear. I remember your voice softening, and your eyes welling with tears, as you confessed to feeling a prisoner in this grandest of palaces."

He smiled at Gulbayez, not with pity but with compassion. "She, who in that moment showed that power need not be arbitrary or cruel, was a woman who had no need to command respect, because she had earned it."

Gulbayez stood silent, and everyone present – Caria, Harry, Juan, even Baba – held their breath. Finally, Gulbayez gestured at Caria. "You would choose a clever slave girl over the wife of an Emperor? Is this the way in your land, to despise rank and to elevate the common?"

Caria's eyes narrowed and, pursing her lips, she appeared ready to speak her mind. Dryden stepped on her foot.

"Sultana, I did not – I do not – choose this girl; at least, not in the way you seem to mean it. We hardly know one another. But we do have something in common, which we share with your grace as well."

"I cannot imagine what slaves might share in common with one revered as Sister of the Moon and Flower of the Khan."

"No?" asked Juan. "Do we not share a wish to chart our own path? To love who we choose, rather than one to whom the giving of love is nothing but a dry obligation? You speak of respect – is it respectful to deny to others the freedom you covet for yourself?" Juan shook his head. "I have seen the Sultana's beauty with my own eyes, and know it to eclipse the splendor of the finest gold. I simply cannot believe that it is alloyed with the base metal of cruelty."

Gulbayez hesitated, and Juan could see that her fists were clenched, her nails sharp on her palm. After a few long moments, she unclenched them, revealing traces of blood.

"Christian," she said, gazing sadly at Juan, "you have acted and spoken in a manner that can yield but one consequence." She turned to Caria. "As for you, I did not pluck you from the Sultan's clutches only to see you betray me."

"I have served you well, and with honor, for more than four years," Caria replied. "Though I owed you a debt, it has been repaid; and now I

seek nothing other than to be free and to return to my home, as I know you wish to return to yours. But if your pride requires that I die, so be it."

Gulbayez stared at Juan, who stood before her with his head held high and his dark eyes steady. Caria stood beside him, and – almost without realizing what she was doing – took Juan's hand in hers, defiantly returning Gulbayez's stare.

Turning away from her own pride's reflection, Gulbayez seemed to decide. "Put them in the boat," she growled, turning to Baba, "and then in the river." She beckoned to Juan, who released Caria's hand and stepped forward.

Gulbayez raised her hand and brushed his cheek. "Such a pity," she whispered. "You rejected the first gift I offered – did you expect a second?" She grasped his hand and pressed her own against it, her blood streaking his palm. His eyes widened, meeting hers. After a moment his gaze flickered to his hand, and – almost imperceptibly – he nodded.

Exhaling, she released his hand and exchanged glances with Baba. Then, without another word, she turned away, returning to her confinement in the most opulent prison on earth.

The torches seemed to flicker as four held breaths were released together. Juan and Harry looked at one another, and at Caria; none of them were quite sure what had transpired, or what was to be their fate. Baba, however, did not seem in doubt. With a glance and a barked command, he dismissed the two guards. "Speak not of their death," he said sharply as they turned to go, "or I will say the same to your replacements."

When the sound of their footfalls on the stone steps had faded, he pulled out his blade, and Juan and Dryden both tensed, ready to throw themselves at the Nubian. "Quickly," Baba grunted, slicing away the cords binding Caria's and Dryden's wrists, "get in." Juan felt a rush of relief as first Caria, then he and Dryden, clambered awkwardly into the bobbing rowboat.

Untying the bow line, Baba lead the craft around the far curve of the dock toward the dark rock wall at its terminus. As they drew closer, Juan was able to make out the faint outline of a narrow channel, and could hear *the soft murmur of flowing water. When the boat was poised at the edge of the darkness, Baba stopped, maintaining his grasp on the line.*

"This channel leads to the Lycos River, which has run beneath this city since ancient times. The flow of the river will carry you to what was once the port of Theodosius, and thence to the Sea of Marmara." He gestured toward one of the burlap bags. "The Sultana bade me bring you your clothes, Christian."

He stepped forward to the edge of the platform, towering above them. "By Allah's grace, you have been spared. Do not abuse this gift by speaking of it to those who might seek to re-cast the Sultana's mercy as weakness. Despite my order, those two guards will whisper, and those who listen will believe that you were all justly sent to the bottom of the Bosphorus. Let your silence – and a few articles of the Sultana's borrowed clothing cast into the water – confirm this as truth."

Baba tossed the line into the boat and, extending his foot, gave it a shove. He watched in silence as Juan, Harry and Caria were engulfed by the hypogean darkness of the river. Juan glanced back as the massive Nubian faded from view. Juan was unsure what role Baba had played in their release but, even more than before, thought him a genii of the highest order.

As the boat drifted along with the current they were silent, astonished to be alive. It was Caria who finally broke the silence, turning to Juan and striking him on the top of his head with the flat of her palm.

"Have you lost your mind?" she demanded. "To speak that way to a Sultana – and not just any Sultana, but Gulbayez, who is known everywhere for her temper?" Laughing, she threw her arms around him and kissed him full on the lips.

Harry Dryden shifted to the center of the bench and, taking the oars, began the process of guiding them down the river in the darkness. He smiled at Caria and flashed a broad grin that Juan could feel more than see.

"I don't quite understand what you did back there, young Juan," he said with a mixture of affection and relief, "but I will say this: You are one hell of a woman!"

CHAPTER 54
The Finest in Antirrio

Between two worlds life hovers like a star
'Twixt night and morn upon the horizon's verge.
How little do we know that which we are!
How less what we may be! The eternal surge
Of time and tide rolls on and bears afar
Our bubbles. As the old burst, new emerge,
Lashed from the foam of ages; while the graves
Of empires heave but like some passing waves.

DON JUAN, CANTO XV

THE TOWN was silent so early in the morning, and as they walked Byron watched the pale smoke of his breath drift before him. Panos led them through pastures crisp with frost, gesturing towards sleeping cattle that looked like huge black rocks. At the edge of the village he paused, crouching behind a lavender hedge as tall as his waist.

"Antirrio," he whispered. They were on a gentle rise above the town, and in the pre-dawn glow the houses looked two dimensional, silhouetted against the sea beyond. Panos pointed past the nearest structures towards the waterfront, where a dozen fishing boats bobbed gently, their lines slipping into the water like eels. "Nico's house is there, almost close to the harbor."

Hobhouse pointed. "That faint line on the horizon. Is that the Peloponnese?"

"Yes. Maybe two miles across the *Korinthiakós Kólpos*."

"The Gulf of Corinth?"

Panos nodded. "Wait here. I will see to Nico's house, and soon to you come back." Slipping through a gap in the lavender he made his way down the hill, carefully edging past a low structure whose odor told of chickens.

Byron squatted in the dirt, reflexively cataloguing the scene before him. The faint pink of the creeping dawn; the floral scent of the lavender, strangely confused with the pungent stench of the chickens; the salty whisper of the wind in the trees, and the glistening frost on the voiceless grass. *Wordsworth would describe this well, and would doubtless imbue it with his usual breathless spirituality.* He chuckled. *That's fine for Wordsworth – for me, it's a perfect spot to set a naval encounter, or an escape from a cataclysm to the sea.*

"What are you thinking, Byron?" Hobhouse asked, turning away from the distant shadow of Mount Panachaikon.

"I was thinking of Pliny the Younger's account of his uncle's bravery at Vesuvius. In the midst of the eruption, he learned that his friend Pomponianus was trapped between the mountain and the water. Hoping to save him, he ordered his ship to the eastern edge of the Bay of Naples, in the shadow of the convulsion. Flaming rock and ash fell like rain, and his helmsman urged him to turn back. 'No,' he said, 'Fortune favors the brave; head for Pomponianus.'"

Hobhouse nodded, impressed as always by Byron's erudition.

Polidori cleared his throat. "Didn't Pliny the Elder die in the attempt?"

"You know your Roman history, Polidori," Byron acknowledged with a wry grin. "Indeed, he did. Gloriously."

Panos was making his way back up the hill. When he was close he stopped and waved, urging them forward. As the sunrise gradually colored the morning sky, they crept down the slope towards the harbor, passing darkened houses and barking dogs.

At the threshold of a house no more than two hundred yards from the water's edge a short round Greek stood waiting, his sparse hair encircling the bald dome of his head like a friar's. Aside from his three-day stubble, he wore only a blue woolen nightshirt.

"Come in, come in!" he whispered, his eyes brighter than Byron would have expected for a man wakened at the dawn. "It won't be long before some nosy old woman peeks out to see what all the barking's about!"

The two-story house stood at the base of the hill. Its walls were solid stone and, when its thick wood shutters weren't closed against the heat, boasted windows that offered a commanding view of the sea. Like most of the houses in the village, the roof of Nico's house was made of rounded clay tiles that were angled to divert rainwater into a stone cistern. As they followed Nico inside, Panos paused to dip a wooden ladle into the cistern and quench his thirst.

"My wife is still asleep – praise God – so best we keep our voices low." Nico glanced around nervously, as though she might suddenly appear, demanding to know who these visitors might be and why they skulked about the town at such an early hour. Nico led them into what Byron took to be the kitchen, where a newly-kindled fire burned in the hearth. Polidori lifted his nose, enticed by the smell of fresh bread.

"Sit,' Nico said, gesturing toward a rough table and chairs. "Panos says you are English – in my youth, I spent four years on a fishing boat out of Padstow." He patted his ample belly. "I was thin as a rail in those days. The food was so bad I ate no more than I had to!" He straddled a chair at the head of the table and shifted to face Byron. "You're the poet? The one with a handsome price on his handsome head?"

"That I am. Iphigeneia said you're a good man, Nico, and one who can be trusted. And yes, the janissaries seem quite eager to see me dead." He grinned. "I seem to be getting that quite a bit lately."

Hobhouse cleared his throat. "Is Patras still in the hands of the rebels?"

Nico nodded. "Except for the citadel, where a few hundred janissaries, *sipahi* and some cavalry reinforcements have been holding out.

They emerge to launch the occasional raid, but at this point they're more an annoyance than a threat. Fortunately, Karatzas and his men got some guns from the British, and they've beaten them back two or three times." He shrugged. "Until they're relieved by Ibrahim and his bootlicking Egyptians, Patras should be safe, and a good place to find a ship to France or England."

"Excellent," said Hobhouse, sighing with relief. "How long will it take to get there by boat?"

Panos and Nico exchanged glances.

"What is it?" Byron asked. "There's a problem?"

"Well, yes," Nico acknowledged. "While Patras is relatively safe, the Turks control the gulf. The rebels have a few ships of their own, mostly taken from the Turks. They've shown great courage in challenging the Ottoman." He crossed himself. "My oldest son – by my first wife Sophronia, may peace eternally be upon her – commands one of these ships. You know how it is," he said, his voice dropping almost to a whisper. "A father worries."

Getting to his feet, he cut five thick slices from a steaming loaf of bread wrapped in a cloth beside the fire. He poured some olive oil from a clay jar into a bowl, which along with a dark brown bottle, some glasses and a jug of water, he set on the table next to the bread.

They ate in silence, each absorbed in his own thoughts. Finally, Polidori asked the question that in one form or another was on all their minds. "So, how are we going to get to Patras?"

Nico lifted the bottle and poured a clear liquid into a glass. He added a little water, and the liquid turned milky white. He took a drink and, with a nod toward the bottle, invited the others to join him. "*Mastikha*, although some now prefer to call it *Ouzo*. The finest in southwestern Antirrio!" The licorice smell of anise was strong even across the table, and the Englishmen glanced at Panos, whose non-committal expression told them all they needed to know. Four heads shook politely. With a disappointed shrug, Nico helped himself to another swallow.

"Each morning," he explained hoarsely, wiping his mouth with his sleeve, "the fishing boats head to sea, returning at dusk with their catch. I have many friends among the fishermen. Perhaps I can persuade one of them to hide you in his hold." Pausing, he again exchanged glances with Panos.

Byron frowned. "But there's another problem."

"You, By-roon," replied Panos. "The problem it is you. Since two days, the janissaries are at the harbor to watching the boats. They ask about Englishmen to the fishermen. It must be they look for you."

Nico nodded in confirmation. "Ten thousand kuruş, I've heard! And they don't seem to care if they pay for you or only for your body." He offered a doleful grin. "For ten thousand kuruş, this wife would turn *me* over to the Turks." He paused, reconsidering. "Maybe for less."

"There are a dozen or so fishing boats, Nico; right?" Hobhouse rubbed his eyes, which ached both from weariness and from the smoke of the fire. "They can't watch them all at once."

Nico took another sip of the *mastikha*, considering the question. "Most of the boats are tied up at the eastern end of the harbor; it's easiest to get to sea from there. But two – Raffi's boat, and Miltos' – are older than the others, so they sleep at the more protected western side. Raffi owes me a favor, and also five hundred kuruş. When the Turks are occupied in the east, maybe we are busy in the west?"

Hobhouse nodded. "Sounds like it could work. What do you think, Byron?"

"It's just a mile and a half across the gulf," Byron replied thoughtfully. "Why don't we just swim it?" Polidori, who'd finished his bread and was wondering if it would be rude to ask for more, looked up in alarm. "Swim across? Are you bloody joking?"

Byron looked at Hobhouse and burst out laughing. "I suppose you're right, doctor – the sharks would probably make short work of us."

Panos grinned and, turning to Nico, asked how long it would take to arrange.

"I'll speak to Raffi today. If he's willing, we'll put you on the boat tonight. In the meantime, you can stay here – there are straw mats in the back room and it stays cool even when the day is hot. You'll not encounter my wife there either, for which you should give thanks."

"My mother did say to be careful about her, Nico," Panos said apologetically. "That the money, you know ...."

Nico sighed, shaking his head. "My sister is a very wise woman, Panos. Best just to stay out of Zehra's way – at least, that's what I try to do." His chair scraped as, rising, he motioned for them to follow him to their temporary quarters.

⁂   ⁂

At the sound of a chair scraping on stone, Zehra slid away from her perch at the top of the wooden steps that led from the ground floor to the upstairs portion of the house. Easing herself back into bed, she removed her slippers, pulled the blankets over her bony shoulders, and pretended to sleep. But her eyes remained open, and for the first time in days, she smiled.

CHAPTER 55
A Danger to His Friends

If people contradict themselves, can I
Help contradicting them and everybody,
Even my veracious self? But that's a lie;
I never did so, never will. How should I?
He who doubts all things nothing can deny.
Truth's fountains may be clear, her streams are muddy
And cut through such canals of contradiction
That she must often navigate o'er fiction.

Don Juan, Canto XV

MOORE, HOBHOUSE, Kinnaird and Murray sat around a burled walnut table in Kinnaird's office. It was late-afternoon on a Saturday and, except for a chimney sweep with a barky cough and a dull-eyed book-keeper poring over dusty ledgers, they had the building to themselves. As Moore poured himself a glass from one of a half-dozen bottles of whiskey that stood on the credenza behind Kinnaird's desk, he whistled with delight. "How do you get anything done, Kinnaird, with so much good whiskey beckoning to you like a whore?"

The banker laughed. "Those bottles are essential tools of the trade. I offer a drink to my counterpart at the outset of every negotiation, and look to top off his glass at every opportunity."

"Aren't you in your cups just as fast? Don't take offense, Kinnaird, but you don't hold your liquor like an Irishman."

Kinnaird shook his head. "That's the beauty of it. I drink from that last bottle, over there." He poured half a glass and handed it to Moore. "Tell me how you like it."

Moore looked skeptically at the whiskey – he didn't fancy the color, which was altogether too faint. He took a sip, his face contorting in disgust. "It's practically water!"

Kinnaird smiled. "Exactly."

Hobhouse cleared his throat, impatient to get started. "We're here to see what can be done about Byron, so let's get on with it."

"What needs to be done?" Moore swirled Kinnaird's whiskey – the good stuff – in his glass. "Is Byron not capable of mismanaging his own affairs?"

"He is, although our good friend Murray here deserves at least some of the credit. After all, up to a point, scandal's good for business."

The publisher frowned. "I'm no better able to control him than you are. You know him – he's provocative by nature, and courts scandal no less enthusiastically than he does other men's wives."

Hobhouse chose not to contest the point. "Still, he's always been resilient." He shook his head, still unable to fathom it. "Through an extraordinary combination of talent, charm, title and – what do the Jews call it? – *chutzpah*, which I understand to mean bollocks – he usually manages to right the ship at the last possible moment."

"God takes pity on the genius and idiot alike, I suppose," Kinnaird agreed. "What's he up to now, Hobby, that's got you so worried?"

"He's on his way to Six Mile Bottom, to see Augusta – it's right by Cambridge, he's probably there by now. He told me he means to persuade her to join him in exile in Italy."

"Italy?" Moore was aghast. "It's a fine place, sure, and the birthplace of Angelica Catalani, the most magnificent soprano ever to grace a stage." He put down his drink and raised his arms operatically. "When she performed Portogallo's *"Semiramide"* at the King's Theatre in London a decade ago, I was unable to speak for hours."

"A shame she's not here now," Hobhouse muttered acidly. "Italy isn't the point, Moore. The point is Augusta. If Byron runs away to set up house in Italy with his sister, it will confirm what for now are merely rumors."

Kinnaird frowned. "I'm not sure what we can do about it, Hobby. Like Murray said, you know how he is. The more we oppose it, the less likely he is to pay heed. I can think of no one as capable of foreseeing dire consequences, or as incapable of altering his course to avoid them."

He rose and walked over to a bookshelf that stood by the wall near the door. Reaching up to the top shelf – where authors whose names began with "B" resided – he pulled down a thin volume. "He rarely asks me what I think of his verse; I believe he considers me irretrievably prosaic. But late last year, on what must have been a whim, he showed me a manuscript of a new poem that he was calling *The Bride of Abydos*."

"Yes, he told me he was working on another eastern tale." Murray removed his spectacles and held them to the light, looking for smudges. "But last I heard it was unfinished."

"As far as I know, it still is. Anyway, it's a story of forbidden love – of incest between brother and sister. When I put it down, with the two siblings in bed together, I asked him whether their love would end in tragedy."

Moore leaned forward, his operatic instincts alert. "What did he say?"

"He said, 'Well, Kinnaird, that's the question, isn't it? To be honest with you, I'm rather keen to find out myself.'"

Hobhouse looked puzzled. "What the bloody hell does that mean?"

Kinnaird shrugged. "But when I told him the ending could be nothing less than tragic, he was indignant. I suppose we can all draw our own conclusions."

"No offense, Douglas – you're thinking like a functionary." Moore raised his glass. "To the irretrievably prosaic!"

Throwing down his whiskey, he set the glass on the table and licked his lips. "Byron is touched by genius, and can write only as quickly as his imagination can dictate. When he said, 'I'm keen to find out myself,' he simply described what many writers feel – that, more often than you'd think, a story emerges unplanned and unbidden, as though self-animated."

"If, by *self-animated*," said Kinnaird, his voice rising, "you mean as animated by his own experience, then I agree – the inspiration for this poem seems all too obvious!"

Murray looked up. "I grant you that Kinnaird's imaginative powers can never be underestimated. Unfortunately, in this case I'm not sure he's entirely incorrect."

"Stop praising me, Murray," Kinnaird said archly. "It'll go to my head."

"More than anyone I've ever published," Murray continued, "Byron writes from his own experience. And say what you will about his conduct, he is invariably an honest reporter, even when his account is unflattering."

Moore shook his head. "I concede he draws on his experience, Murray, but that doesn't mean that he's literal. In the interests of drama, he might easily invent or exaggerate an attraction between brother and sister. Or do you believe that Sophocles couldn't have written *Oedipus* without first murdering his father and sleeping with his mother?"

"Enough." Three heads turned to Hobhouse, who for a moment said nothing, staring down at the polished table. Raising his eyes, he let out a deep breath. "At this point I don't care if he did or if he didn't. It doesn't matter to me if he asserts that he is blameless, or freely admits his transgressions. He's Byron, and for better or worse, he considers himself exempt from the conventions of the times, and from the cant of his enemies, friends, King, and even his God." He paused. "Exempt, at least, here on earth."

"What are you saying?" asked Murray. "That it doesn't matter whether Byron has bedded his sister?"

"No – only that I am his friend and will not judge him. But history will, and if this –infatuation – is allowed to play out on a public stage, it will not judge him kindly. Byron's a lively companion, and easily the most interesting and talented man I've ever known. But he can be selfish, and careless, and a danger to his friends – just ask Hunt."

He lifted his glass and took a deep drink, wincing as the whiskey burned. "It's not always easy to be his friend. Yet here we are. Why?" He looked around at his friends, Byron's friends. "I'll tell you why. Because we've all been entranced by the persona he's constructed, and by the brilliance of the verse he's woven to adorn it. It's like seeing the Himalayas, or the Great Pyramids – it changes you, and mostly for the better."

"He cost you your seat, Hobhouse, and damaged Kinnaird's standing in financial circles. He's been an incalculable asset to John Murray & Sons, I don't deny it, but as scandal adds to scandal, that balance has begun to shift." Murray paused, as if at the Rubicon. "If he's bedded his sister – well, I'm not certain I can defend him any longer."

Hobhouse stared at Murray coldly. "I don't care what he's done, or who. I don't even care what he thinks he wants. There's too much at stake. I won't allow him to destroy himself."

First Moore, then Kinnaird nodded. It was Moore who broke the silence. "Quite moving, Hobhouse – I'm glad you're my friend. When my time comes, I hope you'll be as tolerant of my excesses, and pray for *my* immortal soul!"

"I'll do what I can, Moore, though I must warn you, of late my connections with the Almighty seem to have frayed." He turned to Murray, who sat uncomfortably, busying himself with his glasses. "What about you, Murray? You're his publisher – where do you stand?"

Murray sat silently, avoiding Hobby's eyes. More than any of the others, he felt vulnerable and uneasy. Over time, Byron's verse had become increasingly ferocious and, to his mind, degenerate. Whatever moderating influence he might once have wielded was long gone. Byron's continuing attacks on Southey and Castlereagh were now unrestrained and, in his latest cantos, Byron had even turned on Wellesley, the hero of Waterloo, heedless both of his military achievements and of his enormous domestic popularity.

But it was his personal behavior that troubled Murray most. While he was hardly devout, Murray had been raised in the Church and was appalled that Byron – about whom rumors of all species of sexual degeneracy had swirled for years – now appeared to have engaged in an incestuous liaison with his sister. At a Tory-sponsored gathering a few weeks earlier, Bob Southey had taken him aside. "Murray," the gull-faced poet had whispered, his chin jutting forward in emphasis, "you'd do well to reconsider your professional relationship with Byron." Southey's eyes darted furtively, then fixed hard on Murray's. "You know what's awful about scandal?"

"No, Southey – what?"

"It's like mud flung up by a passing carriage – anyone standing too close is splattered, whether he deserves it or not."

"Well, Murray?" Hobhouse asked again, waiting for the publisher to declare himself. "We need to know if you can be counted on."

Murray cleared his throat. "It is unlikely," he said softly, "that the professional relationship between the John Murray House and Lord Byron will continue." He lifted his glasses from his eyes and slipped them into his coat pocket. "Byron's verse is first his own; but in the eyes of the public it is associated with his publisher as well. And for better or worse, his verse is indelibly linked with the man himself."

Murray's voice hardened. "Byron is my friend, and it is my fervent desire that he remain so. But I will not sacrifice the Murray House to his excesses, nor as a Christian can I condone them any longer. I will not turn on Byron, as some would have me do – but neither can I defend him."

"Why, you bloody self-righteous prig!" Moore leaped to his feet. "The 'John Murray House,' as you like to call it, wouldn't stand among the top ten publishers in England if not for Byron! Or do you honestly believe that you'd reap such handsome profits from your cookbooks, archeological journals and Biblical tracts?"

Moore's face was flushed, and he was almost shouting. "Byron entrusted you with his verse when you were a second-rate specialty house. How dare you abandon him when the provocations that made him famous – and you wealthy – become inconvenient!"

"It's all theatre to you, Moore," Murray replied evenly. "You see everything in black and white, lionizing your heroes, impugning your villains, and resolving it all in the last act with some ridiculous *deus ex machina*! It's a pity, but life isn't quite so neat. Yes, John Murray has profited from its association with Byron – but so too has Byron, and he'd be the first to say so!"

Hobhouse took a deep breath, fighting off the impulse to lash out. He was disappointed in Murray, but well understood how difficult Byron could be. Before Moore could escalate the confrontation, Hobhouse put out an arm. "Best you go, then, Murray. Do what you must. But we need to figure out how to save our friend from himself."

Murray stared at Kinnaird and Moore, whose expressions were hard. He shrugged, pulling himself to his feet. "I would appreciate it very much," he said to Hobhouse, "if you would say nothing of this to Byron; it is a conversation that I need to have with him myself, and not something he should hear second-hand." Nodding to them all, he turned and strode from the room.

There was silence in the wake of Murray's departure, as each of them considered the encounter. It was Moore who finally spoke up.

"To be honest, it's a miracle they stayed together for a decade. The relationship between author and publisher is naturally adversarial, each quietly seething at the impertinence or vanity of the other." He took a deep breath, calming himself. "I probably said some things I shouldn't. For a publisher, Murray's got good instincts. Still, a change in publishers will do Byron good, if he can find one willing to take him on in the present climate."

"Byron has always insisted that Murray's the most timid of God's booksellers," Hobhouse agreed. "As you say, it's surprising it lasted this long. But just as Murray cannot defend Byron's profligacy, I am not sure I can forgive Murray's disloyalty. Although I imagine Byron will."

"Well," said Moore, "we at least remain. As you say, how do we save Byron from himself?"

Hobhouse rubbed at his temple and, reaching for the whiskey, poured himself two fingers. "I haven't the slightest idea. But a number of scattered fires – Melbourne's threatened lawsuit, the increasingly vocal demands of his creditors, the government's pressure on Hunt, and now this thing with Augusta – have combined to become a conflagration."

"This idea of his, to decamp to Italy?" Moore sighed. "I begin to see its merit."

Hobhouse nodded. "As do I. But not with Augusta in tow. That will end badly for all concerned."

"What about another woman?" Kinnaird suggested. "Isn't that how he usually manages to disentangle himself from his lovers?"

"It is," Hobhouse nodded. "But this time it's a little trickier than that. Despite the fact that Augusta is his sister – or more likely, because of it – his feelings for her are of a different nature, and not so readily transferred. It's a shame, really – under different circumstances, she might be good for him."

Moore rolled his eyes. "I don't know – if she wasn't his sister, would he be as attracted?" He sipped at his whiskey. "If another woman will not distract him, then what will?"

Hobhouse didn't answer, lost in thought. For some reason, *Don Quixote* had popped into his mind.

"Hobhouse?"

"A cause, Douglas," Hobhouse said slowly, turning an idea over in his mind. "Or better, a quest. Byron may be ready for a cause, whether it leads him to Italy or to somewhere else. And I think I know of one he's flirted with already, and with which he might be enticed to elope."

CHAPTER 56
An Orchard in Winter

Man's a phenomenon, one knows not what,
And wonderful beyond all wondrous measure.
'Tis pity though in this sublime world that
Pleasure's a sin and sometimes sin's a pleasure.
Few mortals know what end they would be at,
But whether glory, power or love or treasure,
The path is through perplexing ways, and when
The goal is gained, we die you know – and then?

DON JUAN, CANTO I

EVER SINCE she'd received her half-brother's letter several days ago, Augusta had been unsettled. Her children sensed it, clinging more tightly to her skirts than usual. His letter had been innocuous enough – "*I'd like to come out to see you next week, and perhaps stay a night or two, if it's not inconvenient. London has become intolerable; a few days in the country will do me good.*" But she knew there was more to it than that, and as she busied herself with chores that could wait and with children who wouldn't, she felt alternately excited, guilty and afraid.

She'd always been the sensible one, the girl who did what was expected, who tended to the needs of others, who offered not agitation but comfort. She sometimes told herself that it was all an illusion; that below her placid surface, powerful currents ran. And perhaps they did. But she was not a fool, and was honest enough to overestimate neither her talents nor her courage. At root, hers was a nurturing character, not a rebellious one.

Still, she was young enough to remember her dreams. She'd married her dashing cousin George Leigh over the objections of friends and family who warned her that he was a dissolute fool. She hadn't wanted to believe them, and when it all proved true and he left her with nothing of value but her children, she faulted herself, as though the blame for his profligacy lay with her. With the help of her family and a good lawyer she managed to preserve sufficient assets to survive, but she promised herself that in future her conduct would be based not on the reckless hopes of a girl, but on the sober judgment of a mother.

Until Byron reentered her life. Oh, he was so handsome, and cavalier, and clever! How proud she felt to command his attention! How satisfying to be the object of jealousy on the part of women richer, prettier and more titled than she! If alone she was unremarkable, with her brilliant brother she felt extraordinary. She could make him laugh, and her heart leaped when he marveled at how easily he could relax with her and simply be himself.

The shift from affection to desire was so seamless that it almost caught her by surprise, and she found herself carried by the swiftly flowing waters of a river she had never intended to enter and knew she could never safely navigate. Nevertheless, she had to acknowledge, with no small degree of shame, that she had made little attempt to fight the current. To the contrary, she allowed it to carry her away. And now, due to her weakness, it was all she could do to avoid drowning in scandal's rushing waters.

Mrs. Rooney – a fortyish, reserved woman who wore her greying hair in a bun and served as cook, seamstress and whatever else might be needed – stood at the windowed double doors that opened to the parlor, where Augusta occupied herself with a partially-completed embroidery. It was a beautiful Saturday in late-July, and the children had gone off for a picnic with Mrs. Rooney's daughter.

"Lord Byron is here, my lady," Mrs. Rooney announced quite unnecessarily, as Byron strode into the room right behind her. "Augusta!" he exclaimed, a broad smile on his face. "If the mountain will not come to Mahomet, then Mahomet must come to the mountain!"

Augusta smiled and offered her hand. Executing a sweeping bow, Byron pressed it to his lips, breathing deep to take in her scent. "You never fail me, Augusta – for as long as I can remember, you've smelled faintly of oranges! Is your bath water infused with orange blossoms, as was the custom of Queen Amarindra of Siam?"

"It's good to see you too, Byron." Augusta waved him to a chair. "Would you like some tea?"

"It's mid-afternoon, isn't it?" He looked up imploringly. "Mrs. Rooney, is there a glass of ale to be procured anywhere in this household?"

As he expected, Mrs. Rooney countered his request with a look of reproach. "There are the children to think of, my lord. They are so impressionable."

Augusta laughed. "What Mrs. Rooney means, Byron, is that we prefer cider. Clare, would you please bring my brother a glass?"

"A pitcher, if you would, Mrs. Rooney." Byron grinned, pleased to elicit disapproving frowns from both women. "Come now," he chided, "it's a hot day, and a long ride from London. Not even Mr. Wilberforce would deny a man a libation on such a day."

They sat on the sofa and made small talk. Byron had positioned himself to avoid a stain that looked like wine, but Augusta proudly assured him it was her middle son's personal blend of huckleberry and apple juice. She sipped at her cider while Byron, looking rather less settled than usual, downed several glasses in rapid succession. Augusta waited, knowing he'd get to it when he was ready.

Setting down his glass, Byron reached for his sister's hand. "They are determined to bring me down, Augusta, and I have given them more than enough ammunition." He shook his head. "The fault is mine – I have been arrogant, and reckless, and am complicit in my own downfall."

Augusta squeezed her brother's hand, pressing it to her chest. "You have acted in accordance with your nature, and have offended only those who well deserve it." She brought his hand to her mouth and kissed it. "To me, a braver and more honest man has never lived."

"Perhaps," Byron said with a wan smile, "although the merits of restraint have in recent months become more apparent. Still, I regret little, Augusta, except the time I've wasted without you. But I intend to waste no more."

He took a deep breath. "Newstead has been sold – for a miraculous price, and far more quickly than I thought possible. Kinnaird is busy as a mother robin, stuffing guineas into the gaping maws of my creditors. When all is done, I will have enough to live on in Italy – perhaps outside Genoa, or Ravenna." His grey eyes were bright.

"The nights are warm, Augusta, and the air is heavy with the scent of olives and lavender. And the sea – you cannot believe the sea! It's not grey and cold and angry as a bitter old woman. It's blue, the breeze is gentle, and it's warm enough to swim even in the evening."

Augusta smiled. "It sounds lovely, Byron."

"It is. But without you, it would be like an orchard in winter." He hesitated, trying to read her. "Come with me, Augusta. We'll rent a villa by the sea, one big enough for all of us. Your children will speak Italian and learn to eat *stracciatella* and *linguine con vongole*. I'll write in the daytime when the sun is hot, and there'll be dinners and parties and festivals celebrating saints you've never heard of, and who no doubt weren't."

He let go of his sister's hand and, lifting his own, waved it dismissively at the entirety of England. "Come with me, and it won't be long before this grey, puckered little island will be nothing but a grim memory."

"Do you really mean to leave England, Byron? What about your friends? And your work? Who will hold the Tories to account while you're charming the *Contessa* of this and the *Baronessa* of that?"

Byron shrugged, and it seemed to Augusta that his smile was bitter. "When did you last look to the London sky, Augusta? My star is fallen, and my name has become an epithet. Murray knows it – lately, his flattery has grown unctuous, which means he's trying too hard and no longer believes me a reliable milk cow."

Augusta laughed. "Byron, stop it. Since when did your self-estimation depend on Murray's? You know the merit of your verse better than anyone – and if it threatens the liars and enrages the hypocrites, is that not proof?"

She scrunched up her brow. "But perhaps you're right," she conceded with an exaggerated sigh, "and even your genius has deserted you." Gravely, she bowed her head. "Have you considered another trade – you could raise mules – no, I gather they're stubborn – perhaps sheep would be better?"

Byron grinned. "There," he declared. "Do you see why I need you with me? Come to Italy – we'll raise mules together."

Augusta fell silent. She'd heard it said that, done properly, decision-making involves a weighing of alternatives and a careful consideration of logical arguments for and against a proposition. Augusta supposed that might be true of some, but it had never been her way. For better or worse, she acted by intuition and by impulse, a process whose outcomes were, she had to concede, uneven. As she sat half-facing her brother, her hands folded in her lap, she realized in a sudden rush of sadness that she already knew how she would answer; indeed, that she had known it before Byron arrived.

As the silence lengthened, Byron felt the twin stabs of panic and regret. He understood how recklessly he lived, defying both authority and convention, burning bridges over ever-widening chasms of his own making. It had never been his way to check his impulses, or deny himself the pleasures of the moment. Like many possessed of extraordinary talent, he had always been confident he could deal with tomorrow when it came.

He remembered that, in the heat of an argument, Caroline had once accused him of falling in love as an escape mechanism, "like leaping onto the nearest passing carriage – no matter where it might be headed!" And Murray, shaking his head the way he did, begging him to temper his invective "lest you find yourself besieged by your enemies, abandoned by your admirers, and pitied by your friends."

Well, he'd run through dozens of lovers, and antagonized apostates and hypocrites too numerous to count and too powerful to evade. How ironic it was that the woman who finally made him feel safe, who loved him not for his image or celebrity or accomplishments but for himself, could never be his.

There were tears in Augusta's eyes. Byron swallowed, the hollow in his chest painful. He reached for her, and drew her to him, and felt her tears on his neck. "It's alright, Augusta," he whispered, stroking her hair. "It's for the best. Pinched though it may be, England is your home, and your children's – and though I love them dearly, it's far from certain I'm cut out for a domestic life." He took her head in his hands, wiping her cheeks with his palm. "Besides," he said, gravely shaking his head like a tutor addressing a hopeless student, "your Italian is atrocious."

Augusta laughed, which came out as a choked sob. She pulled away from Byron and wiped her eyes with a handkerchief that she produced from nowhere. "I just ... you know, with all the children, and they have nothing ...."

"Hush, Augusta. It's for the best. Besides, who knows where I'll end up? If I live ten years longer you will see that it's not over with me – I don't mean in literature, for that is nothing; and though it may seem odd to say, I do not even think it my vocation."

Augusta cocked her head, uncomfortably reminding Byron of a dog perplexed by an unfathomable command. "What are you thinking of, Byron? There's something you're not telling me – I know you too well."

Silently, Byron cursed himself – he hadn't meant to say anything about the Levant. "Oh, it's nothing really," he said, trying to sound casual. "A few months ago, I was contacted by leaders of a committee formed to support the Greeks' efforts to get out from under Ottoman rule. They thought I might provide some organizational support, and perhaps some financial assistance." He shrugged. "It's a worthy cause, and how often does one have a chance to foster liberty? Anyway, I told them I'd think about it."

"You're going to get involved in a war?" Augusta was aghast. "Do you really think that's a good idea?"

"It's an idea – how good it is remains to be seen. But I've got this handsome Albanian costume – you know, the one I wore for Phillips' portrait? – for which I paid a small fortune, and which hasn't seen much use." He grinned, but stopped short when he saw the stricken look on Augusta's face.

"Come on now, trust me, there's no cause for worry. I may not go at all – so many of my plans wither and die on the tangled vine of logistics. And even if I do, I'll be careful – I won't be fighting, just providing financial and perhaps some organizational support."

Augusta sniffed, dabbing at her eyes with her kerchief. "You can be as dismissive as you wish, Byron – I'm not fooled. When we were kids, you swam for glory, and always – *always* – against the current. I feared for you many times. Nothing's changed."

"I'm not old," he said firmly, reaching out to stroke her cheek, "but I daresay I've lived more fully than most men. Sooner or later, often when we least expect it, we draw close enough to peer into the Void. At such moments, what determines our course? Will our fears drive us, like rabbits running blindly before the hounds? Or will we *choose* our path?"

"Byron, you, I don't–"

"Augusta, you needn't worry. If I travel to the Levant I am unlikely to be there very long, and am as likely to confront the infidel as you are in your garden. But I do not fear death; and when it comes, I don't want my life's work to have been nothing but an inconsequential collection of verse that no one will remember fifty years from now."

He rose, pulling Augusta to her feet. "I may not be Washington, but with any luck I could be a poor man's Lafayette. Besides," he said with a smirk, "think how vexed that miserable sod Castlereagh will be when he hears of it!"

CHAPTER 57
The Note

THE DAWN *broke in oranges and pinks, the wispy clouds fired at their edges by the rising sun. As Juan had promised, Dryden proved his worth as they made their way down the Lycos River and away from Constantinople to the sea. Not only was he strong as an ox and tireless on the oars, he had a soldier's instincts for survival, seeming to sense when danger – a sipahi shore patrol, or a frigate of the Ottoman fleet – might be lurking. His cheerful demeanor was welcome as well, and it did not take him long to charm even the instinctively skeptical Caria.*

"So, lassie," he asked, a grin dappling the auburn shade of his beard, "where do you and young Juan wish to go? I must admit that, in all the excitement, it was enough just to get out with my life, and I haven't given much thought yet to destination." Docking the oars, he allowed the boat to drift as he gingerly massaged his hands. "Haven't rowed like this since I was a boy."

Caria glanced at Juan, who offered only a shrug. She sighed, wondering if she would have to make all the decisions. "Batumi, on the Georgian coast – do you know of it?"

Dryden nodded. "I knew a lad in Gudovich's artillery whose girl lived there." He thought for a moment. "Can't remember his name and never knew hers. I think he may have been blown to bits at Arpachai."

"It's where I grew up; or at least, since I was two. It's been a long time – I'd like to go home." She blushed, surprised by her uncharacteristic reticence.

"*Perhaps Juan might like to come with me, to see my home ....*" Her voice trailed off and, even in the faint morning light, Harry could see the color in her cheeks.

Juan shifted uncomfortably. "*I ... I might like to, to see Batumi,*" he said hesitantly. "*I mean, if Caria really thinks it worth seeing.*" Dryden smiled, amused by the awkward advance and retreat of love's opposing armies.

"*But there's something I need to show you.*" Juan reached into his pocket and extracted a tightly-folded slip of paper, its surface streaked with blood. "*Gulbayez slipped this into my palm when she took my hand, there on the dock.*"

He handed it to Dryden, who unfolded the paper and squinted to read it. After a moment he shook his head. "*Much as I hate to admit it, I can't read this in such dim light. Caria, maybe you can make it out.*"

Caria took the note and angled it to better catch the slanting sunlight. After a few moments, and with a sharp intake of breath, she looked at Juan with astonishment.

"*Well?*" Dryden was a patient man, but also a curious one. "*Read it aloud, would you?*"

"*Sorry, Harry. 'Christian,' it says,*

'you may think that I have spared you out of affection, or that away from the cruelties of my father's court I have grown weak or infirm of purpose. I assure you, neither is true. I have spared you because you may be of use to me. In return for your life, and the lives of the soldier and the clever slave girl, I require that you perform a service. On the back of this paper is a private message to the Tsar Alexander. At the top is the Sultana's private stamp – show this to Alexander's men, so they may know the note to be genuine, and you to be my envoy. Deliver this to the Tsar in St. Petersburg as quickly as you can. Hand it to him yourself, to ensure it is not intercepted or diverted by the Sultan's spies. I believe the Tsar will find it to be of great interest.

'I have little doubt that you will perform this service for me, Christian, as it is obvious that, though you are young, you are already a man of honor. Do this for me, Christian, and your debt

to me is extinguished. May Allah protect you and speed you on your journey, upon which my life and happiness depend.'

Turning the paper over, Caria examined the red wax stamp at the top of the page. "It is her stamp," she confirmed. "I've seen it hundreds of times on financial documents." She squinted, trying to make out the text. "This isn't Türkî, and it isn't Russian. Whatever it is, I can't read it."

Dryden reached over. "Let me see it," he said. "I have a bit of a talent for languages." For several minutes, the big man leaned down to study the note in the lengthening light. Finally, he handed it to Juan, then stretched to work out a kink in his neck. "Well," he said, "little wonder you can't read it. This is in code. The base language looks to be Gheg, which is one of the two principal Albanian dialects. North of the Shkumbin river they speak Gheg, while south of it they speak Gost."

"How do you know it's – what did you call it? – Gheg?" Caria looked at Dryden with amazement. "How would you even know such a thing?"

Dryden smiled. "I know it's Gheg because several words are in the open – probably to make it easier for the Russians to decode the message. But the rest is some kind of substitution cipher." He bent his head as far to the side as he could and was rewarded with an audible crack. "As for recognizing the language, I once spent a month in Kruja, evaluating the fortifications of the castle – if you ever have a mind to lay siege to that town, think again. Anyway, it's hard to buy a drink if you don't master at least a bit of the local dialect."

Caria frowned. "Can you solve it?"

"No," Dryden answered, shaking his head. "I know enough to recognize the cipher, but not nearly enough to break it. Gudovich often communicated with his field commanders through substitution ciphers, but this one is more complex. The Ottoman Turks were the first to develop sophisticated cryptography and cryptanalytic methods. Clever of Gulbayez to use their own techniques against them."

Carefully, Juan re-folded the note and returned it to his pocket. "Harry,"
he said, "when we first met you told me you'd gladly rejoin Gudovich's forces
if given the chance. Would you consider traveling with us as far as Batumi?
Once we're near the town you can continue on your way – Gudovich must
be quartered somewhere to the north, so Batumi will be on your way. I'll
see Caria safely home, then head north to St. Petersburg." Harry opened
his mouth to reply but, hoping to forestall an objection, Juan cut him off.
"Gulbayez knew me better than I could have expected. She's right – I owe
her a debt."

If Juan thought Caria would be grateful, he miscalculated.

"You will 'see me safely home?'" she asked pointedly, hands on hips. "Do
I look like I require an escort from a highborn Spaniard still wet behind the
ears?"

"Uh, no, but I thought—"

"And since when do you make decisions on my behalf anyway? Must
I remind you who engineered our escape from the Palace?" Caria glared,
daring him to disagree.

Dryden laughed. "She makes a fair point, Juan. Although I expect you'd
be in better position to defend yourself if you hadn't forgotten to change out
of those lovely slippers." He reached into the sack that Baba had given them
and tossed over a pair of men's shoes.

"I was getting to it," Juan grumbled, tossing the slippers over the side.
He looked up at Dryden with a crooked grin. "They were very comfortable."
Turning to Caria, he inclined his head, locks of jet-black hair falling over
his eyes. "My apologies, Caria," he said gravely, "I did not intend to offend
you. It's a long way to St. Petersburg – would you do me the honor of accom-
panying Senior Dryden and I as far as Batumi?"

Mollified, Caria nodded. "That's better. Yes, you may accompany me.
But we'll discuss further travel when we get there." She smiled, her blue eyes
softening, and Juan felt the dawn light eclipsed.

"Harry," she asked, gesturing at their fragile craft, "you're strong and
not nearly as old as you pretend. But we can't row to Batumi."

Harry nodded and held up his hands, which had begun to blister. "With these hands, another fifty miles would be too much. Now that we're through the straits we could try to go overland, but that would be slower and much riskier." He cooled his hands in the water, shaking them dry in the brisk morning air. "No," he said firmly, blotting the remaining moisture with his shirt, "we need to get a bigger boat." Reaching for the oars, he angled the craft toward shore. "As it happens, I have a pretty good idea where we might find one."

CHAPTER 58
Ceding the Field

I've no great cause to love that spot of earth,
Which holds what might have been the noblest nation;
But though I owe it little but my birth,
I feel a mixed regret and veneration
For its decaying fame and former worth.
Seven years (the usual term of transportation)
Of absence lay one's old resentments level,
When a man's country's going to the devil.

DON JUAN, CANTO X

WEARY FROM the long ride back from Cambridge, Byron retired early and slept late. By the time he rose it was almost noon, and he took the tea that Fletcher made him to his study, where he sat down at his desk to write.

It had rained that morning, but the skies had cleared and a cool breeze rustled the leaves in the sycamore trees outside Byron's window. However vehemently he might rail against the dismal English weather, there were days in summer that could almost make him forgive London's featureless skies and incessant rains. He looked up from his verse from time to time, distracted by the glint of sunlight on the glistening leaves. At this moment, marriage was on his mind – not his own, which he thought a fate too horrible to contemplate – but the institution in general:

A young unmarried man with a good name
And fortune has an awkward part to play;
For good society is but a game,
The royal game of goose, as I may say,
Where everybody has some separate aim,
An end to answer or a plan to lay;
The single ladies wishing to be double,
The married ones to save the virgins trouble.

I don't mean this as general, but particular
Examples may be found of such pursuits,
Though several also keep their perpendicular
Like poplars, with good principles for roots;
Yet many have a method more reticular –
'Fishers for men', like sirens with soft lutes.
For talk six times with the same single lady,
And you may get the wedding dresses ready.

Perhaps you'll have a letter from the mother,
To say her daughter's feelings are trepanned;
Perhaps you'll have a visit from the brother,
All strut and stays and whiskers, to demand
What 'your intentions are'. One way or other
It seems the virgin's heart expects your hand;
And between pity for her case and yours,
You'll add to matrimony's list of cures.

As he reached to remoisten his pen, he was interrupted by a commotion in the hallway. Before he could rise the door flew open and Hobhouse burst in, his face flushed. "Mr. Hobhouse!" Fletcher called after him in futile pursuit. "If your business can wait two minutes!" He looked past Hobhouse to Byron, who waved him off.

"I'm afraid it cannot wait, Mr. Fletcher." As Fletcher pulled the door closed with a reproachful shake of the head, Hobhouse dropped into one of the chairs that faced Byron's desk. "Lord Eldon and Lord Grey cornered me at Brooks's several hours ago."

"The Lord Chancellor and the leader of – what was that expression you came up with the other night, when we were all in our cups – oh yes – 'the loyal opposition'? I know you mean it truly, Hobhouse, but if ever a phrase lent itself to sarcasm, that one does!" He chuckled. "Anyway, Eldon and Grey remind me of John Byrom's clever little epigram about some meaningless dispute between Handel and Bononcini – *"Strange all this difference should be, twixt Tweedle-dum and Tweedle-dee!"*

"I'm afraid this is nothing to laugh about. They were quite serious, and they asked me to deliver a message. To you."

Byron shrugged. "They know where to find me."

"Eldon thinks himself too important, and doesn't care to get his hands dirty. Grey likes you or, at least, so he claims; but says I'd have greater sway with you."

"George III would likely have greater sway with me than Grey – and he's six feet in the ground." Byron held up the page on which he was working and blew on it gently. Satisfied that the ink was dry enough, he set a clean sheet of paper on top, anchoring it with a small glass globe. "Alright, Hobby, what's this message you've got?"

Hobhouse rubbed at his temple – Byron had seen the gesture scores of times, and knew it meant that his friend was upset. "Come on," Byron urged, "out with it. It's from neither my doctor nor my banker, so how bad could it be?"

"It seems Lord Eldon believes you've 'become an embarrassment and can no longer be tolerated' to maintain your seat in the Upper House. The affair with Caroline is part of it – Melbourne's their party's rising star, and it turns out he may be less broad-minded than you supposed. And I'm sure Eldon and his cronies take more than a little satisfaction in putting it to you, given the savaging you've given the Tories generally, and Castlereagh and the King in particular."

"I've been less outspoken than many," Byron protested. "Sheridan's invective is harsher than mine, and no one's trying to run him out of town. As for Caroline, I can assure you that I have suffered more from that woman's machinations than anyone!"

"Be that as it may, you cannot fuck the wives of the powerful with impunity; at least, not when you have become a more general annoyance."

"Is that in the rules somewhere?"

"It wouldn't matter to you if it were. Anyway, the rumors about you and Augusta were undoubtedly the 'final straw,' as Brougham likes to say. I can't say for certain whether their professed outrage is sincere or merely political, but both Eldon and Grey claim they can defend your participation in the Upper House no longer."

"I was unaware they had defended it previously," Byron sniffed. "As for the Augusta thing, who are they to sit as judge and jury? They assume the worst because that is what they expect."

Hobhouse rose, unable to sit still. He walked over to the window and peered out, half expecting to see a roiling mob, flaming torches and pitchforks in hand. "Your bloody journal, Byron. We must assume they've seen it. Indeed, it's not impossible that they were responsible for its theft."

"Yes, that occurred to me as well. In which case these self-righteous bastards are also responsible for Lyon's death." Byron leaned forward, resting his elbows on the desk. "The journal entry may titillate, but really, it proves nothing more than that Augusta and I share a mutual attraction. Indeed, if anything it's helpful to my case, for it makes it clear that, attraction or not, nothing happened."

"Your case? Good God, Byron, can you not see this clearly? The Lord Chancellor and the leader of the Whig party – your party! – have already made up their minds. If you do not resign your seat, and soon, they will bring a motion to have you suspended for 'disorderly conduct.' I believe they have the votes – it's not Eldon's style to bluff, and with Grey well in step you will be unable to count on support even from the Whigs."

Byron leaned back, suddenly tired. "It's not that I give a damn about the bloody seat, or the bloody House of Lords for that matter. But I don't relish being drummed out – it simply isn't meet." He exhaled, considering his options. "What if I don't play along? Henry Brougham's as good an advocate as I've seen; I suspect he'd see this for what it is."

"And what exactly do *you* think this is?"

"Retribution. You've said it yourself – I've been a thorn in their side, and I'm sure it galls them to no end that Donny Jonny pleases so many at the expense of so tawdry a few. Murray drinks with them – he has a remarkable ability to flatter both sides – and claims the Tories detest me only a little less than they do Fox and Sheridan. This is their chance to even the score, flattering themselves that it is Lady Propriety whose honor they defend." Byron snorted. "Though you and I both know they'd fuck her in the arse if it pleased them to do so!"

"All that may be true, Byron. But you've given them too much ammunition, made it too bloody easy. As for Brougham, he was at Brooks. After leaving Eldon and Grey I sought him out."

"Really? You've been busy, haven't you?"

"Protecting you is a full-time job, and one that doesn't pay very well." He turned from the window. "Anyway, I agree that he's talented and aggressive, so getting his advice seemed wise."

Byron shrugged, deciding not to make an issue of Hobhouse's authority. "What did Henry say?"

"He sees it as I do. Even if Eldon's motion to suspend you rests on shaky legal ground, the forum in which it would be heard is not legal but political. I have little doubt he has the votes. Brougham also made the point that suspension proceedings would be ugly, delving into all sorts of matters that would lend dignity to no one. Even were you to win, you'd lose."

"What does he suggest, then? That I submit to blackmail?"

"Not exactly. He thinks it might be possible to reach some kind of accommodation."

"What kind of 'accommodation?'"

Unwrapping his legs, Hobhouse leaned forward. "Brougham believes it's exile they want, and that humiliating you, while great fun, is of secondary importance. If you were to go abroad – not forever, but at least for a year or two – there would be no need to move to suspend you, or for you to resign."

"Out of sight, out of mind?" Byron laughed bitterly. "Do they think me incapable of plaguing them from the Continent?"

"Brougham made the same point. I daresay you'd have *greater* freedom beyond the reach of the Crown's dogs."

Hobby reached out and, picking up the glass globe anchoring Byron's verse, rolled it in his palm. "You claim to hate it here anyway. With Newstead sold, perhaps an extended stay abroad would be just the thing. It would also bring an end to Melbourne's legal threats; he doesn't care about the money; he just wants you as far from his wife as possible."

"A desire we share. Still, I don't know, it doesn't feel right. It's not my habit to cede the field, and certainly not in response to coercion."

"Oh please, Byron, you know better than that. The *field*, as you put it, isn't London, or even England. Your verse, and *Don Juan* in particular, transcends party, time and place. Sure, you've always displayed a singular talent for skewering our local hypocrites, syco-phants and *poseurs* – there's endless material, and you've observed them close up. But how many times have you insisted to anyone who'll listen that *human* folly – whether tragic, hilarious or both – is your true subject? You don't need to be here to complete that work – if anything, going abroad once again will expand your canvas and keep you from getting stale."

Despite his anger, and a claustrophobic feeling that circumstances were fast closing in, Byron couldn't help but smile. "Hobhouse!" he said half-grudgingly, "I didn't know you paid such close attention."

"I don't intend to – it's just that you like to talk and I can't help but catch some of it. People have it wrong about those of us in public life; they think the critical faculty is an ability to speak. In fact, what's important is to listen."

He paused, hoping his timing was right. "By the way," he asked, trying to sound casual, "how did it go with Augusta?"

CHAPTER 59
A Crescent Moon in Batumi

"SEE? LOOK there! Aren't they beautiful?"

Juan grinned, pleased to see Caria so happy. She stood on the bow of the narrow, single-masted caique, the sleeves of her kaftan fluttering in the wind like flags. Raising her arm, she pointed towards snow-capped mountains barely visible in the distance. "Those are the Caucasus Mountains – my father had a rough cabin there that he built himself. Every summer he'd take me there and we'd fish." She reached out and pulled Juan close. "Over there ... where the coast slides away to the north? That's the old city." She shifted her gaze and pointed to the south. "And there's the fortress – Gonio, it's called. The Romans built it, and they say the remains of the Apostle Matthew are buried there."

"It stands astride the river gorge connecting the city, and the rest of Georgia for that matter, to the Black Sea." Dryden grinned, enjoying once more Caria's astonishment at his wide-ranging knowledge.

"Don't be so surprised, lassie. Batumi's got strategic value, and there was a time Gudovich thought he might be ordered to take it. Anyway, he had me read Prince Vakhushti's Description of the Kingdom of Georgia and summarize for him the sections on Batumi – or Batoum, as the Turks called it." The wind shifted and Dryden trimmed the sail, veering to the southeast in the waning light. "Once it's dark we can tie up below the fortress. I don't expect we'll attract much attention."

As the last glimmers of sunshine flickered on the city's windows, Juan turned away from the shore. "Caria," he asked, "where is your parents' house?"

"It's close, only a short walk up the hill from the fortress."

"We'll borrow a rowboat; or, if necessary, we can swim –"

"No, Juan." Caria smiled, laying her hand on his arm. "It's been a long time since I've been home. Who knows how things are?" She took a deep breath. "I need to go alone. I'll come back for you tomorrow."

"It's not safe. The Georgians and the Turks are at each other's throats these days. I should go –"

"Caria can take care of herself, Juan," Dryden said, winking at the girl. "This is her hometown, after all. You and I can slip ashore separately and find a tavern."

Caria rolled her eyes, but Dryden shook his head. "It's not what you think, lass. No better place than a tavern to gather useful intelligence, especially if we get lucky and happen on a soldier. Maybe we can learn where Gudovich's army is quartered." He gestured at an enormous sack of carrots that lay, now almost empty, on the deck. "And maybe find something to eat. I don't mean to complain, mind you – Juan scrounged what he could when we liberated this lovely little caique from the harbor at Riva, and the salt pork was quite nice while it lasted. But if I never see another carrot, that'd be fine with me."

Juan shrugged. "Best I could do on short notice. Besides, I like carrots."

The night was cloudy, the only illumination coming from lamps in the windows of the houses that fronted the harbor. Dryden struck the sail, using a paddle to guide the caique close to shore. They could find no rowboat or skiff, so Caria removed her slippers and outer kaftan and, dumping out their remaining carrots, stuffed them into the empty burlap sack. She started to remove her şalvar and inner kaftan, and then, with a sharp look at Juan and Dryden, paused.

"What are you two looking at?" She twirled her finger in the air. "Have you no manners at all?" Sheepishly, Juan and Harry turned their backs as

Caria finished undressing and slipped into the water. Calling to Juan to hand her the sack, she held it over her head as she treaded water.

"I'll be back no later than tomorrow night," she called, kicking away from the boat. "Stay out of trouble, will you? I don't want to have to rescue you again."

As Juan watched, she rolled onto her side and, still holding the sack above her head, began to kick toward shore. She was only a few yards away and, even in the near-darkness, Juan could clearly make out the crescent moon-shaped birthmark just below her left shoulder.

⁂   ⁂

It was an hour or so past sunset on the following day when Caria returned, tossing the bag containing her clothing into the caique and pulling herself up and over the side. More sensitive this time to her dignity, Harry and Juan turned away, averting their eyes until Caria dried and clothed herself. When she was dressed and they turned to greet her properly, they knew immediately that something was wrong.

"What is it?" asked Juan. "What happened?"

Caria's hair was wet and hung in long strands around her face, seawater running down her cheeks like tears. "My mother is dead," she answered, her voice flat. "Fever, two years ago." She sat on the narrow foredeck, her feet tucked beneath her. Reaching back to gather her hair, she wrung out the water as best she could, tilting to the side to spare her clothing. "My sister and her husband are living in the house now."

Juan fought back the urge to take her in his arms – he knew it wasn't her way. "I'm so sorry, lassie," said Dryden. "It's not easy, losing one's mother." He paused. "What about your father?"

"Pressed into service by the Russians. I'd have thought him too old, but he's strong, rides very well and looks – well, looked, at least, it's been so long – younger than his years. My sister doesn't know where he is now, but six

months ago she had a letter from him. He said he was attached to cavalry units under a Russian General named Vasily Orlov-Denisov –"

"Orlov-Denisov? I know of him." Dryden frowned, trying to recall the details. "He commanded a Hussar light cavalry regiment that distinguished itself in a terrible fight against Napoleon at Friedland some years ago. I was told that, trapped against the Alle River by Ney's advancing troops, Orlov-Denisov and a third of his men held back the French while the rest of his regiment crossed the river to safety. The general was wounded, but managed to escape with his life, swimming the last hundred yards or so after his horse was shot dead in the water."

He saw the fear in Caria's eyes, and smiled reassuringly. "Orlov-Denisov is a hard man, and willing to pay for his decisions with men's lives. But he is not a butcher, and he's smart enough to understand that men fight hardest when they are treated with respect. If your father has courage – and if his daughter's character tells me anything, he has more than his share – there's a fair chance he's still alive."

Caria nodded, slipping her hands into her pockets and shivering in the night chill. "What about you and Juan? Did you go to shore?"

Harry grinned. "Did you know that Juan here swims like a fish? While I struggled to shore like a whale in a petticoat, he glided through the water smooth as a dolphin. By the time I made it to the beach, he was sitting on his haunches waiting for me, dry as a desert goat!"

"Anyway, we found a tavern and, as luck would have it, struck up a conversation with a couple of Ukrainian swabbies off a Russian merchant ship. They don't know where Gudovich is presently, but heard his regiment has a new cadre of officers. If I know Gudovich, he'll stick close to St. Petersburg until they're fully trained – he blamed his distance from the capital for the Tsar's decision to name Zubov to lead the Russian armies against the Persians." He shook his head. "Zubov! That asinine courtier wasn't fit to hold Gudovich's chamber pot!"

Juan and Caria exchanged smiles – they were used to Harry's tangents. "Harry," he prompted helpfully, "tell her about the ship."

"Yes, right." Dryden turned and pointed to the north. "The Ukrainians are crew on a brig, the Pamiyat Mercuriya, out of Odessa. They claim to have been carrying Russian dry goods, but it'd be a waste of a fast, maneuverable ship like a brig to carry bolts of cloth. My guess is they're running guns to the rebels. Anyway, they're empty now and heading back to Odessa tomorrow. If we play our cards right, I expect the ship's captain might offer us passage, especially if we promise to speak well of him at the Tsar's court."

Juan sat down next to Caria and set his hand on hers. "I too am sorry about your mother. But your father –I don't know, but perhaps it will be possible to get a letter to him, when Harry and I reach St. Petersburg." He smiled, gesturing towards Dryden. "As you know, Senor Dryden is very resourceful."

"When 'you and Harry reach St. Petersburg?' Is it not my father we are hoping to find?" Caria didn't seem angry to Juan, just determined. "There's nothing for me here. My sister and I are very different, and her husband – well, let's just say I don't like how he looks at me." She tossed her head, her side braids flying. "I'm coming with you. When do we leave?"

❧   ❧

How interesting, thought Juan as he and Caria stood at the rail of the Pamiyat Mercuriya and watched the Black Sea slip past, the power of a small circle of wax. Sailing the caique to the north, they had quickly found the Mercuriya, her crew busily preparing the ship for departure. The sight of an Ottoman caique initially raised suspicion among the Russians, but the Ukrainians they'd met at the tavern recognized them and they soon found themselves standing before the brig's captain, a greying Italian named Cavalli who, to Dryden's surprise, Caria's amusement and Juan's consternation, immediately seemed smitten with Juan.

The captain examined the Sultana's seal as Dryden explained in fluent Russian where they were headed. After a quick consultation with his first mate, Cavalli nodded, returning the sealed missive to Dryden. "It will be my honor, Colonello," he replied in English, *"to provide you and your companions passage to Odessa."* He gave Dryden an unctuous smile and leered at Juan. *"Of course, any favorable mention of this vessel and its captain to the Tsar or his ministers will be more than ample thanks."*

Cavalli spat a brief command in Russian, and two junior officers stepped forward. The first he directed to *"show the signorina to her cabin – and be sure she is treated with dignity at all times. If any are remiss in this respect, it will be you who is flogged within an inch of your sorry life."* He ordered the second to show *"Colonello Dryden"* to his cabin. *"Be sure to see to it that he has full access to the ship, and to my personal stores of cognac and rum."*

Turning to Juan, he smiled. *"Giovanotto, I will show you to your cabin myself – no, it is no trouble at all, it is quite close to my own."* Juan nodded politely and then, pulling Caria close, kissed her full on the lips. *"I will count the minutes until we are reunited, my darling,"* he cooed. It was all Harry could do to keep from bursting out in laughter as Juan winked at him and turned to join the disappointed captain.

The sea was perfect for sailing, the prevailing wind strong enough to make good time without churning the insides of those unused to the sea. The sky was clear and crystalline blue and, as they sailed north, Juan and Caria could see Mt. Elbrus to the east, its snowy crest rising more than eighteen thousand feet above the sea. Pirates were common in the region – some operating as outlaws, others acting as privateers legitimized through the issuance of official letters of marque – but Cavalli had assured them that the Mercuriya was fast enough to outrun even the cutters favored by the most sophisticated of the pirate bands. *"Even if they managed to catch us,"* he promised, *"we've got eighteen guns, more than enough to drive them off or destroy them if they persist."*

Now, as they stood together at the rail, Juan leaned to his left until his flank touched Caria. She looked at him dourly. *"Don't think I've forgiven you your presumption, Christian,"* she growled, *"just because I've chosen to take the air with you this morning."*

"Do you think I wanted to kiss you, Caria?" Juan responded. He scanned the deck, making sure no one was close enough to hear. *"It was, I assure you, an act borne of desperation. Say what you want about the depredations of the Circassian pirates – at that moment, I was more concerned about discouraging our captain's advances."*

Caria laughed and punched Juan on the arm. *"Oh? Kissing me is a desperate act? Am I truly so ugly?"*

"No, no, quite the opposite. It's just that my experiences with older women have been – tumultuous." He reached out and pressed a finger to her lips. *"Still,"* he whispered, sotto voce, *"there's much to be said for a woman of experience!"*

Harry had been granted access to the ship's charts and maps, which he wished to study in order to plan their long overland journey from Odessa to St. Petersburg. It was the first time Juan and Caria had spent hours alone together, and Juan marveled at how easily the time passed. He missed no opportunity to make her laugh – not to display his wit, but because he thrilled at the husky timbre of her voice and the spirit that played in her pale blue eyes. He told her about life in Seville and answered her questions about his voyage, shipwreck and rescue. He hesitated to speak of Julia – he was uncertain how Caria would react – but not wishing to conceal, confessed the affair while sparing her most of the particulars.

"You were young, Juan – you are still." Caria scanned the sea to the east, squinting and shielding her eyes against the glare. *"If you and Julia felt love, while Julia and her husband did not, who is to say theirs was the more sanctified coupling?"*

"It's a great relief to hear you voice a conviction I often felt I held alone." He took her hand in his, reassured by the squeeze he received in return.

"You were not a captive for very long," she said softly, *"but I was enslaved for more than a decade. It's an experience that makes you skeptical of what people claim is right. If the Sultan and the Imam can defend the enslavement of children, how can I accept without question any of their edicts?"*

Releasing Juan's hand, she leaned against the rail and bobbed up on her toes, tossing her head back and breathing in the fresh salt air. "They say that over time, slaves become more compliant; that they begin to accept the system that enslaves them. Perhaps that's true of some, but not of me. I have no use for such a system, and will decide for myself what is right and what is wrong!"

Juan took a breath, steeling himself. He had avoided the subject long enough. "I've told you about my boyhood, my travels – even about my sins, though I concede I haven't had sufficient time to catalogue them all. Please – tell me more of you."

Caria smiled. "What do you want to know?

"When we were on the caique, you said something about having lived in Batumi 'at least since you were two.' Did you live someplace else?"

Caria was silent for a few moments. "Look at my eyes, Juan. My mother's eyes are – umm, were – brown, and my father's also. They raised me as their own, but I was not born to them."

She hesitated, her voice halting. Sensing her reluctance to relive the pain of old wounds, Juan almost stopped her, but instead remained silent. He had to know.

"My older sister hated me, she was always jealous – she's the best cook in Batumi and has pretty hair, but otherwise – I don't mean to be unkind – well, she's dull and a bit homely. Anyway, when I was eight and she was eleven or twelve, she told me that our parents took me in out of pity, that I was foreign and unwanted –"

"Caria ..."

"– that no real Georgian would ever want me as his wife, and that I would die unloved and alone."

Caria held her head high, a freshening wind whipping her hair across her back. "I punched her in the nose." She wagged a finger at Juan. "When they say it's always best to speak what's on your mind, do not believe them."

Juan laughed. "Do you know where you came from? If not Batumi, where?"

"I don't know. I asked my parents – I still think of them that way, whether I was born to them or not – but they said they didn't know. All they

could tell me is that I was brought to Constantinople as a small child and sold to an agency that arranges for the placement of orphans. My mother had been unable to bear children after my sister – I like to think she feared a similar outcome! – so they contacted the agency and agreed to take me in."

"Do you know who brought you to Constantinople?"

"I don't know who, but my parents were told I survived a wreck at sea. Somewhere in the Mediterranean."

Juan felt his heart hammering in his chest, and for a second thought he might pass out. Grabbing the rail, he closed his eyes and held on tight until the moment passed.

"Are you alright?" He opened his eyes to see Caria leaning toward him, her brow creased with worry. "Is it the sea? Do you need to throw up?"

He took a deep breath, steadying himself. "I'm fine, just a little light-headed. Caria, that mark just below your left shoulder, the one that's shaped like a crescent moon – have you always had it?"

She looked at him, puzzled. "Yes, always. Why?"

In an instant, Juan thought about Dona Inez; and the burning of the heretics in the plaza of La Giralda; and Miguel, the hidalgo Alfonso's cunning lawyer. He thought about Julia's banishment to La Conventa de Santa Paula; and the loss of the Angelica; and the nights he drifted in darkness on the sea, convinced his death was near. He thought of Gulbayez, defiantly determined to be free; of the emaciated old tar on the pirate ship Panagia; and the nonchalance with which Harry Dryden faced death on the auction block in Sultanahmet Square. And, finally, he thought of Caria's proud independence, and her brave resolve to decide matters of right and wrong for herself. He thought of all these things in an instant, and without deciding, decided.

"No reason, really – I, I just think it's very beautiful." He met Caria's brilliant blue eyes, holding her gaze for what seemed an eternity. Then, inclining his head, he kissed the crescent-shaped birthmark below her left shoulder as she buried her lips in his thick black hair.

CHAPTER 60
Zehra

THE LATE-AFTERNOON sun baked the rutted streets as Zehra hurried through the village, her dark hair covered with a brown scarf and her hatchet face concealed behind a veil. Uncharacteristically attentive, Nico had insisted they go for a long walk along the shore, and it wasn't until after the midday meal, when he left 'to attend to a small matter,' that she was able to get away. Panos, that brat of Iphigeneia's, was sitting on the front stoop as she left the house; he nodded respectfully as she passed.

As she quickened her pace, Zehra clutched a purse to her chest. She had information to sell – important information – and she expected that when she returned from the outpost the janissaries maintained in the ancient fortress it would be bursting with coins.

Constructed in the first years of the sixteenth century by the Sultan Vagiatzit II, the Fortress of Antirrio had been destroyed and rebuilt many times – by the Genoese, the Turks, the Venetians and then once more by the Turks. Surrounded on three sides by water, it guarded the narrow strait that separated the Gulf of Corinth to the east from the Gulf of Patras to the west, its guns set high on a mighty sea wall that commanded the channel. Although many of the towns on the opposite side of the strait were in the rebels' hands, the strategic position of the fortress in Antirrio was favorable, and by controlling the fortress, the janissaries had been able to maintain Ottoman control over the town.

Traversing the busy market square, she ignored the stares of the old women who gathered there most afternoons to pick through the produce and to gossip. They had no use for her – she was *Ahıska Türkleri*, and not to be trusted – and she had only contempt for them. She held her head high as she passed, pretending not to hear their whispers.

Putting the market behind her, Zehra turned a final corner in the old village and, looming before her, saw the battered fortress wall. The area around the gate had been intentionally flooded, cutting the fortress off from the town, but limited access was provided by a narrow, rickety footbridge guarded by two janissaries, one tall, with a thick mustache that drooped below his chin, the other short and burly and with only one good eye.

Hovering impatiently in the shadows until the street was clear, Zehra hurried over to the sentries who lounged, bored and irritable, on stumps that had been placed at the end of the footbridge. "I need to speak to your commanding officer," she whispered urgently. "Right away."

"Did you hear that, Kazim? 'Right away,' she says." The one-eyed janissary half-glowered at Zehra. "Only to the *chorbaji*? Give us a few minutes – perhaps we can arrange an audience with the *Grand Vizier* himself!" He laughed, his belly straining against the belted waist of his şalvar.

"I have valuable information," Zehra hissed, furtively scanning the empty street. "About a man you seek – an English! Ten thousand kuruş is the price on his head!" She saw the tall sentry with the mustache glance at her purse, and – empty or not – she clutched it tighter against her bony chest.

The one-eyed sentry grunted. "Ten thousand kuruş, you say? Tell you what. You tell us where this English is and we'll give you half the reward." He grinned, revealing a misshapen row of blackening teeth.

Zehra hesitated. "I want to speak to your commander, the – what did you say? – *chorbaji*." She glared at the janissary. "It won't go well for you if this man escapes," she warned, "and he learns it was your fault."

"Tosun," the tall Janissary whispered, "maybe we should –"

"He's not here right now, woman," interrupted Tosun, his eye fixed on Zehra. "He'll be back by sundown if you want to wait." He lowered his voice, adopting a confiding tone. "But imagine how pleased he'd be if we had the English here, all wrapped up like a basket of *baklava*. Why, I'll bet he'd double the reward!"

He grinned, but then – his expression sinking – he shook his head. "But if you wait, and this English escapes, I don't know what he'll do. He's a cruel and barbarous man, the *chorbaji*, and looks always for someone to blame, may Allah take pity upon the blameless."

Trying to think it through, Zehra stared up at the fortress, as though hoping someone might appear on its ramparts to tell her what to do. "How do I know I can trust you?" she demanded, her angular features clouded with suspicion. "That you won't seize him and claim the money for yourselves?"

Tosun looked wounded, his one eye doleful. "You're not a Greek – I can see it from your features and hear it on your tongue. *Ahıska Türkleri*?"

She nodded, and his face lit up. "I knew it! Before Allah, you are my sister, and I your brother. Did Abu Hurayra not tell us as the word of the Prophet himself that 'a true believer is he who treats with respect his women?' In his last sermon delivered on the Ninth Day of *Dhul Hijjah*, did the Prophet not say that, while it is true that men have certain rights over women, 'equally is it true that women have rights over men?'"

"Kazim," he asked, turning to his fellow sentry, "do I not observe the words of the Prophet? Do I not strive each day to be worthy?"

Kazim struggled for a moment to untangle the double negative, but then brightened. "Yes! Yes, you do!" He nodded vigorously at Zehra. "He does, I'm pretty sure."

"My sister," continued Tosun hastily, praying that Kazim would say nothing further, "I will split the reward with you equally, as would any honorable man. But we must hurry – unlike the *Ahıska*, who are renowned for their beauty and only grow lovelier with age, information quickly grows stale and soon may be of no value at all."

"We." Kazim nudged Tosun with his elbow. "You said 'I' would split the reward. You meant 'we.'"

"Yes, right, *we* will split it with our sister here." He turned back to Zehra. "Well?"

Reluctantly Zehra nodded, offering the one-eyed sentry a pinched smile. "My brother, I have no choice but to trust you. But," she went on, her face darkening, "may Allah condemn you to eternal torment if you betray me!"

She glanced up and down the street, reassuring herself that no one was watching. "I share a house with a fat, unambitious Greek named Nico, who wants nothing more from life than to fish and play *diloti* for hours with his friends over rounds of *mastikha*. 'Husband,' I scold him, 'is this how you wish to spend your dwindling days? Why can't you be more like Jubaila's husband–'"

"Woman!" Tosun sighed. "Get to the point before our shift changes and the opportunity is lost."

Zehra glared at him for a second, and then – her greed overcoming her pride – got to the point. "The English – with two others – is hiding in the back room of my house. I can take you there."

English or not, poet or not, they approached the house with caution, the two janissaries in the lead, Zehra behind them. "The English hide themselves in the back," she whispered, pointing at the house, "through the kitchen and past the stairs. There's a plank door that doesn't lock – you'll see it."

"Does the room have a window, or a back exit?" Tosun drew his *kilij*, gesturing at Kazim to do the same.

"No, just the one door." She stared at the janissaries' weapons. "Are you going to kill him?"

Tosun smirked. "You said the reward doesn't require that he live, foolish woman. What do you think?"

Zehra blanched but said nothing as the janissaries slid into place on either side of the front door, their backs to the stone. At a signal from Tosun, Kazim opened the door and, pivoting, eased his way through, his *kilij* raised. Encountering no one, he waved at Tosun to follow, and the two janissaries disappeared into the house, leaving Zehra to stand nervously in the street.

Even in the early evening the day's heat lingered, and the shutters on the windows were shut. Tosun and Kazim stood for a few moments, allowing their eyes to adjust to the darkness. They could tell from the close scent of dates and lamb that they were in the kitchen and, following Zehra's directions, they made their way past the table and chairs and out into the hallway. Tosun raised a finger, pointing up at the stairs on their right, then gestured at a narrow doorway past the stairs, at the back of the house.

"Check upstairs," he whispered, "and be quick." Kazim nodded, slid past Tosun in the narrow hallway, and started up the stairs. As his foot hit the second step, the old plank groaned, and both men froze.

"Be careful!" hissed Tosun. "Stay to the edge of the—"

He never finished the sentence. From behind the plank door, they heard a high-pitched cry and then a heavy thump. Waving for Kazim to follow, Tosun rushed to the door and pulled it open, his one good eye scanning the darkened room. Directly in front of him, a chair had been knocked over and, as he burst in, a familiar smell filled his nostrils.

Even if his understanding was often shaky, Kazim could see quite well. "Look, Tosun," he whispered. "Over by the wall." Squinting, Tosun saw a small, pot-bellied goat. The goat looked up disinterestedly and issued a high, thin bleat. Then, lowering its head, it enthusiastically butted a tall stack of boxes in the far corner. The top box wobbled and fell, crashing to the stone floor. With a smooth clatter, a brown tide of almonds spread like lava across the floor. Satisfied, the goat lowered its head and began to eat.

"I like goats," Kazim volunteered amiably. He looked around the room, remembering why they'd come. "Where's the English?"

CHAPTER 61
A Striking of Arrangements

Great Galileo was debarred the sun,
Because he fixed it, and to stop his talking
How earth could round the solar orbit run,
Found his own legs embargoed from mere walking.
The man was well-nigh dead, ere men begun
To think his skull had not some need of caulking,
But now it seems he's right, his notion just,
No doubt a consolation to his dust.

DON JUAN, CANTO XVII

IN THE end, the negotiations were tidy. Acting as broker and more or less trusted by both sides, Henry Brougham managed to architect an arrangement within a matter of weeks following Eldon and Grey's conversation with Hobhouse. Byron agreed to "re-locate" to the Continent, and to allow his seat in the House of Lords to be "temporarily retired." Eldon, in turn, agreed that no motion to suspend or discipline Byron would be offered; that neither he nor any of his Tory colleagues would lend their voices to attacks from any source on Byron's personal conduct; that Addington would drop the sedition charge against Leigh Hunt, though not without a stern warning that future calumnies would not be tolerated; and that Byron's seat in the House – at least in theory – might on some future date be reclaimed with the consent of the Lord Chancellor, whoever might hold that position at the time.

Only one demand – the source of which was Byron himself – required prolonged discussion. "I do not intend to slink off into the night," he said to Brougham when they met in Byron's study to discuss terms. "In return for waiving my right to challenge what would clearly be an illegal infringement on my rights as a peer, I demand the right to address the House before I – what are you calling it? – ah, yes, before I 'retire.'"

"Address the House?" Brougham seemed surprised. "On what subject?"

"Oh, nothing terribly momentous," Byron answered airily. "Tyranny, the Rights of Man, that sort of thing. Shouldn't take long."

"My Lord, why raise such issues now? In Parliament, I mean. You've held your seat for quite some time, but have chosen to speak, what, twice?" Brougham looked over at Hobhouse, whom Byron had asked to sit in on the conversation. "Mr. Hobhouse, have you any views on this matter?"

Byron frowned. "Hobby is my friend and a trusted advisor, Henry, but on this I require no advice. Until I retire my seat, I remain a peer in good standing; correct?"

"Yes," Brougham allowed, "that's quite right. But–"

"And as a peer, I have the right to address the House; do I not?"

Brougham smiled. "You have a gift for the art of examination, my Lord. Yes, as a peer, you have the right to address the House. Of course, if the leadership finds your terms offensive, your status could change rather suddenly, and with it your prerogatives."

"Which is why I have asked only to make a few remarks from the House floor. My fellow peers do this regularly and, as best I can tell, no great harm seems to come of it."

Brougham sighed, jotting a few notes in the scarred, leather-bound journal he always carried with him. "Very well, my Lord," he said, rising from his chair. "I'll see if I can persuade Lord Eldon and Lord Grey. But, as you surely have a notion as to what you intend to say, could you at least tell me this; which are the more likely to be aggrieved by your remarks? The Tories, whose policies you attack; or the Whigs, whose principles you defend?"

Byron laughed. "If I'm on my game, Henry – both!"

When Brougham departed, Hobhouse raised a quizzical brow. "What are you up to? A parting shot?"

"A catharsis of sorts, I suppose."

"I didn't know you needed one."

"Need? Probably not. But no matter how I might rant and rave in verse, condemning the King as corrupt, Castlereagh as a tyrant, Southey as a hack and the Tories as Villainy's baying hounds, the page remains mute, absorbing it all in silence. Bloody hell, Hobby – just once I want to watch the arrow hit the target!"

"That's all well and good, and no doubt great fun. But what then?"

Byron shrugged. "A friend has a villa in Ravenna, on the Grand Canal between the *Piazza San Marco* and the *Rialto* bridge. I may stay there for a while. After that, who knows?"

Reaching into his pocket, Hobhouse extracted a cigar, which he rolled back and forth between his palms but did not light. "Are you still considering the Greek Committee's proposal?"

"I am. Blaquiere and Bowring sent me an accounting of what the committee has raised to date, and how much more will be required to equip and field a Souliote brigade. Looks like another £7500 might do it." He beckoned towards a side table. "Would a glass of port persuade you to put away that cigar, or would it merely incite you further?"

"Well done, Byron," Hobhouse grinned, sliding the cigar back into his coat pocket. "A modest but effective bribe!"

As Byron poured two glasses of tawny, Hobhouse leaned back in his chair, doing the arithmetic in his head. "With the money you've realized from Newstead's sale, such an amount would be well within your means."

"It would indeed," Byron agreed, handing a glass to Hobhouse and taking a sip from his own. "There would be additional expense, of course, and the bloody Albanians will steal whatever they can. Still, to lead men in so glorious a cause? It's tempting. It's just ...."

"Just what?"

Byron gave his friend a sharp look. "Hobby, don't start. You know very well what."

"Augusta?"

"Yes, that's part of it. I left Cambridge resolved to put this infatuation behind me, for her sake at least as much as mine. I haven't written her in weeks, nor have I answered any of her letters, which arrive daily."

"Oh? What is her mind on this?"

Byron threw up his hands. "She's like the rest of her gender, Hobby – she wants what she cannot have and yearns for whatever's most dangerous. But in common with at least the women I've known – and I've known a few – she cannot ask but can only yield. Which, once again, puts it all on me."

"Didn't you make this decision weeks ago, in your sister's parlour in Cambridge? You told me that you had doubts about – how did you put it? – the *domesticity* a relationship with Augusta would entail. And that, to your credit, you realized she could never be happy – not for the long term anyway – away from England."

"Yes, I know what I said. It's just that it isn't how I *feel*."

Hobhouse took a deep breath, weighing how much to risk. "Byron, you bloody sod. Are you so old and lame and, and ... *lovesick* that, rather than championing the cause of Greek independence, where you might actually be able to make a difference, you'd prefer to pine away for your bloody sister in a crumbling villa in Ravenna?" Hobhouse snorted derisively. "That's not the Byron I know!" He shook his head, his voice

368 \ A Striking of Arrangements

dripping with disdain. "It's pathetic and unworthy. It is neither who you are nor who you wish to be!"

For a moment, Byron sat in what Hobhouse thought might be stunned silence. Then he threw back his head and laughed.

"Hobby, *bravo*! That was magnificent!" Lifting his glass in a mock toast, he drained it in a swallow. "But the mere fact that it was a performance – and you the world's worst actor – does not make it untrue. In fact, Hobby, you are correct – I made my decision and will live with it, whether I'm pleased with the outcome or not."

Hobhouse drained his own glass, hoping that Byron wouldn't notice that his hands were shaking. "And the Greek Committee?"

"I've already written to Bowring. After a short time in Italy I will sail to Missolonghi, where barracks and a training ground have been readied. Bowring has secured the participation of several experienced officers, who will be in operational command. I will provide the financing and do what I can to assist with logistics and – for want of a better word – publicity. All on one condition."

"What's the condition?" Hobhouse asked cautiously. One couldn't survive years of friendship with Byron without cultivating an ability to sense trouble.

"The condition, Hobby, is that you come with me – I can't do this alone."

❧ ❧

As Brougham expected, Lord Eldon initially opposed giving Byron the opportunity to address the Lords.

"Who knows what he might say?" the Lord Chancellor grumbled. "If Byron were to level a personal attack against any member, that member would have the right to respond in kind. Before long, this entire arrangement could unravel."

Extracting a silver snuffbox from his pocket, Eldon inhaled a pinch and sneezed. "Not that I care a whit. I'd just as soon see him in the dock."

"Yes, my Lord," Brougham said soothingly, his barrister's voice deep and resonant. "I will stress how important it is that he moderate his remarks."

Grey rolled his eyes. "Good luck with that, Henry. You might as well instruct a scorpion to sting gently."

Eldon muttered darkly – Brougham couldn't quite make it out but thought it sounded menacing. "Brougham, if we allow Byron his little speech – and I must advise you, I would do so only with the greatest reluctance – we would expect him to leave England before a single leaf turns with the season."

"Yes, my Lord. That would be Lord Byron's intent."

"Very well," Eldon grunted, dismissing Brougham with a curt nod. "I will discuss it with those most directly concerned."

Only a day or two later, a messenger delivered a note from the Lord Chancellor. "Byron may address the Lords," it said simply, "but tell him to keep it short."

CHAPTER 62
St. Petersburg

THE LATE-NOVEMBER wind was biting, swirling in petulant gusts that stung Juan's eyes and numbed his hands. Only rarely did the Gulf of Finland freeze over, but not so the Neva River, which entered St. Petersburg in the east, sloughed off multiple channels and tributaries as it meandered through the city, split into the Bolshaya Neva and the Malaya Neva just west of the Winter Palace, and ultimately emptied into the Baltic to the west. The river was already frozen in many places and, as Juan strode along its banks, his frozen hands shoved deep into the pockets of the black long-coat he'd purchased from a French trader in Odessa, three young boys on skates glided past him on the river, their voices fluttering in the wind.

Minutes from his audience with Tsar Alexander, he gave thanks once again for Harry Dryden. St. Petersburg was more than a thousand miles from Odessa, and when they said their farewells to Captain Cavalli and his officers and disembarked at the busy Odessa docks on a crisp autumn afternoon that smelled to Juan like salty apples, he and Caria had spent a couple of days resting and exploring the free port city while Dryden plumbed his seemingly endless network of contacts and friends, making arrangements for this and trading favors for that.

On their third evening in Odessa, he met them for supper at a crowded tavern run by a burly Bulgarian with sharp black eyes and outsized ears. Nodding to the proprietor as he entered, Harry crossed the room in a few *long strides, slid into the narrow booth next to Caria and, reaching across the table, helped himself to one of Juan's roasted potatoes.*

"Sorry I'm late," he said, washing down his potato with some of Juan's ale. "I'm famished! I don't like to complain – it never seems to do much good, so why waste my breath and your time? – but it's hard work, negotiating passage on short notice and with no choice but to dicker with men whose word cannot be trusted."

Harry craned his neck, hoping to find a waiter. "It's bloody fortunate that bastard Kornilov still lives here and owes me money, although I had to remind him of it several times and reacquaint the sod with the concept of interest!" He let out an exaggerated sigh as he eyed Juan's plate, and grinned when Juan pushed it across the table. "That's the spirit, young Juan – live a decent life, kill only those you must, and offer up kindness when you can."

He popped another potato into his mouth and, taking hold of a roasted chicken leg, poked it in the air emphatically. "Do all that, and mayhap one day you too will have the pluck to arrange a coach from Odessa to Riga, and passage from there by ship to St. Pete!"

The journey was long but uneventful, and by the time they arrived in St. Petersburg, the city spires shining in the golden glow of the setting sun, winter had set in and fresh snow lay in great drifts along the Baltic shore. Unlike most of Europe's capitals, St. Petersburg was a new city, founded early in the prior century by Peter the Great, who envisioned his capital as a cosmopolitan mix of east and west. As they made their way into the city from the docks, they were astonished at the diversity of architectural styles, with Byzantine turrets and golden domes giving way to imposing multi-columned neo-classical and Greek Revival buildings that would not have looked out of place in London or Vienna.

They took rooms in a modest hotel only a few blocks from the newly-completed Kazan Cathedral and, at Harry's insistence, paused "to have a look at this lad Voronikhin's handiwork." He shook his head at his friends' blank looks. "The architect. It's an uncommon story; he was born a serf but was so capable it didn't matter."

*They stood on the street, gazing up at the cathedral. "It's impressive,"
Dryden allowed as they admired the enormous vaulted dome and portico
and the graceful colonnaded curve of the galleries, which swept off to either
side like a gull's wings. "But if you ask me, it's a bit derivative, sort of
a combination of St. Peter's Basilica in Rome and – with those massive
bronze doors in the front – the Baptistery in Florence." He turned away to
find Juan and Caria staring at him. "What?"*

*It took only a few minutes' conversation at a local tavern for Dryden to
learn that Gudovich was quartered a few miles west of Schlisselburg, a good
day's ride to the east. When he returned to tell Juan and Caria what he'd
learned, he had already formulated a plan.*

*"The best way to approach the Tsar will be through Gudovich. I'll ride out
to see him; I imagine he'll be pleased to see me, if somewhat surprised to find
that I'm still among the living. I'll need to show him the Sultana's note," he
added apologetically. "Even Gudovich might fear the consequences were he to
facilitate a meeting with the Tsar on false pretenses, so he'll be careful and will
want to see it for himself."*

*Procuring a sturdy horse at a nearby stable, Dryden departed at dawn
for Gudovich's camp. He was gone for three days. When he returned, he wore
the blue jacket, red leggings and high black boots of a Russian cavalry officer.*

*"Well, I found Gudovich," he grinned, falling into a cracked leather
chair in the hotel lobby. "Once he realized I'd been dragooned and wasn't a
deserter, he was so pleased to see me he decided not to have me shot!"*

*Inclining his head to Caria, he reached into his coat pocket and pulled
out a small, carefully wrapped package. "When I told him about you and
Juan," Harry said as he handed her the package, "and how bravely you
acquitted yourself in Constantinople, he insisted that I present you with a
token of his esteem."*

*Caria put her hand to her mouth – it was perhaps the first time Juan
had seen her taken aback – and, opening the package, removed two delicate
earrings, each in the form of a golden cross. Reaching for the earrings, Juan
carefully fit them into Caria's pierced lobes.*

"Did I hurt you?" he asked with alarm, seeing the tears on Caria's cheeks.

"No, no – not at all," she whispered, her voice quavering. She took a moment to compose herself, wiping her cheeks with her palms. "I think I like this Gudovich," she announced, her voice firmer. "Now, what did you learn about my father, and what did the Marshal say about getting us in to see the Tsar?"

❧❧   ❧❧

Three days later, in accordance with the instructions that Dryden had received from Gudovich, Juan dressed in his finest things and readied himself for the walk to the Winter Palace, at which he had been told to arrive at sunset.

"Juan, I really should come with you," pressed Caria as he smoothed his jacket and checked his teeth in the mirror. "I can be of use, and – who knows? – may be able to keep you from saying something stupid." She scrutinized Juan's clothing through critical eyes and, reaching up, adjusted his cravat. "They shoot people here, if what they say is stupid enough."

Juan laughed. "I'm a messenger, Caria, nothing more. Traveling on papers signed by Gudovich himself." He stroked Caria's hair, his fingers lingering on her cheek. "Besides, I survived my encounter with the Sultan, did I not?"

"Only because you were disguised as a woman and didn't say a word. You don't have that option now, do you?"

"Oh, I don't know," Juan replied, "perhaps it's not too late to change my outfit. Maybe something low-cut, in a rose and cream chiffon?"

Unamused, Caria hmphed and turned away, her arms crossed. "It's not like I have nothing at stake, Christian. Yes, my father is safe for now, praise Allah for that, and Harry for finding him in the ranks of Gudovich's cavalry. But unless the Sultan resolves the situation with the Greeks soon, Harry thinks Alexander is likely to mobilize his troops. If he does, Gudovich's

Hussars will be in the vanguard. My father's life may depend on what you say and how you say it."

Juan set his hands on Caria's shoulders. "Caria, we've been over this. You heard Harry. Gudovich was clear, as was the Sultana; as Gulbayez' message is for the Tsar's eyes alone, he will expect it to be delivered solely by the one to whom it was entrusted. You know," he grinned, brushing his hair out of his eyes and batting them coyly at Caria, "that good-looking Spaniard you've taken up with?"

Caria hesitated and then gave in, kissing him hard on the lips. Even as he pulled her close, his hands sliding down her spine, he felt once more the unwelcome tug of guilt.

⁂   ⁂

Hurrying along the Neva's embankment, Juan skirted the edge of the Summer Garden, its bordering trees now bleak and leafless, and passed the Marble Palace, the wind whistling through the two dozen marble columns that fronted the river like the strings of a harp. It was late-afternoon on a Sunday and few people were out– Juan had heard the peal of bells as he made his way through the city, and thought perhaps they rang to summon the faithful to Mass.

As he approached the imposing white and green façade of the Winter Palace, he heard the shouts of workmen from across the river. Squinting into the sun, low in the sky in the winter months, Juan saw the partially-completed Stock Exchange building originally commissioned in the last century by Peter the Great, and still under construction on the easternmost tip of Vasilyevsky Island. Inspired by the ancient Temple of Hera in Paestum, the Exchange's imposing Doric columns were enclosed by scaffolding and, looking up, Juan could see a small wooden platform dangling uselessly in the wind. Shielding his eyes, he saw that a crowd of workers had gathered at the foot of one of the columns, directly below the broken platform.

As he watched, several uniformed soldiers emerged from the crowd, struggling to carry off what appeared to be a body. Another half-dozen soldiers stood by, their swords at their sides. The gathered workers watched in silence, hunched against the wind and cold. No longer a stranger to death, Juan wondered how many were summing up the ledgers of their own lives. When the soldiers disappeared around the building's corner, the workmen gradually dispersed, until Juan could see no one at all.

It was getting dark and even colder, though Juan hadn't thought that possible. The winter sun had dipped below the nearly-completed Admiralty Building to the west, and Juan shivered and pulled his coat tight as he hurried to the southern side of the Winter Palace.

"Who do I ask for?" he'd asked, as Harry and Caria helped him prepare for his audience with the Tsar.

"No need to ask," Harry had assured him, "they'll find you."

Just as Harry predicted, Juan had no sooner turned the corner onto the expansive Dvortsovaya Ploshchad – Palace Square – when he found himself flanked by four soldiers, each dressed in the long white leggings and dark, cross-sashed tunic of Tsar Alexander's Imperial Grenadier Guard. Including their ceremonial helmets, which extended more than a foot above their heads, they seemed impossibly tall to Juan, who smiled up at them bravely.

"Umm, good evening," he managed to say, hoping his chattering teeth wouldn't be misunderstood. "My name is Juan Pedro Calderón de Castilla, from Seville." He handed over the papers that Gudovich had provided to Dryden. "It's cold out here," Juan continued, looking up into the soldiers' expressionless faces, "and I've traveled a long way."

After the soldiers had had a moment to examine his papers, Juan gestured at the imposing trio of arches that dominated the southern entrance to the Winter Palace, whose doubled-colonnaded façade rose above them like an extravagantly gilded cliff. He still could hardly believe how cold it was.

"Do you fellows mind if we go in? I carry a message for His Excellency the Tsar."

CHAPTER 63
Where Danger Lies

Heaven and his friends knew that a private life
Had ever been his sole and whole ambition,
But could he quit his King in times of strife,
Which threatened the whole country with perdition?
When demagogues would with a butcher's knife
Cut through and through (oh damnable incision!)
The Gordian or the Geordian knot, whose strings
Have tied together Commons, Lords, and Kings.

DON JUAN, CANTO XVI

HENRY ADDINGTON didn't bother to acknowledge Reilly's existence, much less his stammered greeting. Brushing past the lad's spotless desk – Castlereagh had become obsessed with orderliness in recent months, and Reilly had no intention of provoking him – Addington let himself in.

The office lay in shadow, the drapes drawn. At the far side of one of the windows, peeking past the edge of the drape to the street below, stood the Foreign Secretary. Looking over at Addington, he put a finger to his lips.

"Softly, Henry," he said, his voice barely a whisper. "One never knows who's listening." He peered down at the street. "Did anyone follow you here?"

"No, Robert – no one." Addington gestured at the window. "Who do you expect to see?"

"That's the thing, Henry; I don't know. But someone has been spreading rumors, and I have little doubt I'm being watched."

Addington nodded. Castlereagh's behavior over the last couple of months had become erratic, but Addington knew how hard he was working and the pressures he was under. He assumed his colleague was suffering from the effects of stress, and had urged him to spend some time with Emily in the country. Castlereagh would have none of it, staring at the Home Secretary with enough suspicion that Addington had immediately changed the subject.

"Is anyone out there now?" he asked carefully.

"No, no – never mind, Henry." Castlereagh released the edge of the drape and turned to Addington with a weak smile. "Probably nothing, just the normal gusting of the political winds." Extracting a silk handkerchief from his breast pocket, he wiped the sweat from his forehead. "Damnably hot in here. Can I get you something to drink?"

"Kind of you but no. You wished to see me?"

"Quite so." He settled into his chair, Addington taking one across from him. "I received a note this morning from Byron."

Addington arched his brow. "Really? What, is he seeking to save his seat – or perhaps his soul – with an eleventh-hour conversion?"

"No. Say what you will about him, he has always stood by his convictions, however misguided."

"Yes. Byron is to perversion what Thomas More was to Catholicism. A pity you're so set on sparing him a similar end."

"There are worse things than death, Henry," Castlereagh murmured. He sighed and, reaching across his desk, lifted a folded note.

"A week or so ago, as a condition to his accepting a voluntary exile, Byron asked for an opportunity to address the House of Lords. After discussing the matter with the Lord Chancellor, whose reluctance I well understand, I was able to convince him to allow it." He handed the note to Addington. "I received this note today."

Reaching into his jacket, Addington found his glasses, which he carefully slipped over his nose. He raised the note and read it aloud.

Lord Castlereagh,

As you know, I have been granted the 'privilege' of doing that which as a peer is entirely my right. In making my remarks to the Lords next week, I may express opinions hostile to your own, and which may cast you in an unfavorable light. Therefore, as a matter of honor I wish to advise you of this possibility so that – if you choose – you may attend and respond. Whatever my feelings may be regarding your policies and conduct, your office deserves respect, even if its present occupant does not.

Byron

With an impressive degree of contempt given the simplicity of the act, Addington tossed the note onto the desk. "Cheeky bastard, isn't he?"

Castlereagh shrugged. "I don't know. In his own way, it's rather thoughtful, don't you think?"

"Of course, you're going to ignore his speech, aren't–" He stopped in mid-sentence. "You're shaking your head. Why are you shaking your head?"

"I intend to be there, Henry, although I suppose that whether I rise in reply will depend on what he says. I asked you to drop by only to make sure that – no matter what Byron says on the floor – no action is taken against him."

Addington stared at his long-time colleague as though he'd lost his mind. "What on earth are you up to, Robert? Byron has raked you over the coals in his damned verse and, as you and I both know, in dining rooms and parlours from here to Liverpool. You'd have long-ago made an example of anyone else. Like that Irish journalist you sued for libel, what was his name?"

"Finnerty. Peter Finnerty. I had no choice there – he accused me of sanctioning the use of torture to put down the Irish Rebellion in '98. While I don't deny that mistakes were made, they were the product of chaos, not policy."

"In the face of rebellion, one does what's necessary. But, more to the point, hasn't Byron said the same or worse? Why are you protecting him?"

Castlereagh grimaced, closing his eyes against the sudden pain and pressing his thumb and middle finger to his temple. "I have my reasons, Henry. Trust me, Byron has a higher purpose, whether he knows it at present or not. Let him say what he will about me, it doesn't matter."

He looked up at Addington with narrowed eyes. "I hear the dark whispers – the filth they seek to pass as truth – to undo me, Henry – to destroy my work. Nothing Byron says can cut as deeply as the knives of men who pose as friends."

"What whispers? I've heard nothing, other than the concern of your friends that you push yourself too hard."

Castlereagh rubbed his eyes, trying to focus. "Never mind, Henry – too many late nights. When the bloody Eastern Question is resolved, perhaps Emily and I will have some time to relax, maybe even travel. But for now, can I count on you to stand down on Byron, no matter what he may say in the Lords?"

"If that's what you want. It would be complicated to prosecute him for remarks made in Parliament anyway. It seems that notions of Parliamentary privilege have become quite fashionable. To my mind we've got it backwards – we punish those whose words are barely heard, while tolerating blasphemy and calumny on the floor of Parliament itself."

"Thank you, Henry. I can't tell you–"

"Don't be so quick to thank me, Robert. It's true that prosecutions for sedition fall within my portfolio. Nevertheless, like you, I must answer to Jenkinson and to the Crown. If Byron goes too far, well, my hands may be tied. The Regent – bloody hell, I've got to stop doing that, the *King*.

The King has already complained at least twice about Byron's parody of Southey." Addington rolled his eyes. "Seems your boy may have struck too close to the mark!"

"But you said it yourself, Henry; what Byron says in the Lords is privileged."

"I said a criminal prosecution would be *complicated*, not impossible. Besides – and I seem to recall you making this same point quite recently – a prosecution may serve political purposes whether or not a conviction is obtained, particularly if it is conducted in a manner calculated to drain the purse and tarnish the reputation."

Castlereagh frowned – he preferred to avoid unnecessary risk, and usually managed to orchestrate events to his liking. But Byron was unpredictable and – particularly if provoked in the give and take of Parliamentary debate – who knew what he might say? He remembered Southey's smug assessment – *'Given enough time and freedom, he will destroy himself, no matter what you and I may say or do.'*

"I understand, Henry," he said, his headache beginning to pound once more. "If Byron begins to go too far, I will intercede."

Although Addington appeared unconvinced, he chose not to press the point. He rose to leave but Castlereagh remained seated, his fingers pressed to his temples.

"Are you alright Robert? Is this situation with Byron more serious than it appears?"

Castlereagh didn't look up. "No, Byron's no problem, Henry. He's gifted, no question, but more forthright than devious. One can see him coming." His voice, already soft, trailed off so that Addington had to strain to hear him. "It's the others; the ones you can't see but whose poison is more insidious. That's where the real danger lies."

CHAPTER 64
One Finger at a Time

DARKNESS, BYRON had once lamented, descends no less gradually than the first glimmering of dawn brightens into daylight, but without the hope that attends the sunrise. It was dark now, down by the water's edge, but as they crept along the quay, concealed behind barrels of olives and fragrant crates of lavender and sage, he felt more hopeful than he had any right to expect. Once more they had cheated death and, if their suspicions were correct, the sinister machinations of their own government. He wanted to live – he wasn't half in love with death like poor Keats – but neither did he contemplate his end with terror. Hobhouse and Polidori, however, were a different matter. No matter the cost, their deaths must not be on his hands.

He had been sleeping in Nico's house, leaning up against the cool wall alongside Hobhouse and Polidori, when he felt a hand on his shoulder.

"By-roon. Come, we must go." Panos moved on, hurrying to wake Hobhouse and Polidori in turn.

"It's time? Already?" Byron stretched, his back sore from the hard floor.

"Nico's wife – Zehra? I do not trust this woman, so when she goes from the door I follow. Where does she to go? To the bloody janissaries! She will bring them to here. For the reward." Panos gestured at the door, where a small goat stood patiently, chewing on an old ear of corn.

"We must go – hurry. I leave here Nico's goat – maybe she makes them busy for some time."

They'd departed quickly, closing the door behind the goat. The Turks would be coming up the hill from the harbor, so they climbed further and watched from a safe distance as Zehra and the janissaries approached the house.

"That bitch!" Hobhouse spat, furious at Zehra's betrayal.

"We've no cause to complain," Byron observed equably, "she owes us nothing. Nico, on the other hand, may wish to re-think his marital vows."

"Speaking of Nico, where is he?" Polidori whispered, turning to Panos. "We need him to get us to Raffi's boat."

"He leaves the house close before Zehra – to talk to Raffi. After the dark, he says to meet him to the western end of the quay."

They'd circled away to the west, then followed the hill down toward the harbor. Now, as they crouched behind a line of olive barrels and surveyed the docks, they could see half a dozen janissaries spread out at intervals. A horse-drawn wagon stood in the road at the eastern end of the quay, a placid white mare in harness. A sizeable pile of hay lay at her feet, with the rest mounded loosely in the wagon's bed. The mare bowed low as she ate her supper, looking up from time to time to shake her ponderous head.

As they watched, the janissaries questioned returning fishermen as they sorted and cleaned their catch. Byron sniffed the air, which smelled like pitch. Peering between the barrels, he traced the odor to an iron kettle of hot tar perhaps sixty yards down the quay. Blackly viscous, the tar had been used to fire torches that stood at intervals in metal brackets. A few unlit torches, their ends sticky with pitch, stood in a pail beside the kettle, awaiting the fire.

"Look," said Hobhouse, pointing. "It's the sods Zehra brought to Nico's." Craning his neck, Byron saw the two janissaries – the one tall and thin, the other short and round – speaking with an elegantly dressed senior officer with thinning hair and a greying beard. The janissaries gesticulated, first pointing up the hill toward Nico's house, then out to the western side of the harbor. The officer listened carefully.

When the two janissaries completed their report, the officer barked an order. In a matter of moments, a junior officer leveled his sword at the two janissaries, relieved them of their weapons and, over the short one's shouted protests, led them away.

"They know we're here," Byron noted grimly, his optimism beginning to evaporate, "and Zehra no doubt told them what we're up to."

Sure enough, as the sounds of protest faded, the senior officer summoned two of his men and pointed out into the harbor towards a fishing boat whose dim outline they could just make out in the distance.

"This is not good," Panos whispered. And quickly, the situation grew worse. Heralded by the gentle slap of oars on water, a small rowboat emerged from the darkness, a stout Greek in a loose blue smock working the oars.

"It's Nico!" Polidori hissed. "Do you think he knows–"

Polidori's question was interrupted by shouts, as two janissaries rushed down to the dock. Nico looked up as though surprised. "*Teşekkür ederim!*" he shouted jovially as he eased the boat alongside the dock. *Thank you!* He slid the oars into the boat and tossed the bowline to one of the janissaries, who scowled as he secured it. Flanked by soldiers, Nico waited as the grey-bearded officer strode to the dock's edge.

"My name is Demir," the officer announced. "Colonel Demir. And if I'm not mistaken, you are Christopoulos?"

"Nico Christopoulos, Colonel."

"Are you related to Anastasios Christopoulos?"

Nico turned his head and spat. "My cousin's third son? A bad seed, that one." He extended his arm, palm down. "Haven't seen him since he was this high. Is he in trouble again?"

"You might say that. He's been active in the current rebellion, and is wanted for treason. But that's not why I had my men detain you."

"Oh?" Nico was solicitous. "How can I assist you?"

"Two of my men were informed that an Englishman – three Englishmen, in fact – were in hiding at your house. Now, I have long known these two to be dim-witted, a fact they demonstrated once again by failing to inform their superiors and by failing to establish a perimeter before approaching your house." Colonel Demir smiled sadly, as though pained to have to acknowledge such stupidity. "Nevertheless, I do tend to credit the informant's account."

Nico turned and spat again. "I know nothing of any Englishmen, Colonel. Why do you credit one who would concoct such a story?"

"Because, Mr. Christopoulos, our informant is your wife." Casually, Colonel Demir pulled a short dagger from a sheath on his belt and ran his finger along the flat of the blade. "Now, enough of this nonsense. Would you like to tell me where these men are hidden, or must I extract that information one finger at a time?"

CHAPTER 65
Influence in Certain Circles

WHILE JUAN had only limited experience in the matter of palaces, he had spent at least a little time in the Sultan's alcazar in Constantinople and expected to find the Tsar's Winter Palace much the same. But as his footsteps echoed down the polished marble corridor, the Tsar's Grenadiers flanking him two by two, he was struck not by the similarities between the Sultan's and Tsar's palaces but by their differences. Although both were magnificent beyond measure, the Sultan's had been an animate hive of activity. Men and women laughed, debated, danced, worked, ate and drank, and as music from one room faded behind a passing visitor, music from another took up the refrain.

The Winter Palace, by contrast, seemed almost empty save for the guards posted at the confluence of corridors and outside elaborately carved doors that led who knew where. As they proceeded, they passed paintings as large as tapestries, which Juan recognized from his studies in Seville as the works of Rembrandt, Rafael, Van Dyke and Rubens. Above his head, hanging from a ceiling he estimated was at least thirty feet high, were crystal chandeliers that looked like enormous wedding cakes and which glowed softly in a golden frosting of candlelight.

They passed through an archway and into a grand gallery whose shining, intricately stenciled floor stretched out before them like a polished wooden sea. Rising sets of twinned columns lined each side of the cavernous *room, supporting an upper gallery lined with windows. But unlike the Sultan's palace, in which all manner of men and women were busily engaged in each 'room' defined by the interspersed columns, here stood only empty urns and pensive busts.*

At the far end of the gallery, atop a platform fronted by a set of semi-circular steps, stood a red velvet throne. Behind it, emblazoned on a rich red tapestry shaded at its top by a red and gold canopy, was Ivan the Great's double-eagle, long the symbol of imperial Russia. When they were within a dozen feet of the throne, the Grenadiers came to a sudden halt.

They stood at the terminus of the gallery for several minutes, directly in front of the empty throne. Juan was conscious of his own breathing, and wondered if it sounded as loud to his escorts. Finally, just as he felt sure he could endure the silence no longer, a door to the left of the throne opened and a small man in brown robes stepped through. The man lifted a finger and, without a word, the Grenadiers pivoted in unison, retreating down the corridor.

The cleric – for that is how Juan took him – approached and inclined his head ever so slightly. "I am Brother Mikhail. I understand you have a message for the Tsar?"

Juan nodded. "I do, and though I mean no disrespect, it is for the Tsar alone." He shrugged his shoulders in apology. "I am nothing but a messenger, but this much was made quite clear."

Brother Mikhail did not seem to take offense. "Of course." He took a half-step to the side and gestured towards the door through which he had entered. "Please, follow me."

They passed through a small antechamber and came to a richly-stained double door guarded by two Grenadiers. "Raise your arms," Brother Mikhail said apologetically, watching as a Grenadier patted Juan carefully from neck to toe. Satisfied, the soldier nodded.

Brother Mikhail stepped to the door and knocked twice. Turning to Juan, he smiled. "The Emperor of all the Russia's will see you now. If he asks you a question, my advice is to answer it fully. The Tsar dislikes equivocation." Opening the door, Brother Mikhail once again inclined his head and then withdrew. Juan took a deep breath, patted his pocket for the thousandth time, and stepped through the doorway.

He found himself in a spacious wood-paneled office. Paintings in gilded gold frames adorned the walls, a deep red and gold carpet cushioned his feet, and a fire crackled in a weathered brick hearth. On the far side of the room was a massive oaken desk; at its side stood Tsar Alexander I, Emperor of Russia. He wore a military uniform of a green so dark it looked almost black, with gold epaulets on both shoulders and a row of ribbons across his chest. He wasn't a tall man, and his thinning auburn hair had for the most part retreated to the sides of his head. Juan had expected that a Tsar would be severe in aspect; but when Alexander smiled, his eyes were more curious than menacing.

"Good evening, young man," said the Tsar, motioning Juan to one of the chairs that faced the great desk. Juan waited as Alexander circled the desk and settled into his straight-backed leather chair, then sat down himself.

"Thank you for seeing me, your Excellency," Juan replied, furiously trying to remember the protocols in which Caria and Harry had coached him. His mind was a blank – he couldn't remember a single one – and he resolved to say as little as possible.

"Your name is Juan Pedro Calderón de Castilla, and you are from Spain. Do I have that right?"

Juan nodded. "Si," he said, cursing himself for lapsing nervously into his native tongue.

"You have travelled here from Constantinople?"

"Yes, your Excellency."

Alexander waited patiently. When Juan remained silent, the tiniest hint of a grin turned up the corners of his mouth. "You have a message for me?" he suggested helpfully.

"Yes, your Excellency." Juan feared the Tsar had already marked him as a slow-witted dolt, but there was nothing to do but press on. "It is from the Sultana Gulbayez, the Ottoman Sultan's seventh wife. In return

for allowing my companions and I to escape with our lives, she bade me deliver a message to you directly." Reaching into his pocket, Juan extracted the Sultana's note. "The note is in code," he added, remembering Harry's parting admonition – "make damn sure Alexander knows that you haven't the foggiest notion of what the message might say."

Juan passed him the note. Unfolding the paper, Alexander studied it carefully, finally reaching up to pull what looked to Juan to be a bell cord. Within seconds, Brother Mikhail appeared at the door.

"Mikhailovich, I have a note here that employs a substitution cipher." He handed over the note. "How long will it take to have this decoded and translated?"

"Perhaps an hour or two, your Excellency."

"Good! See to it. And Mikhailovich, have someone bring in food and drink." He turned to Juan. "Are you hungry, young man?" While Juan didn't know how to respond – what was the protocol for dining with a Tsar? – he hadn't eaten since morning and was famished. "Umm, well sir, since you mention it, your Excellency. Yes."

"Good!" Alexander seemed pleased. "We'll have cold fish and iced vodka, and you'll tell me all about the Sultan's palace, and how you came to be a Sultana's messenger. And when the message is decoded, if I have any questions, you'll do your best to answer them." The Tsar rubbed his hands together briskly. "Won't you?"

⁂ ⁂

Over cold poached salmon and caviar, Juan recounted his adventures since leaving Seville. Alexander listened attentively, picking at his fish while asking what it was like to watch the Angelica go down; how the captain of the pirate ship Panagia maintained discipline among his crew; whether Sultanahmet Square was larger than Dvortsovaya Ploshchad; why the sipahi officer Tokaskh chose not to kill Juan and Dryden; what the Nubian eunuch looked like and what he wore; whether or not he'd met the

Sultan and what kind of man Juan thought he was; and more. When Juan told Alexander of Gulbayez, he omitted any mention of the Sultana's desire to bed him, but the Tsar was quick to interrupt.

"She had her eunuch disguise you as a woman and bring you to her inner chamber? Why?"

"I can't really say, Excellency. She paid a pretty price at the auction – perhaps she wished to inspect her latest acquisition."

"She didn't have your friend Dryden brought to her, though she paid for him as well." Alexander lowered his voice and leaned forward. "Her interest in you was of a different nature, wasn't it?"

Juan lowered his eyes and made no answer.

"Ah," the Tsar said, chuckling. "You display the chivalry for which Spaniards are so well known! But you are an intelligent young man and, if our conversation is any indication, well-educated. You've read Cervantes, yes?"

"Umm, yes," Juan answered hesitantly. He wondered where this was going.

"What does Don Quixote tell us of chivalry, and the knight-errant?"

"That a man who cannot distinguish what is real from what is imagined is a fool."

"As concise a summary as I've heard – and quite right. The essence of judgment, and the key to survival, lies in that distinction. Now, let us take the next step. Can you tell me how to distinguish what is real from what is not?"

Juan thought on it a moment. "Well," he said slowly, "a threat can be real or it can be imagined. Whether or not the worst occurs will tell you which."

Alexander nodded. "Yes, I suppose it will – but far too late." Lifting his glass, he sipped at his vodka. "My generals warn me of the British, and the French, and even the Austrians. Do you know which of these is the greatest threat?"

Juan thought of Harry Dryden, and how he might answer the Tsar's question. After their narrow escape at the slave market, he'd been curious.

"There were so many arrayed against us, Harry – which did you think the greatest threat?"

"The closest, young Juan – almost always, the greatest threat is the one beside you."

The Tsar was waiting for Juan's answer. *"Your generals, Excellency. They are the greatest threat." Juan saw surprise register in Alexander's eyes and recalled Caria's admonition not to say anything too stupid. 'They shoot you here if you say something too stupid.'*

"Except of course for Marshal Gudovich," he added quickly, thinking that perhaps he should have brought Caria with him after all. "His honor and loyalty are beyond question."

Alexander's eyes narrowed and his lips tightened; for what seemed to Juan an eternity, he sat in silence, staring at the Sultana's messenger. Then, as the corners of his mouth once again began to betray him, he burst out laughing.

"You may be young, Juan Pedro Calderón de Castilla," he said, lifting his glass, "but you have wisdom and, even less common, courage enough to trust it." He motioned to Juan, who exhaled in relief as he lifted his own glass. "To dangers both real and imagined," toasted the Tsar of all the Russia's, clinking his glass against Juan's, "and the wisdom to tell the one from the other!"

※   ※

It took the Russian cryptographers longer to decipher Gulbayez's message than Brother Mikhail had thought, but at last the task was completed. Juan waited with Brother Mikhail in another room while the Tsar reviewed the message with several of his advisors.

Finally, just as Juan thought he could fend off sleep no longer, the door to the Tsar's office opened. "Mikhailovich," called Alexander, his voice echoing in the vast chamber, "I'd like to speak with our Spanish friend for a few minutes more. But stay close, this won't take long."

Alexander gestured towards an ornate chair that faced the hearth and settled wearily into its twin. "The message you've carried may prove useful, young man. That the Sultana entrusted such a thing to you is remarkable."

Juan sat in silence. He wondered what Gulbayez had felt it so vital to communicate to the Tsar, but knew better than to ask.

"I wish to thank you for your role in facilitating a rather sensitive communication. I have but two questions for you. First, besides yourself and your two companions, who else knows of this message?"

"Only Marshal Gudovich, Excellency – even with a message bearing the Sultana's stamp, we saw no other way to persuade your Excellency's guard to take us seriously."

When the Tsar made no reply and the silence began to lengthen, Juan cleared his throat. "Excellency, you had a second question?"

Alexander nodded. "You've done well. I will have Brother Mikhail see you out, but before you go, is there anything I can do for you?" He grinned. "While the perception that a Tsar has unlimited power is exaggerated, I do have influence in certain circles."

It was the opening he had hoped for. "Well, Excellency, there is one small thing...."

CHAPTER 66
The House of Lords

The consequence is, being of no party,
I shall offend all parties. Never mind,
My words at least are more sincere and hearty
Than if I sought to sail before the wind.
He who has naught to gain can have small art. He
Who neither wishes to be bound nor bind
May still expatiate freely, as will I,
Nor give my voice to slavery's jackal cry.

DON JUAN, CANTO IX

THE LORDS' chamber – generally referred to as the White
Chamber – was located on the second floor of Westminster Palace,
long the seat of Parliament. Prior to 1801, the Lords met in a chamber
so small and crowded that, as the joke went, future seats would be
inherited not by a peer's oldest son but by his thinnest. But with the
passage of the *Acts of Union*, which united England and Ireland and
added the Irish peers to the Lords, the situation had become impossible, and the Court of Requests had ceded occupancy of the White
Chamber to the Lords.

Not that it wasn't crowded still. The chamber was divided into
three sections, with tiered wooden benches on either side; one for the

government, the other for the opposition. Between them on the floor of the chamber stood non-partisan cross-benches.

Occupying the southern end of the chamber was a raised dais framed by a richly-embroidered red and gold canopy bearing the royal coat-of-arms, a quartered shield. In the center of the dais stood the King's red throne and, below it, the Lord Chancellor's woolen chair, a physically uncomfortable tradition dating back to the time of Edward III. With the addition of the Irish peers the extra space was quickly taken up; at the sensational adultery trial of Queen Caroline earlier in the year it had been necessary to construct temporary balconies to accommodate peers, parties and counsel.

With Fletcher's assistance, Byron spent the weeks prior to his speech preparing for his departure. He sold off most of the Newstead furniture and art; packed his clothing, books, claret and other personal possessions; and said his farewells.

Satisfied that all was ready, Byron arrived early on the day he was scheduled to speak, taking a seat at the rear of the opposition benches. For the next two hours, he watched as the House debated a bill to regulate the transportation of perishable goods on British merchant shipping. As the debate droned on, he recalled with horror his boyhood ambition to achieve fame in politics. He was thankful the impulse had passed before boredom could dull his senses or crush his spirit.

At last, as night fell and the new and comparatively smokeless Argand oil lamps were lit, the Lord Chancellor looked up from the sheet containing the session's agenda. "If there is nothing further with respect to the matter at hand," he announced in a bored tone, "Lord Byron will *briefly* address the House."

As Byron stood to speak, it pleased him to hear a murmur among the peerage. Before he could begin, Dudley Ryder, 1st Earl of Harrowby and a Tory stalwart, rose to his feet.

"Point of order," he called in a thin voice. "May we be informed as to the subject matter of Lord Byron's contemplated remarks? And whether they will be framed in prose or in verse?"

Byron smiled, ignoring the scattered laughter on the Tory side of the chamber. "If the honorable gentleman will indulge me, I believe the import of my remarks will soon become apparent." He nodded to Ryder, who as Lord President of the Privy Council was the minister responsible for education. "As for your second question, I shall speak plainly. Sadly, I fear that for some, the affective gain to be realized by verse would be offset by a corresponding loss in understanding."

As the earl's gaunt cheeks flushed with indignation, Byron turned to face the Lord Chancellor. Out of the corner of his eye, he took note of the late-arriving Foreign Secretary, who slipped into his customary place on the Tory front bench. *He looks disheveled*, thought Byron. *As though he's slept in his clothes.*

"My lords, I address you today for the first time in several years. If any of you believe that the infrequency of my appearances reflects satisfaction with how this body performs its functions, or how this realm is governed, you have neither read my verse nor had the misfortune to endure my rants at Almack's."

"In fact, Lord Byron," called a minor peer from Surrey whose name Byron could not recall, "I find them indistinguishable."

Byron ignored him. "The truth – a commodity which in my experience is not valued highly enough – is quite the opposite. From 1783 – five years before my birth – to the present year, our island suffered under the rule of a sovereign who, however amiable he may have been in his domestic relations, lacked the qualities of mind required of a monarch. Indeed, I believe that with perhaps one exception, all would acknowledge that for the last decade of his life, our late King wasn't entirely in possession of his faculties. The exception, of course, is our fawning *poet laureate,* who fancies himself a successor to Milton but has in common with that old lion only blindness." Byron had to smile as peers from both sides of the chamber laughed. Apparently, dislike for Southey transcended politics.

"Unfortunately, the cure may have been worse than the disease. A regency! Which, if we speak true, is nothing more than a constitutional device for allowing trusted 'advisors' to enrich themselves at the nation's expense. And now, as we bid a horrified farewell to a year in which the old King died and the Prince Regent ascended to a tarnished throne, we find that the son has learned his lessons well, assuming his first and rightful place among those who suckle at the Exchequer's teat."

A buzz could be heard in the chamber. As Byron paused to take a sip of water, he did not miss the terse whispers being exchanged within the Tory ranks. He glanced at the usually unflappable Castlereagh who, to his surprise, tonight seemed entirely flappable.

"Of course," Byron continued, "given the increasing preeminence of Parliament, it shouldn't matter so much, should it? If, in the service of mercantile interests and favored clerics, a monarch threatened to bankrupt the treasury, deprive his subjects of their liberties, and engage in expensive adventures abroad, surely Parliament would assert its prerogatives? If ruinous policies – a punitive import tax on corn, for example – left thousands to starve, surely Parliament would take steps to ameliorate their suffering? If – in a nation that purports to cherish the freedoms declared in the *Magna Carta* and the *Declaration of Rights* – critics questioned those policies, surely their words would be heard, and not summarily silenced by intimidation and imprisonment?"

"Indeed, Lord Byron," shouted Lord Henry Pelham-Clinton, the 4th Duke of Newcastle and a so-called 'Ultra-Tory,' "the fact that despite your blasphemies and perversions you stand before this assembly a free man is proof enough of this government's tolerance!"

"It is proof," Byron shot back, "only of this government's hypocrisy and cowardice. As Home Secretary, Viscount Addington has been diligent in prosecuting those whose opinions he deems 'seditious' – whatever that means – so long as they lack the power or means to defend themselves." Although his voice remained calm, Byron felt his anger rising. "You speak of 'this government's tolerance?' Ask the families of the scores of unarmed workingmen and women massacred by their own government's cavalry at Peterloo last summer about 'this government's tolerance!'"

Lord Pelham-Clinton stared at Byron coldly. "When seventy-five thousand men and women gather illegally and ignore directives to disperse, it is not merely the government's right, but its duty, to restore public order. While we all regret the unfortunate loss of life –"

"Regret it? Oh, I hardly think so. Only a week after the massacre, with the ground still soaked with his subjects' blood, the Prince Regent had the Home Secretary send a letter to the Manchester magistrates by whose order that blood was spilled, thanking them for their actions 'in the preservation of the public peace!' If they continue to preserve the peace so efficiently, there will be no more room in the Cross Street Chapel cemetery."

Byron extracted a paper from his breast pocket. "Nor were the dead the only voices silenced; within a few months, Viscount Addington had dozens of reformers arrested, many of whom now languish in His Majesty's gaols. James Wroe – twelve months; Henry Hunt – thirty months; Samuel Bamford, Joseph Healey, Joseph Johnson – twelve months; John Knight – twenty-four months."

Sliding his notes back into his pocket, Byron shook his head. "You speak of regret? What is most regrettable, my lord, is that when conditions become so intolerable that the poor and dispossessed have no alternative but to raise their voices in protest, the government's solution is not to ameliorate conditions but to silence the protestors!"

Castlereagh exchanged glances with Addington, who sat on the ministers' bench only a few feet away. Addington wore a scowl that left little doubt as to his mood. Despite the fact that Castlereagh had prepared him for this, he wasn't entirely confident that the Home Secretary might not have Byron arrested on the spot. Shifting his attention to Eldon, he saw that the Lord Chancellor sat in silence, his arms crossed, glaring not at Byron but at him. *Eldon's angry I prevailed upon him to allow Byron to speak; it would seem he intends to leave me to the consequences. This has the makings of a disaster.*

"Lord Byron." Castlereagh spoke softly, but somehow his voice carried. "The character of your remarks is passionate. While that is not a crime, such address is more fitting in the Commons than in the Lords. As you have not attended these sessions for quite some time, your deviation from this chambers' customs is not surprising. However, it is to be hoped that as you proceed, you will keep our traditions in mind."

Ah, the serpent slithers from its den. Byron inclined his head to the Foreign Secretary. "Lord Castlereagh, it is not my intent to disrupt these proceedings. I only wish I had your equanimity! For most men, orchestrating policies that doom youthful thousands in order to preserve institutions already writhing in their death throes would be unendurable."

"You go too far, Byron," sputtered Pelham-Clinton, his features clouded with rage. "Would you have the government sit idle as radicals like Hunt and William Hone fan the embers of dissatisfaction into a conflagration of rebellion? As for Lord Castlereagh, there is no man living save Wellington to whom England owes a greater debt. While you sat comfortably in London penning silly rhymes, Lord Castlereagh defeated rebellion in Ireland and ensured a more lasting peace in Europe."

Byron responded with a sardonic smile. "Lord Castlereagh's exploits in Ireland are indeed well-known, my lord. Or, as some would say, notorious. Among the Irish his name evokes loathing; and why not? Three thousand Irishmen shot down at Gibbet Rath after they laid down their arms to surrender. Three thousand captured Irish murdered at New Ross, many of them burned alive. Men tortured to death in the shadow of Dublin Castle, where for weeks, their screams could be heard from dusk to dawn."

Byron turned to the benches occupied by the Irish peers. "You all know the rest. Through a fraudulent combination of bribes, patronage and promises, Castlereagh and Pitt managed to secure the cooperation of the Irish Parliament in its own dissolution – the Acts of Union. At which point the Tory government infamously reneged on its promises of Catholic emancipation, adding the stain of betrayal to Lord Castlereagh's already irredeemable reputation."

Heartened by the angry protests that issued from the Tory benches, Byron launched a further broadside.

"As for Europe – how did you put it, my lord? – ah yes, I believe your claim was that Lord Castlereagh has 'ensured a more lasting peace.' To be sure, after decades of conflict, relative peace has prevailed for the past five years. It is too soon to say how long this peace will last. Whether durable or not, however, we know its price – the succor of despots in Prussia, France, Austria and Russia; the suppression of republican movements in favor of corrupt monarchs and decaying empires; and the callous disposition of lands and peoples tossed like hunks of meat to the howling jackals of State and Church."

Byron stared at Castlereagh. "In Ireland it was men who died; in Europe, the aspirations of incipient nations. Tell us, my lord – what is it like to play at God?"

As Byron's accusations echoed through the chamber, all eyes shifted to Castlereagh, who sat woodenly, gazing at nothing. In his younger days, he had responded to provocations such as these with force, suing one detractor for libel and famously wounding another in a duel.

Byron, he knew, was trying to goad him – but were his charges unfounded? Castlereagh remembered the screams in Dublin, and sometimes woke in a cold sweat with their echo in his ears. He hadn't ordered the killings at Gibbet Rath and New Ross, nor any of the others that occurred on a smaller scale in towns and villages all across Ireland, but he had been unable to prevent them. In Europe the situation was more complicated, but Byron wasn't wrong – together with Metternich, Alexander and Talleyrand, he had orchestrated a balance of power that preserved – indeed, depended upon – autocratic rulers he privately despised.

As the silence lengthened, he felt his neck and face flush with heat, and dimly perceived a strange vibratory hum, like swarming bees. His heart was pounding and, as he scanned the gathered peers, he perceived far more enemies than friends. He wondered how many held knives behind their backs. God help him if only a fool like Pelham-Clinton stood by his side.

Slowly, he rose to his feet. "Do not deceive yourselves, my lords," he began, spreading his arms to encompass both Tories and Whigs. "While Lord Byron may speak more boldly than some, his sentiments are shared by many and, in a better world, would be laudable."

He took a deep breath, steadying himself. "The seeds of liberty and self-determination that took root in our former American colonies and in revolutionary Paris were inspired by ideals shared by all of us, ideals at the heart of England's traditions. As Lord Byron reminds us, England has been a model for those who seek to broaden prosperity by lifting the mantle of poverty from the backs of the working class. For make no mistake, my lords – in the coming years, governments that serve only the wealthy, and that fail to create opportunities for all their people, cannot prosper and may not survive."

Castlereagh paused, conscious of the lengthening shadow of disapproval darkening the Tory side of the chamber. He knew that these men, ensconced in their privilege and secure in their prejudice, saw the future as nothing more than a continuation of the past. The only common men they knew were servants, and they had no patience for those who wade into the waters of history and feel the inexorable pull of the tides of change. He had spent a lifetime fortifying them in their arrogance, and he sometimes wondered whether it might not have been better to stand with Fox and Byron. But for the Jacobins, he thought ruefully, he would have.

With a start, he realized that his mind had wandered. He tugged at his cravat, which felt tight as a noose. "Nevertheless," he said, forcing himself to continue, "Lord Byron simplifies matters that in practice are far more complex. However noble their ideals, the separatists in Ireland committed no less than treason by plotting with the French to invade Erin's shores. Although foul weather frustrated their aims, the rebels seized towns and destroyed property across Ireland, committing atrocities of their own."

Castlereagh turned to Byron. "Surely Lord Byron has not forgotten the two hundred loyalist men, women and children who were locked in a barn in the village of Scullabogue and burned alive?"

"I have not forgotten the dead, my lord, though it is not my name that lingers like a curse on their cold lips. Still, I am always struck by the generosity with which the authors of suffering seek to share the credit."

Castlereagh shook his head. "I do not excuse the excesses you describe. They are a stain upon England. I merely wish to emphasize that war – and especially civil war – is a terrible thing. Indeed, the unavoidable horrors of war are the reason why this government's measures to prevent violent insurrection, though they may seem stern to some, are in fact essential."

Byron laughed. "Your logic is circular, my lord or, perhaps more truly, perverse. Do you actually believe that liberty depends upon the suppression of dissent? And that order depends on the preservation of tyrants, whether in France, Italy, the Levant or in Albion itself?"

"I would urge you to curb your tongue, Byron!" shouted Pelham-Clinton, leaping once more to his feet. "Such disrespect threatens the dignity of the Crown, and is, in my view, the most dangerous species of seditious mischief!" He turned toward Addington, who sat glowering on the ministers' bench. "Those responsible for ensuring public order will not long tolerate such misbehavior, which brings disrepute not only to the speaker but to the Lords itself!"

Byron looked at Pelham-Clinton as though he'd farted. Shrugging, he turned back to Castlereagh. "As I was saying, Lord Castlereagh, and as the Duke of Newcastle has just demonstrated, only a fool would credit reasoning such as this. And whatever you may be, you are not a fool. So, let us all speak plainly."

Byron gathered himself, raising his voice to be heard above the cries of the Tories and the whispers of the Whigs. "In fact, my lord, it is not violence that you fear but disorder. And why? Because the order you defend favors a privileged few, while the freedoms you deny deprive the many." Raising his arm, and feeling suddenly like Milton arisen, he pointed at the empty throne, which loomed above the assembly like a graven idol.

"The days of Kings," he thundered, "are drawing to a close. There will be blood shed like water, and tears like mist; but the peoples will conquer in the end. I shall not live to see it, but it shall come to pass!"

As dozens of Tory peers rose to voice their outrage, Byron fixed his gaze on the opposition seats, where the Whigs sat hunched in uncomfortable silence.

"And *you*, who claim to be the party of Locke and the champions of liberty! You sit on your hands and do nothing while those with the courage to speak are vilified as 'seditious' and broken like horses. Locke observed that 'the only thing that gathers people into seditious commotion is oppression.' Yet it is plain to me that many of you *prefer* oppression to commotion!" He raised his voice so that his words echoed throughout the chamber. "I suspect that Locke would have as little use for you as I do!"

Amidst the riotous tumult that engulfed the chamber, Addington edged past several shouting ministers to where Castlereagh sat glumly, his head in his hands. As the Lord Chancellor vainly called for order, Addington put his hand on Castlereagh's shoulder.

"Quite a show," he said, his features grim. "This exile you've arranged for Byron? You may wish to suggest that he expedite his departure. When word of this reaches the King, he will demand Byron's arrest." Addington surveyed the uproar in the chamber and looked up to see Byron, a pleased smirk on his handsome face, standing at its center. "I expect you're aware, Robert, that he and Jenkinson will look for someone to blame."

Castlereagh groaned. The drone of the bees had become deafening, and his head was pounding. "I'll get word to Hobhouse," he gasped through the pain. "Byron should sail as soon as possible." He looked up at Addington. "Perhaps I'll join him."

CHAPTER 67
The Last Friendly Face

WHERE DOES courage come from? As he realized what lay in store for Nico, Byron remembered a conversation he'd had once with Caroline. Spent from their lovemaking, they lay in Caroline's bed, her head on his chest. *"Are we brave to risk so much,"* she'd asked as his fingers played in her curls, *"or are we simply foolish?"*

"There's a difference?"

"You don't believe that – you're just being cynical, which you imagine earns you the admiration of men and the affection of women."

"You know me too well, Caro!" he said, laughing. *"But courage is complicated. It is the sources of courage I find interesting."*

Caroline propped her head on her elbow. *"And those are?"*

"It depends. The French courage proceeds from vanity – the German from phlegm – the Turkish from fanaticism – the Spanish from pride – the Dutch from obstinacy – the Russian from insensibility – the Italian from anger."

It was Caroline's turn to laugh. *"And what of the English? From what source does our courage spring?"*

"The English? We're obsessed with appearances; when chaos swirls around us and Danger's hand is at our throats, our self-conception requires that we remain unperturbed. We act with courage because even death is preferable to embarrassment."

They watched as two janissaries pulled Nico from the boat. Sensing movement at his side, Byron saw that Panos was preparing to rush to Nico's defense, his hand on his pistol. Byron extended his arm. "Panos," he whispered, "killing one or two of them accomplishes nothing. I have an idea." It took him only a few seconds to explain what he had in mind. When he finished, Panos nodded gravely. "Move quick, By-roon," he whispered, gripping the Englishman by the arm. "Iphigeneia will be very anger if you be killed."

Hobhouse, who was crouched next to Panos and had heard Byron's plan, reached for his friend's shoulder. "That's insane! There must be anoth–"

"There is no other way, and – no offense Hobby – I'm the only one who has any chance of making it. If all goes well, we'll meet on the fishing boat." He grabbed Hobhouse by the neck, pulling him close and kissing him hard on the cheek. "If it doesn't, remember what I told you about my papers." Byron looked over at Polidori and winked. Then, picking up a loose stone, he hurled it as far as he could into the harbor.

The janissaries turned at the sound of the splash, peering into the darkness. Behind them, Byron leaped out between the barrels and ran eastward down the quay. Colonel Demir spun at the sound, shouting at Byron to halt. Demir's men looked to their colonel, who gestured impatiently as Byron raced along the dock. Within seconds, the janissaries were in pursuit, the astonished Nico forgotten.

Byron ran down the dock as fast as he could, his flank aching. As he passed the burning torches he ripped each one from its bracket and tossed it onto the wooden dock. When he reached the simmering kettle, he paused to kick it off the fire and onto the dock, the pitch pouring out in an acrid torrent.

He glanced back to see that the janissaries were getting closer. Moving quickly, he seized two of the unlit torches – he could tell from the odor they'd been dipped in whale oil, a natural accelerant – and thrust them first into the fire and, when they caught, into the spilled pitch on the dock. Within seconds the whale oil ignited and the pitch began to smoke. As he lit the last torch and took off running, he prayed the dock's rough planks would ignite as well.

He was getting close to the eastern end of the quay. Behind him he heard shouting. As he approached the horse and wagon he saw a janissary step out of the shadows, his *kilij* in his hand. Byron was close enough to see the man's dark eyes, and he could hear the janissaries behind him. He didn't understand their words, but he knew what they must be saying – *we've got him now, he's trapped!"*

Byron skidded to a stop. He was breathing hard, his side ached, and the torch he held smelled bloody awful. He glanced at the janissary blocking his path and, turning back, saw that his pursuers had stopped a dozen yards behind him. They had managed to leap over the burning pitch, but the dock behind them was now ablaze, orange flames leaping in and out of the wind-whipped smoke. The janissaries looked for all the world like hell's executioners, and he would not have been surprised to see Mephistopheles himself emerge from the fire at their backs.

"It's over, Mr. Byron," panted the Turkish officer, struggling to catch his breath. He held a pistol in his hand, its hammer cocked and its barrel aimed at Byron's chest.

Curious, the mare looked up from her supper and, as Byron met her eyes, it occurred to him that she might be the last friendly face he would ever see. He thought of Lyon and wished the big dog was by his side. Every detail of the scene – the pursuing janissaries, backlit by dancing flames; the reflection of the fire on the rippling waters of the harbor; the white mare's snort as she returned to her meal – appeared to him with crystal clarity. He could feel his heart pounding, and he marveled at the realization that he had never felt more alive.

"That's *Lord* Byron, *esek oglu!*" he shouted, hoping that really meant 'son of a donkey.' It was the only Turkish insult he knew. Without waiting for a response, he took a step toward the wagon, raising the torch. Demir shouted and two janissaries leaped forward, their swords raised. Before they could reach him, Byron tossed the torch into the hay in the wagon's bed. As the dry straw burst into crackling flame and the frightened mare whinnied and bolted, he turned and ran hard for the water. With a guttural curse, Demir aimed his weapon and fired.

⁂   ⁂

The instant the janissaries rushed after Byron, Panos stepped out from behind the barrels, urging Hobhouse and Polidori forward. Moving quickly, they crossed the dock and, with Nico right behind them, leaped into the rowboat, which teetered precariously beneath them. Even as questions began to form on Nico's lips, Panos slid onto the center bench and grabbed the oars. "Get the rope!" he almost shouted to Polidori, who was closest to the bow. Stumbling forward, the doctor untied the line and pushed them away from the dock. Working the oars, Panos swung the bow to sea, pulling hard for Raffi's fishing boat.

Nico sat heavily on the stern bench, perspiration shining on his grizzled face. "Just in time, Panos," he muttered, holding both hands up and wiggling his fingers as though they were a gift. He peered past the young partisan. "No," he said, pointing. "Further to the left, over there. Toward Miltos' boat."

"I thought – you did say in this morning, Raffi's boat?"

Nico grunted. "True. But when I walked with Zehra this morning she acted very strange, and seemed too eager to get back. She must have heard us last night. The Turk, just now. He said she–"

"Told them? She did, didn't waste any time about it, either." Polidori nodded toward Panos. "If Panos hadn't followed her and warned us, they would have had us."

Another grunt. "I'll deal with her. Anyway, I spoke to Miltos. In return for a good milk cow and the use of my stall in the monthly market, he agreed to take the English to Patras." He looked back over his shoulder to the burning quay. "Byron?"

"Leading the Turks away from us," said Hobhouse. "There was no time ...." He fell silent, staring at the smoke and flames behind them. "He said he could get to the water, swim out to meet us." He felt Polidori's hand on his shoulder, and turned to the doctor. "He's a strong swimmer, Polidori," he mumbled, tears running down his cheeks. "If anyone–"

They all jumped as the sharp crack of a gunshot sounded across the open water. As its echo faded, all that could be heard was the rhythmic slap of Panos' oars as their boat slipped through the darkness towards safety.

CHAPTER 68
A Boy Aglowing

All that the mind would shrink from of excesses,
All that the body perpetrates of bad,
All that we read, hear, dream of man's distresses,
All that the devil would do if run stark mad,
All that defies the worst which pen expresses,
All by which hell is peopled, or as sad
As hell, mere mortals who their power abuse,
Was here (as heretofore and since) let loose.

DON JUAN, CANTO VIII

"**WHERE DID** you put my bloody kit?" Castlereagh shouted in frustration. "I've looked everywhere – someone must have moved it!"

"It's right here, Robert. You're looking in the wrong drawer." Emily Stewart handed her husband of almost thirty years a toilet kit from which the razor had been removed weeks ago. She forced a smile and reached up to stroke his cheek; scowling, he turned away.

The slow deterioration in the Foreign Secretary's faculties that had begun almost a year ago had accelerated in recent weeks, leaving Emily fearful for her husband's safety. The doctor had given him something for his nerves, but it hadn't seemed to help, and Castlereagh now spoke little and slept less. He still worked long hours – at times she thought it might be the only thing keeping him sane– but the burdens he carried weighed more heavily than ever before. The Eastern Question in particular had become an obsession; in letters to Strangford he demanded better and more timely information, while his correspondence with Metternich focused on military options for which he often felt himself the only proponent.

Castlereagh returned to his study, closing the door behind him, and slumped into the chair behind his desk. He stared for a moment into the fire burning in the hearth. Then, for the third time, he re-read a dispatch he'd received that morning from Metternich. *"My dear friend"*, it began,

> ... *the despair so evident in your recent letters saddens me, for it is wasted energy. If I have learned anything in the course of my long service, it is that history cannot be rushed, though on occasion it may be possible to prod it a little. This is not the first time – nor will it be the last – that statesmen fixed on the future must wait on politicians who care only for the present. Despite our efforts, it seems unlikely that our governments will bestir themselves to intervene until the ongoing violence provokes precisely the crisis we had hoped to avoid. So be it – all we can do is to prepare ourselves and pray that, when our opportunity comes, it is not too late.*
>
> *An interesting aside – our agents in the Filiki Eteria report that in martyrdom your poet Lord Byron has become a hero amongst the Greek rebels. From what I understand of this Byron, another poet's words seem apt – 'Nothing in his life became him like the leaving it.' Still, it is a shame that his death seems to have changed nothing. I suppose I should read some of his verse someday.*
>
> *With warm regards and affection,*
> *Klemens*

The window was open, and he heard Emily puttering about in the garden. As he looked up from Metternich's dispatch, he was shocked by a vision – it lasted only for a few seconds, but that was enough – of a young lad emerged from the fire, glowing but unharmed. He gasped and leaped to his feet. His heart was racing and, for a few seconds, he thought he might faint. It wasn't just that he'd had a vision – what stunned him was that he'd seen this boy once before, during his posting in Ireland.

It was something he would never forget. He had gone hunting and, caught in a violent storm, had sought refuge in the house of a local land-owner. During the night he awoke with a sense that he wasn't alone. Sitting up, he saw a naked young boy with golden hair standing by the smoldering hearth, glowing as though in flames. Castlereagh tried to cry out but the boy vanished as suddenly as he had appeared. Castlereagh never encountered him again – until now.

Outside the window, the warm summer sun shone on Emily's roses, rich with fragrant color and the hum of bees. The breeze was from the west, carrying scents of cut grass and honeysuckle. *The boy in the fire – a foretelling of death, to be sure. Surpassing strange that the end should come in the guise of a young boy aglowing.*

In the moment, he realized that the agitation and paranoia that had become his constant companions had subsided, and that all he felt was tired, more tired than he could ever remember. Sighing, he reached into a spare satchel beneath his desk and extracted a pen knife he'd been given as a boy. They'd missed it in their search for blades.

He opened the knife and felt the edge, ensuring it was sharp. Then, wondering why he'd waited so long, he leaned back in his chair and drew the blade sharply across his throat.

CHAPTER 69
The Judgment of History

In twice five years the 'greatest living poet,'
Like to the champion in the fisty ring,
Is called on to support his claim or show it,
Although 'tis an imaginary thing.
Even I, albeit I'm sure I did not know it
Nor sought of foolscap subjects to be king,
Was reckoned a considerable time
The grand Napoleon of the realms of rhyme.

DON JUAN, CANTO XI

"WHERE'S THE body now?" asked John Ireland, Dean of Westminster Abbey. In a lifetime of service to the Church, Ireland had come to appreciate the importance of logistics when decisions were required.

"On its way to England. If the weather holds, it should arrive in London within the week." Attired in his Sunday black, Robert Southey shifted in his chair. He had never been inside the Dean's office and, in the vastness of the Abbey, was surprised to find it so cramped.

"Have you spoken with Jenkinson?"

"Of course. But he's in an awkward position right now – he's counting on Whig votes in the Commons on Emancipation. He'd prefer that you take the lead."

Ireland frowned. As an Anglican prelate, he saw no reason to extend rights or liberties to the bloody Papists, who would undoubtedly abuse them. Still, he owed his post to Jenkinson, and it was in any event a question within his province to decide.

"I'm sure he would," he said dourly. He contemplated the man before him. "You obviously have views on the matter, else you wouldn't be here."

"Yes. As an individual my views are unimportant. As *poet laureate*, however, I have an obligation to make my opinions known. After all, the entire purpose of Poet's Corner is to recognize poets and writers whose work has honored England and God." Southey caught himself. "Not necessarily in that order, of course."

"And your opinion is?"

"That Byron has no place here – let him be buried elsewhere."

Ireland frowned. "There are many – including, I am told, your friend Wordsworth – who consider Byron to have been among the most talented of poets." He peered at Southey over his spectacles. "You disagree?"

"I believe that he was clever. But greatness in a poet requires more than wit. To lie alongside Chaucer, Spenser, Dryden and Johnson, one must be exemplary both in verse *and* in conduct. Even if Byron's verse qualified him for the Abbey – and, in light of its blasphemy, I hardly think that so – his conduct was nothing short of scandalous. To bury him here would degrade virtue and be an affront to God."

Ireland chuckled. "Man thinks in years; God in millennia. Had it been left to King Charles II after the Restoration, there would be no monument here to Milton."

"This is not about Byron's politics, your Grace. I would not have come to see you if it were. Byron had talent, I cannot deny it. But he used it not to champion our Lord, but to denounce His servants. To bury him here, in God's house?" He shook his head. "It would be an abomination."

Ireland shrugged. "Byron's name has indeed become synonymous with scandal. Whatever the merits of his verse, I cannot risk bringing disapprobation upon Westminster. Particularly when it is the *poet laureate* himself who entreats me to bar the Abbey's doors."

Southey exhaled. He'd helped drive Byron out of England, and now – even in death – had ensured that lasting honor would be denied him. Rising, the *poet laureate* nodded to the Dean and turned to go, smugly confident in the righteous judgment of history.

CHAPTER 70
The Decision

IT WAS early morning when the Tsar's coachman delivered Juan to his rooms, and he was asleep before his head hit the pillow. When the sunlight that streamed in through the window finally awakened him, he dressed quickly and went out for a walk. The air was brisk, and Juan turned up his collar against the freshening Baltic breeze. He needed some time to think, and found it easier to do so on his feet than in his bed.

When he returned to their lodging, he found Harry and Caria sitting on a wrought iron bench in the small garden at the rear of the building. "We wondered when you'd emerge," Harry said in greeting, a broad smile on his face. "Were you and Alexander up late drinking vodka?"

"How did you know?" Juan replied innocently. "It turns out the Tsar favors iced vodka with cold salmon."

"You ate and drank with the Tsar?" Caria was incredulous. "Really?"

"He was quite genial. While his – I don't know what to call them, the people who interpret encoded notes – while those people decoded Gulbayez' message, we had a late supper. He was interested in our travels, and I told him about you and Harry. We probably talked for an hour or more."

"What about the note?" pressed Caria. "Did he tell you what it says?"

"No. But he seemed pleased. He said that our services were of great value and, if there was anything he could do for us, we had only to ask. Oh,

and he said that while there were limits to his power, he had 'influence in certain circles.'"

Harry grinned. "Please tell me you asked him for a dacha on the Crimean coast." When Juan tilted his head, Harry shrugged. "No harm in asking, my friend – it isn't every day that a Tsar of all the Russia's asks what he can do for you."

Caria lowered her gaze, her hands folded in her lap. Her lip trembled but she said nothing. Juan guessed she was afraid to ask.

"I told him of your father," he said gently. "I asked him whether, in return for services past, he could be permitted to return home. I told the Tsar that your father is all you have left."

Caria did not look up, and scarcely seemed to breathe. Harry put his arm around her protectively. He searched Juan's eyes but detected neither sadness nor joy. As a man of experience, Harry took this to mean that the answer must be complicated.

Juan knelt and reached for Caria's hand. "He has to speak to Gudovich – your father is under the Marshal's command – but said that, subject to one condition, your father would be free to return home. He said that Harr–"

He got no further. Caria lifted her head and, with tears running down her cheeks, launched herself at Juan's chest. He fell back laughing in the morning frost, a sobbing Caria astride him. As she smothered him in kisses and hugged him so tightly he worried for his ribs, he could have sworn he saw Harry rub a weathered palm across his eyes.

Caria sat up, wiping her cheeks with her sleeve. Her sobs had turned to giddy laughter and, as she started to rise, she changed her mind and collapsed onto Juan again, wrapping her arms around his neck. "I love you, Christian!" she blurted, then sat up, her hand at her lips. Quickly, she got to her feet and turned away.

Harry extended a hand to Juan. Helping him up, the soldier brushed grass from his young friend's back and shoulders. When he was satisfied, he clapped Juan heartily on both shoulders, almost driving him once more to his knees. "Young Juan, you have done very well." He looked him in the eyes.

"I found you interesting when we met on the pirate ship. I did not suspect you would be this interesting!"

"What condition?" Caria had composed herself and had rejoined them in the garden. *"You said that Alexander agreed to your request on one condition."*

Juan cleared his throat, pawing at the grass with his toe. "It was late, and he was tired – he may not have meant it, or he may change his mind." He glanced at Dryden. *"When he said your father could return home, I thanked him of course, and said that we – you and your father and me – would leave for Batumi as soon as matters here could be settled. Harry, I figured you would need to rejoin Gudovich's Hussars."*

Dryden nodded. "Gudovich said he has plans for me in the Crimea."

Juan shook his head. "They may have to wait. Alexander said that you should escort Caria and her father to Batumi."

"Why Harry and not you?" Caria asked, concern in her voice. *"Is it something to do with Gulbayez?"*

"No, nothing like that."

"Then what?"

"The Tsar wants me to do something for him. In London."

"The Tsar wants you to do something for him?" Caria stared at him, her mouth agape. *"Did you tell him you're busy?"*

Juan shrugged. "That didn't seem an option."

"So, what exactly does he want you to do?"

"There's a poet in London named Byron – he's a lord or something. According to the Tsar's daughter Sofia, this Byron is supremely talented and very handsome. Apparently, he's become quite famous."

Caria gave him an arch look. "You met the Tsar's daughter?"

"No, of course not! Alexander told me she thinks him handsome." Juan pressed on before Caria could interrogate him further. *"Anyway, she is smitten with this Byron, and the Tsar wants me to extend him an invitation – in person – to give a talk here in St. Petersburg."*

꙰   ꙰

Hobhouse lowered the manuscript and looked up at Moore, Kinnaird and Murray. "That's it," he said with a wry smile and a hoarse voice. "I suspect that last bit proved too much even for Byron!"

Laughing, Moore finished off his remaining claret and set his glass on a side table. It was well past midnight, and Hobhouse's parlour was suffused with a soft orange glow from the fire in the hearth and the candles that flickered in sconces on the walls.

It had been more than three months since since Hobhouse and Polidori returned to England on a merchant ship out of Marseilles, and the night was warm. The windows were open, the still broken only by the passing chatter of an occasional carriage in the street below.

"Well," Moore said, "it's a rollicking tale, I'll give him that, and not without charm. But I think we can all agree that it wants the brilliance of his verse."

Murray nodded. While his relationship with Hobhouse and the others remained strained, as Byron's longtime publisher they felt they had no choice but to involve him in the disposition of the poet's literary estate. And with the passage of time, the cooling of passions and the lubricating influence of some of Byron's best claret – bequeathed by the poet to a grateful Moore – the tension of their initial meetings had dissipated. For this, Murray was grateful – the renewal of their acquaintance allowed him to feel that Byron too might have forgiven him for distancing himself from the scandals that helped drive the poet away to Italy and, ultimately, to the Greeks' rebellion in the Levant.

"It would sell, I can say that with confidence," he mused, turning the matter over in his mind. "There's sex and violence enough to hold the attention of even the most impatient reader, and some of the characters are memorable – Dryden, for example, and Iphigenia, and Caria as well."

"It's pretty obvious that Byron modeled Harry on me," Hobhouse declared with confidence, a twinkle in his eye. "The martial prowess, the erudition—"

"The receding hairline!" Kinnaird interjected, laughing.

"What about his Juan?" asked Hobhouse. "What do you make of him?"

Kinnaird sipped at his wine, considering the question. "He's more than a bit like Byron, wouldn't you say? Younger, of course, and without our friend's relentless self-indulgence."

"It seems to me," Hobhouse ventured, "that Byron invested Juan with those of his qualities he thought most worthy. His curiosity about the world; his courage in the face of danger; his capacity for adventure and for friendship; and of course – when he wasn't being insufferable – his wit and charm." A sad smile made a brief appearance and then was gone. "As for Byron's faults? Well, it *is* a work of fiction, is it not?"

Grinning, Murray returned to the issue at hand. "But the question isn't whether it will sell; the question is whether we should sell it. When Byron first raised the possibility of recasting *Don Juan* as a serialized novel, I advised against it." He nodded toward Kinnaird. "You did as well, if I'm not mistaken. I think our advice was sound, and perhaps Byron felt the same – he made no effort to have it published, so far as I know. I doubt he spent much time on it; he didn't even finish the last scene."

"It's hard to be sure, isn't it?" asked Moore. "After all, it *was* stolen and out of his hands." He gestured at the manuscript. "If I didn't recognize his handwriting, I'd have suspected that Castlereagh's man – what was his name, Hobby?"

"Turner."

"Yes, right. That Turner wrote some or all of this story. It would explain the difference in literary quality, now wouldn't it?" He shook his head. "But it's Byron's hand, no question, and just good enough to believe him capable of it. As we've all said, he was best at verse."

"I still find it astonishing," mused Hobhouse. "This fellow – working class, rough clothes, no education to speak of I'd guess – turns up at my door, a package in his hand. 'Mr. Hobhouse,' he says, polite as can be, 'my name's Turner. I'm the man wot stole Lord Byron's journal and killed his dog.' Before I could say a word, he hands me the package. 'I've done things I'm not proud of,' he continues, very calm, like he's been thinking about what to say for a long time. 'But I never meant to hurt 'is dog, and it's been on my mind so's to keep me up in the wee hours.' Then he points at the package. 'I can'a make that right, but I can return wot I stole.' I didn't know what to say, just stared at him. Then he turned and strode off, just like that."

"Strange that he held on to it in the first place," mused Kinnaird. "I would have thought he'd have given it to Castlereagh with the journal."

Hobhouse shrugged. "Who knows? After Castlereagh–"

"The bloody coward!" spat Moore. "Too easy for him, is what I think. As for Turner, it seems he may have had more of a conscience than Castlereagh realized."

"Maybe." Murray shrugged. "But it's in our hands now, along with his journal, which with just a little bit of editing could readily serve as his memoirs. The novel fragment, I think we can all agree just to put it on the shelf. But the journal – let's just call it his memoirs – that's the real issue. We need to decide – do we publish it? Hold it for publication at some future time? Or, as Hobhouse has urged, destroy it?"

Moore leaned forward. "I'm his bloody literary executor, a responsibility he no doubt foisted upon me because he knew how much I'd hate it. In any event, I am not at all certain we would be justified in burning his memoirs. It's part of a historical record, isn't it? Do we have the right?"

"Nonsense." Kinnaird gestured at the handwritten volume set conspicuously on the table before them. "This is nothing more than the excess clay and stone that remains once the sculpture's completed. If meant for public consumption, the artist would have left it in the work."

Moore shook his head. "These aren't discarded fragments, Kinnaird. As a memoir it stands alone. Whether we like it or not, it provides insight into Byron's character."

"Insight? Byron may not have been able to defeat his demons, but he understood their nature, and catalogued their objects and effects with painful candor. The public is already generally aware of Byron's appetites; for better or worse, they account at least in part for his celebrity. The, the – *salacious* – matters detailed here contribute nothing new."

Kinnaird lifted the volume and waved it at Moore and the others. "Publication would only titillate the *voyeurs* and confirm the prejudices of the self-righteous."

"There's even more to it than that," Murray added. "From what I hear, the King is still furious over Byron's speech to the Lords, which all agree was a debacle for everyone but Byron. Byron and Castlereagh may be beyond his reach, but Addington is not, and clings to his position by a thread. Any publisher bold enough to publish this material would quickly find himself under arrest."

"No, Murray – not again." Moore wagged an accusing finger. "You surrendered to expediency once – do you really counsel doing so again?"

"You'd be wise," Murray retorted, "to tread carefully yourself. Not only is this material salacious, it contains Byron's comments and observations concerning the character of persons of prominence, some of whom hold high office. If – no, *when* – they sue for libel, they will not limit themselves to suing the publisher, but will undoubtedly sue Byron's literary executor as well. Do you really wish to spend the next several years in court?"

The silence that answered Murray's question was broken at last by Hobhouse, who spoke deliberately, seeking the eyes of everyone present.

"This is all beside the point. In his last words to me, Byron asked that I make sure his papers were destroyed. He viewed them as private, and understood that their disclosure would cause damage. We are his closest friends, and the men he trusted most. Would any of you deny him his last request?"

Kinnaird shook his head, as did Murray. They all turned to Moore, who shifted uncomfortably. No one spoke. At last, Moore sighed.

"I cannot endorse this, not as an artist and writer and certainly not as Byron's literary executor." Rising to his feet, he reached for the claret and refilled his glass. "I am going out for a brief stroll," he announced. He looked to Hobhouse, who returned the slightest of nods. "I will be back in fifteen minutes or so."

"Moore, wait." Hobhouse lifted his glass, and the others lifted theirs. "To George Gordon, the 6th Lord Byron. May he be remembered by his friends, mourned by those who loved him, and forever honored for his works."

When their toast was done and Moore had left the room, Hobhouse took Byron's papers in hand and cast them into the hearth. The fire flared. Too soon, spent by the intensity of its combustion, all that remained were glowing embers.

Afterword

THANK YOU, Reader, for spending some time with Byron, Caroline, Hobhouse, Juan, Harry, Iphigeneia and the rest. As I noted in the *Author's Preface*, my primary objective in writing this novel was to tell a compelling story. But the decision to set the novel in a specific time and place, and to draw characters premised on actual individuals, imposed an obligation to be faithful to the setting, culture, habit and politics of the time, and to what we know of their character. To the extent consistent with my story, this was an obligation I did my best to meet.

That being said, the events described in the novel depart significantly from the historical record. First and foremost, Lord Byron was not wounded on the battlefield, nor did he die at the hands of the Turks. Byron did indeed travel to the Levant in support of the Greeks' insurrection against the Ottoman Empire, where he spent a good deal of his remaining assets on the outfitting and support of a Souliote fighting force. While quartered in Missolonghi he contracted a fever which, in keeping with accepted medical practice at the time, his doctors exacerbated by bleeding him both with lancet and leech. Dying and delirious with fever, he called out for Augusta, his daughter Ada, Kinnaird, Hobhouse. Lord Byron died on April 19, 1824, with Fletcher by his side. His body was returned to England, but – after Dean Ireland refused to allow his remains to be interred in Westminster's Poet's Corner – he was buried in the Byron family vault at the Church of St. Mary Magdalene in Nottinghamshire. Although his funeral procession was attended by his closest friends, of the more than forty stylish coaches sent by England's noble families to accompany the procession, almost all were empty.

A word about dates. In service to the demands of the novel's plot, I have compressed and, at times, rearranged events that took place over a longer span of time or in a different sequence. Byron's affair with Caroline Lamb, for example, commenced and ended in 1812; Byron departed England – first to Italy, and only later to the Levant – in 1816; the first cantos of *Don Juan* weren't written until late 1818, after he fled England and while he was living in Italy; and the outbreak of the Greek rebellion against the Ottoman Empire, including the murder of the Patriarch Gregory V, did not occur until 1821. To those offended by such deviations I apologize, and can offer as a defense only a weak denial of agency: it was the story that did it, not I!

While the antipathy between Byron and prominent Tories of his day, including British Foreign Secretary Robert Castlereagh, was a matter of public record, there is no evidence that Castlereagh or anyone else in the British government conspired either to drive Byron from England or to have him martyred at the hands of the Turks. Rather, it was Byron's abysmal behavior during a brief and disastrous marriage to Annabella Milbanke – which, in bitter divorce negotiations initiated by Annabella, included allegations not only of incest but of homosexual and hetero-sexual sodomy as well – that ignited a scandal from which he escaped only by decamping to Italy, never to return. Some of the salacious details regarding Byron's sexual predilections, which included homosexual trysts with fellow students at Trinity as well as Byron's incestuous relationship with Augusta, were provided to Annabella by a vengeful Caroline Lamb.

After he ended their relationship, Caroline poured out her resent-ments in a novel – *Glenarvon* – that savaged a thinly-disguised Byron. Characteristically, neither did Caroline pull her punches in depicting the hypocrisy and petty vanities of the leading lights of Whig society, offending some of the most prominent figures in England. One of these, the rich and influential Lady Jersey, retaliated by banning Caroline from Almack's in 1816, completing her determined journey from socialite to outcast. To his credit, William Lamb never entirely abandoned Caroline; under intense pressure from his family, the future Prime Minister and mentor to the young Queen Victoria quietly divorced her, but then allowed his ex-wife to live at Brocket Hall, the Melbourne family's country estate in Hertfordshire. Struggling with depression, Caroline abused both alcohol and laudanum, developed a serious edema and died in 1828. William was present when she passed, having rushed from his posting in Ireland to be at her side.

As the 6th Baron Byron, Byron was entitled to a seat in the House of Lords. Early in his tenure he delivered several speeches, including a blistering address criticizing a proposed measure to hang discontented workers – the so-called *Luddites* – convicted of the criminal destruction of industrial machinery. He did not, however, deliver an address to the Lords prior to his final departure from England. Nevertheless, had he delivered such an address, I believe the event would have been both acrimonious and entertaining.

Although their relationship was tested by Byron's increasingly erratic and destructive behavior, first with Augusta and then in connection with his marriage and its emotionally bloody dissolution, Hobhouse remained one of Byron's most loyal friends, playing a major role in the burial and other arrangements following the poet's death. This included the controversial destruction of Byron's memoirs – an act in which John Murray, Byron's literary executor (not Moore, as in the novel), acquiesced – in the parlor of Murray's home on Albemarle Street. Overcoming the political inconvenience of their friendship, Hobhouse was elected as a Whig to a seat in Parliament and is credited with originating the expression "His Majesty's loyal opposition" in a speech in 1826. Hobhouse went on to hold positions in Lord Grey's and Lord Melbourne's governments, and in 1851 entered the House of Lords as Baron Broughton. He had three daughters by his wife, Lady Julia, who died of tuberculosis in 1835. Hobhouse died in 1869, having lived a life whose achievements, substantial by any fair reckoning, were nonetheless eclipsed by his long association with the incandescent Byron.

Robert Southey, Byron's nemesis in the novel, was in fact a more complex figure than his critics cared to admit. His talent as a poet, while not inconsiderable, did not approach that of his more famous contemporaries; but many of Southey's essays, biographies and histories were works of substantial scholarship, a fact acknowledged by Byron himself. In a delightful bit of trivia, he is also credited with having written *The Story of the Three Bears*, the first Goldilocks story. Yet Southey's wholesale conversion from impassioned radical to sanctimonious conservative, and the financial and political benefits that accrued to him as a result, earned him the scorn of many of his contemporaries, Byron chief among them. In the end, it was distaste for the *poet laureate's* apostasy that led essayist William Hazlitt to remark that Southey "wooed Liberty as a youthful lover, but it was perhaps more as a mistress than a bride; and he has since wedded with an elderly and not very reputable lady, called Legitimacy."

And what of the Eastern Question, the crisis created by the potentially destabilizing dissolution of the Ottoman Empire? Owing in part to the partisan sympathies of Russian Foreign Secretary Ioannis Kapodistrias, who was of Greek origin and actively urged Tsar Alexander to move against the Turks, the danger of Russian intervention on behalf of the Greeks was for a time very real. The Ottoman sultan, however, made certain political and territorial concessions to the Tsar, and the crafty Metternich managed to persuade Tsar Alexander that Kapodistrias was acting in concert with the revolutionary Italian *carbonari*, leading to Kapodistrias' resignation. In the end, George Canning, Castlereagh's successor as Foreign Secretary, was able to engineer a military intervention; and a joint British, French and Russian fleet routed Egyptian and Turkish naval forces in 1827 at the Battle of Navarino, paving the way for a settlement and the creation in 1832 of an independent Greek state. To this day, Byron is honored in Greece as a hero and martyr to the cause of Greek independence.

Castlereagh, however, did not to live to see the Eastern Question resolved. Exhausted from overwork, and assailed as a tyrant for his role in supporting Addington's repressive measures, Castlereagh showed increasing signs of paranoia and mental collapse. Finally, in 1822 – after insisting that he had been visited by visions of a 'radiant boy,' which he interpreted as a harbinger of death – the Foreign Secretary slit his own throat. Not surprisingly, Lord Byron did not mourn Castlereagh's death, penning his own cruel epitaph for the gravesite:

> *"Posterity will ne'er survey, a nobler grave than this.*
> *Here lie the bones of Castlereagh: Stop, traveler, and piss."*

The Virtues of Scandal	Source
"The poem will please if it is lively – if it is dull it will fail – but I will have none of your damned cutting and slashing!" (Chap. 3: The House of Murray)	*Byron to John Murray, April 6, 1819 (Marchand, Leslie A., ed. Lord Byron: Selected Letters and Journals (Harvard University Press, 1973-82) (hereinafter "Marchand")*
"There are times, William, I have been tempted to blow my brains out, but for the recollection that it would bring pleasure to my mother-in-law. Even then, if I could be certain to haunt her..." (Chap. 11: Melbourne)	*Marchand; Byron to Moore, Jan. 28, 1817*
"I dined with Sheridan, Colman, Kinnaird and I can't remember who else. Like many of these affairs, it was first silent, then talky, then argumentative, then disputatious, then unintelligible, then altogethery, then inarticulate, and then finally and irretrievably drunk." (Chap. 17: The Predictability of Vice)	*Marchand; Byron to Moore, Oct. 31, 1815*
"Maybe you heard about his response to the watchman who found him wandering one night recently, drunk and for the most part senseless? He – the watchman – asks 'Who are you sir?' – no answer. 'What's your name?' – a hiccup. 'I say, sir, what's your name?' – Answer, in a slow and deliberate tone – 'William Wilberforce!'" (Chap. 17: The Predictability of Vice)	*Marchand; Byron to Moore, Oct. 31, 1815*
"Wake up, Hobby! This is England. Here, the only homage paid to virtue is hypocrisy." (Chap. 23: Only a Mortal Sin)	*Marchand; Byron to R.B. Hoppner, May 11, 1821*
"The verse may be bawdy – but is it not good English? It may be profligate – but is it not Life, is it not the Thing?" (Chap. 28: The Judgment of Milton)	*Marchand; Byron to Kinnaird, Oct. 26, 1818*
"I did very well, Caroline – until you took abundant pains to cure me of it." (Chap. 29, A Shiver in the Cold)	*Marchand; Byron to James Wedderburn Webster, Sept. 18, 1815*
"But what is Hope? Nothing but paint on the face of Existence. The least touch of Truth rubs it off, and then – too late – we see what a hollow-cheeked harlot we have got." (Chap. 35: Rivers of Blood)	*Marchand; Byron to Moore, Oct. 28, 1815*
"If I live ten years longer you will see that it's not over with me – I don't mean in literature, for that is nothing; and though it may seem odd to say, I do not even think it my vocation."	*Marchand; Byron to Moore, Feb. 28, 1817*
"The days of Kings," he thundered, "are drawing to a close. There will be blood shed like water, and tears like mist; but the peoples will conquer in the end. I shall not live to see it, but it shall come to pass!" (Chap. 66: The House of Lords)	*Marchand; Byron's Ravenna Journal, Jan. 13, 1821*
"The French courage proceeds from vanity – the German from phlegm – the Turkish from fanaticism – the Spanish from pride – the Dutch from obstinacy – the Russian from insensibility – the Italian from anger." (Chap. 67: The Last Friendly Face)	*Marchand; Byron to Murray, Aug. 31, 1820*

Attributions

THE VAST majority of the dialogue in *The Virtues of Scandal* is the sole product of this writer's imagination. However, in a few instances I borrowed or paraphrased lines from Byron's correspondence or from his journal – both entirely in the public domain – as the best expression of his feelings or views regarding the subject matter. These are catalogued in the table on the opposite page.

Acknowledgements

AS I pen these words on precisely the one-hundred ninety-sixth anniversary of Lord Byron's death, I need to express a debt of gratitude to the Byron and other scholars whose research and writing offered unparalleled insight into the poet's opinions, attitudes and character, as well as invaluable detail with respect to his relationships with family, friends, associates, rivals and lovers. Leslie Marchand's comprehensive thirteen volume collection of Byron's letters and journals was an endless source both of material and – as anyone who has had the pleasure of reading Byron's letters can attest – amusement. If, through some wondrous alchemy, I could meet any historical figure, it would probably be Abraham Lincoln; but if offered the opportunity to correspond with any figure, Byron would be my unhesitating choice.

Several other works on Byron's life were of great value as I tried to wrap my head around a figure who, as Harold Bloom put it, was "the most antithetical of men, and one of the most self-divided of poets." These include Benita Eisler's *Byron: Child of Passion, Fool of Fame*; Leslie Marchand's *Byron: A Portrait*; Fiona MacCarthy's *Byron: Life and Legend*; and, with respect to his final months in the Levant, Richard Edgcumbe's *Byron: The Last Phase*. In addition, in developing the characters of Robert Castlereagh, Robert Southey and Caroline Lamb, I relied on and found inspiration in John Bew's *Castlereagh: A Life*; W.A.

Speck's *Southey: Entire Man of Letters*; and Paul Douglass' *Lady Caroline Lamb: A Biography*.

The Virtues of Scandal was my first novel, and – perhaps a quarter of the way in – I realized that virtually everything I knew about novel writing came from a lifetime of reading. Determined to master – or, at the very least, to wield more or less purposefully – the tools of the trade, I was fortunate enough to take Lynn Stegner's *Novel Writing* class at Stanford University, which opened my eyes to many of the crucial subtleties of the novelist's craft. I am extremely fortunate to count Lynn both as an early editor and as a friend. To the extent *The Virtues of Scandal* succeeds, she deserves much of the credit. To the extent the novel falls short, the fault is entirely mine, as there was little else she could have done.

Many of my friends and family were kind enough to read the novel at various stages of its development, and their comments and encouragement were consistently helpful, sustaining me even when I wondered what could possibly have led me to embark on such a project. Sara Abramson, John Shepard, Cheryl Shepard, Leslie Cannold, Jeff Rothstein, Keith Ehrman, Diane Hailey, Michael Abramson, Mira Kopell, Holly Brady, JoAnneh Nagler, Marcia Sterling, Julia Weiner – thank you for so generously contributing your time in helping me to figure out what worked and what did not. I can think of few gifts of greater value to a writer.

Finally, during the three years it took me to write *The Virtues of Scandal*, I enjoyed the unceasing support and encouragement of my wife and best friend Lisa Green Abramson, whose comments on the developing draft were both insightful and rich in wisdom. Lisa, I am deeply in your debt and – after thirty-four years of marriage – still just as deeply in love.

Richard Abramson
April 19, 2020
Palo Alto, California

About the Author

RICHARD ABRAMSON was born in New York but has lived most of his adult life in Northern California. Squandering his undergraduate degree in English Literature, he spent thirty-five years practicing law, first as an intellectual property litigator and then as General Counsel of a major scientific research institute. Since retiring in 2015 he has been teaching at the Stanford University Graduate School of Business and spending time with his wife Lisa, his sons Jonathan and Michael, and his golden retriever Bear. A longtime reader of Romantic poetry in general and Byron in particular, this is his first novel.

CPSIA information can be obtained
at www.ICGtesting.com
Printed in the USA
LVHW110900130920
665255LV00005BA/217/J